A LICENSE TO KILL

STEVEN TURNER

Author: Steven Turner

Cover photography and design: Steven Turner

Printed in the United States of America

Second Printing: August 2019

ISBN- 978-0-9959937-0-9

"To better understand our ancestors, we may try to rekindle their lives. The surprise is that in so doing, we learn to better respect ourselves."

–Louise Champoux

For Aaron, Charlotte, Victoria, and Jasper

CONTENTS

ACKNOWLEDGEMENTS

Acknowledgements are due. First to my wife, whom I've subjected to neglect and frustration for many years yet now I've reached this point, has become my most intrepid defender and biggest promoter. To my sisters who encouraged me and provided feedback, and to my supportive family and friends. To the many who have written about the game laws and gamekeeping, including: Sir Wm. Blackstone, Knt.; Edward Christian; W.B. Daniel; E.L. Darwin; Richard Jeffries; T.B. Johnson; David S.D. Jones; Owen Jones; John Locke; P.J. Mackie; P.B. Munsche; James Paterson; and John Wilson. A debt of gratitude is owed the internet, and anyone found there whose work is relevant to this story. I may have relied upon your contribution to further my understanding of the subject matter. Also thank you to FamilySearch, Ancestry, Findmypast, The National Archives, The Norfolk and Suffolk Record Offices, GENUKI, Google Books, A Vision of Britain Through Time, Faden's Map of Norfolk, The Suffolk Family History Society, British History Online, and The Breckland Society to name only a few. To so many others, I am grateful to you all as if named.

I simply hope this modest exploration will become a stepping-stone on your personal journey of continuous learning.

A warning! This story is not for the delicate of body, or of spirit.

Now off wit' youse, tergether!

CHARACTERS

Astley, Sir Edward, Bart. – Knight of the Shire, Norfolk
Babington, Henry – Manages Mountrath Properties in England and Ireland.
Bacon, Catherine (Kitty née Sallett) –Cook Weeting Hall, Marries Nate Bacon
Bacon, Nathaniel (Nate) – Overseer at Weeting Hall Estate, Husband of Kitty
Band, Jonathan (Jon) – Head Gamekeeper, Weeting Estate & Gooderstone Estate
Bigley, Jason – Solicitor for the Defence
Capell, Hollis – Earl of Essex, Squire of Gooderstone Manor, Justice of the Peace
Colhoun, William - M.P. (Bedford), of West Wretham, Squire of Wretham Hall
Constable, The – Elected Official for Gooderstone, see Garwood, James
Coote, Charles Henry –Earl of Mountrath PC, Irish peer, Squire of Weeting Hall
Cowper, Rebecca – An Interesting Serving Girl, The Greyhound Inn, Swaffham
Cranefield, Henry – Master Carpenter at West Tofts and Poacher
Farrow, Augustus – Barrister for the Defence
Feetom, William – Head Gamekeeper, Gooderstone
Forrester, Solomon – Judge Thetford Court of Assizes
Garwood, James – Elected Gooderstone Constable
Haldimand, Sir Frederick – British Governor of Quebec, Canada
Hambling, George – Magistrate's Clerk, Court Clerk Thetford Assizes
Hennessy, James – Manages Mountrath Dublin Banking Interests
James & Davie – Assistant Warreners to Thomas Turner
Lady Ann – Wife of Sir Edward Astley, Bart.
Leveritt, Edward – Thatcher, Poacher, Newport Furriers, Husband of Sally
Leveritt, Sally (Sarah) – Wife of Edward
Manning, Ardley – Father of Mary, Grandfather of Henry, Flint Merchant
Manning, Henry – Protégé of Lord Mountrath
Manning, Mary – Mother of Henry
Osborne, Gabriel – Owner Black Feather, Mundford, Victualler, Husband of Mary
Osborne, Mary – Wife of Gabriel, Victualler's wife & Poacher
Pulsford, Dr. Morris – Physician of Mundbridge
Sallett, Catherine (Kitty) – Cook Weeting Hall, Wife of Nate Bacon

Salmon, Ernest – Steward of Mountrath Estate, Ireland
Shafton, John – Butcher, Mildenhall
Shinn, The Widow – Generous Woman, Widow of the Late John Shinn
Smith, The Revd Mr. Charles – Vicar, Saint Mary with All Saints, Weeting
Spinks, Edmund – Curate of St. Ethelbert, Poacher
Starling, Samuel – Assistant Gamekeeper, Gooderstone
Stokes, Samuel – Manages Mountrath London Banking Interests
Swift, Cecil – Steward of Weeting Hall
Taylor, Aaron – Presiding Judge Thetford Court of Assizes
Took, John – Warrener, Wretham Warren
Took, Lydia – Wife of John
Turner, Elizabeth neé Tuffs – House Maid, Weeting Hall, Marries Thomas Turner
Turner, George – Brother of Thomas, Warrener turned Gamekeeper
Turner, Martha neé Pressland – Wife of Thomas senior, Mother of Thomas
Turner, Thomas –Warrener at Bromehill & Wretham, Husband of Elizabeth Tuffs
Turner, Thomas – Warrener at Eriswell, Father to Thomas, Husband of Martha
Walpole, George – 3rd Earl of Orford, Squire of Houghton Hall
Wembley, Josiah – The Coroner
Windward, Phillip – Leader of the Mundford Gang of Poachers

MAPS

For Contemporary Maps of Norfolk & Suffolk, visit:

http://www.historic-maps.norfolk.gov.uk/mapexplorer/

www.historic-maps.norfolk.gov.uk/mapimageviewer/

http://www.fadensmapofnorfolk.co.uk/

https://maps.nls.uk/index.html

https://maps.nls.uk/view/91577050

https://maps.nls.uk/view/101168069

www.stedmundsburychronicle.co.uk/hodskinson/map2&3&14&15.jpg

www.visionofbritain.org.uk/maps/

http://www.bl.uk/onlinegallery/onlineex/ordsurvdraw/f/zoomify82509.html

BACKGROUND

A T THE HEART OF THIS STORY lies a chapter of English law commonly referred to as *the game law.* It had an outsized effect on the lives of people of different classes: particularly the landed gentry, sometimes called the squirearchy, and those who lived by their estates. Some have claimed more ink and emotions were spent in the fight over it than almost any other aspect of the law. Nevertheless, it remains little understood even in our day. It was even once popularly allowed to have been the final vestige of the "Norman Yoke" suffered upon the English by William the Conqueror, his Norman noblemen, and their descendants, following their victory in 1066.

A reputed huntsman, William I of England enacted The Forest Law to protect all noble beasts of chase and their habitats from destruction and to protect the exclusive right to take these beasts for himself, and later for his nobles and the senior clergy. Promoting noble methods of preserving and killing game was as important to him as enforcing the royal prerogative.

The monarch's warrant, or free warren, was given exclusively to those who met the threshold for property qualification or held a certain rank in society. This ensured only significant landowners qualified. In addition to nobles, the senior clergy and virtually every monastery, abbey and convent met the qualification. These were all granted free warren privilege in their demesne lands; that is, land attached to their manor or order, and used for their own purposes.

Those granted such a warrant as a sign of his favour, or who purchased one in times of royal need to raise money, shared in the monarch's prerogative to take game in a gentlemanly manner within the bounds of their defined preserve. Holding such a franchise was not without cost. Franchisees were obliged to shoulder the monarch's responsibility to protect the noble beasts and their habitats from any depredations, and to seek redress for offences against his privilege through the Courts established for that purpose.

These habitats were then more populated by wildlife than by humans, and consisted of large tracts of heath, wetland, grassland, and forest that William had set aside as sporting preserves. Given the nature of agricultural practices of the time, there was no competition for land, as the little in use for this purpose satisfied the needs of man.

William's successors continually added to these preserves through afforestation, ensuring not without some pushback that all who resided within and on the verge, or who ventured into these 'forests', respected the law as it applied to the vert (vegetation) and to the venaison (noble game). Eventually realizing the value of these forests to their coffers and to consolidating their influence, kings awarded specific rights to sport (hunt) through franchises of (free) chase and (free) warren. They later added gamekeeperships, giving holders the right to kill game within the grantee's demesne lands on the written orders of, and for the landowner.

James I was the first monarch to appoint royal gamekeepers. His warrant to preserve the King's game within a specified preserve, usually one near the gamekeeper's own seat which served as the basis for his qualification, allowed him to hunt there in an appropriate manner while preventing others from hunting. If he did not adequately preserve the habitat and prevent illegal killing by men of mean quality, which often meant confiscating their guns, dogs, nets, and other equipment, or if he lost favour with the King, he lost the right to hunt.

Though the earliest known English records of the rabbit date to the Romans who imported them for personal use, it was the Normans who introduced them with deliberate intent to be farmed. So fond were they of coney, denoting a rabbit sufficiently plump to be taken, they brought with them the practice of building warrens for the purpose of breeding them in number. This they did wherever the English climate was sufficiently mild, and the earth sufficiently soft for these beasts of warren to dig their tunnels.

During the Middle Ages, warren-raised coney was intended to satisfy the need of manor and monastery. Rabbit was reserved for only noble tables, and the skins for their finest garments. No great meal or feast was a success unless lavishly furnished with coney. By the records of prices paid, it was doubtless considered a delicacy. As with any luxury item it was also bestowed upon others, but never to exaggeration. To gift a brace of coney was to make a powerful statement.

However, before the 17th century, owners began to raise it in greater numbers for commercial purposes in enclosed, or domestic warrens. These were not the warrens of old, which were not necessarily enclosed and may have also protected a variety of species. When in the next century the human population rapidly grew, landowners quickly seized on the prospect of increased profit from ever larger numbers of rabbit. For instance, the New England Company operated vast warrens to generate funds to pay for its colonial activities, just as many lords used the profits from their warrens to cross-subsidize such activities as shooting and hunting.

Where parks were the enclosed, chases were the unenclosed havens for the noble beasts of chase; being the hart and hind (red deer), buck and doe (fallow and roe deer), hare, fox, boar, and wolf, though the two latter were long ago hunted to extinction. Those beasts and fowl sheltered in warrens for the purpose of hunting were the hare, coney, partridge, and pheasant. Fish also enjoyed royal protection in a system that reserved for the elite classes the responsibility to preserve wild game in all its forms, with the help of hired foresters (eventually called gamekeepers) while giving them liberty to take that game for the landowner.

Over time, the law became less strenuously enforced, and by the early 17th century the law had become all but abandoned, though it remained in place until the Game Act of 1671 as a useful source of royal patronage, and as a reminder of the monarch's privileges and powers. This Act and its many amendments governed every aspect of the protection, taking, distribution, possession and sale of game, deer, and rabbit; though the penalties for illegally taking deer and rabbit had long fallen within the more severe common law of the land.

By this time, both deer and rabbit were raised almost exclusively in private enclosures as the private property of the wealthy landowner. This effectively permitted landowners who operated parks and warrens to engage in commercial activities, and to protect them with armed men: gamekeepers and their lesser but equally protective brothers, warreners.

Gamekeepers were both instruments of and governed by The Game Act of 1671 and its many amendments. In their capacities, gamekeepers were the gentry's chief weapon in its battles against violators of the Act. Some have argued that whether by rank, role, or reason, there were no limits when attempting to justify a violation of the Game Act as everywhere, the unworthy struggled to acquire a commodity the law withheld.

The issue at the core of this story is the prerogative associated with free warren and gamekeepership. Some have seen the social history of the coney, and of all game as defined by law, as a reflection of English social history wherein all privilege was distributed according to birth right and rank, to the exclusion of the many who by birth alone were deemed unworthy. Law and social mores enforced a strict hierarchy within which rank was once manifest by the colour of rabbit fur worn, and the availability of prized meats at one's table. All who failed to achieve sufficient rank of manor or monastery were prohibited from wearing rabbit fur and eating its meat, and that of other noble beasts.

The years 1750 and 1790 are more than just convenient bookends to this story, for between them lies the period of history from which emerged disciplines associated with modern politics and governance, agriculture, medicine and public health, economics, city planning, business management, and of course, manufacturing. Although England is often depicted as the centre of much of this advancement, what to this day may be less known is how much was effective adaptation from elsewhere, including some ancient civilizations.

This project is challenge enough without attempting to have characters speak in the dialect of 18th century East Anglia. Such would be a distraction to you and a disservice to all East Anglians, resulting in your unhappiness and their disdain. It will therefore be in short supply. You are encouraged to use the accent of your choosing.

BOOK THE FIRST: KILLER RABBIT

CHAPTER I

> Hush, baby bunt'n,
> Far's gorn a-huntin,'
> Gornter tearke uh rabb't skin
> To wrap his baby bunt'n in.

TO REJOICE IN THE LORD'S BLESSING, to only then suffer the anguish of its loss, was a sorrow she had no will to relive. So consumed was her strength by fear, Sally Leveritt was unable to prevent the quavering that had taken over her voice. As she sang to the baby in her arms, "E'en he," she thought to herself, "must surely sense the futility of my efforts."

Her first was almost a year old when he'd grown quiet, but for his winces whenever sharp pain cut short his attempts to complain. Then came the fever and the vomiting. The midwife had returned, bringing with her plasters, advice, and comfort; but she had tried to care for him herself, and Sally now knew she had waited too long. Her ill-informed efforts had cost him his life.

The midwife later put a name to his misery. Scarlet fever was so-called because of the red spots and the pink tongue it gave to its victims.

Himself too late to be of any real help, the vicar nevertheless baptized him before performing a short cleansing ceremony over the tiny, white-clad body. In view of their little means, he did take upon himself to arrange for the baby to share old John Shinn's coffin. With the blessing of his widow, who proved generous with her late husband's eternity, the two were laid to rest together.

"I know me John 'd like o' the comp'ny," she said. "An' he'll keep safe in Heav'n yorn cock-farthin' o' like name. For that is surely where they now are, tergether."

More than a year had now gone and the memory of the loss of John was still as fresh as this day's picked apples. It was pulling her down that dark hole she had come to know too well.

Despite all the precautions she had taken with this baby, named in the manner of the day for his lost older brother, he too had become weak and feverish before the vomiting began. Her grandmother had taught her much about remedies. She had been a strong woman, and so respected by people they would travel many miles for her advice and her remedies. Sally tried to remember her lessons and had worked feverishly to make up what she thought might cure him and ease his pain.

"I've tried all I know, my poor, poor Johnnie. Though I've failed to cure what ails you, surely the Lord will not suffer me to lose you as well," she complained.

> Hush, baby bunt'n,
> Far's gorn a-huntin,'
> Gornter tearke uh rabb't skin
> To wrap his baby bunt'n in.

"Think, Sally. What did he say that may help us now?"

More than two years had passed since she first went to Mundbridge in search of a physician recommended by the midwife. Then only a few months gone with this child, she had resolved her ignorance would not be the cause of losing another baby. Dr. Morris Pulsford was youthful and seeking to grow his own practice. Already, promised the midwife, people agreed that despite owning some outlandish ideas and practices, his interventions provided them comfort and satisfaction.

When she explained the reason for her visit, he offered his sympathies for her loss, before his congratulations on her pregnancy. Much later, he admitted to her he found her determination to be inspiring. He proved kindly, even agreeing his fee could be paid at her convenience.

She did find his concern for their home and how they lived, a curious thing.

"Where do you live and can you rely on family to help, should you be in need?"

"What is the state of your cottage, and how is the ground on which it stands?"

"Are there any open fields, fens, running water, or a wood lying nearby?"
"Where do you fetch your water?"
"Where do you keep your livestock?"
"Where is the garden planted?"
"Where do you collect your edibles in the open, and how do you use them?"
"Have you sufficient to eat?"
"Where, and upon what do you sleep?"
He also asked about their muckup.

As she answered his questions a young woman, perhaps only a few years older than herself, brought him something he had evidently been awaiting. From a basket she extracted several small coloured bottles containing the potions, unguents, and tonics she had promised to concoct for him. He appeared very satisfied and listened until he understood her explanations of their purpose, and how to administer them. Sally noticed she was paid handsomely in coin. As Kitty Sallett took her leave, apologizing for the interruption, it struck Sally that this young woman reminded her of her grandma.

"I know every one of those plants you named," she bravely ventured, before Kitty reached the door. "Grandma took me whene'er she'd go collectin', but she minded me always to be careful, as people could be suspicious of her secrets."

Kitty's response immediately confirmed Sally's first impression. Warm and interested, she proved genuinely pleased to find a sister spirit with whom to share her passion for unlocking the curative secrets of nature.

After Kitty had gone, Sally resigned herself to believing this encounter would be unlikely to translate into a fruitful relationship, despite their obvious affinity for each other. "Edward and John are everythin' to me," she said to herself, "and my life already has more than I know to deal with." To her way of thinking, their survival could only be assured should she be sufficiently diligent and not become distracted. Yet she had enough of her grandma in her to sense she also needed a little fortune on her side. "Perhaps," keeping a ray of hope alive within her, "that fortune will be found in Kitty Sallett."

Because he had witnessed this affinity for himself, the doctor took pains to explain to Sally the ways in which his patients, thanks to Kitty, enjoyed relief from their ailments. He also informed her that Kitty could also be helpful in another way as well. With some circumspection in consideration of the still dangerous nature of this subject, he admitted he had personally experienced her talent. When cajoled by Sally, whose curiosity was now fully aroused, he explained Kitty's gift to stanch the flow of blood, should she only be asked for assistance. She may keep this in mind, though it must never be repeated, for dangerous people were still about.

After consideration of the Leveritt household's situation, Dr. Pulsford wrote out for her a list of tasks to be completed before the arrival of her baby. She was satisfied with his genuine concern for their well-being; so much so, that before she departed she willingly promised to fulfill his every charge without delay, though she did not truthfully understand the purpose of some.

Edward and Sally lived among a clutch of old cottages by the common waste at the edge of the village of Bromwell. Much as everyone of their status, their quarters were small, poorly built, and ill-equipped. Edward was a thatcher, and Sally spun wool in the manner of all cottage women. They otherwise earned their meagre way toiling in the fields, working a small field on the waste, and using their cunning.

The weather of the past year had not been generous to farmers; gleaners found the pickings unusually meagre. People everywhere suffered under these conditions, meaning there was a scarcity of money to go around and labour of any sort was no easy thing to find.

Sally swept, and thereafter kept tidy the dirt floor; above which she now kept all foodstuffs safely on the shelf. Using mud and straw, Edward blocked holes in the walls and stuffed the cracks around the windows and the door. He also found a glass to finally fill the space left when, in her fury at their loss, Sally had blindly thrown a jug through it.

The son of a thatcher and not without skills, Edward made sure the roof would not leak in the coming winter storms. Their tiny home was happily built on a small rise, so water would flow away from it and easily drain from its sides during rainfall. Despite the floor being of beaten earth, it proved comfortable enough when they could keep it dry.

Morris Pulsford warned against leaving the baby on the floor, even when in a basket. He said, "It should be raised in a manner to protect it from vermin as they would predictably be attracted to the scent of a newborn." When thinking of how to resolve this, Edward was reminded of how they protect game in the larder over at the big house. He then built a staddle stone on which to sit the baby's basket to keep it free of vermin.

The garden where she grew vegetables and tended a few apple trees was off to the side of the cottage, on the same raised area. The doctor seemed pleased to hear they kept a cow and some fowl. He took great interest as she explained her use of water to make beer, cider, and soup, and to occasionally scrub the mud out of clothes. On one subject she noted, Edward was unyielding: they should not wash themselves often in water. He believed it unnatural as it went against all they knew about keeping a body protected from every manner of ill.

Edward had been frowning as Sally recalled for him the doctor's queries about their source of water, and how they disposed of their waste. As most other folk in the country hereabout, they drew water from a shallow well dug near the cottages, and their waste flowed from outside the door to a small shallow where it collected. Sally was in the habit of skirting it on the way to the well, lying just beyond.

They were both struck by his summary with respect to water, relayed as best she could, given the doctor's accent. "If the Lord had wanted water and waste to exist in such proximity, he'd not of placed our mouths so far from our bottoms." She understood him to mean they should find another source of water, preferably a clear spring or a deep well, and to ensure the flow of their muck settled as far removed from any well as possible. This proved challenging, as the slope that ensured water flowed away from their cottage, also carried it to the pit beside the well they shared with neighbours.

John was now eighteen months old and all their preparations had seemed fruitful. As he daily grew strong and healthy, so too, Sally grew in confidence. Nonetheless, just five days since she was visited by a neighbor, whose eager but grimy children competed to carry John like he was a sack of wool, he was well into a sickness.

As she now sat with John in her arms, Sally no longer seemed to take breath. She imagined her vision was beginning to fail and that tiny sparks danced before her eyes. When his little body jolted, John shivered in her arms and his gasp brought her back to him.

Last night, a freezing wind blew and shook them all night long. They awoke to find the leaves were all blown to the ground throughout the night, to now lie amassed in the crooks and lees where they would be left to decay. The burnt yellow and warm russet clouds that yesterday floated between heaven and earth, were given way to a multitude of black spidery limbs, climbing to a cold and bright blue sky. Thankfully, Edward's repairs to their wattle and daub cottage and its openings held them against this blow. The thatch, too, held. The doctor would approve of Edward's efforts.

Unable to think of more to do for John, Sally's confidence completely evaporated with the arrival of the dreaded squits that her mam so feared in children. She had failed her first; was she now to fail his little brother? Going against everything left in her body, she pulled herself out of her state, resolved to fight as never before.

She pleaded with Edward to think of something. He understood nothing of sickness except it often came suddenly and most often took what it came for; sometimes quickly and sometimes not, leaving emptiness and sorrow behind. Edward was less equipped than Sally to help John, though he was equally determined to be helpful. In the absence of better ideas, he resolved that if nothing else, his son would be shielded from the advancing cold. Thus, he set out to find some warm skins to replace the miserable swaddle in which their baby was huddled.

> Hush, baby bunt'n,
> Far's gorn a-huntin,'
> Gornter tearke uh rabb't skin
> To wrap his baby bunt'n in.

As she sang, she heard her own mother's voice singing to her as a girl. Sally looked around her modest home as the cold descended upon them. There was little to look at save a few pieces of furniture; some of which Edward had fashioned himself. She'd brought to their marriage the few eating utensils, cooking implements and iron pots that served them well enough. They also had a covered tub and firkins to store the beer and cider she made.

She was proud of the few personal items that belonged to her mam, and her mam's mam: a piece of lace, large enough to adorn the small table in the middle of their one room; a glass ball given by her mam that had always hung in her window; and an old quilted bed cover, now so threadbare it failed to keep them warm during these cold nights. Tonight, it served meagre purpose as she huddled with her baby on the bed, hoping her own body might keep John warm.

Here and there were touches she and Edward had together brought to their home: bundles of herbs and several teasels were suspended from a rafter to dry for later sale; a fistful of flowers, long wilted, were stuck in a tumbler by the window; and Edward's scythe and apron that lay by the door. Sitting between the grate and the chair was a large slice of oak where they rested their feet to warm by the fire.

On the shelf were breads, cakes, cheese, and the last of a roasted pigeon they had been slowly working at. The corner table held small sacks of grains, salt, sugar, and assorted herbs she liked to use in her cooking.

Other than seasonal work gleaning, and gathering faggots and berries, Sally worked her spindle and distaff. These stood leaning against her chair by the fireplace, where also stood an armful of long teasels Edward had found on a day when cutting reeds for thatching. A sack of wool sat well out of reach of the fire, waiting for her to spin it into yarn. What she earned at her work was used to supplement their existence.

Sally had some benefit of her grandmother's teachings. Edward had learned the rudiments of thatching from his father before being turned out by his parents while still a young boy. Taking what he knew, he struggled on his own to become competent at his craft. Along the way he came to understand he was valued as a quick learner and a hard worker, even resourceful, though he worked to his own rhythm.

Setting out, Edward had convinced himself his son's salvation would come from the warmth of a rabbit fur covering. In the absence of any resources or wealth, and without her knowledge, he made the only arrangement that came to hand. Edward had bartered the exchange of a half dozen rabbits for a finished fur coverlet; one he estimated to be sufficiently large to also warm Sally.

However, there was only one way he could see to keep his part of the bargain, and it would mean having to break one of the most violated yet fiercely defended laws of the land. The unintended result of his arrangement was that Sally would now fear for his safety and well-being, in addition to little John's.

In pursuit of his aim he reached out to Phillip Windward of nearby Mundford, a man he knew only as one whose reputation was suspect. Phillip responded by inviting Edward to accompany him as he went to spy on a promising thicket, hard by a field of clover. Phillip's easy confidence and the sight of such bounty discovered were indeed encouraging, for this Breckland warren provided plenty of opportunity for the placement of nets and engines.

The art, as Phillip explained, would be escaping with enough rabbits to make it profitable for all, while avoiding confrontation with the warreners who would stand between them and the rabbits. Warreners, cautioned Phillip, who enjoyed the right of force in preventing their theft.

Readying himself for the evening's work, Edward remained resolute in his decision while Sally pleaded her case, only reluctantly submitting to his decision as she watched him depart. He did give her his solemn promise to remain vigilant and avoid unnecessary risk. After sitting in the dim light, she thought of something else she could do: Sally prayed for divine intervention on their behalf.

Well after dark, Edward was at the appointed rendezvous before setting out on their mission.

> Hush, baby bunt'n,
> Far's gorn a–huntin,'
> Gornter tearke uh rabb't skin
> To wrap his baby bunt'n in.

She blew out the rushlight and nestled with John under the cover. Still, he would not take her milk.

Sally wrapped her arms around her newly swollen belly, urging herself to sleep.

CHAPTER II

A POACHER THIS WAY COMES, SEPTEMBER 20, 1782

BUT FOR ITS UNIQUE situation in the community of Bromwell next Weeting, *THE THREE CONEYS* would be no one's choice for a place to meet. Long, low, and thatched, it sat by the roadside servicing the few coaches and riders who frequented these parts of necessity. Captive to its charms were also the local tenants, agricultural labourers, and for some time now, the many tradesmen come to work at Weeting Hall.

The food was dreadful, the beer indifferent, and the fire so mean it posed no burden to patrons, even in summer. Clumps of greasy dust adorned the exposed beams and chandeliers. In its favour a few upstairs rooms did provide welcome refuge for needy travellers, and the locals found within, where there was none other about, a place to meet or socialize.

The publican and his wife were perhaps not proud, but they did know everything about their neighbours. One can't help overhearing things, and one overhears so much more after customers have been in their cups. Cheap gin was the drink of choice for most, having the known facility to unhinge tongues, leaving them to wag freely. The proprietor was sure to always have a good quantity of it on hand.

Phillip Windward sat alone at a long table with his back to the wall, carefully eyeing everyone inside. It might appear from a distance he was simply given a wide berth by those present. He preferred traditional English ale to gin, and that only in small quantities. Phillip did not tolerate undue interest in his activities. He lived in relative ease with his family but as to his means, little was known. This was how he wanted it, yet despite his every caution many suspected he lived outside the law. In such times this was not beyond imagination; he simply wanted his affairs beyond wagging tongues.

The room did not respond when the taller, leaner, blonde and blue-eyed Edward entered. When he stooped to pass through the door, he simply became another drop of water in the pond. When he noticed Phillip, he was struck by his manner that so resembled a beast in the wild. For even as he sat in the best lit of corners, there was nothing to distinguish him from his surroundings: as though he hid in plain sight of all who entered.

Phillip concealed himself under a wide-brimmed black hat that sat tilted to one side. Approaching him, Edward made out his dark curly shoulder-length hair tied at the back with a black cloth. His ample neck cloth was double-wound for warmth above a knee-length great coat and a double-breasted waistcoat. The remainder of him was hidden below the table, yet what was above was as unremarkable as the stubble fields and hedgerows found hereabouts.

"Edward, sit and have a tankard, won't you?" This was not a question. Edward acquiesced, hoping it would settle his nerves. He assumed Phillip must have just arrived, as his own beer was not yet touched. "My friends arrive shortly, when we shall discuss our excursion."

As it happened, two men just then came through the door. They exchanged greetings with several other patrons on their way to Phillip's table, where he greeted them without rising.

"Lads, this here's the gentleman Edward Leveritt I spoke to you about. Edward, this here's Edmund Spinks, and that's Henry Cranefield."

Edward was more than unsettled by their arrival. He had assumed this evening to be a strictly private affair. Now his illegal and unsavoury act, the sole purpose of which was to save his son, would be witnessed by two more strangers whose discretion was not assured.

He found himself sitting face-to-face with a stout and cheery curate, The Rev. Mr. Edmund Spinks of St. Ethelbert, and a quieter sort by the name of Henry Cranefield, whom he knew by reputation as a master carpenter. They were all four from different towns. When two more tankards arrived, Phillip raised his to toast their new partnership; which declaration further surprised Edward.

He was now in unexpected and unfamiliar waters, and as Edward soon learned, the relationship of the other three was longstanding and close. He understood these men were once four, yet the fate of that missing person was impossible to determine. For just a moment he suspected his connection with

Phillip was not of his own making after all. Perhaps some malevolent force had worked to bring them together.

He felt trapped. His breathing became short and his head began to throb. He realized this was more than a simple case of two gentlemen leisurely snatching up a sack full of layabout rabbits, as he had been led to believe. This had all the appearance of organized industry; full of menace, and long-term implications. How could he possibly walk away now? He could not, came his own terrible response, not if he wished to complete his bargain.

The undoubted leader, Phillip, laid out his plan for this night's work on Starston Warren. The plan seemed plain enough for Edward, but he at first failed to grasp the number of rabbits intended to be taken. When it did register with him, he expressed the view that it seemed almost an impossibility. The others politely ignored his concern.

The night remained clear and the sky was slathered with crystal lights. Along the way they retrieved their equipment from its hiding place. They then stopped to collect a pair of lurchers, those specially bred dogs favoured by every poacher, from an unspecified residence. By the time they reached the border of the warren they were still teasing the tyro. Henry smiled confidently, "Just you wait and see, young Edward, when they come out at night to graze you will hardly believe your eyes. They're all just there for the pickin'. Afterwards, if we're separated, we're to meet up where we conceal the equipment."

Phillip stopped. He faced Edward such that they were square to each other. His words were slow and in a faint voice to prevent them from travelling on the night air.

"'Tis like that Edward. The cullin' season is not yet upon the warren, so puss is at her most plentiful and tender, 'cept there's much more to it than you may know. Time I told you what to do and o' the dangers, it bein' your first time."

From their previous visit they knew where the burrows were to be found. Edmund and Henry would place purse nets and snares, and otherwise stop up as many of these holes as they could find in the dark to prevent puss finding a bolt hole. His specific instructions to them were concise and clear.

Phillip and Edward would set up two parallel hayes, or long nets of different mesh between the burrows and the grazing fields to trap puss as she bolted home. The lurchers were sent to range from up wind, to drive everything before them. All the men had to do was pick them out of the nets, dispatch then bag them, and clear out after retrieving their equipment. They did not want to be greedy, but their experience had proven this to be the quickest manner to secure their measure and make their exit before the warreners appeared.

Edward was to keep watch during the whole operation. This was a most vital role as the matter of their safe return, prize in hand, rested with him. He was to take up a position of advantage from where he would keep a sharp eye for any warreners out to protect the rabbits. If anything, he repeated, anything seemed amiss, he was to give a low short whistle and they would decamp as quietly as possible.

"What are the dangers you speak of?" Edward's voice broke as he spoke.

"All right, lad. You must know the warreners have the advantage. They know this land better 'n us. They mayhap 're already in place, waitin' to get the jump on us. They may be armed with guns. We've only these here cudgels to fight 'em off if needed. You mustn't be caught, or they'll prosecute. The penalty could be a stiff fine or prison with hard labour. As you're new at this, they'd perhaps go easy on you.

"If they suspect we're here, they'll holler 'Stand!' But they shouldn't shoot if we don't shoot first. If it comes to a struggle or blows, save yourself and meet us where we agreed. Be careful you don't lead them to us. Take a roundabout way to get there. We'll look out for ourselves. Old Sly here, he'll find his way home on his own and bring his mate with him.

"Also, only move if necessary, and then step very carefully and quietly. There may be nasty surprises hidden in the coverts.

"Should all go well, you'll soon be helpin' us recover our equipment and carry everythin' off. Come, let us not be out here longer than need be."

Edward was numb, and uncertain he had taken everything in. He had questions he wanted, nay, needed to ask about his role and how to extricate himself, but no sound came from his mouth. What were these nasty surprises Phillip spoke of? How should he find his way back to the hiding place, when this was not his parish and he knew not the direction to take?

Phillip showed him his post for when that time came, leaving him with some words meant to encourage. His partners were taking a risk, he explained, but he had assured them Edward would do right by them. His own reputation and surety were in Edward's hands. They all counted on him.

The work got under way. So expert was this band, that Edward found his own contribution in setting the nets was soon finished and he was placed at his post to keep watch. From here he saw the whole operation come to its deadly climax. Rabbits scattered, their broken and halting runs visible by the erratic movement of their white tails. He could not count the number of casualties, so fast old Sly and his partner herded rabbits for the men to dispatch.

He became so distracted by all the action he forgot the reason for his watch. When it came back to him, he carefully scanned about. Far and near, above and below the horizon he searched for anything that appeared unusual or in movement. For now, all appeared quiet. Surely, he thought, if there were warreners about at this time, they would not wait until we had completed the destruction of so many rabbits.

The bags were filled, and the nets and other engines were now folded, ready to carry away, when suddenly the hair on Edward's neck stood straight and his ears pulled back.

Did he hear something move over to his right? He looked as carefully as he could and slowly shifted his weight to gain a better view. What he saw made his guts turn to water. Sitting not twenty paces away were two men with guns at the ready, their muzzles standing starkly against the night skyline. They had waited till now. Had they seen everything? Were there others about? How did they approach without him noticing them? Perhaps they had not seen everything, for they seemed fixed on the others, apparently unaware of his presence.

Collecting his thoughts, he remembered his instructions. Yet it seemed in the moment that by whistling, he would surely give himself away. How then, to warn the others?

He surprised himself when he reached to the ground to search out a rough stone. As quickly, he launched it in the direction of the intruders for it to crash into the gorse by which they were hiding. Surely this would be heard by his fellows.

The warreners started, such that one inadvertently discharged his cocked weapon into the air. This was enough to startle the whole warren, for everything took flight at once. Trees erupted with birds taking to air. The warreners stood in confusion and frustration looking for the source of their undoing as our villains took flight, but not without taking up what they had come for, and much of what they had come with.

After some moments everything returned to calm.

Then just as suddenly it erupted once more, the warreners by now having regained their senses and their bearings. As the poachers stepped rapidly over the heath, the less burdened warreners took off in all haste after them, crying

"Stand, villains, we are determined to take you. If you will not stand, we will shoot!"

Another shot rang out and then came more shouting and crying aloud. Edward distinctly heard Phillip crying, "Stand back, we are armed. You go on about your business and we'll go on with ours."

To which someone replied in a menacing and slow voice, "We are about our business. It seems you are also about our business. We are determined you shan't escape. You had better surrender."

"Do you mean to shoot?" cried Phillip.

"We do not mean to shoot if you do not mean to." came the reply.

Immediately, the crying increased as the poachers must have taken their cudgels to those men, unaware they had been lying in wait for them in the dark.

Edward thought he should now leave his hiding place and make his way back. As he came upon the scene of the crime, he saw something lying in a heap. The long hayes and purse nets were folded, ready to be taken, but were left behind when his partners abruptly fled.

This must surely be unintended, he surmised, so he slung them over his shoulder and made his way in the general direction of their flight, careful to stay well clear of where the cries last came.

Sometime later he heard what could only have been the aggrieved warreners coming towards him as he walked, he thought, safely along on the track. Where to hide? There was nary a leaf to provide cover, and the gorse was so thick to one side not even a rabbit would enter. This left only the field of stubble to the other side. He surmised, though, that should he attempt to run across the field, he would but make a perfect target.

"There's nothing for me now," he thought. "I'm done for, unless I can make it into that field and make myself as small and still as possible. Perchance they will pass me by without any notice."

As they came opposite his new hiding place, one of them noticed something in the field that should normally not be there. This night they had suffered a defeat in failing to take the poachers. An excess of ill humour now ruled their spirits and this was something he could avenge himself on. Letting off a bang would release some of his frustration. After all, his was the one piece still charged and loaded, not having had the opportunity to fire at the poachers. He turned back, aimed and discharged his weapon. As nothing stirred, they proceeded on their way.

Phillip, Henry, and Edmund made it safely back to their hideaway. Edward was not there. He had not been seen or heard from since taking up his position. "This don't look good," said Henry. "I wonder where he's got to, then?"

"S'ppose that first bang got him? 'Twas over to his direction. Perhaps a spring gun hit him if he moved about, though I told him not to. That old warrener was present. He don't usually go out himself, and now he's got his bile up we shan't be goin' back that way for a while, boys."

As Edward had correctly determined, these men were full of purpose, and it soon turned to sharing the haul for the night. When he was readying everything for their next outing, Edmund noticed the hayes and purse nets were missing.

"Damnation!" spat Phillip. It'll not do to return for them as they'll have a watch. If they fail to trap anyone in the next few days, they'll take 'em in the name o' their lord for their own use."

"That's a loss we'll have to make up," said Henry. "Hayes come at a pretty price."

Much later, as they were just about to leave, a sound was heard without. "Hush." Phillip put his finger to his lips to signal silence to all.

The sound came ever closer until Edward finally stumbled through the door. In the next instant he slumped to the ground, exhausted and barely conscious. Their short-lived relief was now turned to distress.

Within minutes, Edward was supported on either side by Edmund and Phillip as Henry led the short way to the home of Sly's owner. There, they hoped he would receive attention.

Once Edward was safely reposed in the home of Gabriel Osborne, victualler, they noticed he was bleeding profusely, which explained his weakened state. "This is most unwelcome. You are putting us at grave risk by coming here like this," quarrelled Mr. Osborne. "Your man requires more assistance than I can provide. I cannot have him here. If they come looking for you, it'll be enough I've the lurchers. And his wounds will surely give him away."

Phillip agreed he was a danger to have nearby. "Let's first give him some strength and see what he can tell us. We know not how he came to this state, as he hasn't been seen since he took up his watch. What can you give him, Gabriel?"

"I'll fetch some bread, cheese, and a bit of whiskey to revive his spirits. I propose we all have the same, as I find it quite restorative. Smugglers bring it from Oban, a small village in Scotland. Phillip, you look to his wounds. Mother will fetch some cloth and water to swab him down some, but we must return him home afore light, when it'll be too risky to travel about."

Whether from the shock of being struck by the shot, the loss of blood, the effort of carrying about the hayes, the trauma of his experience, or all of these, Edward knew he had not one step more in him when he collapsed before his fellows. Now somewhat restored, Gabriel Osborne's wife was cleaning and assessing his wounds which she estimated to be slight. All seemed to agree, although one did bleed such that Mrs. Osborne declared it required a tourniquet.

She tried to reassure Edward by chatting to him, running on as one does without provoking a need to respond. In this manner he learned that Mr. Osborne operated a tavern in nearby Mundbridge. His business was brisk enough that he found it financially advantageous to supplement his provisions with game, deer, and rabbit. And yes, Edward would be correct in assuming this was illicit but it was everywhere being done. Phillip and his men did the work, but her husband was behind it, providing the capital to purchase the equipment. He also trained the lurchers. There were others like Sly. He relied most on men of stout heart and body for this work, as Edward surely now knows.

"What brings a lad like yourself to take up with our boys?" Her tone changed, signalling that a response was now expected.

Edward explained his story: the illness of his boy, and the misery of his wife who faced the loss of their second son.

She could see he had little strength but asked regardless, what had happened to him that night.

Edward described, in a brief and not entirely coherent fashion, his actions on the warren, and his subsequent flight with the retrieved equipment. He spoke sufficiently of the shooting that they could envisage the scene for themselves. Heeding Phillip's words, he said, he had taken an indirect route back, which caused him to lose his way in the dark, undoubtedly adding to his torment.

Mrs. Osborne was not without sympathy. "What are your intentions now? Will you wish to withdraw, now you're proven to them? You did a fine and loyal thing this night. They will look to show you their gratitude."

In fact, already realizing their earlier haste, the others had begun re-distributing their haul of that night. Gabriel always received the largest portion. This was by reason of his underwriting their activity, and paying any fines assessed should they ever be convicted by the Court. Phillip took the next share as their leader and planner. The balance was usually given out in equal parts, except that on this night Edward's agreement was for only six rabbits.

Mrs. Osborne chose her moment to slip away to speak at length into the ears of the others. Gabriel's situation was unlike that of his men. Although the top man here, he cleverly avoided any connection with the nets, gins, and other equipment that are stored away from his property. Neither did he poach, kill, expose for sale, or buy any beasts or fowl of warren. Should he be convicted of having such in his possession, or of maintaining lurchers, both of which would bring stiff fines if not much worse for repeated convictions, he could happily suffer the financial consequence, as the reward for him far outweighed the risk. Besides, he had practice packing up his traps to elude being caught if need be.

When Phillip put aside Edward's agreed share, Henry was the first to speak up for him. "Boys, the lad did well by us. His thinkin' and action saved us and permitted our escape. At risk to himself, he also delivered the nets from their hands, that Gabriel will not now oblige us to replace. I say Edward's more 'n earned a full share. I can stand the loss, though I'm in this for the money as much as for the sport of it, truth be told." He said these last words with a smile. "Are we all in?"

Edmund Spinks was foremost a man of God, and charity was his constant companion. "I'm in this for my rage against a class that e'en today subjugates those who, by misfortune, are born into lower classes. 'Tis doubly outrageous to restrict access to wild creatures God put on this earth for men to profit from equally. 'Tis un-Christian to my mind. 'Tis for such reason I distribute my reward to the needy of my parish. On this occasion I'm thus willing to be a benefactor to Edward, for he has more than paid his due this night, as you say Henry."

"And you, Phillip. You are quiet. What say you to this?" Mrs. Osborne's voice was solicitous, not challenging him.

Phillip glanced at Gabriel for an indication of how he was leaning on the subject, but his face told him nothing, one way or the other.

"Edward did agree to a half dozen. Had the haul not been as 'twas, I'd 've been required to pay out o' my share. An agreement should be held to by both parties." The others left him time to continue at his leisure.

"I'm only in this for the money. Yet, 'tis truth Edward was clever in warnin' us. And he did recover the hayes. He could've escaped unburdened and he is now wounded for his trouble. He showed an inclination for this business and we are in need of a new partner."

"A full share 'tis, then." Mrs. Osborne showed yet another side of her.

"Now see to it he returns safely to his wife."

The night sky was taking on the first blues of early light when Edward was slowly being helped home. No words remained to be spoken. He thought instead of the last hours and what they meant to him, to his wife, and to his son whose father had gone for a rabbit skin to keep him warm. Should they rest comfortably and survive, then it would prove to have been a very good thing for himself. It was now left to make the exchange he had bargained.

Despite this, he was deeply unsettled. Sally would be displeased by the danger he'd found and the injuries he had suffered. One wound appeared to be quite serious, even though his partners went to some lengths to diminish its gravity, his loss of blood was worrisome. Mrs. Osborne, he reckoned, had the better measure of it.

His mind turned to the others walking with him. "Do these fellows now believe me their partner? I know little of them, or whether they will look after my well-being despite their generosity on this day."

He sensed he was enmeshed in a situation he could not easily unravel.

And why, he wondered, was there seemingly more to Mary Osborne than was avowed?

CHAPTER III

THE DOCTOR DOES A GOOD DEED, SEPTEMBER 21, 1782

EDWARD SOON HAD THE OPPORTUNITY to know if these fellows would be faithless. In the event, they showed themselves to be steadfast in his support, remaining to see to his well-being and to help him explain what had transpired. They did not fail to provide every detail meant to assure Sally of his stalwart performance. His full share being laid out for her to witness, was also in their manner of disarming her.

Sally reached deep within herself to resist falling faint upon seeing the poor state of Edward in his blood-stained clothing. Her first instinct was to examine how badly he had been struck. She was not reassured by the method used to stop his bleeding. In her experience grave danger lurked, for a tourniquet either anticipated a deadly experience, or itself caused more harm than good. This was not the outcome she had prayed for.

"Hush little John. I must put you aside to see to your da." Was she up to this? These men were unknown to her, but all the help she would have for now. She could not allow her rage and fear to push them away until matters were in hand.

She willed them to continue with their tale while she examined Edward's wounds. Without knowing their names, she gave directions for water and wood to be fetched, and the fire to be stoked to heat it. The largest of them was pressed into propping Edward in a seated position. As the water heated, she tore a skirt into strips to bind his injuries.

"He appears comfortable enough," offered Henry, hoping to keep things on the even.

Unwrapping him, she found four punctures and three deep scratches where the shot had grazed his skin, all confined to his upper arm.

"He'd been squinched behind the hayes when he took the shot," said Phillip. "His shoulder must've been for'ard; a little more and he'd 'a been missed altogether. This last one is a trouble, methinks." He held her eye for an instant.

Edward considered it best to not add to the distress in the confines of their home, preferring Sally to use her energy in his aid. For this reason, above all others, he remained silent.

Below the tourniquet was a puncture of the elbow where a piece of shot had struck bone and caused a most distressing bleeding. Carefully, Sally began to loosen the tourniquet when suddenly, from below the wrapping, a stream of blood shot out spotting the far wall. Quickly recovering, she retightened it to stop the flow. "This is vexing. He's in need of help without delay. I can't leave my baby. You must fetch doctor Pulsford at Mundbridge. He'll come to see Edward." Sally then added, "But we've nothin' to pay him."

Edmund's nature and calling showed when he offered, "There are young and fat coneys aplenty here on the floor. Surely the doctor would enjoy having one or two for his pot. In my life I've known men do much more for much less. If that is not sufficient, then we'll add some coin to help, as you've the babe to look after as well."

Sally's nerves were beginning to settle. Edward was not out of the thick of it, but she now knew the extent of the danger to him. It could be worse, and these men seemed true to him, which was not a bad thing for now.

One more thought struck her as Henry and Edmund were setting off to fetch the doctor. "Edward, that skin needs to be fetched this day. You must explain to them your bargain."

Minutes later the carpenter and the cleric set off, pockets bulging with rabbits. Despite the danger of walking about with such in daylight, they agreed to make the exchange and to summon doctor Pulsford; a summons Sally prayed he would heed.

Phillip agreed to stay with them until the doctor arrived, though he too had a family waiting for him. Sally kept her humours in check so they would not spill over, forcing him away. Besides, she wanted to know more about these men and their intentions for Edward.

"S'ppose he'll be needin' a new shirt and coat, now these're destroyed. Won't do any good him walkin' abroad like that. People will seek answers."

Whether intended or not, these opening words had an immediate effect on

Phillip. "We are true to each other, Mrs. Leveritt. Your Edward did good by us tonight. We don't want him to suffer more 'n need. And truth, we don't want to rouse more questions than necessary. I'll send over garments tomorrow."

"Will you take a cup, Mr. ...?" Putting John down, she reached for their only two cups from the table to draw some beer. She handed him one; the other she would share with Edward who was still quiet.

"Windward, Mrs. Leveritt, Phillip Windward. Truth be told, I could use a cup, thank ye."

"What are you, then, Mr. Windward?" Her frank look into his eyes left no room for evasion. He was in her sights.

To his credit, which Sally would later comment favourably upon, Phillip told her much, omitting only the roles played by the Osbornes, spring guns and mantraps. He spoke of his family and how he supported them from his poaching. He came to this as the son of a poacher, learning under his father's careful eye. He gave up the stories of his accomplices, Henry and William, whose full names he neglected to provide out of discretion. In all, she thought they are not unlike her own kind. They may be outlaws, but they are not beyond honour, discretion, and humanity.

"Are you not afraid of the law, then? They can hang you for stealin' rabbits and partridges. I cannot lose Edward for the sake of these coneys."

Phillip knew the game laws were widely understood to be needlessly harsh in preserving the ancient and exclusive right of the gentry to all game. To protect this right, they had the power to create the laws, use deadly force against those who would flout them, and devise severe penalties for any breach of their laws. Further, they sat in judgement of the accused and sentenced the guilty. A growing consensus amongst the people declared this to be an unfair system.

Yet this system perversely made it possible for some to make a good living. "'Tis well known that a man will desire that which he cannot have. Thus, should his direct access be obstructed, he will seek access by any means possible. Whene'er the reward remains to their advantage, men like me 'll take the risk to provide what others seek," admitted Phillip. "For most, reward is financial; for some 'tis the opportunity to provide for others, especially family; and for yet others, 'tis a means to rebel against an unjust system."

Fortunately, the laws were less onerous than once they were. Phillip explained that taking these beasts was a matter only of trespass or stealing, which may result in a fine, a flogging, or confinement at hard labour. Much was dependent on the judge. It was helpful to have a person of standing speak to one's good character or circumstances, unless of course one had been repeatedly caught in the act. Judges were not all without sympathy, and many sentences proved light when the judge appreciated the poaching was done in a sporting manner. "He will always take exception to poachers firing upon keepers, blackening their faces, and poaching in gangs."

"You're poachin' in a gang," Sally was listening, thinking this sounded more like the tales told by her father of Robin Hood, than of something she should find objectionable.

"Yet we find that sufficient and well-placed coin will assure us leniency. If e'er we're taken and found guilty, I assure you, we'll be dealt with leniently.

"How can you say so?"

"I am able to provide payment needed. As I say, the rewards can be great."

"Edward only went along last night as he desired a warm blanket for our little boy."

"I truly hope he will do better for it. His father earned it for him, and in so doin' he's proved himself. 'Tis my wish Edward would join with us."

"I don't wish to be ungrateful, Mr. Windward, but this night may not prove to be a blessin.' We shall have the blanket if your men are true, but Edward is in a bad way. If I lose him, we're not blessed at all. I don't care for him to go out there again."

Judging this the wrong time for such a discussion, Phillip held his tongue. In this manner, they passed the next several hours taking turns administering to Edward who was still not sufficiently revived. Phillip did replenish the water barrel and the wood pile, and even held John for brief periods, allowing Sally to do what she needed.

Suddenly, there was a sound without. Coming along was a horse, stepping carefully on the ill-kept and root-infested pathway pulling Dr. Pulsford aboard a dogcart whose wheels humped across the terrain.

To simply say that Sally was relieved, would be to underestimate the effort she had been making. Though most anxious for his examinations to begin, she greeted him warmly and invited him to take a seat, handing him her newly filled cup to freshen him from the trip.

"Mrs. Leveritt, I have come with all possible haste. Your men did not find me at home when they first arrived. They left there on an errand to return afterward. They pray me give you this, apparently 'tis the subject of much effort by your husband." Whereupon he handed her a bundle, which she discovered to be the prized blanket of rabbit skins. "I believe I have two patients to see to. I should make haste, as neither can wait a moment longer. I shall begin with your son."

Dr Pulsford had studied life at his father's feet. A successful farmer who had implemented several new practices in agronomy and animal husbandry, he taught his son that mankind can benefit from the application of similar practices. "We are all beasts of this celestial body, simply attempting to survive as best we may," he would repeat. His teachings carried forward into his son's vocation as a physician, where today they influence his practice of the art of healing.

One habit for which the good doctor was noted was his constant recording of every pertinent detail regarding his attentions to patients. From this, he hoped to learn to repeat his successes and avoid repetition of his errors.

Another was his fervent belief in the efficacy of concentrating expertise and facilities to the benefit of the surrounding population. Dr. Pulsford was one of a small group of men campaigning for a hospital to be situated in a nearby town, perhaps Norwich, or even Thetford.

He examined John, all the while asking questions of Sally to keep her mind occupied and focussed. When finished, he said he believed the boy would be fine in two to three days, provided she give him as much of her milk as he would take and keep him in the fur blanket, well above the floor as planned. He should also be placed out of doors whenever the climate proved mild.

She, however, must drink much more and eat well for fear of drying up her milk. Should she ignore her own needs, it would be dangerous for both. He gave her a small bottle filled with tonic. When provided a few drops at a time on the end of her finger, he promised it would return John's appetite and strength. It would not do harm should she also administer it to herself.

He then turned to Edward. After his examination he excused himself to fetch tools, bottles, and cloths from the cavity in the dogcart. "This will take some time, he predicted. I did inquire of your men the nature of Edward's injuries and of John's ailment. That was providential, as I first visited Kitty Sallett who has provided me with salves and tonics."

"You must be Mr. Windward. I have a message from your men, who promise to tell your good wife you have been detained on an urgent matter but that you are well and will return forthwith."

"Thank ye kindly, sir. My wife does worry, e'en she's ne'er had reason to worry. She's a good woman, who cares well for me."

"Apparently so. Shall we now see what is to be done for this soul? If you would sir, I need him to be laid on his side for examination."

The two turned Edward on his side, fully exposing his wounded right arm. "This will be very uncomfortable for you. You may wish to place this between your teeth such that your cries do not frighten your son."

After probing with a metal stylus to determine the depth of the wounds, he reached for a tool that resembled two long and very thin fingers bound at one end. The other he placed inside each wound to pinch and extract the piece of shot therein lodged. The last he addressed was the vicious wound on Edward's elbow.

"Hmnn. This will be more difficult. I feel where the bone has broken apart."

He took a glass from amongst his articles of practice and wiped it clean on his linen shirt. He then asked Phillip to bring a candle closer, though it was full daylight without. Using a polished steel to reflect the light onto the wound, he proceeded thus to examine it.

"Steady, sir. I must extract the shot and attempt to replace the bone such that 'twill heal in its natural position. Should I succeed, you may again have full use of your arm."

When he was satisfied, Dr. Pulsford heated little glass bowls which he placed over each tear in the skin. When they had done the job of drawing more blood, he turned to bandaging the wounds. For this he took several cloth bandages that were pungent with the smell of Kitty's work. These he applied over the tears in Edward's skin, followed by a splint to brace the arm. The lot was then bandaged very snugly with the clean linen strips made by Sally.

"That should do nicely. I have removed the offending shot, cleansed the wounds, and placed the bone in its native position. The poultices from Kitty will soothe the pain and provide the necessary essences to help the flesh regain its vitality. He must remain like this for several weeks. Should the arm not be held fast in this position, 'twill be of no use to him as a thatcher, for 'twill set crooked.

Kitty also provided this tonic should he have trouble sleeping. Only a few drops each time will be sufficient. He needs rest, water, and meat for several days to regain himself. I will see him from time to time to follow his progress."

"Doctor, I earlier tried to examine this same wound and on lettin' off the tourniquet, it bled so the far wall's been spattered, as you can see. How is 't that just now, when you did the same, there was no such flow?"

"I'm afraid I cannot explain, for 'tis beyond me to say." Dr. Pulsford gathered his things and cleaned after himself. "Mr. Windward, I return to Mundbridge. Should it be convenient, might I offer to see you home? 'Tis a simple dogcart, quite unlike the splendid machines of my London colleagues, but it does navigate these country roads satisfactorily. For me 'tis also much safer than riding atop a horse, or in a whirly gig, both of which are found to be quite mortal to country doctors."

"You are kind. It has been a long day. Please, allow me to place your equipment in the cart."

"I have no money, doctor, as you well know. And with Edward infirm as he is, I do not foresee soon payin' you for your troubles, though I have here plump coney. I pray you may take some against our account." She revealed to him what were, indeed, very plump rabbits.

Dr. Pulsford regarded Sally with a kind expression that also showed a hint of sadness. "Dear Sally, what have you got yourselves into? How did Edward come by these injuries?"

"He was by a hedgerow when a gun nearby banged 'im. A mishap. And the rabbits, they're payment for some thatchin' he did fer those fellows."

"Very well, shall we agree two brace of coney for this day, one of which will settle my account with Kitty for her concoctions, and your former account with me remains."

"Thank you, to you and Kitty, tergether."

"You may recall we once spoke of Kitty's special gift. You remember it can ne'er be spoken of, and she can ne'er receive any gratitude or remuneration. 'Twas she who stopped Edward's bleeding. I thought you should know."

"How'd she do that?"

"As I said, I cannot explain. 'Tis beyond me to say, and for you to e'er speak of."

Phillip appeared at the door.

Bowing his head slightly to take his leave, doctor Pulsford turned to take Phillip by the arm. "Come, sir, we must depart."

There was little conversation on the return. Dr. Pulsford wondered aloud how the Leveritts would do for the next months with Edward unable to cut thatch or climb onto roofs. There was certainly nothing put away for times like this. Phillip owned that he too failed to see how they would survive, but he promised to put his mind to finding an answer.

Phillip asked to be left at a crossroads, from which point he said he would find his way. In truth, he estimated that the less the doctor knew of him, perhaps the better.

When Sally was assured they were sufficiently distanced from their home, she went outside and loosed a cry of anguish. She then slumped to her knees, sobbing.

CHAPTER IV

AS THE FIRST RAYS OF THE DAY'S SUN painted a blush on the brow of this, the highest point in the parish, Bromehill Lodge oversaw a life that had changed little in almost five hundred years. Certainly, the scale of it had increased and there were now crops succeeding where others had failed, but otherwise life on the warren had changed little throughout this time. The Lodge could be seen from afar in all directions as it stood proudly and in defiance of any who would violate the lord's privileges, and his property.

As a symbol, it was an appropriate one given the purpose of the warren, for Bromehill was as prolific and as much a living and breathing creature as any beast or man. The proof of this lay in the variety of life it supported in a continuous cycle of life and death. Herein lay the secret of Thomas' success, for having been raised on Eriswell Warren, one of a score of such *Grandes Dames* for which the Brecklands were famous, he understood their need for respect and for assiduous attention.

The Lodge itself was home to the Turner family. Its two floors stood tall and square, protecting more than one thousand square feet within. Its walls were faced with knapped flint and like most ancient stonework, were not as they seemed. Between two surfaces was a hollow core, filled as they did hereabouts with clunch and flint rubble. Only a single door and two high slit windows broke its exterior. Their outlines of dressed limestone matched the cornerstones, and they could all be barred from within.

Since the arrival of the Normans, the rabbit had been greatly esteemed and protected: its flesh was once reserved for only noble tables, though clothing and felt makers still used its fur to make sought-after apparel for these same nobles. Until not very long ago, the colour and quality of rabbit fur worn was an indication of a person's rank. These attributes had long made the rabbit a property worthy of vigorous nurturing, and protection from thieves.

In recognition of this, man developed a sophisticated array of bespoke earthworks and structures with these specific requirements in mind. The warren was at once the place where rabbits were raised in a safe environment, to be then harvested for their attributes.

It was known that certain men of long ago had a culinary preference for the very young, even unborn foetuses of rabbits. The long-standing practice on this warren was to harvest only suitably mature beasts. Called coneys, for their lush fur and most succulent meat, they were distinguished from the still young, referred to as rabbits, and the too old that were left for breeding stock. Timeless and silent, the Lodge stood watch over a creature that lived and died in accordance with the treatment it received.

Behind three-foot thick walls at its ground level was a large working area. Here the warrener stored his equipment, tools, lanterns, and engines with the racks to hang carcasses and drying pelts. The sole entrance to the lodge was punctuated overhead by an embrasure, through which deadly fire or boiling liquids could be launched at anyone attempting a forced entry through the door below. With the recent adoption of firearms, the nature of these projectiles was now more deadly than any of those ancient methods.

Although ferrets and small terriers had always been used to flush rabbits from their burrows across the warren, the once noble method of killing them with the hawk was now replaced with the flintlock. When shooting parties found themselves on the warren they could rely on being perfectly accommodated in this room, where a warm fire, hot food, good drink, and excellent companionship were reliably provided.

Two long tables sat before an expansive fireplace that burned without cease, if most often only slightly. Here, where coneys were dressed, no role was too small for every member of the family to contribute. Dressing was a matter of flaying and gutting, then huddling the carcasses in baskets for market. So little light came through the two slit windows that even in daylight, and despite any glow from the fire, several candles were needed for Elizabeth and the other women to work with precision.

Their family quarters were reached on the second level by a winding stone staircase from which strategic and secure position it could resist assault by armed poachers. Although Thomas had yet to face such an attack, increasingly brazen incursions were whetting his nerves; the fear that one was imminent grew. Of the four rooms above, one was furnished with two large bedsteads for the family. This was where they spent their little personal time together. Of the others, one served the warreners in planning the culls, and the final two were for storage and use by warreners taken on expressly for the culling season, or for labour to mend the boundary.

These rooms were open towards bared oak rafters and riven-oak battens that supported the Collyweston slate roof. The underside of the slates was covered in a layer of lime mortar and horsehair torching to protect against the roof's susceptibility to the Norfolk winds. These were known to blow seeping rain and melted snow beneath the tiles, or to lift them away altogether. The torching by now was fallen away in places, exposing certain of the Lodges vulnerabilities.

Looking up, one could see the rising course of stone chimney on one side, and the ladder on the other leading to a parapet from which vantage point the warrener could survey the whole of the warren, day, or night.

Certainly the most impressive on the warren, the Lodge was by no means the only structure. Flanking it were two far less ambitious siblings. One housed a barn and overhead granary to service the family livestock consisting of great cattle, swine, and goats. The other stored carts and wagons and also stabled the dray horses and nags used to haul fodder out to the rabbits, carry equipment and carcasses about on the warren, and transport the dressed product.

Near the lodge were also found several enclosed garths. Here, Thomas grew fodder for winter feeding and herbage for the pasturing of livestock while Elizabeth grew vegetables, fruit, and herbs for the kitchen. Fruit trees bearing varieties of apples, pears and plums were planted in rows. With their fruit Elizabeth made her cheeses, puddings, biffins, ciders, and wines. These enclosed fields were adjoined by various sheds and lean-tos, all strategically placed to store implements and equipment and to kennel the dogs and ferrets.

Further afield on the warren were two cottages, each with an attached barn, its own deep water well, latrine, and enclosed fields for livestock and growing crops. These outposts served to provide some privacy for their inhabitants, as well as to create a defence network of warreners.

The most considerable of the earthworks had the twin purpose of enclosing the farmed rabbits and of repelling vermin and poachers. The whole of the warren's eleven hundred and fifty-six acres was circumscribed by an almost six-mile long perimeter bank, called a baulk. Thrown up to a height of five feet, these twenty-foot wide banks consisted of turves cut from the land. These were laid in offset courses and stacked such that grass showed on the vertical inside wall and on the sloped outside wall.

To disincline rabbits from burrowing to freedom, a planted topping of furze and hawthorn was encouraged to grow down the sides. An invasive plant, furze was controlled on the open warren as it would provide a vantage from which stealthy vermin could spring. Completing these works, and in a further attempt to foil any escape was flint rubble, here and there embedded into the inside wall.

Preventing the illicit entry of poachers and vermin onto the warren was a chief responsibility of the warrener. Against poachers, the above measures were proven to have considerable success. Unfortunately, vermin had other, more discreet routes to their hunting grounds. To deter the four-legged kind, warreners built traps of stone and board at every vulnerable location without the perimeter. Such defences were nothing, however, to winged vermin whose preference for perching where they could see below presented their own special challenge.

Few boundaries have withstood man's preference for a straight route over a circuitous one. In recognition of this, two gated roads through the warren were maintained. Named in the manner of most roads for what lay at their far end, the Brandon and Swaffham Gates controlled traffic along one road, and the Grim's Graves and Brick Kiln Gates, the other. Built in a manner to prevent rabbits escaping, they were easily secured after one passed through.

Despite all the above measures, the elusive rabbits proved capable of escape from their protected area. Those whose paths they crossed were only sometimes delighted; for others their presence was a major point of contention. When inadequately managed, this fury could lead to serious conflict in the community where Thomas was often singled out as the villain; being subjected to legal and physical retaliation of all manner.

Within the boundary meer were other earthworks used in managing the herd. Four variously situated sets of smaller and unadorned rows of parallel trapping banks served to round, or trap, the rabbits with the aid of hayes. Ancient mounds, like blemishes on her face, joined small, more recent enclosures along the perimeter bank called clappers. Here, the breeding does and their kits were kept safe from vermin and harsh weather. By their fertility, these nurseries determined the success of the warren.

No exception to the requirement of all creatures for sustenance, the warren had proven its great appetite for provender of all manner and to avoid disaster, Thomas' methods must satisfy the year-long needs of the herd. Within fields delineated by low baulks to discourage raiding by the rabbits, he broke up fields to be sowed with crops such as corn and hay for winter fodder. Throughout the whole of the warren sheep were folded, since they would eat what rabbits did not and they manured the otherwise poor earth. He would then encourage the broad sowing of herbage for grazing.

This was the current state of the warren. Alas, some time before the arrival of Lord Mountrath, Bromehill had succumbed to years of neglect and misfortune. Left to languish, she became a derelict, adrift on this sea of sand. The waning interest of the wealthy in rabbit would have been discouragement enough, but the coup de grâce may have been dealt a century before the arrival of Thomas. It was then that a period of shifting sands buried many places under dunes higher than the tallest waves at sea, according to one who claimed knowledge of such things. Strong and violent weather like that experienced when he was a boy, may have been the final discouragements to its owner.

In Thomas' day, modern methods and infusions of fresh capital were helping warrens in general and our Bromehill in particular, outpace their old form. Rabbit meat and its fur were of growing economic import, and the rabbit itself was appreciated by shooters for its considerable sporting interest. For these reasons, the Earl of Mountrath invested in the warren within his broader rehabilitation scheme for the parish; a scheme that would feature excellent shooting of walked-up game.

A competent head warrener was an asset worth keeping, and Thomas was well kept. He received wages of £15 12s. for fifty-two weeks, payable yearly on the 23rd day of January, though he knew it to be most often delivered months later. His wages had risen a mere 6s. since he began at Bromehill on the 26th day of February 1774. Regardless, his contentment remained, the more so in view of the perquisites he was entitled to. Chief among these were lodging and a few acres for livestock, poultry, crops, and gardens.

He also received various emoluments and vermin killing bounties that, when added, almost doubled his wages. Bounties received for vermin killing on the warren and throughout the manor, including about the manor hall, were substantial and payed out against proofs in the form of tails and beaks. These symbols of his mastery he would then nail to his gibbet as a warning to all that threaten those under his protection.

His own compensation was less for his labours than for the knowledge and skill he brought, and for being a man who could resist temptation while living in dangerous isolation. His status, he was aware, did not necessarily translate into respect and admiration from others in local society. As the guardian of an ancient seigneurial privilege, he stood between them and what they viewed as theirs to freely take, by force if necessary. After all, was not the rabbit a beast of nature, free to roam the earth? He received no sympathy from villagers for his pains, or for the danger to himself and his family who often endured the taunts and torments of neighbours.

From time to time he took on extra labourers, such as when he periodically required Elizabeth's brother, Robert Tuffs from South Pickenham, to cut and cart furze bundles. More often he required extra warreners during the trapping season that would soon be upon them. He was generally certain to find the best of help, as his lordship's account unfailingly provided immediate payment for such services rendered.

Thomas brought to his warren the knowledge of what to do, and the skills to deliver the results that could only be acquired through a life-long association with the profession. If he was not first a good husbandman, the rest was for nought.

By nurturing his charges and ceaselessly promoting the conditions for successful breeding, Thomas had successfully reversed the fate that befell our old lady and it was his duty to now maintain this form.

His knowledge and skills were of little consequence without also the strength of character and presence of mind to enable him to perform his duties without concern for the time of day, the weather, or the nature of the threat.

Good judgement, according to the squire himself, enabled the warrener to take those steps to ensure durable success. Thomas Turner, above many of his comrades, was recognized for his forethought, economy, and prudence. He respected the warren as the living creature it was and remained attentive to its every need and threat.

Should any one or more of his adversaries have gained the upper hand, or taken him by surprise, the warren could have been irretrievably set back. It was against their ceaseless efforts that he struggled to protect the rabbits, until the day he would himself take their lives. The warren eventually took the most of everyone who lived on it, whether man, woman, child, or rabbit.

The day-in and day-out tasks of trapping coneys and killing vermin were aided by some very ordinary yet effective tools and engines that have been used by warreners since early days. They included traps and snares, dozens of purse nets for blocking burrows, hundreds of yards of long haye nets to place across coverts or at the trapping banks, shovels of various shapes and lengths for digging burrows or fetching a ferret that had laid up, staffs for prodding holes or transporting the hocked carcasses, bags, and lengths of measured line for working the ferrets and the dogs.

A special-purpose dog, the lurcher, was favoured by warreners and poachers alike. A cross between a greyhound and a collie, its chief characteristics were its herding agility, speed and ability to stay quiet. When let upon the warren it would identify a target and quickly round it up to be taken by its master or the net. Used alone, or in combination with ferrets or small terriers to flush rabbits from their burrows, they were an efficient means of harvesting the farmed coneys. For this reason, a good warrener was an effective breeder and trainer of these dogs.

When Elizabeth added her own to that of Thomas, the total family income was considerable. From her fruit trees and gardens she sold fresh damsons, apples and herbs, or transformed them in her kitchen into fruit cheeses, sauces, and pastes. Although the big house was her priority customer, she was becoming a favoured provider to many of the village households. When she could, she also carded and spun wool into yarn, for which labour she was paid by an agent.

Perhaps for Thomas, her most helpful contributions were to the warren itself, for she not only helped with chores, it was Elizabeth who organized and directed the transformation of carcasses into the meat and the pelts for market. Thomas referred to her as his partner.

With the arrival of every September, Thomas commenced planning and organizing the cull. From Michaelmas to the end of March he would have the proof of his skills, for this was when the daily routine he had devised was set into motion. Like a clockwork, it was meant to deliver an almost constant yield to satisfy the demands of the market and the manor alike.

This year, a new tool made its way onto the warren. With the news of armed gangs laying siege to warrens and their lodges, Lord Mountrath was concerned for the safety of his warreners and the security of his property. Never troubled by those who might take a few rabbits to fill an empty stewing pot, or to bring in a few desperately needed shillings, his concern was now the growing number who targeted the lodges intent on making off with the considerable numbers of dressed carcasses and pelts stored therein. Reverberations were still felt from the depredations last winter on Eastwyk Warren. It was there, of a dark evening, poachers forced their entry into the lodge where they shot and killed a warrener and severely wounded his son who was standing watch with his father. They made away with thirty dozen coneys.

Lord Mountrath responded by purchasing new flintlocks to protect his cherished warren. These were now delivered to Thomas with instruction to ensure he and his men become competent shooters without delay.

For this, Thomas would do something unaccustomed. He would reach out for help.

CHAPTER V

EXACTLY WHEN HE WAS BORN was unclear to him. His mother had said he was only a few months old when baptized on the 7th day of January 1749. When still a boy learning to count, he once calculated that according to the new Gregorian calendar that day should now be the 18th day of January 1750. By his mother's account, he was likely born in October or November of 1749. He was now in his thirty-third year.

His mother remains proud of one fact. Shortly after his baptism their county was visited by ladybird insects in numbers not before seen. The old women attached their presence to the early warm weather, claiming it to be a sign of good fortune, while pointing to the wall flowers already in blossom as evidence of this wisdom. Everyone learned to live with them that year, even the children who were forbidden stepping on them out of superstition.

Not to contradict the wise women of Eriswell, it must be noted there were also unusual floods that same month. They must have been to the disadvantage of many, but thankfully the water levels did not come close to the higher ground their family occupied. The old men said the water was not a sign of impending good, or evil. They, whose lives were spent in the examination of all that might affect their well-being, attributed the high waters to the moon, which they claimed appeared larger than normal.

There was no such divergence of wisdom or attribution when, in July of 1750 there was a sudden great canicule responsible for the sudden deaths of many people and horses. This was accompanied by storms so violent they brought all manner of strange happenings: thunder that made animals bolt, and people jolt; lighting that melted lead and torched thatched roofing and left many a stack of hay in flames; wind that blew over steeples; and hail the size of a man's fist that left fields and villages in ruin. In the fens, fish were found floating and bloated in the waterways. Crops of every kind were laid down in the fields. Of note were reports, not believed by everyone, of balls of fire moving across the land between black clouds and windswept land.

This was followed, a mere month later, by a scarcity of water.

Whether these events were good signs or bad, he was not certain. What he did know with perfect certainty growing up, was these events could destroy a warren and as it was his destiny to be tied to one, he understood he must learn to pay attention to them. Having learned his lessons well, he has fulfilled the promise of his birth.

His father is also named Thomas, and with his mother the former Martha Pressland, they form a team. Love between married partners may not often be emphasised, but as close as he could tell, Thomas and Martha had always been in love. They know what the other is thinking and most often resolve disputes without anger. They even finish each other's sentences. His father tells him not to worry if ever he hears harsh words between them, as that is a sign they still care enough to suffer vexation. Surely, Thomas junior believes, this must be what love is. If not that, it is certainly a praiseworthy friendship.

Along with his older brother George and his much older sister Martha, he grew up in the Lodge on Eriswell Warren. He came to Weeting-with-Bromehill, at the time a warren in name only, on the recommendation of his father's landlord.

When they met, Lord Mountrath took immediate comfort in Thomas' knowledge and demeanour. He also valued the recommendation of a respected local squire, William Schutte, Esq., of Milden Hall, who had long known of the family's good reputation.

Thomas Turner senior, a man of good character, unstinting industry, and unsurpassed knowledge of warrening, was descended from warreners since before the earliest memories that have been passed down in the family. No challenge was too great for him, and his sons were raised in his own image.

George was taken on at Downham High Warren in 1765. By 1770, the younger Thomas was more than ready to take on his own responsibilities when given the opportunity to warren at Bromehill, where he rose to become Head Warrener in a few short years.

This was how things had to be done. Children provided a source of reliable labour for their parents in exchange for the opportunity to apprentice under them, learning the skills that would serve them in life. Cobblers' sons made shoes; blacksmiths' sons forged iron; gamekeepers' sons protected the lord's game; and, warreners' sons raised rabbits. If an informal apprenticeship, it was no less effective than a contracted relationship, since they learned from the cradle on. Thomas senior, being from such a long and successful line of warreners, found his children to be worthy apprentices.

Every warreners' daughter and wife had to acquire the skill to dress coneys and prepare them for market and the squire's table. His sister Martha learned from their mother. Most often starting later in the day when coneys were brought in from the warren, their work continued until the day's cull was prepared for delivery at the next opportunity.

On the ground floor of the fortified lodge, with only small high windows, a fire, and candlelight by which to see, Martha's strong arms, good back, and swift fingers worked alongside the others for hours without stopping. Her skills were amplified by the tidiness with which she sped through to consistently flay each coney, such that pelt and carcass would each fetch the highest price at market. This was of immediate advantage to their squire, and of ultimate advantage to the family.

When Martha married, the match was declared a good one for Giles Beeton had grown up on the same warren. Born in the year 1729, he was eight years her senior. Of their four children, one died in a most unfortunate accident. Little Mary Beeton was trampled by a bolting nag in the summer of 1778 as she watched her father stable the horses. She died just before her tenth birthday, from that which her father had prayed that day to avoid, the lightening before the storm.

Although they would have their youngest daughter for several more years, they would lose her on her twenty-fourth birthday due to complications following childbirth. Jane had married and moved to Bury where her husband lived. William Harvey, following in his own father's path, had set up shop as a poulterer in the market and cathedral town of Bury St. Edmunds. He well knew that running a successful business required getting to know his suppliers personally, and on just such a mission, he met young Jane Beeton. They were married within eight months. Within the first year she was gone.

William had not known how to help Jane, when, within days of giving birth she began complaining of a burning, incessant pain in her belly. As the pain worsened, so did she, until they were both no more. The midwife complained she had seen these progressions many times previously, yet knew not from where they came.

The young widower now lived with his daughter who was named in honour of his late wife, and who would herself take up the family business.

Thomas senior and Martha Turner continued their work to this day on a warren south of Brandon, albeit in diminished capacities given their ages. Martha and Giles Beeton resided with them since George and Thomas had moved away in search of their own fortunes.

When Thomas arrived in Weeting he was immediately impressed by Lord Mountrath and his agent, Mr. Swift. The warren perhaps not so much, though it so fired his imagination that within a year many changes had been already wrought. The first profits came at the end of the third year when the harvest brought in sufficient quality coneys to bring to market. This year's cull was the most promising yet, which knowledge pleased his lordship who has increased his expectations now the warren flourishes.

Over the years, Lord Mountrath's impact on the parish steadily increased. Buying up land, he hired the displaced tenants and agricultural workers in a variety of new roles as his initiatives took hold. There was no shortage of work, as even new labourers with new skills were relocated to the parish. As a result, the community changed shape as it became vibrant and productive.

Thomas' few close friends included some of the parish, and some new to it. Nate Bacon was the overseer on building sites across the estate. Kitty Sallett was the cook in the Hall. Jonathan Band was the estate gamekeeper. Elizabeth Tuffs, now his wife, had been a maid in the Hall.

Kitty was the first. He always found her approachable, having such an easy manner. His relationship with her developed as they regularly met to discuss her needs for the kitchen. Their shared knowledge of plants led to improving the roles played by different grasses, clovers, vetches, legumes, and root crops in the health and the taste of the coneys he would bring to her kitchen.

In return, he once shared with her a recipe his father had given his mother after they wed. Passed down through many generations, it required boiling cut pieces of dressed coney in a fine broth made with blanched and brayed almonds. Then a mixture of powdered sugar and powdered ginger was prepared in which the coney was boiled. Before serving, it was scattered with sugar and powdered ginger.

This recipe came from an ancient time when coney was an extravagance even for noble tables. Their discourse led to a significant improvement to the dish that quickly made it a sought-after preparation for his lordship's dinner table. To improve the richness of the dish, Kitty and Thomas devised a broth by simmering the remains of cooked fowl with onions, a bouquet of parsley, thyme, rosemary, sage, and bay and a quantity of salt and pepper to add dimension. They adjusted the broth by employing at times warren fowl, either pheasant or partridge, or a domestic fowl from the manor's stockade.

Thomas senior always enjoyed telling his favourite story of a nobleman's wedding feast, having taken place more than two hundred years ago, being provided with twenty-one dozen coneys at a cost of £5 5 s.; an amount he once valued at nigh £100 in his own day.

Of course his mother, more practical than romantic, was always on hand to point out that while certainly a great deal of money at the time, the price of coney had now fallen. "At this rate of decline we should soon be obliged to pay people to take them away." Then, her eyes would twinkle and his father would put his arms around her, pulling her close to steal a pinch.

Thomas and Elizabeth Tuffs had known each other for four years before they were wed. In that time they experienced change, unfulfilled promise, and forced separation. When marriage was often a matter of necessity or convenience, Thomas considered himself fortunate to be married to a woman he knew was right for him in all ways. He still admired her eyes that projected a shine and an openness like his own mother's, and understood this to explain part of his attraction to her. For a man his age he was well placed and it pleased him to provide Elizabeth a situation that was suitable for her.

They already had two healthy young children, which was also not a given in those days. There was reason to believe these would soon be followed by more. While one-year-old John showed little personality, Mary who was now three, showed plenty of it. Just recently she gave them all a terrible fright. Unable to find her within the Lodge where she was last seen, people were sent out to search for her. After some time, a young girl came running back to the house in tears. All she could summon was a cry of Mary's name, and to point in the direction of the stockade where poultry was kept.

The posse arrived on the scene within minutes. The startled gapes from the search party, followed by several awkward moments of confusion, were evidence of their struggle to understand what they witnessed. Little Mary was sitting on the ground amidst chaos. "Dancing. See. They're dancing, mammie."

Reaching for one after the other of the score of hatchlings she had gathered up, she took their fragile wings between her thumbs and forefingers, her little fingers pointing skyward. Thus cocked and ready, she gave a sharp whirl. The frightful cheeping and the frantic flailing that ensued was so amusing to her, she kept repeating the event until her mother brought it to a halt.

Amused she undoubtedly was, but she unwittingly caused great pain to the hatchlings and distress to their parents, not to mention to the other children present. She had destroyed months of work and cost her father considerable loss, which he was obliged to pay in restitution to the warreners whose chicks she had destroyed.

Her parents were cross with her, but being a child she did not understand. Thomas was fond of saying that adversity is the mother of all good tales and as he lay in bed that evening, he wondered what tales would result from this day.

Within days he had his answer. A warrener's child became angry at his mother and in frustration, he raised his dirty dimpled hands, little fingers raised to the sky, and imitated Mary's gesture bringing instantaneous laughter from the adults.

The broken chicks, so entertaining to Mary's eye, were distressful to others. Yet the gesture itself was amusing to an adult's eye and Thomas and Elizabeth would often enjoy a chuckle over the memory of it. From that day forward, the family had a new way of signaling vexation. Knowing eyes would meet, and then most assuredly someone would repeat Mary's gesture with little fingers raised to the sky; the meaning clear to all.

CHAPTER VI

ELIZABETH STOOD BEFORE THE LARGE DESK as the man, gazing at her over the top of his spectacles, readied his hand to write. "So, Miss, shall I make that ff, ft, or fft afore the s?"

"I don't know, sir," replied Elizabeth. "Father ne'er learned me to write it."

"Well then, let's just say it's 'fts,' shall we?" The administrator took fresh ink in his quill and carefully wrote her name into the ledger as Elizabeth Tufts. "This way we may be only partially wrong, as I cannot determine with my ear any difference. In any event, how a name is written is all in the ear of the writer."

"Very well, sir." Elizabeth said with a smile in her eyes, "As long as you will call my name, I will respond equally no matter how 'tis written."

"And how old are you?"

"I was born at the beginning of the year 1753. My father told me 'twas in the first full year of the new calendar."

"Then you are twenty-two, almost twenty-three years old. Very well, young lady, for what position do you believe yourself qualified?"

"Well, I do have a little experience looking after people. I mean, if they are sick, if they need fresh bed clothes, if they need to be fed, or if the house needs cleaning. I am not lazy, sir."

"Miss Tufts, such may be said by anyone of themselves to justify their employment. Is there nothing to distinguish you from the other young women?"

"I think everyone has to deal with a great many challenges placed before them by the Lord. I've tried to deal with mine in the best way my parents, especially my mother God bless her soul, knew to show me."

"Do you mean to tell me your mother is deceased?"

"I don't mean to tell you anything, sir. Yet that is the plain truth. She's been gone ten years. I think a broken heart took her from us. She was a sweet and caring mother whom I loved dearly."

"How so, a broken heart?"

"Well sir, I don't mean to burden you with my situation, but she buried three of us, you see. First there was me. And well, here I am sir, fit as you can see. Then there is Robert, he is the last. He's named for my father, Robert. There was James, followed by the first Robert, and Mary, between us. They all died as children."

"I do believe I see, Miss Tufts."

"I'm not certain I see, sir. I helped my mother with the three young ones, but they passed in any event. Then I helped with my mother. It broke my father. When she too passed, I mean to say."

"And what has become of your father? You are his only daughter. A son, as everyone knows, will be of little comfort to him when he is old and infirm."

"Well sir, a few years back, after trying his best with me and Robert, he met Miss Ransome. They married as he said we ought to have a woman in the house. I mean not a girl, like me, sir. Though she was already with his child when they married. Then the baby, Sarah, she died too."

"And what did you do in the home throughout all this time, Miss Tufts?"

"Everything, sir, as I was the oldest and only girl. There was nobody else and my father is on the warren at Pickenham. I also card and spin wool like all the girls, for the money it brings."

"Miss Tufts, do you believe yourself capable of great discretion and energy?"

"Certainly, sir."

"And do you believe yourself to be a proper young lady with exacting standards of propriety and cleanliness?"

"I do."

"Well then, Elizabeth Tufts, I will take you on as housemaid in the personal chambers of Lord Mountrath. We shall see whether you fit in. Can you begin immediately?"

"Sir, I have no other place to go this night."

"Then welcome to Weeting Hall, Miss Tufts. I shall have someone find you accommodation and help you settle in. Perhaps you have not taken supper as you have been on the road? Let me take you to the kitchen, where I feel certain we shall find something for you."

On that Michaelmas eve when Elizabeth left her family forever, she established a relationship that would affect the rest of her life. In the kitchen she was introduced to Kitty Sallet, with whom she struck an immediate and lasting bond. They spoke at length about Kitty's mother, her work in the kitchen, and of Elizabeth's fears. Never having left home and uncertain about trusting people she did not know, it took some time, but she was finally able to repeat to Kitty what she had conveyed out of necessity to the agent upstairs. There were things she felt strongly yet lacked the means to express. In her experience, those near to her tended to the impermanent, and during their time, to be reliant on her strengths. As such they contributed little to her becoming a woman. Unless, of course, they did so without her noticing their contribution.

It was the year 1775, and now in personal service to Lord Mountrath of Weeting Hall, it did not take long for Elizabeth to gain the confidence of her superiors for her qualities in service, and the admiration of her fellow servants for her compassion and discretion. In truth, she had a pleasant way with her voice and her mannerisms that people took to without hesitation. Perhaps due to her experience in treating others at their weakest, she was adept at picking up on the smallest of cues. It seemed she knew what was to be said before the speaker himself. And her smile, which was not a smile, framed as it was by blonde curls and punctuated by topaz blue eyes, made her perfectly agreeable to all those around her.

Little time elapsed before Kitty introduced her to Thomas Turner. They were at first reticent to engage in conversation, neither having had much such exercise before. However, once they found common ground in the business of warrening, and after making discreet enquiries about each other, they arrived at similar conclusions: they would be good for each other. A Courtship ensued, and as everything proceeded on its natural course there soon came talk of a permanent union.

Then fortune stepped in. On an evening when Elizabeth was going about her business, enquiring of each bedroom's occupants whether anything was required before retiring for the night, she inadvertently startled a guest in his lordship's rooms. Because of the partially drawn bed curtains, she in fact saw nothing untoward. Her assurances to this effect were in vain, as was soon confirmed. One suggested in her presence that the knowledge she was presumed to have gained represented a great danger to them. It would be intolerable for her to remain in the hall. Her fears were proven when only days afterwards, on the 17th day of June 1776 she was summarily turned off. She was given one month's pay in lieu of the usual warning.

Stunned, she was unable to contact Thomas on such short notice. In any event, fearful any displeasure he might feel would only taint his affection for her, she left without a word of explanation to anyone save Kitty, who knew only of her destination.

Elizabeth bundled her meagre belongings, and tied a knot in the cloth so she could carry the whole as a sack. She struck out on foot, savings and severance in hand for Emneth where her brother Robert had found labour at nearby Banyer Hall. She also carried with her a letter confirming her satisfactory performance as a housemaid. This she had extracted from the manager of the estate as he paid out her severance, satisfied her departure was immediate. In truth, he also felt sorrow for Elizabeth as she was well-liked and found to be wholly satisfactory at her functions.

Based on her answers to queries, more than on the letter of recommendation from her previous employer, Elizabeth found some relief from her situation when she was immediately taken on as a maid at Banyer Hall.

As time passed, her grief continued to weigh on her for despite a naturally pleasant and obliging character, Elizabeth began to wonder what life might ever have reserved for her. The same ugly and painful sickness took most of her siblings. A broken heart then took away her mother. Now, she was alienated from the friends with whom she believed she could make a life for herself. Her only comfort proved to be Robert. Yet despite her miserable state she resolved to push forward, one more time.

Elizabeth soon fell into the rhythm of the household and quietly went about her work. With time, she found the numbing routine provided a shield against her feelings, though the manner and the suddenness of her dismissal still stung. As a wounded animal might, she kept quiet and to herself, interacting with others only after lengthy consideration. Her superior and her brother were the only exceptions to this. A newly acquired aspect of her routine was held to firmly. Henceforth she habitually knocked and waited before entering any bedroom.

Elizabeth earned respect for her diligence and her efficiency, however the distance she maintained eventually eroded the usual perception of warmth in her relations. Though in the privacy of their home Robert enjoyed her as she truly was, he noted the change in her when others were present.

Despite his probing, she remained perfectly discreet about the cause of her departure from Weeting. And despite his prodding, she would not surrender to happiness. It seemed the two might be destined to grow old together, the bachelor brother and his spinster sister. He regretted that she who had given so much of herself to their family, seemed so unlikely to ever have one of her own.

Well over a year after her departure from Weeting, Thomas' ceaseless enquiries finally led him to her. His first reaction was to blame himself, and yet despite all his searching, he found no suitable blame to lay upon himself. Was it possible he had misjudged her feelings for him? It took several months for Kitty to convince him Elizabeth's sudden and unexplained departure had nothing to do with him. Only when Kitty's protestations had relieved the weight of self-doubt, did he set out to determine from Elizabeth herself the reason for her departure.

His persistent and overwhelming sense of loss made it clear she meant a great deal to him. He therefore resolved to attempt to restore their relationship. Or, if he had his measure right, to put it on an even stronger footing.

After months of discreet enquiry he became convinced her departure was due to Lord Mountrath's personal intervention. The reason for this however, he could not determine, save to understand the subject was of considerable sensitivity. Thomas thus bided his time for the right moment to speak directly to his lordship.

One day in early autumn while they were scouting coverts with an eye to organizing a shoot, he introduced the subject of his admiration for a former housemaid who some time ago had left the Hall. He admitted to finding her charming, and in her absence, he longed for her in a manner he could not have predicted. He was now decided to find her with the intention of becoming betrothed. When prompted, he provided her name. As the response was dispassionate, even mildly congratulatory, Thomas decided the time had come to pursue her more vigorously.

Upon receiving an encouraging response to his written enquiry, Thomas travelled to her Emneth home. Even before they were seated, he commenced awkwardly, asking about everything truly of no interest to him. Beneficially, this allowed him to rein in his emotions, and to get his mouth to form the words he wished to say. When he arrived at the matter, he stated: "Elizabeth, I was bewildered by your sudden departure. You left with no word or explanation, or knowledge of where you might be found. I believed we had an understanding that we was, at least I was, contemplating a future together and that we should one day be betrothed. Did I misunderstand?"

"My departure was as abrupt as the loss of my welcome at the Hall. 'Twas demanded of me. I could not stay a moment longer, yet I did not wish any presumption of mine to burden you towards me. I was fearful any feelings you might have towards my situation would merely taint your feelings for me. I could not go to my father as he and his wife are not able to take me in. I therefore sought my brother's aid. He was my only hope, and he has proved good to me."

A pause was interrupted when Elizabeth continued, "I'm happy you sought me out, and e'en happier now to be found. I have missed our friendship, Thomas." As she finished saying this, Elizabeth reached out to lightly brush the arm of his coat. Their eyes met briefly, probing in search of answers.

"I need only know that much, Elizabeth. Why you left only concerns me if I was in any way responsible, or if there is any remaining danger to you or your reputation. Is there anything you can say to put my thoughts at rest?"

"I can say I was discharged without warrant. 'Tis in someone's fear of my presence, though I remain unable to understand what they fear. But you are here now, and if you wish it as well, I pray we may continue to see each other. I also miss Kitty. I miss our talks and her laugh. She is a dear friend and I wonder shall I e'er see her again."

"Elizabeth, if there is any justice, you will assuredly see us both again. I am determined to let her know of your friendship and to find the way for you to return to us." They parted with a shared feeling of renewed hope.

Although he had not yet received a formal blessing, Thomas assumed from the reactions, or perhaps the lack of reactions to his persistent remarks on the matter, that Lord Mountrath would not object to wedlock between himself and Elizabeth Tufts. That is, he did not appear to find fault with the clear implication she return to the parish to reside with him at the Lodge. Perhaps happily for the promised couple, the Lodge was at some distance, in all senses pertinent to this issue, from the manor house and its rumour mill. One final opportunity for his lordship to object came and went when Thomas announced his intention to ask Father Smith to publish the banns beginning Sunday after next.

Banns were simultaneously announced on three successive Sundays in the churches of St. Edmund, Emneth, and Saint Mary with All Saints, Weeting.

One day before that first Sunday publication, as Elizabeth was happily going about her business in Banyer Hall, the housekeeper approached to advise she would be receiving an important visitor in the person of Lord Mountrath himself. It transpired that while visiting with Mr. Wainwright, the owner of the Hall, he specifically asked if he might pay his respects to her. While strictly not her business of course, the housekeeper stressed Elizabeth should not depart the Hall before meeting with his lordship.

When they met, Lord Mountrath prayed her be seated. He then offered to pour her tea. Given their history Elizabeth was unsure what to expect, but she saw the situation required civility, if not quite her once ready smile. She accepted tea with a manner pleasant enough.

For a man accustomed to taking the lead, Charles Henry Coote, 7th Earl of Mountrath PC, was uncomfortable just now in the knowledge this situation demanded more delicacy of him than he was accustomed to showing. He knew that Elizabeth, despite his fear of her as a witness, had proven discreet even in the aftermath of her own dismissal and banishment from the parish. At this moment, and in a flush of heat and colour that surely gave him away, he realized for the first time the full implications of her banishment. It had not occurred to him that losing her membership in the parish must surely have led to her ruin had the only person she could turn to not provided her shelter.

However afraid he had been for his reputation; he was now determined to put that aside in favour of attempting to salvage their relationship. Lord Mountrath also wanted to avoid alienating Turner on whom much of his financial, and therefore social success, rested. He chose his next words carefully.

"Miss Tufts, I do not wish to detain you more than is necessary. Neither do I wish to abuse of your kindness in granting me this visitation. I will get to the point. I am aware you and Thomas Turner are betrothed. If, pardon me, when you indeed wed, you shall return to Bromehill Warren. As you must know, I am very partial to Mr. Turner and am thankful for his accomplishments there.

"I am also aware you was suddenly, and without explanation turned off at the Hall for a reason that remains unknown to you. I wish to be candid with you out of respect for yourself, for Mr. Turner, and for your future relations in the manor. I was the cause of your dismissal.

"I am afraid, while simply going about your business you surprised me in a moment of impropriety, an indiscretion let us say, the public knowledge of which could have meant the ruin of my guest's reputation, as well as my own. I reacted to protect my interests, the manifestation of which was your banishment from the manor, the parish and the protection you deserved. I have come to regret my decision, not least because of the virtue you have proven in the face of my own shameful attempt to protect my reputation.

"I am aware of the discretion you have shown these past two years. Another man might have simply prayed it had been long forgotten, ne'er to return. I am, however, a careful man and do not enjoy leaving loose threads. I am not here to apologize or to ask your forgiveness. I am here to ascertain your intentions regarding your newfound knowledge, now I have spoken to you plainly."

Elizabeth was at first unbalanced by such candor, and by the information just now imparted to her. Equally destabilizing was his lordship's manner, for not before had anyone ever been so solicitous of her intentions. "Your lordship must know I was happy at Weeting Hall and my friends are terribly missed. Since my estrangement we have only recently found each other, and it requires great effort to meet.

"I wish to impress upon your lordship I will remain constant to any discretion I may have shown. I have no desire to interfere in others' personal matters or to spread rumour. I now see your lordship has suffered on my account, without cause, for I understand not what I witnessed upon entering your rooms and have only suspected a connection with my dismissal."

"In that case, Miss Tufts, I regret my actions and I mean to cause you no further harm. Nay, I offer you and your future spouse my best wishes for your life together at Bromehill. I trust we have an understanding and if you agree, I shall conclude my business here and look forward to your happy return to Weeting."

"I too am satisfied my lord, that we understand each other. As the wife of Thomas, I should want only contentment between us."

"From this day forward I assure you Miss Tufts, there is that. As a demonstration of my support I will arrange with Thomas for my coach to be at your disposal. You shall not return in the same manner in which you departed."

He reached for her hand which when given, he saluted before taking his leave.

Despite all that had transpired she began to feel lighter than she could ever remember. She resolved the memory of this day would stay locked within her forever: her promise of discretion would be a promise respected.

Their day came on Monday, the 19th of October 1778, one day following the third reading of the banns. Thomas and Elizabeth were wed in a small ceremony presided over by the Reverend Charles Clarke, rector of St. Edmund, Emneth. Thomas was recorded as a parishioner from Weeting and Elizabeth, of St. Edmund. Being somewhat educated he signed his name in the register while Elizabeth made her own crosshatch mark against her name, Elizabeth Tuffs, by which spelling she would thereafter be known. As was the custom for people of their class the marriage was a perfunctory affair, attended only by a few friends. In their case these were John Stone and Elizabeth Robinson, acquaintances of Elizabeth from Banyer Hall.

Throughout the short ceremony on that bright Monday morning they were looked down upon by carved angels from the wooden rafters above. At its close, they walked down the aisle for the first time as husband and wife, oblivious to the disfigured poppy headed pews where Cromwell's men had executed all religious symbols. Upon exiting at the side and passing through the hinged carved doors, they came face-to-face with potent reminders of why we must make the most of our time here on earth. On such a day, perhaps only the most thoughtful would be struck by their walk along the tombstone-lined walkway of the churchyard, and to their lives beyond.

Lord Mountrath did not forget his promise to Elizabeth. Thomas made the trip to Emneth in his lord's post-chaise early on that still autumn morning. As he set out it was barely light enough to see the road ahead and the fields rolling between the tree lines. The vivid greens of summer were being overtaken by yellow and the stubble in the fields was turning beige, signalling change.

The cooler air of the night refused to release the smoke it held in a layer of light grey, like small flat wisps that stretched through the hollows leaving the highest roof, tree, and hill tops to catch the first rays of sun.

Still too early in the day for the warming air to carry it away, the air was sharp with the heartening smell of peat and furze fires being lit in cottages coming to life, rising with the crowing of the cocks. Wild birds had been stirring for some time, but with the warming of the sun their songs grew more animated and carried over great distances.

The return to Weeting by late afternoon was a much different journey, now they were two. Arriving home for the first time, they found a small gathering of cherished friends. Lord Mountrath had sent a basket of fruits, cheeses, breads, smoked meats, and a cask of French wine brandy. That evening their friends and fellows in the warren celebrated with them until, taking to their bed, it seemed as all in the world was where it should be.

Upon awakening the next morning, slightly unsteady from the previous evening's celebration, they found a bright sunny day which normally meant one thing during the harvest season on a warren. He had taken the previous day to be wed, but Thomas was now reminded of his commitments to the squire. They may now be two, which would undoubtedly be of benefit in getting the work done, but taking two days away from his work would be irresponsible.

The projected take of coneys in the autumn and winter of 1778 numbered only a few thousand. The warren itself was by then refurbished and the new stock was beginning to take hold, though it was not yet sufficiently mature to endure a heavy culling. This proved fortuitous as an unusually cold winter drove the rabbits deeper and coaxing them from the safety of their burrows proved difficult, even for the terriers. By the end of winter the loss to cold and severe storms became evident.

Despite these hardships, Elizabeth found the lighter work suited her condition for as Thomas happily discovered, however competent she was at dressing coneys, she was beginning to strain under the weight of her own expectations.

Their first child was born at the end of August. Given her previous experiences, Elizabeth hastened to have the baby baptized without delay. Unexpectedly, sadness over the loss of her younger siblings had been renewed with the birth. Foremost was the image of their swaddled bodies being laid inside the coffins of older men so her father could avoid paying the church fee. To her relief, their first daughter was successfully christened in honour of her departed mother at Saint Mary with All Saints on the 20th of September 1779. Mary Turner's godparents were Nate Bacon and Kitty Sallett.

With time, Thomas proved to be equally diligent in caring for his family as he was in caring for his beloved warren. Contentment reigned throughout their lives and as it thrived, so did they. In September of 1781, a son John was born. This time, perhaps influenced by the bloom on their lives, Elizabeth waited out the culling season before having him baptized. On the 13th day of March 1782, almost to the day the end of the culling season, John was brought to church to be purified and named.

Now eight years since he arrived in Weeting, Thomas felt life had thus far treated him fairly. His successes were not gratuitous, but earned through forethought, diligence, and arduous labour. The warren was successful, his squire was satisfied, he and Elizabeth shared belief in their relationship and their children, and they enjoyed genuine friendships with a few good people.

There was every reason to believe their circumstance would continue like this for a very long time.

CHAPTER VII

A WEETING OF THE MINDS, OCTOBER 7, 1782

THE CLOCK HAD JUST STRUCK FIVE of the evening as six men sat around a large table in sumptuous Mayfair, London's new and upscale residential district for the distinguished. The table, now cleared of their meal, was covered with documents and papers of account laid out for examination and discussion.

They had dined first on Fish, Calf's Head, boiled Fowl and Tongue, a roasted Saddle of Mutton served on the side table, Scotched collops, and Swan served with a Currant Jelly Sauce. This was followed by Dun Fowls, Larks, Blancmange, and Puddings, with also a sweet note of Pies, Plum Tart, Fruit, Damson Cheese, and Macaroni with Toasted Parmesan. The whole was accompanied by wines, including a sweet white wine to satisfy their palates.

There also stood six glasses of a wine brandy with the opened bottle before them. By the whiteness of their stockings and the cleanliness of their shoes, they had evidently not arrived on foot. As expected of men of distinction, they were conveyed door-to-door to attend this important meeting.

"A toast! To our brilliant endeavour gentlemen, and the jewel in the crown, Weeting Hall." The speaker rose from his armed chair, glass raised. One after another as they rose to meet him, he touched his glass to theirs, sending a clear and crystal ring throughout the room rising above the hearty sounds of affirmation.

"And thank you James, for this splendid liquor. You say 'tis from France?"

"A region they call Cognac. 'Tis reputed to be the finest of that country and available only by virtue of my Irish kinsman's efforts, who despite the hostilities, has stayed in that country to oversee his family interests. Some consider it contraband, and thus not to be widely acknowledged." He flashed a rogue's smile at his host.

The man at the centre of attention was dressed in a three-piece suit of burgundy velvet, trimmed with narrow silver braid. The collar of his frock coat stood tall before falling, and the front sides swept away as they descended to finish behind in a squared and vented back. He was not particularly tall. His slim build allowed the tight sleeves with narrow cuffs to flatter him with a younger look than some past fashions. The single-breasted waistcoat flared just below his waist and was fully buttoned, yet one did not fail to notice the quality of his white linen shirt beneath. Breeches finished just below the knees, from which point to his black silver-buckled calfskin shoes, his legs were clothed in white silk stockings. Around his neck was a fine white linen stock held in the back by a silver pin with polished garnet stones. The powdered toupee on his crown was of the newest style.

Impeccable if not fashionable, the overall appearance of Charles Henry Coote, 7th Earl of Mountrath, at fifty-seven years was appealing and confident. He was a careful man; so wary of contracting smallpox he had acquired several homes that he might travel between Norfolk, London, Devon, Dublin, and Mountrath, without having to sleep at an Inn.

Of Anglo-Irish descent, Lord Mountrath was the last of a line of men who held senior trusted offices as overseers and governors in the interests of the ruling British in Ireland. As Irish peers they sat in the Irish House of Lords, though some also sat as Members in the House of Commons of the Parliaments of Ireland and Great Britain. Most had received appointments as Privy Counsellors of Ireland, which sign conveyed to all the trust of their monarch.

Charles Henry was the only child of Algernon Coote, 6th Earl of Mountrath and Lady Diana Newport. Lady Diana was a woman of some renown and complexity, having elicited comments from a notable contemporary for her avarice, lewdness, dignity, and fondness for claret. Widowed in 1744, she had arranged to be entombed with Algernon in Westminster Abbey beneath a life size monument she had made accommodation for in her will. Commemorating their eternal love, it depicted Lady Diana rising from the tomb to be taken even higher by a hovering angel, to where her beloved Algernon awaited.

During his political career, Algernon sat for several years in the British House of Commons as member for Castle Rising in Norfolk. It was as a boy, accompanying his father throughout his constituency that Charles Henry formed his impressions of the Brecklands, and its people.

It happened that Charles was at once the commonest of sons and the rarest of persons. Uncomfortable with the fierce anti-Catholic and unionist actions of his forefathers whose opposition to Irish independence had assured their prominence as leaders of the landowning class, he did what many an independent-minded son would do. He set his own path in pursuit of political and social reform, and fiscal responsibility for Great Britain. His breed of man with the power and skill to influence was yet very small in number; though on the rise.

Exposure to people of all classes throughout Great Britain had long ago convinced him that if men came in all manner of size and shape, they were not so diverse in their disposition with regard to that most basic of desires; to survive without undue suffering. Along the way, he encountered those willing to share and help their fellow man. He was also introduced to many who would willingly step on their own mother's head to gain an advantage. Since his early life he watched the growing upset as the ancient rhythms in the lives of people were destroyed by changes introduced without any forethought of impact on people.

The result of this was now evident. The survival of the many was in jeopardy and it was his resolution to be one of those who reached out with a helping hand. He had decided to use his privileged position to promote humanitarian business practices and legislation.

The others present were James Hennessy who managed the Earl's banking interests in Dublin; his London counterpart Samuel Stokes; Ernest Salmon and Cecil Swift, respectively his stewards for Mountrath and Weeting Hall Estates; and Henry Babington, who represented his other properties throughout England and Ireland. Together, they represented a new breed of Englishman. They were businessmen and reformers too, unafraid to take initiative, and to a man supporters of emerging practices and skills.

Their day began early. They had met to review the past year's business and to examine current issues of note with the aim of taking any decisions necessary to assure the future well-being of the Earl's properties. A chief interest in their examination was the most industrious and profitable of his assets, Weeting Estate in Norfolk. At the conclusion of their examinations they enjoyed a leisurely dinner, during which they arrived at the obvious conclusion that Coote's portfolio of properties, investments, and various business interests had largely performed well since the national disasters of 1778-1779.

In that year, a severe early frost destroyed what was not already stacked or brought in from the fields, greatly diminishing what could be gleaned by labourers and the poor. The frost lasted a full eighty-four days and when the thaw finally came, it was accompanied by the discovery that many weak and poor in all parishes had perished from the cold. Stocks of peat and wood were pilfered to depletion in the attempt to repel the cold. Of concern to their business interests, it ravaged the still immature population at Bromehill where rabbits starved within the snow-covered warren for want of food to be spared. Adding to this crisis, poaching became rampant as men turned to rabbits to feed their families.

To compound this misery, in January of 1779 the whole of Great Britain was hit by the fiercest storm in any living man's memory, or as later determined, ever recorded. Haystacks and granaries were blown away, chimneys and steeples tumbled, and thatched rooves were ripped away. Much livestock was lost as animals took shelter under trees that were blown over onto them. Everywhere, the ruin proved so shocking the country's recovery efforts were slow to get under way.

To mobilize his own recovery effort, the Earl established an advisory board comprising the men who were associated with attending to his wealth. This was the board's third meeting since that grievous year and despite the obvious air of satisfaction in the room, each secretly entertained a feeling of relief.

Their leader confirmed as much in his conclusion to the formal proceedings. "I am grateful for your constancy in shepherding my affairs. Despite these trying times, I believe our endeavour has now returned to a solid footing, with the path to continued prosperity lying before us. At your pleasure gentlemen, I propose we agree our mandate become permanent, with the sole proviso that upon every third year it be re-examined to ensure it remains pertinent."

As congratulations circulated, Charles Henry Coote recalled to himself how even before he first laid eyes on the Weeting countryside, he knew of its reputation as poor ground and barren heathland where rabbit warrens, sheep walks, abandoned brecks, the ruin of Weeting Castle, and the former Bromehill Priory that once belonged to Cardinal Wolsey before passing to Christ's College in Cambridge, testified to its traditional uses. At its western end, the parish once fell away to join the marshes and the fens that were now recovered through drainage projects.

In the northeast of the parish lay a twelve-acre Neolithic mining centre called Grim's Graves, so named, at least in part, for the pockmarked surface of the site. Who or what was Grim nobody now knew, though most believed it to have been the site of an ancient Danish Encampment. The surrounding area was once the source of high-quality flints used in ancient toolmaking. Now abandoned, the most recent extraction activity had been for making strike-a-lights and gunflints, and for building walls.

The parish was now dotted with recent mining sites of the modern horseshoe-shape, flanked by mounds of chalk and flint debris. This characteristic shape reflected the technique used by indigenous miners whose pits, including the burrows and galleries, were filled in after exploitation to prevent cave-ins. This likely explained the pockmarked appearance of the surface at Grim's Graves.

When he first visited Weeting, he was reminded of a sea of sand with nothing on all horizons save an occasional tree, sheepwalks on the heath, and a few of the older warren lodges standing proud. The loose, sandy topsoil was so consistently barren that a devastating sand blow had once completely obstructed the flow of the river Lesser Ouse and buried several homes at Nearby Santon Downham. Farmers reported that during strong blowing days, they could see their fields billowing as they moved downwind.

Yet to a man with vision, Weeting parish offered hidden opportunity. The Earl of Mountrath was such a deliberate and reflective man, whose satisfaction was best achieved when his enterprise contributed to the welfare of his fellow man, as much his own.

In the year 1756, he purchased a house in the village of Weeting. He followed this with several small property acquisitions and the lease of the warren from Christ's College. He continued until he had secured exclusive rights of use throughout Weeting and Bromehill as the squire of some six thousand contiguous acres; virtually the whole of the parish, with more holdings a little further afield in West Dereham.

Returning from his reverie his lordship began to speak, "As I recollect, I first found the whole of Weeting-with-Bromehill barren and sallow, even impoverished. Many of my acquaintances believed there was then nothing to recommend it as a destination. Still, our enterprise has wrought many improvements to the character and the complexion of the parish."

"You saw that which others failed to see." replied James Hennessy, "Many of your peers are followed in your path, transforming the Breckland into numerous shooting properties. I should add, these changes are to the profit of all inhabitants who remain."

Cecil Swift added, "Being one of those inhabitants, I assure you there was a time a tenant farmer was hard-pressed to survive one year to the next. Nor had he the means to keep a property in good repair. Yet today, Weeting stands apart for being much more than a shooting establishment."

"I have heard similarly," Henry Babington followed, "the land was suspect of being exhausted from over-grazing by the many sheep. And the warrens, once so prolific, had become rabbit-sick. The little arable available did not provide for the tenants. I should believe that in the absence of all else, even much appreciated coney soon became poor fare."

Samuel Stokes, one of the new breed of bankers, added, "The problem was in holding on to the old ways. The many small landowners enforced old methods, repudiating the benefits of inclosure and modern practice through contracts that constrained their tenants. This relentless poor state simply left individual landowners vulnerable to your offers of purchase."

"I concur. Where there was an abundance of barren heath and unproductive lands, I saw fields of newly flourishing arable. Where there were small, as you say Henry, feeble warrens, I saw regeneration. And where there was land unsuitable for either arable or warren, I saw plantations of pine and fir to provide for game coverts and future profit.

"Examine the warren for a moment if you will. I had previously witnessed a once fruitful warren become wholly restored in the number and quality of coneys taken. This was done by employing modern methods and though yields did not at first impress, the earth did improve, permitting rabbits to be introduced once more. This is the very course our Turner has chosen. He ensures the vigour of the warren by subjecting the land to rotations, where each course will strengthen the soil as it nourishes the rabbits. He then introduces several foreign does of excellent constitution, every year, to keep the strength of the warren's blood line."

He paused to reflect.

"Much is also owed the success of the flint mines, which have proven singularly successful. Though long a favoured building material in the Brecks for its convenience and cheap cost, I foresaw greater profit from its reputation as Brandon Black: the most reliable gunflint. The war against our New England colonies and France is an unfortunate affair indeed, yet it provides us with lucrative contracts to provision our armies."

He took a draught of his brandy and set his glass on the table. This supplied the pause for the discussion to be taken up by another.

"I am curious, my lord," says Stokes, manager of the Earl's vast London-based fortune, "about your views on the state of agriculture. I am struck by the variances in evidence throughout Norfolk where, apart from the changes you and other early adopters of new methods have instigated, the Breckland adheres to an antiquated open-field system. Certain business relations give me to understand the movement for inclosure is resisted in the Breckland. Surely, a broader harmony must be found for the whole of the region to profit."

The Norfolk man Swift, with a shift in his glance towards the Earl, was given a nod of assent to address this comment.

"Our host permits me to address your question, in recognition more of my enthusiasm, than of any expert knowledge of it I possess. Gentlemen, I have given fair warning!

"You may be unaware, the Breckland is named for the fields that are temporarily carved from the vast poor heath for cultivation. So droughty are the sands and gravels that make up the soil in these brecks, they are suitable only for irregular sowing after much manuring by the flocks. After an unsatisfactory yield or two, they are surrendered back to the vast open heath, as they are now exhausted.

"As you witness, the Breckland is a country of accommodation, where approaches unfold to suit local variation and opportunity. Hence a confusion, rather than a single system of cultivation once dominated. The paucity of arable previously ensured a low value for the land; the effort to improve so grand that inclosure gathered small interest among the landowners. This, as the Earl has beforehand discovered to his profit, created opportunity for those willing to suffer the expense of improvement.

"There existed designated commons and wastes, with occasionally a few strips of every year land that were intensively cultivated to produce successful crops of corn, which is our way of saying, all grains. The success of these select infields was due one important contribution, the constant presence of vast flocks of sheep."

Swift proceeded to explain the Norfolk old open-field system and its associated rights and privileges for owners, tenants, labourers, warreners and flockmasters. He noted how these contributed to an unreliable and wasteful field rotating system that left most fields barren or lying fallow, even after much hardship and investment. The result was poor yields and growing frustration by all.

An engaging and intelligent man, Cecil was known by his colleagues to test the endurance of his audience. Ultimately he would become exhausted of information, but never of energy.

He commented on those physical boundaries so curious to foreigners and often mistaken for parish boundary markers. They were in fact, the armour-clad baulks that have been thrown up to enclose the warrens. While largely effective, tenants constantly complained they failed to wholly constrain the overabundance of rabbit whose presence amongst the crops caused severe damage. Unless sufficiently requited by the warrens, tenants were obliged to endure both the loss and the discouragement of their depredations. Swift appeared somewhat sympathetic to their cause.

Babington interjected, "I know of a warren's baulk being ploughed up, and elsewhere of parish boundary markers being unlawfully moved. I believe extinguishing these legal marks is explained as attempts to merely gain deceitful advantage."

"Indeed!" exclaimed their host, who cheerfully relayed the following tale. "Worse than the law may await such disturbance. An Abbot of Bury, at St. Edmunds, once responded furiously upon hearing how a person, whom he declared to be clearly incited by Satan, had altered the boundary of the Liberty of St. Edmund. In consequence, the Abbot condemned him to be anathematized, or drowned in the fires of hell. Undoubtedly, the Abbot's banks were of foremost importance to him. Happily for himself, the malefactor was not apprehended. Unhappily for the outraged Abbot, he was later murdered in Mildenhall during a peasant's revolt."

"The poor Abbot's frustration notwithstanding, there are many boundary changes agreed lawfully, your lordship. We are a country of accommodation, after all."

Swift continued, imparting other ancient practices, leaving his listeners with a mixed understanding of what might be required for the concurrent success of crops, livestock, sheep, and rabbits.

At this juncture the Earl asked in a light-mannered fashion whether Swift might be abusing the patience of his fellows. He was reassured his concern was ill-founded. To the contrary, his audience remained greatly interested.

"My wife will unhesitatingly ridicule my enthusiasm for husbandry. However, I pray all will be clear should I bring you to understand the system that brings together field, rabbit, and sheep.

"Now Stokes, I shall address your question regarding the new system for cultivating fields. But I must first make a point."

Unexpectedly, Cecil stopped first to quench his thirst, exclaiming,

"Gadzooks! this is excellent wine brandy, Hennessy, and so preferred to the tea we now enjoy. I wonder, when hostilities with France end if we might contemplate the importation of it in quantity?"

"I shall happily inform my cousin of your appreciation and inquire of him the possibility of such a venture, Swift," replied Hennessy.

Acknowledging their conspiracy with a nod, Swift continued, "We owe a debt to the likes of Lord Townshend, or as his lordship has become known, Turnip Townshend."

Standing to stretch his long legs before re-settling himself with his glass, he took another sip before resuming in this manner.

"'Tis a matter of considerable pride to British subjects their compatriots are recognized for developing and spreading the use of improved farming and animal husbandry practices. You will recall our lordship's good friend and neighbour, Thomas Coke, Earl of Leicester. He has been influenced by the late Lord Townshend and has notably adopted many of his practices, to the immense improvement of his estates.

"Some ancient machines are now being adapted to the conditions of different earths. Others offer new, mechanical means to perform labour. We now enjoy the benefit of improved threshing mills, the seed drill, and the cast-iron mould board, or plough."

Cecil Swift catalogued the merits of sowing improved strains of turnips, grasses, clovers, wheat, barley, oats, corn, and legumes. He delved into the use of cover crops in improving the soils and relieving the stresses of winter for game. He did not forget to explain the use of various catch crops now frequently exchanged for, or undersown with another crop.

He left no doubt that the modern Norfolk four-course regime, whereby farmers maintained healthy fields without the need for fallow by sowing root, legume, and two cereals in rotation for four crop cycles, was even now being overtaken by the new six-course rotation system.

"Handsome dividends flow from the application of this complex logic," his lordship advanced, "wherein the selection and sequence of sowing must consider..." and here he pointed successively to his fingers, "... the nature of the land; the season; the availability of labour and engines; the ability of a crop to add to, rather than subtract from the quality of the earth; and which crop gives the best to its successor in the field."

"Quite so, my lord. The tragedy of the commons has been reversed as turnips, to take our finest example, are now grown throughout winter to provide forage for ruminants. Clover as another example, is excellent for grazing, or for turning back in to benefit the soil. These practices permit the intensive use of all fields, such that little is left to waste.

"The essential ingredient is the most natural of all, for in the absence of manuring, there would be no dividend at all. It comes in many forms, be it the dung of livestock, great cattle, and sheep, rotting course fish, river ooze, dead leaves, the wastes from the warrens and kitchens, turned in crops, stubble, and marl. However, the most promising of all appears to be certain sowed grasses, the burning of which provides a superior effect. The obvious consequence and benefit of keeping all fields constantly under the plough is greater crop yield, to satisfy the growing appetite of man."

Intrigued, Babington added, "And obviate the ancient need to slaughter most livestock after harvest. With winter fodder now available to sustain it, livestock is bred throughout the year, thus breaking with the necessity of pickling, salting, and smoking meat to keep it through winter."

"A laudable achievement," interjected James, "and one permitting adventurous attempts at improving our breeding stocks. However, I am curious to know why the folding of sheep should not provide sufficient manure to transform the heath when, as we plainly see, they exist thereabout in vast numbers."

Enthusiastically, Swift drove into the world of sheep. Foldcourse, tathing, shackage and sheepwalks were explained along with their associated rights which he concluded thusly.

"There is a mounting frustration between livestock owners, flockmasters, and tenant farmers over competing, I daresay, confounding rights to the manure of great cattle and sheep through folding and tathing on the fields. The same confusion and frustration reigns over the means to sustain these beasts through adequate access to pasture, shack meadow and fodder. An unnecessary frustration is experienced where tenants block the free movement of animals by erecting hurdles for fear of the damage they cause on fields that no longer lie fallow. The owners of these beasts then complain there are fewer fields left fallow for their animals to cross. Alas, accommodation appears impossible to achieve."

Lord Mountrath advanced to speak. "And there, Swift, I believe we come to a point that is critical to our success. Our agreements and contracts are consistent with our desire to migrate all tenants, proprietors, and flockmasters toward the modern system. Many small fields are thus made contiguous, permitting the new sowing techniques you speak of to bring in previously infertile land to the likewise benefit of crops and livestock.

"Achievements are numerous, undoubtedly, although they come at exceeding cost to many."

He stopped to check the light without and then stood.

"Gentlemen, I see the afternoon is growing late, and our carriages are without. You must oblige me for one hour, as I have arranged a short excursion to profit from this fine autumn day. 'Twill also permit us to stretch our legs after so long a discourse. Let us take our overcoats, as the air has a bite against which we are not yet sufficiently braced. This is no criticism of your fine French brandy. We shall return to it anon, Hennessy."

"This looks promising," said Ernest Salmon. "What are we to visit?"

"As you all know, Mayfair is now extended to Hyde Park with the whole district being virtually developed for residences. The most modern and the grandest mansions and townhouses in London, in other words all the best addresses, are here within these few square miles. I wish you to see Grosvenor Square, not long completed, and just now showing signs of a maturity that is quite charming to the eye. On such a day we shall find everyone out for a stroll or a ride."

Their carriages twice ambled around the square, affording the occupants the opportunity to take in the vistas and the sights of other visitors. Unlike other early Georgian-styles enclaves, Grosvenor Square had been built to last. They alighted from the carriages onto the walkway forming the outside perimeter of the square.

Others such as Hanover Square had been built stylishly, though to a standard not meant to outlive their land leases. For this reason, certain areas of modern London were already in need of demolition and replacement. This process had been exacerbated by a variety of financial troubles resulting in the collapse of much new, and even much more old wealth. The South Sea Bubble was one such trouble.

Another problem was the landed aristocracy's ancient preference to build grand mansions and palaces on country estates, rather than on small lots governed by time-specific leases. This same phenomenon went hand in hand with their on-going interest in preserving the shooting privilege for their class.

"As you see, the square has an overall appealing aspect. I put it down to the scale of the place and the style of the mansions erected here. I am also fond of the park at its centre where classically laid lawns, and trees that will grow with time, make this in my view, the most appealing of London's residential habitats. One can almost conjure up visions of the countryside we all love.

"You may argue my sentiment in its favour over other fine examples, is doubtless influenced by it being the first of the grand residential squares.

"Come, let us stroll to enjoy the different perspectives. Mind you remain on the walkway, behind the bollards. Horses are discouraged from passing there, which will no doubt be to the benefit of our footing. Afterwards we shall rejoin the carriages here."

Stokes was familiar with Grosvenor Square, and indeed the whole West End of London. Aimed at no one in particular, he contributed to the moment by offering this, he believed, appropriate comment.

"The old May Fair once took place in nearby Shepherd Market. 'Tis this event that gave its name to Mayfair where we now stand. In its day 'twas the site of much levity as well as gravity, for fairs and public executions both took place there. Unfortunately, with time it attracted an undesirable element that preferred coarse and unruly behaviour over civility. Now, 'tis being built over with prestigious residences for the upper class. Hence, your own fine residence, my lord."

CHAPTER VIII

IN A LAND WHERE THE VALUE of an educated population was increasingly understood to be in the national interest, the children of well-paid warreners often found themselves among the fortunate. Some may have read Shakespeare's *Much Ado About Nothing*, wherein Benedick describes Count Claudio being, '... as melancholy as a lodge in a warren.' Yet on this morn, there was no such poor sentiment. Thomas rose early with a clear head, thankful there had been no trouble yesterday. These days, poachers had taken to raiding on Sundays while the faithful warreners were at service. He took a meal of stale bread soaked in hot bacon fat and washed it down with a beaker of poor beer.

Elizabeth would remain abed until the men were departed. When she did rise, she would break her fast on similar fare before commencing to sharpen knives, ready the cloth bags, and clear the tables. Later in the day, she and the warreners' wives would dress the coneys killed that day by their husbands.

* * *

Every part of the coney was put to use. After dressing them, the carcasses were sent to market towns as far away as London and to the colleges at Cambridge. Although less prestigious than it once had been, the appetite for coneys was still relied upon during the winter months.

Pelts were hung to dry before being bundled off to factories in Brandon, where the fur was shorn and felted for hats, and the skins were transformed into gloves and other articles of clothing. The finest pelts were made into exclusive robes, collars, coats, and other fine pieces for those who could afford them. Everything else was ground up to become fertilizer, or cut up and fed to the dogs, ferrets, and swine. Nothing was lost.

To answer his lordship's demands, the trapping in the early part of the season needed to begin in earnest and maintain a steady rhythm throughout the autumn and winter months. This year's expectation was for twelve thousand coneys, a number agreed after their assessment of the health of the warren and the needs of poulterers, butchers, and the manor. As costs grew more slowly than the growth in production, the warren was becoming an increasingly profitable activity for the estate. That Thomas would reach his target this year was in little doubt, if his plan was not interrupted.

Rabbits bred from February to September when the weather suited them, with the first born of the season coming in late March. Owing the prevalent disdain for eating rabbit when they were pregnant and milking, and thus to the depression in price from the 25th day of March to the 30th day of September, they were left to themselves during this period to mature.

Coney was harvested when at its best for the table, and therefore its price was highest: from the earliest of October to the beginning of February. To be successful, a warrener must master this cycle and ensure that as one season closed, he retained sufficient healthy stock in the appropriate ratio of bucks to does, to meet the expectation for the next year's cull.

Too much rain could dampen their spirit, but when the elements were favourable a doe produced four to eight litters per season, of about eight kittens each. Blind and helpless at birth, they were nursed by puss once daily for only a few minutes. After four weeks the kits were weaned, being now able to fend for themselves. Each healthy doe produced about forty surviving kits per year. Making some accommodation for loss to poachers, vermin, and harsh weather, the warrener could establish how many does and bucks of the right ages to retain as seed.

Although coneys appeared peaceful enough, bucks were often seen doing battle for supremacy of a territory when mating. Their violence extended to boxing, shrieking, biting, and kicking out with their hind feet. A successful buck would command a large area with several does, visiting different burys to make his conquests.

Does were temperamental when giving birth. Seemingly more comfortable, and certainly more successful when separated from the main colony to give birth, they were kept in segregated areas called clappers. Here, they dug short tunnels for their nests which they then lined with wool pulled from their chests and marked with urine, as a warning that this dam would protect her young.

Clustering them in this manner also made it easier to monitor their progress, to feed them, and to protect them and their young from predators, especially the bucks who tended to prey on the vulnerable kittens.

Thomas was uncertain of its origin, though he was certain the Norman French were so exceeding fond of its sweet and tender meat, and its furs for clothing, they brought it with them in large numbers, establishing the farming of rabbit on a large scale.

The effects of the cold, wet and snowy English climate could make their numbers pall as they would not vigorously search for food under these conditions. Rabbits did not dig in snow for the food that lay just inches below. Thus, a chief duty of the warrener was to plan for and provide sufficient food to see his herd through the winter. Yet in this same season, when coney's fur was thickest and its meat at its sweetest, he was simultaneously busy culling the herd for market.

Rabbits grazed within the pale of the warren where there was relative safety and planned abundance. Although nocturnal, they often grazed intensively in the late afternoon. Finishing up after light with a select diet, they then expelled their final hard, dry pellets.

The Head Warrener worked hard to ensure his charges flourished, having long ago adopted practices that were now finding favour more broadly amongst warreners. He broke up the heath to plant fodder crops and lopped whitethorn, ash, and willow to provide them with bundles of the branches whose bark they consumed in winter. He folded sheep and knew the value of the rabbits' own manure and urine to ensure adequate fertilization of the warren's cropping fields. Care had to be taken, for should customers become disaffected by an altered taste of the flesh, he could only blame himself for an injudicious application of these methods.

The year's cull began today, but the waiting crew was reminded that the plan for the day began several months ago. It would now be up to his trustworthy men to make good his promise to his lordship.

Each lurcher and terrier was beforehand examined for any detail that might render it unsuitable for the rigours of the chase. Foot pads must be clean and uncut and there must be no limp or sign of slowness. Each must show an eagerness to chase or for terriers, follow a scent through the burrows, and teeth were to be healthy. The dog should show good appetite when fed, for only those in the best of health were retained for the cull.

Ferrets were bred only for this time of year. Keeping a healthy and lustrous coat free of the mange was so important, each was regularly examined to ensure it remained free of this curse. Thomas rejected any whose signs of good health did not include clean feet and tail and a thick glossy fur, free of black dust at the root of its hair. His insistence on clean wheat-straw bedding and a daily change of litter helped keep them clean and dry at all times.

He did not tolerate any ferret improperly trained or socialized, for it was then of little use in working the burrows. Its character should show signs of playfulness. Most appreciated was when its dance steps carried it off in that strange sideways manner they have. When handled, he wanted it to show curiosity and energy, but to not bite its handler. To aid in this, they were given to the children as playmates weeks in advance of the season.

He liked to provide his ferrets with a diet of milk, bread, and the meat of small birds and vermin, but on the morning of a working day they were given only bread and milk to ensure their keenness as hunters.

* * *

Approaching, Thomas saluted his waiting crew in his customary manner.

"Davie, how're we this fine day?

"Will, has your mum her apples and plums stewed and put up for the year? Tell her I have some Damesons for her, should it not be too late.

"James, how's your boy's broken arm? Tell him he can come 'round and give us a hand if he's feelin' up to it. I'll pay him for his time."

Then he turned to Henry Manning, the youngest at sixteen years and the natural son of Mary Manning, whose father is the head of a prominent Brandon family. Together they had taken pains to ensure Henry was provided an excellent education and raised in an environment where the affairs of the nation and the matters of business are openly discussed, and in which he is encouraged to partake.

Ardley Manning and Lord Mountrath were partners in turning the Brandon black into gunflints and strike-a-lights that were increasingly in demand. For eighteen years his knappers had been working the Weeting flint and when it came time, he turned to his lordship to seek advice about his grandson's future.

Lord Mountrath appeared quite satisfied when he agreed to introduce Henry to his warrener and gamekeeper who were always in need of brave, independent young men in no great need of social contact. Henry was presently in Thomas' charge.

"Come along, Henry, we have work. You'll need to keep your wits about you and continue to work hard. Now tell me what you would do with these ferrets, then?"

Henry confidently reached into a box and pulled one out by the shoulders. He examined its feet and tail, then brushed its fur against the grain with his hand. He put the tiny face up to his own to give it a greeting, to which it responded with curious tiny bright eyes and alert ears. On the ground, it wanted to play and showed no hostility towards him. Satisfied, he placed some clean straw in the bottom of the carrying bag before placing it inside and drawing the string. When gently he placed it in the cart he turned to Thomas, awaiting his assessment.

"Well lads, I think master Henry has learned well. We don't want any mangey rascals spoiling our rabbits. Finish off the rest lad, and we'll be off. Out there," as he nodded towards the expanse of the warren, "we'll put you to many more tests before this day is done."

As they rode on the cart to the day's designated area, Henry was asked to review some of the things he had learned in his time on the warren.

This was how he began. "There is nary a moment of rest as there is as much to do throughout the night, as the day." He then listed everything he had grasped during his apprenticeship.

Thomas added that it took many years to know how to best feed his coneys. This year quantities of hay would be stacked about the warren. Wheat, rye, barley, oats, corn, and shifts of turnip and other root crops whose tops were grazed, would provide fodder throughout winter.

"I've also sowed thistles, dandelions, groundsel, and parsley to be there for them when needed.

"Before my da's time warrens were small, for only nobles and clergy was provided for. In our time we also provide for the growing number of wealthy gentry and townspeople, and for this reason winter fodder must be ensured lest the coneys starve."

"Starvation is not the only enemy of the coney." Henry reached to rub his lower back. "I've near broke my back, tearing gorse from the fields to eliminate any shelter for vermin. It now lies aside to dry for firing. I have dealt a blow to vermin, but as for the poacher, I shall not interfere directly should I see any unauthorized person near the warren. Rather, I shall hail you immediately."

"'Twould do no good to confront danger recklessly and fetch more trouble than needed."

"I'm for that. I believe I am afraid of no man when it comes to a fair fight, but poachers will have the advantage of us if we do not use good sense. I have much yet to learn, though my wish is to also know other aspects of this business. I wish to know of our customers, and of theirs in turn."

Thomas thought before replying with a question of his own. "And why should you wish to know this, Henry?"

"I think it only proper to see how our coney compares to others, and to see to what purpose we work. To become a head warrener, I must know how to fetch the best price for my coneys."

"I will not argue this. I shall see what can be done for you. For now, let us get to the business of trapping some, so we have something to take to market.

"Now, what has been done to prepare for this day?"

"The horses, ferrets and the dogs was examined. The equipment and nets was repaired and laid out. Repair to the carts was made good in readiness for hauling equipment and coneys. For the day we've food and water for man and beast, and within the Lodge, Mrs. Turner has all in readiness for our return."

"What have we done out on the warren?"

"We've trapped and destroyed plenty of vermin. Is this your meaning?"

"'Tis not my meaning. What have you done to aid in trapping the coney?"

"Ah, I now see. I've been watching their grazing habits to find where they spend the night, then where they spend the next day. I found their freshly marked trails to know where they are active. It was around these active burys and trapping banks we planted poles. I've marked the burrows without active nests so to not disturb the kits. And, I helped set the passage boards in the banks so the coney is in the habit of moving freely through to the other side. I am eager to see what this brings."

"You shall see soon enough. With some effort we shall finish the day with our carts filled. Once we have set a good pace to the season you shall take a load to market, perhaps e'en Mildenhall." Smiling, he added, "I believe I could convince Mrs. Turner to go along. She does take joy in such visits."

"Now, master spy, where do we begin?"

"I believe the best advantage would be beyond the Grim's Graves gate where many have been foraging only a few hundred yards from their burrows. Last evening, I went with Will. After the rabbits had left to feed, we strung the hayes and nets on the poles previously struck in the earth. If we succeeded, the nets have prevented their return to the safety of their burrows."

"Then, set the course. Let us see how you have done"

The others followed in their carts as they filed out of the Lodge yard, travelling towards the northeast corner of the warren along one of the many well-worn pathways created over the years.

"The heart of a warren is in the buries, for here the coney finds community, shelter from severe weather, and safety from vermin. An important aspect of every bury is its many holes, some of which provide a bolt hole when coney is under attack. We will now take advantage of those bolt holes, Henry. The land here is high and sloping to the Lesser Ouse. Do you remember why this is important?"

"Rabbits do not tolerate damp and wet. They have no like of water; thus, good drainage keeps them healthy in their burrows and prevents the kittens from drowning."

"Hmm." As they progressed, Thomas surveyed his domain, soaking up the growing warmth from the now rising sun. It would be a clear, and dry day. This was a good sign, as rabbits were difficult to put up when wet reigned over their land.

Inside the warren were small rolling mounds on an otherwise flat surface. Here and there a bush grew. Beyond the pale could be seen the rising pines, oaks, and beech of the plantations.

Upon close inspection of the land one noticed a multitude of small black clumps. These were the coney they had come for. Near each was a bare, sandy hole around which was a ring of short-cropped grass and lichens. A few wildflowers persisted, even at this time of year. With so many rabbits, no long grasses were able to survive unless they were in the protected fields that provided winter fodder.

There were some deliberate exceptions to this flat surface. The trapping banks, and the boundaries protecting the arable fields and the clappers, were clearly visible. There were also several burys that had been thrown up in earlier times to determine their usefulness in the Brecklands. In the event, these proved unsuccessful in the omnipresent light sandy soil where puss could easily dig downwards to thrive.

Once arrived, they off-loaded the equipment and nets before organizing the dogs with a minimum of commotion. Any dog let upon the warren must first be trained to obey commands. There was no need to put up the coney before his men were ready for it.

Thomas surveyed Henry's work from a distance. Fully five hundred yards of hayes had been positioned in an arc, blocking the pathways back to their burrows. He found nothing to criticize. He explained Henry's tactic to the lads and gave instructions for working the lurchers. The harvest season was about to give up its first rewards.

They walked the lurchers around to the far end of where the coney had been grazing so as not to alarm them. They were trained to follow signals and to remain silent even though provoked. This was essential to avoid disrupting the herd. They were positioned about one hundred yards apart with a view of the nets in the distance. On command, the dogs were released to give chase.

What happened next was of no surprise but to Henry. He had heard of, though not yet witnessed scores of coney simultaneously bolting in the same direction.

Trained not to take them in their mouths, lurchers ran hither and thither in pursuit of rabbits as they attempted to reach the safety of their burys. Their flight was predictably interrupted by the awaiting long nets in which, after a brief flurry, many were caught; the remainder having successfully found refuge in a hole.

All the dogs but one, and it to chase down any stragglers, were returned to their leashes. Being secured to stakes this prevented disruption of the next operation.

The warreners proceeded down the line to dispatch the entangled coneys one by one, releasing the dominant bucks, pregnant does, and any still insufficiently mature. Thomas extracted and destroyed those too long in the claw, showing grey, or whose front knee joints were too close together. These were too tough to be sent to market and too old to continue a strong bloodline. They were, however, useful for the Lord to fulfill any number of obligations within the parish.

Dispatching was done quickly to avoid prolonging any suffering, fright, or commotion, and without bruising or breaking which only diminished the coney's value at market. The method involved gripping its hind legs with one hand and placing the thumb of the other hand behind the neck with two fingers under its face. With a smart movement the coney was stretched and the neck was snapped by pushing the head back. Working on the warren brought constant reminder of the respect due each living thing, and a good warrener tolerated no abuse of the principal that all life was sacred. Thomas had immediately turned off any man who failed this test.

As the cart trundled along beside the line of working warreners, the pony being led so to avoid stepping into a rabbit hole which could prove disastrous, one further thing needed to be done.

"Here, Henry, there's one more thing to do 'fore loadin' it onto the cart. Take it by th' ears an' run yer thumb down its belly."

"What's that for, Davie?" asked Henry.

"Ya don't want spoiled fur."

Henry looked at the others who stood there, expecting Henry would do as Davie had told him. "I'd rather you show me first," he said, not sure how to proceed.

"Nah, you'll do it easy 'nough."

Henry looked wary, though he did as Davie had urged. He took a rabbit by the ears, stared into its now blank eyes, and rubbed his thumb straight down the middle of its belly.

To his surprise a stream of warm urine came shooting out and splashed over the front of him.

The other lads burst out into great laughter, slapping their thighs and each other's back while Henry looked sheepish and annoyed. After a minute, even he was caught up by their laughter and broke into a wide grin, chuckling at their little jape.

"Now ya know why they 's called slops," said Will. "Here, we'll show ya' how it's done so's ya don't get pissed all over."

Each coney was held on its back facing away from the warrener in one hand, while the thumb of the other hand ran firmly down the length of its belly to evacuate its urine. This was often a surprising amount for rabbits do not drink, rather they get their moisture from the succulence of vegetation. This evacuation was done to preserve the fur and to keep the flesh from acquiring any unduly strong tastes.

Once the nets were cleared, Henry took a long pole and balanced one end on the side of the cart for support, while the others hocked each coney before suspending it upside down from the pole. He watched as they slit the thin part of the lower leg between the two bones and pushed the foot of the other leg through this slit to form a loop with the legs. He quickly learned to do the same, and one after another they suspended the coneys with their legs interlaced until the pole was full of the coneys hanging freely. If done correctly, the cart would be well balanced.

They counted nine dozen coneys taken this morning, which augured well for the season. Henry then learned to his dismay their day was just beginning, for more harvesting awaited before they would return to the lodge.

Before leaving this place they collected the hayes, removing them to be positioned on another set of poles they had previously planted alongside the nearest trapping banks, opposite the side from which the rabbits tended to approach. Once their hayes were in place they left for the next site, to return later in the day for a final attack.

Trapping banks at Bromehill were a few hundred yards in length and about two to three feet high. Each was made by placing grass sods or turves on top of each other as one would place courses of stone, leaving occasional short gaps. These gaps were fitted out with boards, weeks before the culling season, and more sods were added to hide their presence from the rabbits. All was intended to encourage them into a routine of passing freely through the hole in each board. This routine was to be their undoing, for with the nets in place on the far side, and the chasing lurchers setting them in flight, the coneys found only treachery where they sought refuge.

The next site was sufficiently distant that the earlier commotion had not disturbed the population. It was chosen for the number of burrows where rabbits would have taken shelter in the approaching midday.

Holes were chosen for the placement of purse nets to capture anything trying to bolt from them. With the men working in two teams, ferrets were unleashed into the burrows where a final purse net was placed over this last hole. A struggling rabbit could not go far, as purse nets were staked in place and as it struggled, the drawstring was pulled tighter.

This method worked satisfactorily, if not as efficiently as the first. Other than using muzzled terriers, which they did from time-to-time to give the ferrets a respite, this was the only way to force the rabbits from the security of their burrows. A Jill was usually a safe bet as she was smaller and more able to work quickly to flush rabbits. A Hobb was muzzled and leashed with a measured and marked length of cord. His unfortunate tendency to kill and eat the rabbit before falling asleep, left the warrener little choice but to dig him out whenever this happened. By the length of cord, he knew where to dig, which he did until he broke into the nest area where the ferret, and usually the remains of his feast were to be found.

If a Jill laid up, it was most likely because she had not frightened the rabbit out and there was a standoff within. After some time, the rabbit and the ferret were located by the rabbit's thumping, which sound it made to signal alarm or anger. Again, they must be dug out, but in this instance an ear to the ground was used to locate the thumping.

Astonishingly, he took uncommon pleasure in the thudding of the rabbits. Since his arrival on the warren in early summer he had not encountered such a sound. At times there was no need to put an ear to the ground as the sound came from near an entrance. At other times he was required to sleuth around, running his ear on the ground back and forth in different directions, until he identified the exact spot above the source of the sound.

Digging out was laborious and if it were not for the need of the ferrets for further trapping, it would be avoided. The sandy soil was easy to work yet when the nest was deep, as some were, Henry was sent headfirst down the hole to retrieve the ferret and the rabbit, or its remains. To Henry's relief, this only happened twice.

When they had taken a goodly number, Thomas signalled it was time to leave off this area. It did no good to exhaust it completely. Fortunately, the warren was constantly growing and the emptied burrows would soon be filled with new tenants.

"Come lads, we've something waiting in the cart yonder."

Thomas strode over and from a sack pulled several items wrapped in folded cloth and handed them out. Inside each was a dark bread, cheese, a thick slice of bacon, and a few plums. He then opened a cask in the back of the cart, filled a wooden beaker with Elizabeth's small beer and passed it around for the others to drink. He filled it up a several times before slaking his own thirst.

"I believe we have nigh on thirteen dozen. What say you, Davie?" Thomas' remark was said with cautious satisfaction.

"Well, I reckon we've that at least. Them last holes flushed out many and we got 'em all," said Davie. He took a swig of beer to wash down a mouthful of bread and cheese.

"I count a hunnert fifty-nine," stated James. "I says that makes more 'n thirteen in all. A good mornin's work by my count."

"I grant you that, 'tis a fine morning's work."

Thomas thought for a few moments. Silence was not an issue with these lads. They were not long on conversation and most at home in the silence of the open heath. Their days were usually accompanied by the soft sounds of the wind, birds, and bleating sheep that seemed to carry for miles in this region of Norfolk. Rabbits didn't make much noise unless the bucks were fighting for their territory, or their lives. Their shrill screams could be short-lived as a dominant fighter would make swift history of his competition.

Still, his responsibility for Henry meant he was willing to enlist the unwitting help of his men in support of his aim. He therefore took this time to engage them in discussion of the various means of capturing coney in the harvest. There was plenty of time to return for the day's final assault.

The short of their exchange was that some means of capturing coney take more effort and time than others. Yet there is a means for each time of day and for each part of the warren. A familiar technique much used in the past was simply to surround a bury or a selected area with long nets, before flushing the rabbits with ferrets and terriers. The bolting rabbits are caught in the nets, but sometimes they simply run in and around their holes in a merry-go-round, with too few actually being taken.

Importantly, it was acknowledged Henry had correctly identified one of the more efficient methods for this warren. It was also effective when recovering escaped rabbits that have found refuge in a coppice or a covert. The additional incentive in capturing these rabbits is in avoiding the wrath of nearby farmers.

Henry spoke, "I've heard in the yard, should a dog run a rabbit to ground 'twill ne'er then bolt, e'en you ferret it."

James responded, "In Norfolk, 'tis true. Only way to git a rabb't thus run to ground is to dig it out." He went on to explain his own calculation that rabbits felt so safe in the deep dry burrows of the Breckland they could not imagine one would take the trouble to then dig them out.

"But if yer ferr't has laid up, if ya got the time, place a trap with bait at the hole and next mornin' ya got yer ferr't."

Evening was approaching as the men worked their way home along the warren's well-worn paths between the Lodge and its many killing fields. The carts were laden with poles strung crossways on the beams. In his mind, Thomas was already planning the evening's work and the distribution to markets. In all they had two hundred and seventy-five coneys: twenty-one market dozen with a pair left over for the squire's table.

Thomas was gratified. He well understood that every occupation had pleasant and unpleasant aspects to it. In his experience, today was the part of the warrener's job some did not take to. Henry Manning had not faltered.

✳ ✳ ✳

However hard the men had worked to bring home the carcasses, it was here in the Lodge where the real demonstration of skill took place. Any soiling or damage to the furs, or tainting of the meat by pooled blood, urine, or fecal matter, would make waste of the day's efforts and represent a loss for the estate. Tonight, two hundred and seventy-five carcasses would be dressed using skill, care, and strength before they could take to their beds.

Weather permitting, and with few exceptions until mid-March, this day would repeat itself over, and over, and over again. Henry knew that becoming a successful warrener required mastering many skills. He now realized it also required strength of body and character. For the first time, he questioned whether he was a man for the job.

As they unloaded the carts, two men to a pole, the waiting women began dressing the coneys. While three cased, two paunched, and two more finished the dressing while the oldest children huddled them by the dozen in clean cloth.

All equipment was cleaned, sorted, and stowed and the animals were given their rewards. Dogs and ferrets were cleaned and fed morsels of liver, kidney, and heart washed down with water. Horses were fed, brushed, and stabled.

As he had estimated when watching the setting sun, they would be at it again before first light. Thankfully, the intense winds that had blown sporadically for some weeks, were now abated.

Thomas looked to Henry, who answered before his question reached his lips, "As you showed me, there is a place for everything, and everything is now in its place."

Thomas nodded with appreciation.

Henry knew of different ways to dress a coney, yet here all was repeated with an identical economy of motion and deft use of knives and fingers. The meat was valuable enough, but as the skins were valued at 18s. per pound weight, or sixteen furs, spoilage could soon undercut profits. For this reason, only those trained to the satisfaction of Elizabeth were involved in this process.

Before the fourth hour had come, the only signs of the day's industry were the baskets of huddled carcasses and the hanging skins. And a tired crew. As everyone sat to a hot meal prepared by the women that afternoon, Henry privately celebrated his first harvest. It was no small beer on this night. Elizabeth served her wheat beer, made the more satisfying for her manner of serving it cooled.

There being several married couples at the table, conversation was lively and only somewhat mindful of Henry's presence.

CHAPTER IX

CHARLES TURNED SUDDENLY to his right hand man in Weeting, "Am I mistaken, Swift?"

"I believe not my lord, for such is my understanding as well. Although their traditional rights are extinguished, they continue to enjoy others granted by your agreements. They enjoy, as an example, unstinted rights upon the heath, and rights to cut turf, furze, brush, and ling for fire sufficient for the needs of each tenant. I should not forget you have set aside poor's land to the benefit of the needy."

The Earl and his guests were returned to the comfort of his hearth where it was agreed the intermission was greatly appreciated for its exhilaration and the pleasantness of the views. Throughout their excursion Swift was most impressed by the noises of workmen as they clattered, hammered, sawed, and chipped away at their labour. He discreetly remained silent when he computed the evident source of ideas now being applied to Weeting Hall.

They had returned to the issue at hand when they earlier broke off, leading to a discussion of the various rights and privileges of flockmasters and herdsmen. Swift considered his earlier explanations had somehow fallen short and he desired to correct that failing. "'Tis a matter of confusion that the uses and practices related to the rights of liberty of fold, foldcourse, foldage, shack and sheepwalk do not refer to the same right or practice in all counties. Moreover, some have long changed meaning through the force of common usage in each county."

His examples illustrated his meaning and he soon sensed from the questions that his explanations were beginning to take hold. One that was particularly illuminating came in response to James, when he asked why a sheepwalk in the Breckland was elsewhere known as a foldcourse.

"A foldcourse connotes the land over which sheep feed, and in which they are folded within a perimeter of hurdles, or boundary markers, that are constantly shifted about to ensure the benefits of tathing are well distributed over the lands. Tathing is the valuable working of the land when beasts both manure and trample the earth. Where villages contain more than one manor, or where heaths are expansive, separate foldcourses are allotted by agreement. From these fold areas, sheep are daily led to their grazing, or after harvest to their shack fields, where they feed on the stubble and wastes.

"With time and common usage, tenants came to assume the privilege of foldcourse was exclusively theirs to fold and turn their sheep out by day to pasture. In Breckland, it came to be claimed by tenants as a right of common, when in fact this was only incidental to the lord's right to fold all the tenants' sheep to tathe his own lands.

"Thus, foldcourse, sheepwalk and common of pasture became synonymous in Breckland. This only became a matter of contention when livestock and great cattle far exceeded the immeasurable sheep in number.

"We now arrive at the crux of it. For the rivalry Hennessy has identified became too distracting when the vast herds and flocks vied for increasingly limited grazing as improvements converted outfields, or brecks, to productive infields. Thus, foldcourses overflowed. Great cattle and sheep encroached onto each other's sustenance. Even the once-impervious heath proved susceptible to erosion under these conditions.

"I pray I have made clear that the lesson propelling inclosure is one of excessively varied and competing rights and interests to the satisfaction of none. 'Tis thus inclosure demands the extinguishing of rights of common, sheepwalk, shackage, and other rights and interests over any common lands and grounds so inconveniently situated they are incapable of any improvement."

Salmon reflected upon this Weeting stratagem to eliminate chaos. Addressing Charles, he said, "Mountrath tenancies are drawn up on advantageous terms to the estate wherein a complex field cropping, folding and tathing system, in truth all other interests, are subordinate to, and at one with your own. Ownership of the whole permits such subjugation.

"Undeniably, 'tis to the eventual satisfaction of all. The resulting increase in crop yields and sustenance for beasts justifies your higher rents, which tenants and owners submit themselves to for profitability is now in their own hands. The strength of this stratagem is evident in the increased sums derived from rents."

Saying this, Salmon leaned forward to identify on the table those statements of account which supported his point.

Stokes reached for a document on the table immediately before him. "I recall rentals previously did not exceed £5,000 per annum." As he glanced down, adjusting his double spectacles, he specified, "Yet this past year have exceeded £25,000." Having drawn out the twenty-five thousand pounds, he looked around the table. "This is due the increase in crop yields by, let me confirm, one-third per acre with many more acres now sown. The total crop yield milord, is considerably more than a twofold increase."

Swift ran on vigorously, "Such, in sum, is the promise of inclosure. As Stokes argues, the Weeting scheme consolidates fields, reduces waste areas, and ploughs together the boundary meers and the grass baulks upon the heath of ancient warrens and folds. This permits improved rotation of crops and manuring, of which 'tis believed burning holds much promise, such that fallow is all but eliminated."

"We should expect some brecks will fail, only to be returned to the heath or converted to plantation," added the Earl to curb runaway enthusiasm, before Swift continued.

"Indeed, the hand in glove nature of the thing has led to successes elsewhere. With winter fodder now assured for the warren, Turner has taken on additional warreners to assist in the trapping and to stave off poachers." The Earl conveyed his satisfaction with this decision.

He continued. "A final word from me on this. Since taking up cross-breeding that black beauty the Old Norfolk Horned, with the Southdown, our efforts hold great promise it will be highly appreciated at fine tables."

Babington took this slight deviation to interrupt with a thought that had been steeping in his mind for some minutes. "We must not overlook the benefits derived from these successes by the families of our tenants and labourers. Each farmhouse and cottage now has a sufficiently large and bountiful garden. I am also given to understand there is widespread enjoyment of tenants, especially of their women, in keeping greater numbers of livestock from which to derive quantities of sweet milk, cheese, and meat so essential to the vigour of the young."

Ernest elaborated, "I'll wager the proceeds of their labour are claimed to permit them to acquire needles, pins, cloth, and other necessities to clothe their families."

Babington continued, "I can attest that upon my last visit I found the changes visibly arresting; for the landscape itself is much altered from my first travels to Weeting. I noted the many wells now dug to provide for the multitudes of man and beast, particularly your precious game fowl and rabbits, my lords, who require great quantities of water in this dry land. Yes, I too previously found it the poorest of open heathlands and warrens where ..."

"Where now we may find vast fir plantations of pine and larch," interjected Swift.

"Indeed," taking up this thought Babington continued. "Larger fields are now distinguished by long rows of banks being thrown up, to be topped with dense plantings of pine and beech."

"They are proved effectual in reducing the amount of soil carried off by the blows that imperil exposed fields," said the Earl.

"Undoubtedly they also provide excellent game cover and contribute to the quality of shooting." Salmon thus reminded them this had always been uppermost in the mind of Charles Coote.

"Quite so. That which we set out to accomplish has been achieved and notwithstanding this success, there remains one aspect of the plan I find dispiriting." The Earl stood as he spoke, taking a turn toward the window to catch the dying light.

"I deplore the fate of those tenants and labourers turned off for want of finding labour among the remaining tenants. Some have found refuge with kin, to live constrained by inadequate lodgings. Yet others have migrated to the towns so ill-equipped to take them in. Those unfortunately too ill, young, or old to work, continue to suffer and so have been removed to the Poor House. The remainder have fallen upon the parish. Not all then, have shared in the benefits of our project."

"Yet the Parish Officer reports the poor are better now than ever before. He assures me the rents from two lands and the interest of several sums bequeathed the poor are substantial. Mayhap your concern will be somewhat assuaged by this knowledge," affirmed Stokes. "Surely the benefits we enumerated, and the profits we examined this morning, justify the improvements made."

"Let us not forget the many more mouths now fed due the increase in crop yield and the abundance of sheep and rabbits." offered Salmon.

Swift interjected, tapping the table with his finger in emphasis of each point. "The remaining tenants are undoubtedly much improved for the new arrangements. Labourers enjoy greater income now their work carries on throughout the year, rather than a few short seasons. Livestock enjoy pasture of a quality not before achieved. Every soul keeps a garden plot where they yearly introduce new and varied vegetables, herbs, and flowering plants. Fruit trees now grow where previously none were possible. Estovers, secured by arrangement, now provide wood for heating and repairs to cottages. All this wellbeing is enjoyed by those we have retained."

Charles Henry Coote responded, yet in such a manner the others knew to move the conversation to another subject.

"I accept your verdict: those who remain have benefitted. 'Tis fitting these tenants and labourers, either by chance or by ambition have shared in the benefits. Yet I remain ill at ease for having extinguished the ancient rights of people whose families had lived in Weeting."

Now Charles began to tap his fingers on the table.

"'Twas intolerable for those forced to leave as they lacked the purpose or the opportunity to stay, or perhaps was unfit to withstand the changes. Where did they go and how did they provide for their families?

"You spoke earlier, Swift, of our friend Coke. Know you he was foremost a believer in the moral, if not legal obligation of a landowner to ensure the quality of life of all who live on his estates? The landlord is to provide fields, roads, bridges, buildings, and certain engines. The tenant is to give seed, minor implements, and his labour. Labourers are to provide their toil in return for wages. I may favour this model, yet the changes it demands are disturbing for the injury suffered by many. I question whether a new model will not soon be required."

"Of what do you speak? Surely not of upheaval." Mr. Salmon shifted in his chair at the uncomfortable thought.

"Many lament the passing of older ways so necessary to forging improvement. When an existing order becomes uprooted, some will thrive in the chaos and derive benefit. Too seldom acknowledged is the displacement and loss suffered by the many more. Our old order staggers under the obligation to feed a populace that grows more rapidly than we know. To remedy this, we require new systems with new tools without delay. Yet uncertainty lies before us.

"Though we Britons are increasingly numerous, we are limited by the seas that surround us. Gentlemen, we share a tremendous responsibility. If we fail to do well by our countrymen, we may come to experience a most remorseful season."

There was a momentary pause as unpleasant images of his meaning were conjured. Rumblings and dissent were indeed rampant. To a man, they understood his meaning. Responsibility for the interests of all citizens must not be taken, as the Earl intimated, lightly.

"How do you find the shooting this season, my lord?" Hennessy bravely took up the challenge of broaching a different subject. "I have news of my cousin in France who laments the failure of game and rabbits to provide a pleasant experience, not having recovered from the recent depredations everywhere reported in that country."

"Well, this is a subject that pleases me greatly and of which I am prepared to speak. Let me fill your glasses gentlemen, as we steer a course for more pleasant thoughts." Saying so, Charles Coote poured each a generous dose of the delightful therapy provided by his Dublin man.

"I'm given to understand you now maintain a permanent staff at Weeting Hall. Surely, this is encouraging." Babington supplied this contribution while their host concentrated on reaching everyone's glass. He too was eager to move the conversation along.

"That is so," he answered as he sat. "The shooting is excellent throughout the whole of the parish with the game being luxuriant and in good fettle, which fact guests comment upon favourably. As well, the warren flourishes with that single breed of black that does extremely well in the pot. We shall enjoy many fine shooting days on the warren this winter."

Hennessy was reminded of his familiarity with shooting at Weeting, having at times even attended the Glorious Twelfth, that day in August marking the opening of grouse shooting. This season witnessed the Prince of Wales attend, as did the recently resigned Prime Minister, Lord North. It was widely known but never admitted openly, that Weeting was not renowned for its grouse for the inability of that game bird to propagate on the dry heath. Lord Mountrath's invitations on that occasion were taken up more for the quality of society and the evening entertainment, than for the bagged game.

Meanwhile, Lord Mountrath held the floor. "I am deliberate in keeping only the Muel, for its rich black fur so esteemed by furriers and felt makers in Brandon. Its meat, long desirable for its flavour in our market towns and at Caius College, will soon be found in Leadenhall Market where rabbit is more generally sold than in earlier times. Epicures shall soon account for one thousand two hundred dozen Bromehill coneys per annum.

"This shall bring almost five hundred pounds income annually. Turner reported a satisfactory first week of harvest, and there was seemingly room to improve should we agree future contracts at twelve, rather than thirteen coneys the dozen."

"'Twould seem poachers are so smitten by your coneys they now represent a great menace. What say you to this, my lord?" Swift was aware of recent interactions between poachers and the keepers resulting in appalling incidents.

"You are quite correct, Swift. Fortunately, the ill suffered is limited to the loss of a few score rabbit and the beating inflicted on one of Turner's men. I have nevertheless taken additional precaution. For one, you will have encountered the Notices posted along the warren boundary. Turner has also taken on two additional men with modern guns. He is himself now armed with a superior fowling piece fitted with a three-foot barrel. These should prove somewhat discouraging to further trespasses."

It was now the host's turn to move the subject along. "There is one aspect of shooting we all agree on: the black flint produced on the estate is superior to all else for its reliability. As I earlier alluded, the Board of Ordnance has recently agreed a contract for the provision of one hundred thousand flints of the best sort from our mines. We can thank Stokes, whose timely intervention with Lord Wellesley conveyed to us the specification for the platform flint newly adopted from the French. We also owe a debt to Mary Grief and her company of knappers for acquiring the skills for their production. At the current rate, we shall soon complete the terms of the contract."

Hennessy, for his part, had not ventured far from his recent thought. "This recalls to me an inquiry I formulated when recently shooting at Weeting. I was then resident in the Hall where I was impressed with your improvements and the competence of your staff, for which I complement your establishment, my lord." A remark of this nature from Hennessy did not go unnoticed. Having travelled with his cousin throughout France, experiencing the finest of that country's luxury, fine food, and excellent wine, he had gained the reputation of a fine gueule.

He continued, "I questioned, however, why you did not take advantage of the native flint for your new Hall. It has been in use here since before Weeting Castle was built for the Earl de Warenne. The warren lodges hereabouts make good use of it and have stood for several centuries. Should you not have availed yourself of the parish's natural stuff?"

"You make a point, Hennessy. 'Twould indeed have been a fitting substance had I desired a sturdy house consistent with the tradition of the Brecks. My goal, however, was to the contrary. I desired to create the sensibility of a modern, well-proportioned, and welcoming Hall. I therefore shunned the use of it for my home, though it has proven useful in building and repairing our farmhouses and cottages."

The well-travelled Hennessy concurred with his lordship. "I believe the white brick of your Italianate style is from your own kiln?" Seeing the lifted eyebrows, he said, "I quite thought so! The bold portico and the large stone columns enhance the façade, affording it an entirely noble and inviting appearance. 'Tis one I believe pleasing to your peers. Do I understand the workers sent down from London will soon complete the interior finishing?"

"That is indeed the promise of their overseer. When completed, the Hall will be surrounded by vast lawns, treed park land, and planned gardens comprising forty acres. The enclosure will be of native stone augmented by those recovered from the ruins of Bromehill Priory. The ruin of Weeting Castle, lying opposite, will provide a pleasing aspect to the gardens being planted."

"I should wonder," queried James, "whether such a number of workers would overtax the wherewithal of the parish?"

"I might respond to this." stated Swift.

"People are proving very resourceful, but undoubtedly the weight of so many has taxed the resources of the parish. To alleviate some of the strain we have laid in new roads that employ pioneering techniques. We are assured these roads will better resist the climate and the blows of Norfolk, and thus be of lasting benefit to the parish. They have proven essential to the expeditious movement of men and supplies, as well as sheep and great cattle, without disruption to the tenants. Their surfaces, being impervious to the churning caused by the passage of wagons and animal hooves, permits them to be built at a width half that of dirt roads.

"Other works have been assumed. Where possible, workers are lodged with the families of parishioners who are grateful to receive the additional proceeds. To accommodate other workers we have thrown up rows of cottages. These are solidly constructed of clunch and flint nodules, or rough stones. Rooves are well thatched with native water reed, where the ceiling overhead supports straw above for increased comfort in the cold. Tenants and labourers are no longer suffered to endure bare earth floors where water pools, or unfinished walls with doors and windows that prove insufficient as barriers against the rain and snow. The result is thoroughly modern and comfortable. When vacated by the temporary workers, these will remain as living quarters for those agricultural labourers whose own cottages are beyond repair.

"These undertakings have required a high order of organization, coordination and oversight of execution. I can think of several men whose presence has been essential to this, Nate Bacon being one who stands out for his knowledge of the environs and its inhabitants."

"And has this all transpired in harmony with the inhabitants? Surely, the many tradesmen and labourers have brought with them foreign ways disturbing to the natural order of Weeting." Babington, although stewarding affairs for the Earl at other properties, was aware of recent friction between estate and agricultural labourers. Such was a predictable consequence of assembling people of differing habits in such proximity. Although workers at Weeting came with excellent references, the cockneys exhibited a slyness beyond the experience of rural folk. By comparison, they appeared rough and selfish.

The Earl of Mountrath responded to the astute question in this manner. "'Tis not the friction between people that most troubles me. I am most vexed with the serious damages suffered by myself and our men at the hands of a villainous and treacherous few. Thievery cannot be tolerated; thus, I am occupied with the countering of such acts, including the persecution of those caught in the act."

"What is in your power to do?" asked Stokes.

"I can attempt to prevent further acts by expressing to all workers my expectations for probity at all times. This, I have personally done while reminding them of the consequences of being discovered.

"I have also, just this day deployed another tactic. I have unleashed our vicar upon them."

"How so?" asked the others almost in unison, equally astonished at his tone.

"I recently requested of Father Smith an uncommonly emotional and thoughtful sermon. His subject is to be the recent execution of the traitor Tyrie, at Plymouth, and I am assured no detail of that butchery will be too grisly for him to recite. The devout will doubtless be impressed by his words."

"Prince Machiavelli would himself be impressed," said Hennessy.

"If it reaches the ears of those for whom 'tis intended." replied the Earl. "If it reaches their ears with effect, I should concur."

CHAPTER X

EVERYONE PRESENT RECOGNIZED where this would lead. The slowing of his speech, the careful enunciation of each syllable, and finally, the rising pitch of his voice confirmed it for all. The Reverend Charles Smith was rounding the last corner for the home stretch. "Perhaps now we shall know his message," he complained to himself as he listened.

"And when he was demanded of the Pharisees when the kingdom of God should come, he answered them and said, 'The kingdom of God cometh not with observation. Neither shall they say, lo here! or, lo there! for, behold, the kingdom of God is within you.'

"And does it not say in the Book of Proverbs, 'For as he thinketh in his heart, so is he.'?

"As you go in Peace, I pray you remember these words, for they tell us if a man will find the kingdom of God within his heart, his actions will be worthy of that kingdom. I say to you, everything that enters a man's life has the opportunity for good or for evil, yet we know whether a man will enter the kingdom of God by the sum of his actions. A man who chooses good will be doubly blessed. But a man who chooses evil will pay both here on this earth, and in everlasting damnation."

Solemnly, and with outstretched right hand he directed his final blessing at his congregants. At each extremity of the cross he touched them with two crooked fingers, "Go with God." The vicar turned over the last of his papers. He then gestured towards the rear with outspread arms that made wings of his surplice, bowing his head silently to invite them to take their leave.

One by one, the pews emptied as parishioners turned slowly to leave. No benevolent reminder of God's grace and forgiveness was theirs on this day. In its place was the burden of anxiety and the fear of damnation now laid upon them by their shepherd's words.

Once met, the eyes of two of his sheep communicated the desire to meet outside. After the obligatory greetings and small talk at the door, Nate Bacon and Thomas Turner excused themselves from their immediate company. They stepped aside for privacy amidst the tombstones.

"Those are words to think on, Thomas. What do you make of them, then?"

"They was certainly enough to put the fear of the law in people, if not the fear of the Lord, do you agree?" replied Thomas. "I do not grasp the meaning of the subject our vicar has chosen this day."

The parishioners of Weeting Saint Mary with All Saints were accustomed to their vicar using his sermons as weapons in the fight against evil. At times striking suddenly from beneath a veil of allegory, he wielded arguments like a blunt weapon, without naming either the crime or its perpetrator. These sermons left everyone feeling equally culpable.

At other times his complaints came as from a blind sheepdog attempting to herd its flock over the moor. On these occasions he only confused everyone as to his expectations.

In neither instance did he hit his mark, for every congregant could see a way clear of his strike. He was an obscure and unsubtle cleric, yet this flock's leader had, on this Sunday, thrown down an uncommon challenge.

'Twas now only weeks since the public execution of David Tyrie in Portsmouth on the 24th of August 1782. David Tyrie was convicted of High Treason for having corresponded with the French during the American Revolutionary War. For his crime he was to suffer one of the most barbarous penalties ever devised for he would be hanged, drawn and quartered.

On that day, he was drawn in a wicker hurdle to his place of execution and slowly hanged by the neck until not quite dead, then cut down to have his private members cut off and his bowels taken out before his own eyes. This lot was burned in front of him before having his head severed from his body, which was then cut into four pieces. The head and quarters were par-boiled and disposed of according to the pleasure of the King.

While he still could, he reportedly maintained an even conversation with his gaoler, showing concern for the welfare of his father. He held his head high and refused to gratify the crowd by speaking to it. His execution was so badly managed that the necessary equipment had to be scrounged at the last minute, the fact of which made him smile and comment on his executioners' preparedness. In the meantime, David read from his bible on the sideline.

David's head and parts were buried in a rough coffin among the pebbles on a nearby beach. Within minutes the place was swarmed by a thousand sailors who descended upon his remains to take away each a small piece to be exhibited in their mess halls.

Untold spectators were later claimed to have witnessed the whole event and so affected were they by its gruesomeness, it would become the last such execution in British history.

The vicar had not failed to administer each recorded detail of the event with appropriate emphasis in his voice.

"He's something a' mind. And he's no heed, Thomas, for the delicacy of the women and the children. What's the meaning of such a terrible thing to us, who live here in the Brecks?"

Nate Bacon had recently come to Weeting to find work. He was a friendly, forthright, and competent young man who was becoming a fixture in the parish.

It happened that an older home and some lands had been purchased by Charles Henry Coote, 7th Earl of Mountrath, an Irish peer and wealthy landowner. He continued to purchase properties and buy up leases of the surrounding lands until he had amassed a considerable estate. His intention was to turn a smart profit by adopting newer methods to farm and also create a shooting destination worthy of receiving his peers.

All the attendant activity required architects, engineers, masons, brickmakers, carpenters, thatchers, gamekeepers, farmers, warreners, and all manner of labour from man and beast alike. Some were already of the parish, but many were not, and the increased numbers fairly strained all regional capacities.

One party, however, was enraptured. The Revd Charles Smith was currently riding the wave of new-found affluence created by the influx of workers and tradespeople. This not only provided the capital for badly needed repairs to his church, it also provided him with the capital for greater influence with the Bishop. Perhaps becoming rector, with an attendant increase in tithes, was in the wind. His flock now considerably grown; ambition raced where neglect had slumbered.

A region of traditionally meagre prospects for work, Weeting was now calling like a beacon to young men and women of talent. Nate was one such youth, who until recently had lived all his twenty-one years in the nearby village of Feltwell. Known as Nate, a distinction created by his mother as he shared the name with his father, he'd grown up with his parents, an older brother and four younger sisters in a home in the parish of St. Nicholas, at the north end of Feltwell.

His father was a successful tradesman, a carpenter who took pride in believing his own father's declaration of the family's descendance from Sir Edward Bacon, the half-brother of Francis Bacon. Even if true, Nate saw little advantage in claiming a relationship that provided him neither property, money, nor connection. All the same, old Nathaniel prayed his son keep his eyes and ears open as he proceeded through life. "Advantages," he would say, "coming often in disguise, can catch one up who is napping." The pragmatic young Nate came to understand his father's advice to be a useful doctrine to live by.

He apprenticed under his father who judged him to have become a capable carpenter, though he remained concerned Nate's exposure to the world beyond Feltwell was limited to the knowledge imparted by family and community. Rarely had he visited market towns to experience the excitement and the challenge of new ideas and relationships. He preferred the company of his father and his tools. Nate was known by all as a man of many qualities but of one good direction: Nate was earnest.

If asked, he might have guessed himself to be unambitious. His interests were usually restricted to the here, and the now. On his father's recommendation, he was recruited to work on the estate where his higher skills quickly manifested themselves. He was first put to work on repairs to the hall; from which major undertaking he was occasionally offered up to contribute elsewhere. A preferred task was working on repairs to the bridge-crossing with Brandon, where the estate was bound on that side by the Lesser Ouse river.

His role was now grown to include supervising work gangs and organizing the timely delivery of building materiel. He was paid well in money, benefits and prestige. People now sought his advice and companionship, and with his new prospects came greater attentiveness to the world around him. This included being attentive to anything in it which might upset his plans.

This morning, the whole world came to know of Nate Bacon's plans. His intention to wed a young woman of his new parish had just been announced through the first reading of the banns.

Nate's mother, Elizabeth Fuller of Feltwell, married the elder Nathaniel

Bacon when she was just of age, some twenty-three years ago. Her family were long-time residents of the town where her father was a farm labourer.

Marrying Nathaniel had been a step up for her, although her modest origin was never evident in her bearing and her manners. Comely, graceful, and always constructive in her interactions with others, Eliza was much admired in the community. Her husband was deeply proud of her and would say, if he were obliged to tell the truth, that her attachment to him made him stand above others. Though he remained concerned about his worthiness, her civility was such that it was impossible to tell whether she understood this about their relationship.

In a few weeks, their son was to wed Catherine Sallett of Weeting village in the parish of Weeting-with-Bromehill. Since Kitty's father died when she was a girl, she had lived in the village with her mother. Charlotte Sallett was a natural woman and midwife whose success permitted them to continue living in the house Kitty had known since childhood. The family was not originally from Norfolk.

Aside from helping give birth, Charlotte was a practitioner of physics. She concocted potions that were reputedly effective tonics, salves, balms, and purgatives. While she was eager still to learn from others, most of her results came from somewhere inside her. She resisted speaking about what guided her or from where her insight came and remained, thankfully, careful about her every interaction and transaction with others. For instance, she had been taught the art of misdirection by her own mother to keep other folk from finding their prized locations. After all, it was not long ago that her kin were being persecuted for suspicion of cunning. She wisely shunned the spiritual, in favour of the mortal world.

Importantly for herself, she was guided by a code of ethics that prevented her from selling anything she would not herself have consumed, if in need. If a remedy was ineffective, she attempted to work with the patient until satisfactory improvement had been reported, if not actually achieved. She used only the natural ingredients cultivated in her garden and gathered in the countryside.

She also collected leeches, using herself as bait. For this she waded thigh-deep through any of the many waterways and leats, allowing leeches by the score to attach themselves directly to her legs. Once removed, using salt or the flick of a purposely fashioned fingernail, survivors were kept in glass until collected by the agents of her customers. Doctors heartily paid her price, to which most unfailingly added a healthy profit at the expense of the bountiful sick.

Kitty's skills and knowledge were learned from her mother. From the time she first walked, villagers had become accustomed to her following in her mother's footsteps in search of precious ingredients. Whether shoot, flower, fruit, leaf, stalk, bark, tuber, fungus, moss, sap, nut, or seed from the many plants growing on land and in the water, they would be collected. Insects too, at all stages of their lives. In the garden patch they kept, Kitty could be seen making certain the weeds did not take over, and that if too dry, the plants received a few drops of water to satisfy their thirst.

Inside, she watched and repeated the instructions her mother knew from memory as she stored, sorted, cut, measured, ground, roasted, boiled, steeped, and mixed things into her various remedies.

When it came time to preparing meals, Kitty learned of the benefic effects of plants and other natural ingredients, as well as the ways in which they could improve the taste of food when added alone, or as a concoction.

This proved fortuitous, for when the Earl's agent wanted to staff his kitchens with local women, an early recommendation was Kitty. Despite her relative youth she proved to be extremely helpful in all aspects of preparing the meals, including the planning, cooking, and even the preserving of food. Where she truly differentiated herself from the others was in her creativity in finding new and interesting ways to prepare the meats, their sauces, and the accompanying fruits and vegetables.

Thomas Turner had pondered Nate's question for some time, before thus answering. "The war with the revolutionaries and the French strains the country. People are discomfited by the increasing bad news from abroad. I have heard it said officials now regret both the traitor Tyrie's sentence, and the way 'twas executed. They say their hands was tied; they was compelled to set an example."

"Why should that be?"

"I believe they fear the humours of the public; if unrestrained, they may affect events such that society is tested beyond the point it can be salvaged."

"Once more Thomas, how is that connected to us, here?"

"The changes in Weeting bring many people from distant places to the upset of the old community. Look at us, who are come from elsewhere to take up responsibilities that will forever change our lives. Our work will continue until we are both older men and our families are grown. Not all have fared so well.

"I now have a wife and two little ones to think of. We all pray you and Kitty will soon have a family of your own. This parish has taken us in, and as we settle, we must also give back.

"Yet among us are many who come from London, or e'en more foreign parts. Their manners are said by many to be rough, and quite different. They ask more than what is their due and their grumbling over their share leaves many to suspect their fidelity to our community. Are they justified in their wants, or are they merely grasping?"

"As children of God we are taught to share and to trust equally. Yet this is not the way of some people. I ask why this is so. Why do we not share and trust, equally? Are we not equally deserving, Thomas?"

"I have no answer for you. I suspect the Earl himself must not trust everyone equally. He is a man of great learning and experience, yet his experiences in this place are making him e'er more cautious. Have you not noticed the new night watchman at the hall?"

Nate had, in fact, noticed the new guard, and that all deliveries to the estate are now carefully accounted for. He also admitted hearing of many who now bar their doors at night, where such had never before been considered.

Thomas continued, "I have taken on more warreners and we are to be armed, as poaching is becoming more frequent. The squire tolerates some small level of theft, for I believe he is not without sympathy for those with mouths to feed. However, the great quantities now stolen are doubtless solely for profit. If this theft is not stopped, the warren will suffer for it.

"His lordship's wealth has brought us much. Though not all for the good, 'tis unjust he suffer such losses and I should wager this upset is caused by some among the new parishioners." After a moment's hesitation he added, "We shan't resolve this question today.

"Enough, my young friend, you are now promised to wed, and 'tis more pleasant to discuss your marriage on this, the Lord's day of rest."

Thomas turned to the ladies. They were examining the plants growing among the headstones dotting the little rise surrounding the church. "Elizabeth, on this uncommonly pleasant day of rest, mayhap our last before the wind and cold return, can we not offer our friends some of your best brew and a bit of supper as we pass the day together? I would not object to a game of cards, or dominoes. Besides, our Mary is now three, and little John is nearing his first year. Let our friends," he added with a quick smile, "see what 'tis to have little ones at their feet. If you've a mind for it, please join us."

Nate was returning from a place deep in his thoughts, when he added, "It troubles me that all men are not to be equally trusted. Yet should this be so, how does one determine who is worthy of trust?" It was now his turn to hesitate before finishing, "We must return to these questions, but for the moment, we thankfully accept your offer."

"Come Nate, we shall remain mindful and watchful. We may yet come to understand the purpose of our good priest's words. Whether for the better I know not, but as this parish is now our home, 'tis ours to protect."

On this bright Sunday morning and on this day at least, the breeze blew gently across the heath. The leaves had already changed their colours and the yellow and russet flakes had recently been blown to the ground in a strong blow. The first smell of decaying leaves was in the air. Elizabeth and Kitty rode on Thomas' cart to the Bromehill Warren Lodge, a short mile and a half on such a pleasant day.

Upon reaching their home at Bromehill Lodge, Thomas did not at first follow the others inside. "If you will allow, I should first inquire of my men whether any poachers have presumed to take advantage of my attendance at church."

CHAPTER XI

THE ART OF SHOOTING, OCTOBER 21, 1782

THE MUNDFORD ROAD, just north of the Bromehill Road crossing at the eastern limit of Shadwell's plantation proved a convenient spot to meet. Only five years since the leafy trees were planted, they already provided adequate cover for game. It would suit the purpose they had in mind. Daylight was almost upon them and by the time they would be in position, all would be clearly visible.

It was not the most convenient time of year, but there was an urgency to their purpose, so with foresight they had taken measures to avoid leaving their chief duties unattended.

"'Morning Band."

"That's a fine piece you've there. We'll put you to the test today, together."

"Such is my expectation. I should not wish to leave Elizabeth a widow yet."

Band had ten years on him. Thomas knew his own eyes were destined to age like his father's hooded green orbs. He could at times be mistaken for being in a stupor when he was simply, as he would explain, "resting my eyes." Band's wide and clear blue eyes took in the low-angle morning light like pools of water. His skin showed all the signs of a man who had embraced his life outdoors. He stood tall and held a fierce countenance.

His dog stood by him. With eyes alternating between the approaching Thomas, and its master from whom it awaited a signal, its tail swayed in a sign of acceptance. "She's friendly," he said, confirming what Band already knew. "What's her name?"

Jonathan Band, the Weeting Gamekeeper and Thomas Turner, the Bromehill Warrener enjoyed similar responsibility for raising and protecting animals to the exclusive benefit of their lord. Any differences in their mandates was due a complicated and constantly moving body of law that many have complained has always been ill understood.

Of the many similarities, one was the need to master the gun to ward off vermin of all sorts, the most dangerous rapidly becoming the two-legged variety. Protecting game was increasingly fraught with danger for these men and their families, as poachers became ever more numerous and their methods ever more enterprising and rude. Poaching in armed gangs, ambushing unsuspecting keepers or warreners and their families, and shooting rather than laying down their arms were on the rise. Particularly unsettling, defenders could not trust that in their midst was not one felon to precipitate a fight through alarm, restlessness, or antagonism. There were other means than direct intervention with arms to fend them off, but these could be more cruel to the victim.

"She's Norrie, and she's friendly. Nary 'nother good as her. I found a mate with the same blood she must have taken to, for she gave up a litter some months back. If I can break them, the squire should be pleased to have six more like her." Saying this he held up a hand and rubbed his first finger against his thumb. "They tend to be headstrong, though once trained, they'll be steady and true 'fore the guns."

Jonathan took a few steps and Norrie stuck to his heels.

"Doesn't fancy me leaving her behind. She'll stay at my side 'til I command her. Retrieves from water too, though we've little o' that hereabouts. Today we'll brush along the hedgerows and covers. That'll hold her attention."

He stopped to look at Thomas. "'Tis fortunate his lordship discourages the participation o' novices. Whether man or dog, 'tis alike. All them bangs, and birds flushing, and shouting should you have the wrong kind o' shooters, can excite a dog to the ruin o' the day. Thus, I've trained her to be the finest near a gun I know."

As he listened, Tom smiled at her and reached to scratch behind her ear, at which Norrie's brows rose towards her master in search of permission. As no restraint was signalled, she leaned into his hand and wagged her tail effusively. Norrie stood sixteen inches and her long shaggy white coat was speckled with liver spots. She had a white forehead and dark long satchel ears. Her sturdy body was evidence she could work all day long. "Will you join in my instruction then, Norrie? Good girl. We should be off."

"We'll brush in the manner most favoured by guests. Dogs can be rough beaters; running too far afield, jumping at the game, or giving chase at their own will. Our Norrie here's a good springer and I wager, you'll not 've seen wing shooting like this. You'll be pleased by what she brings your way."

"I expect I will. I've heard his lordship to declare the rage for shooting is presently at a very high pitch, and that Mr. Swift believes the art of shooting flying at Weeting is arrived at superiority over most."

"Let's hold here. Afore we commence shooting there's things I must show you. Even a modern flintlock is a precarious weapon, full o' whims and hazards. Though you say you have some knowledge o' ancient guns, I must see you master the weapon itself, as you master shooting it. The failure of either could mean a life."

Jonathan's first rule of using a weapon was to give it a look over. Any piece lacking the proper marks stamped on the barrel, or showing signs of a chink or a crack, should be shunned. Two Crowns, one over GP and the other over V, showed the barrel was proofed and warrantied its quality. Failure to examine a gun for defects or fouling has resulted in guns misfiring or exploding in the face of shooters. These two men were fortunate to possess fine pieces. Their first duty he made clear, was to ensure they remained intact and clean.

His next rule was to charge his weapon only when his emotions were under control, so as not to make any potentially fatal mistakes. Tom was next introduced to so many related dangers he began to wonder why a man would take up a gun. Misfires were common. When shooting game they were merely an unfortunate occurrence, but in action against a formidable foe they could prove fatal.

The merits of their very own Brandon blacks for their spark and durability concluded a sermon on maintaining properly knapped flints to reduce the possibility of a misfire, and of never setting out without additional flints, as they will wear.

The flash pan not being truly rainproof as promised, Thomas should beware using a weapon in damp of any sort. Moisture on the frizzen, or damp in the powder would prevent firing, thus he should always flash off a partial charge of powder in each barrel to eliminate any damp or wet. Then he should charge both without delay to ensure dry charges.

To avoid an inadvertent frizzen strike igniting the main powder charge, though the pan might not yet be primed, a leathern pouch, much like the hood used in falconing may protect the pan from inadvertent firing, as well as from wet. However, it was not a sure thing and the practice greatly diminished loading time.

Embers were particularly treacherous when left in the barrel as they would most surely ignite a powder charge loaded into the barrel. Before loading the next charge, one should wait until the powder burned itself out. If time permitted, one might ram the barrel with a patch of clean cloth.

When shooting game, the best guns would attempt to load and fire as many as three charges each minute. As this pace did not permit the shooter time to assure there was no lingering ember, inadvertent discharges were quite frequent. Jonathan recommended this should normally only be attempted when life was in the balance.

When fired, the flintlock had the uncomfortable habit of showering sparks forwards from the end of the muzzle, and sideways from the flash-hole. There would be no end of discomfort should the shooter and his eyes be subjected to these showers, which was common when shooting into the wind, and for wrong-handed shooters.

Loading became more difficult through the day. This was due the black powder that increasingly fouled the barrel, preventing the shot from being properly seated. The interstice between powder and shot could be fatal. Should any air remain between the charge and the shot, from either fouling or any shifting of the charge out of its tight confinement in the barrel, it would cause a short start, resulting in an unattended explosion.

Not quite discouraged, Thomas listened dutifully as Jonathan pursued his anthology of warnings about sparks that could set off black powder, dampness that would render it useless, and the equipment needed to prevent both: leather, copper and brass were preferred.

Thomas began to wonder if he should shoot at all this day when Jonathan removed all doubt about the corrosive nature of damp, when combined with the sulfur contained in black powder. To avoid decay within the barrel or the lock mechanism, he would be obliged to thoroughly clean and oil his weapon after each use, cork the ends of the barrel, release the lock spring to its easiest position, and store it with his powder in perfectly dry conditions.

Jonathan warned that his lordship would be most displeased should his fowling piece be destroyed for lack of due care. In such circumstance he could foresee him rightfully demanding Thomas replace it at his own expense.

He finally turned to his procedure for arming and firing the weapon, which Thomas imitated as Jonathan explained.

The flint, firmly seated in the cock to produce a true shower of sparks, was rotated to half cock while ensuring the sear fell into the safety notch on the tumbler to prevent any accidental discharge.

The corns of powder were loaded into the muzzle, ensuring they were dry and of uniform size for best results. Using the ramrod, the wadding was rammed home and then followed with the lead shot wrapped in cloth or paper. Jonathan showed him to gauge the amounts of powder and shot required for an advantageous result.

Next the charge was set by pouring a small amount of fine black powder into the flash pan, making certain to also fill the touch hole and close the frizzen. The gun was now loaded, primed and ready to shoot. "Come, let's get you acquainted with the trim o' your piece. I make it forty paces to that posted notice by yon tree. Shot falls over distance. We'll see if she's true."

The notice was well known to Thomas, for they were posted on all access points around the parish. More than a legal nicety, they were a pre-requisite to any successful persecution for trespass, and read as follows:

To all those attempting to trespass on these lands.

I do hereby give notice, and require you not to enter, or cause or procure to be entered, any of my closes, lands, or premises, situate and being in the parish of Weeting with horses, dogs, or otherwise, in order to beat for, follow, or pursue, any game, or for any other purpose whatsoever; and in case you do not as yet know the local situation of such, my said closes, lands, and premises, I hereby give you notice, that the same will be pointed out and shewn to you, upon reasonable application at my dwelling-house, situate at Weeting Hall. And I do hereby further give you notice, that in case, after your being served with this notice, you shall commit any trespass upon any part of my said closes, lands, or premises, you will not only be proceeded against as a wilful and malicious trespasser, pursuant to the statute, in that case made and provided, but will also be otherwise prosecuted for such offence according to law. Dated this 30th day of June, in the year of our Lord 1782.

Charles Henry Coote

Some further instructions about holding, cocking, and aiming the fowling piece preceded Jonathan's authority to fire when ready. Thomas held his breath and steadied his aim before slowly pulling the trigger to release the cock holding the flint.

In an instant a series of actions was unleashed. The flint struck and forced open the frizzen permitting the showering sparks to ignite the dry powder in the flash pan, before passing through the touch hole to ignite the main powder charge.

The ensuing delay almost made Thomas turn, his piece in hand, to ask Jonathan if there had been a misfire. Thankfully, he held steady as his fowling piece finally discharged; the kick near putting him to the ground.

The notice was untouched. Thomas required two additional attempts before taking out his victim and another five to find his gun's pattern. Jonathan was only satisfied when three or four pellets struck an area the size of his fist in a pre-determined corner of the notice board, "For that is the ideal distance and load for shooting game in our conditions. You'll vary the amount o' powder, load and shot size according to the distance and strength o' game as well as the conditions on the day."

In little time he found the proper dosage of powder to set in the pan and how to hold his stance and his breath until the discharge. He now had some feel for what to expect. Jonathan judged his fowling piece to be true.

"Not to worry, Tom. Proficiency will come before comfort. You'll then be able to shoot flying with ease. A final essential, ne'er direct it at anything, or anybody you don't wish to kill.

"That should get us started. With time you'll learn to estimate the measures and weights for each occasion, though I believe you've no need to worry for you'll not be required to take more than a few well-placed shots, whate'er you're shooting at."

"I'm doubtful, Jonathan. I had imagined guns to be a safe and assured protection against poachers and villains. I now see their use may come at a price, for these weapons should be for only the very responsible in character and qualification. Letting them into malevolent hands intent on harming the innocent and the unwitting is to be avoided. There ought to be assurance they will find only responsible use."

"I came to shooting early, so I've given it nary a thought. Pater put a fowling piece in my hands when I was but a lad. Plainly, there are parts o' society quite accustomed to their use, while others are surely not. Many are they who believe every man has the right to own and use a gun as he alone sees fit. And many are they who fear their use in the hands o' madmen or organized revolutionists. We must look to Parliament where men have taken the oath to govern in our best interests, and pray they do proper by us."

Jonathan stepped toward the plantation. The fully risen sun had begun to burn away the early morning cold. In respect of the cool late autumn weather, Jonathan wore a high black felt hat whose wide brim was curled where it suffered his customary grip. Greying sandy hair was gathered in a thick braid and tied at the back of his neck with coarse twine. His brown felted wool overcoat featured a well-worn collar that may once have stood proudly folded, but now fell limp and wide over his shoulders. In view of the day's promising weather and light work, he left behind his heavy cape and leathern leggings that fit over the tops of his black, thick-soled boots. A substantial dark green waistcoat covered his shirt to his thighs and a neck sock, all of which had long ago lost any appeal to fashion, completed his attire. The whole fulfilled Jonathan's requirement for service, rather than style.

Thomas wore similarly serviceable attire and boots although the overall effect on him was considerably less substantial. In part, this was due the difference in their ages and their outward aspect. More so, it was due their different requirements.

Thomas' introduction to the art of shooting completed, they proceeded to the secret of shooting with accuracy at a moving bird, or what Jonathan called shooting flying.

"You'll want to avoid any unintentional discharge when carryin your fowling piece, Tom. Best keep the frizzen back, with the hammer down against the pan. Should it catch on something, fall as you walk, or fall from being leaned on something with the hammer half-cocked and the frizzen down, the hammer would then fully cock and discharge your piece. I've heard guns and soldiers alike have been wounded by many o' their brethren thus.

"The leaves being down, I expect we'll have good pheasant in the brush and under the hedgerow, or warming themselves in the stubble. Look for a covey o' grey partridge basking, or a coney from your warren just yonder. We'll take this side, where the early sun has warmed the air 'tween the cover crop and the hedgerow to the far coverts by yon wind break. The trees aren't so grown the going will be light work."

"Might we encounter other game?"

"Woodcock are plentiful only after their moon in a few weeks. They're difficult quarry though, Thomas. Only the best guns have a chance at them, for their flight is difficult. Quail, grouse and landrail don't thrive hereabouts.

"We'll pace ourselves as Norrie brushes ahead. Know where they will seek cover and take that as the line o' their escape. Keep your fowling piece ready. Look just above and ahead o' Norrie. When she's on a scent you'll know. Pheasant suffer you to walk right up before rising to take you by surprise, or they may run some 'fore taking flight. Partridge prefer to run longer first.

Norrie may stop to encourage one with her nose if it refuses to spring, but she'll get it up. If its coney she's on to, it'll run well before her."

He winked, "Mind you don't shoot our Norrie."

"Lead on, then." Thomas was beginning to feel an apprehension brought on by an intense desire to show up well on his first shoot. He imagined hands now covered his ears, for all he could hear was the muffled sound of his beating heart.

As Norrie enthusiastically yet quietly worked the field ahead of them, Jon directed her movements by hand signals, whispers, and short low whistles. She searched methodically at twenty, moving to thirty paces on either hand of them, adjusting as they advanced their position. Jonathan called this quartering. She kept her head up and beat up wind to use the little wind to advantage, and when she did scent a bird she slowed slightly, wagged her tail, and moved to encourage it to spring, rather than run. In the event, it chose to run. She turned to hinder its path and thus place the bird between Jonathan and herself. This would have provided Tom a better shooting situation. Tom believed he was ready.

So disoriented was he, the bird rose and flew out of range as he failed to even get his shot off. "Ne'er the mind, Tom."

Jonathan whistled. When Norrie came to his side he gave a quick hand signal and she sat, looking at him for his next command.

"Why do you whistle, Jon, and not call to her?"

"Whistle travels better if the wind is up, and it's the sound birds make. It doesn't startle them, you see. Ne'er like to use my voice in the field. Not natural.

"See here Tom, choose any bird on the wing and point your finger at it. Follow it with both eyes open. That's what you want to do with the gun: cock, point, fire, and hold steady. Pater taught me it's like throwing the gun at the bird.

"Take hold o' your piece as I do. Your arms closer to your sides 'll take the great weight off yet remain at the ready to lift, just like pointing your finger. As you see the bird spring, place your left foot in the lead and turn your body slightly to lead with your left shoulder for balance.

"Let's keep on this way. The day is young, and you've a way to go yet. Allow me to take the next shots to show you. I believe you'll learn a lot by watching." At his signal Norrie was off, head towards the ground, searching for scent.

Jonathan took the next three pheasants as Tom watched. With every one of Jonathan's movements, Thomas began to feel his own muscles twitch. By the time the third was in the air, for just seconds before plunging to earth, his muscles had synchronized with Jonathan's, mimicking his actions. As the signal to retrieve it came, Norrie was on to the fallen bird, her soft mouth proven when she offered it up directly at Jonathan's feet.

Thomas improved markedly from that point. Norrie diligently brushed up and down, back, and forth, following Jonathan's signals. As each bird sprang it provided them with excellent shooting. By the time they stopped for nourishment, Thomas no longer completely missed his mark. He did wing one bird that had to be chased down by Norrie before being dispatched. However, the last saw him make a clean shot of it to bag his first cock pheasant. It was a young one he now knew to determine, by the lighter colour, softer texture, and blunted shape of its spurs.

To rest they chose a site beyond the edge of some arable for its excellent view of nearby activity. On the way to it, Jonathan summed up Thomas' progress. "You seem comfortable now, Tom. With little time I expect you'll make an excellent shooter. Your movement is natural and quick, showing little motion in the manner of an experienced sportsman. Game should be shot clean with nothing wasted, 'specially not powder and shot."

They reached the pile of boulder stones and removed their shoulder bags. As soon as their fowling pieces were given a quick cleaning and wiped down, they loosened their coats to sit. Choosing two appropriate stones, they broke out their provisions.

Chewing, Thomas said, "You spoke of your pater. He was a keeper as well?"

"He was. I suppose keepers and warreners are something alike."

"Hmnn. I suppose we are. I believe you know my home was beyond Brandon, on the warren at Eriswell by Coclesworth. My family have been warreners since anyone can remember. As with you, the only thing was to follow my father who required me to work from an early age. I've no complaint, as I suspect you've none either. I'm happiest outdoors where the work is hard, yet not backbreaking. Can't say that for every man's life. You're from Shropshire?"

Jonathan swallowed. "By Drayton, over to north Shropshire. My granda had accounts o' his forebears. To a man they preserved the game for their lords, but keeping has changed since then."

"In what manner, Jon?"

"In their time they'd preserve the forest and the game for the lord's personal privilege, perchance bring in faggots o' favoured brushes in demanding times, kill vermin and take the game as the lord required. They would, too, go about the manor under power o' warrant, searching and seizing."

"What did they seize?"

"Guns, gins, nets, and all equipment. Greyhounds, ferrets and setting dogs as well, for they was being used only for poaching. I too may search and seize on the estate whene'er I've a suspicion o' someone who's about poaching."

He took a bite before continuing, speaking haltingly between chews.

"In our day, the law permits the squire to invite shooters to take game according to the season. He must still register, with the clerk o' the peace, his own appointed keeper. Being our squire's appointed servant, I'm to preserve game on his estate until I kill it in his name, though I must use force to prevent others taking it unlawfully.

"You must know that on the same day each year we begin killing prodigious numbers. On the Glorious Twelfth o' August we take grouse, but as it will not thrive here I'll arrange for bagged ones for the first week alone. Partridge begins on the 1st o' September, and pheasant on the 1st o' October. In this way each bird has time to mature undisturbed 'till the guns take them. Here at Weeting the pheasant, partridge, hare and rabbit are most plentiful."

Thomas added, "Our breeding schemes and excellent coverts ensure the abundance of game. Together, we raise and protect our beasts, fend off poachers, prosecute all who trespass, and then kill what we've raised, though we are governed by different laws."

"As the warren is enclosed by the baulk, coney is deemed the property of his lordship. Stealing it is thus akin to taking it from his house."

When Jonathan lowered his hand to share some choice morsels with Norrie, Tom continued.

"The common law of the land protects a man's property from those who want to take it unlawfully. Punishment can be more severe than for trespassing or taking game under the game law. Desperate men abound now they are forced off the land, and in their despair, with mouths to feed, they take greater risks and do not hesitate to take up arms. Plainly, poachers are now more dangerous for they do not respect any law as before."

Jonathan grunted. "I ask myself if, as keepers, we don't encourage them. We raise e'er more than our fathers to satisfy our masters' competitions; all to attract the best shooters and obtain the biggest bags. Yet the consequence, as all can see, is game in such abundance it attracts more poachers as well."

Jonathan chewed on another bite before continuing, while Tom enjoyed the lack of interruption to his own feeding.

"We employ stratagems not needed by our fathers. Bespoke coverts attract and hold game. In March and April, I'll search out nests and pay a small sum to every lad or field worker who'll point to one. I may also procure pheasant eggs from dealers, and partridge eggs from abroad to add to nests for the hens to care for. When they haven't the instinct or are taken by vermin, I'll pay to have broody hens sit on the eggs."

Jonathan swallowed what he had in his mouth and washed it down before finishing.

"I'll then watch over them 'til they're old enough to fly, direct which cover crops be sown for their feed, secure fodder to last the winter, and preserve their coverts and trees from villains who would fell them for the wood. I have at times even placed grain in the hedgerows to hold them for the shooters."

"'Tis truth we are obliged to raise more game, and we know no hour of the day or night, nor season of the year that doesn't call us to duty. My Elizabeth tells me 'tis arduous for her as well."

"We're fortunate to have good and capable wives, Thomas. And we're our own men, for the most, which I appreciate greatly." He looked thoughtful for a moment before continuing.

"When not game, 'tis vermin we kill, and whether winged or four-legged, I trap, poison, or shoot it, 'fore nailing the carcass to one o' my gibbets as a warning to others. 'Tis no sure thing, though 'twas always done, and the Earl's then certain I'm protecting his game. He pays a bounty for each o' them."

"I kill anything trying to get within the pale of the warren, and all assuredly finds its way to my gibbet as well. 'Tis winged vermin that vex me as they strike often at night, when rabbits are grazing. They're unhindered by the baulk that keeps other vermin out, yet are found to be uncommon shy and suspicious. My father destroyed birds of prey by arranging naked stumps and hillocks in various parts of the warren. Preferring a view free of obstruction, they settle on the high points where he placed his traps to ensnare them."

At Jonathan's suggestion, he agreed he might now shoot them as well, if only to develop his skill.

Jonathan added, "The fox most plagues me, though interest in it permits me to easily find keepers to pay my price for cubs. The coin is always welcome in my pocket, and 'tis so plentiful here I find it simply a nuisance." A wink communicated to Tom what he suspected: the Earl derives no benefit from these transactions.

"Against any fox in my coverts I'll place poisoned bait by its earths, rather than chance any loss to it. But if it will remain at a distance it may save itself and its cubs, till I catch it up for the hunt."

"There appears no absence of menace for us to fight off. Jon, you speak of reward. I believe myself doing well. Still, against the growing menace from poachers, I wonder are we adequately rewarded. Poachers grow bolder; now roving in gangs at will, unafraid of armed battle. A keeper's boy, over to Thetford, was ambushed and shot in the face as he left to see to his beat."

"I've no complaint. My keepers are armed and ready to assist when they must. Presently, 'tis poachers who threaten the diversion o' the gentry and their shooting, such that a capable keeper can readily find himself in a good situation. Pater alone fended them off when they were less determined.

"The old girl and me, we're comfortable in the lodge with a few acres free o' rent, bounties for vermin killing and a set o' new clothes and hat each season. I yearly receive £20 plus all the perquisites I'm given, or can arrange on the side. I have no complaint and Jane seems happy 'nough. She contributes her own and she keeps the pot filled. There's no shortage o' pudding on the table and she's rightfully proud o' her garden and larder.

"I should be truly ungrateful if I'd not mention I receive a gratuity from each shooter at the end o' their visit. Also, the squire has given his permission to take older cock pheasants and all the woodcock and pigeon I may desire."

"You should indeed be ungrateful, Jon," said Thomas, as he smiled wryly. "I do believe keepers now have the advantage of warreners. 'Twas not thus in my father's time. I suspect credit for this is due the increased imperilment to keepers arising from the desire of gentry to vigorously defend its privilege. By their numbers and by their knowledge of our ways, poachers appear to now enjoy an advantage over us and they intend nasty business."

"If they come 'round my bailiwick, Tom, I've set mantraps and spring guns to gain surprise o' them. They'll have to be determined to get past my devices. I'll show you just now as we pass by a spring gun I've placed in yon covert. Best you know, to avoid the danger. They're not loaded to kill, but we don't want to be harming you now, do we?"

With these last words, Jonathan turned to Thomas with frank blue eyes, in part conveying the humour of brotherhood, in part searching for answers to unasked questions.

Having already stowed what he did not eat, Thomas stood to stretch, then picked up his weapon before responding to Jonathan's tease.

"We should be on our way. I believe I'm getting the feel of it and I'm keen to see the effect of your expert instruction."

"It has become a welcome habit to take my pipe after I eat. The wind in our face will convey the smoke away from our shooting. You may proceed; I'll be right along. Mind you keep an eye on the stubble, I'll wager you'll find something there this time o' day."

He pulled his clay pipe from his pocket and with practiced movements pulled and spread on the rock a small quantity of cut leaves to dry while he took out his tinder box and strike-a-light. When the bowl was filled to the brim he tamped it down with his tobacco-stained index finger before lighting it with the now burning tinder. After a few shallow draws on the stem he re-tamped the tobacco, before re-lighting for his smoke. He drew a long breath and enjoyed the proclaimed healing powers of the Indian fume.

CHAPTER XII

THREE SUNDAYS HAD COME AND GONE since the first reading of the banns for Nate Bacon and Kitty Sallett. As required by law, the banns ordered anyone with knowledge of any reason in law why this couple may not be joined in matrimony, to bring such knowledge forward. Having now cleared all obstacles, they were about to be married on this morning of Tuesday, the 29th day of October 1782.

All the previous day and night the wind blew stiff, but unworrying. As people stepped outside in the morning, they immediately realized the force of the wind had been seriously underestimated. Perhaps it had crept upon them gradually, or perhaps it was due the absence of ominous clouds and rain. For whatever reason, one had difficulty walking without leaning heavily towards the wind or bracing oneself with a stick.

Regardless, this was a joyful day for the promised couple. The wind would prove insufficient reason to delay their union a minute longer than necessary. Saint Mary with All Saints stood waiting for the appointed hour where Father Smith would legitimize yet one more relationship before anything went amiss.

In his experience, the woman in these parts were often with child before any formal agreement to wed. It appeared the father would sooner pay for a license to marry without delay, as it came with a guarantee of parenthood, than to accept the delay imposed by the free publication of banns with no such promise. As a man of God, he was also a man of some practicality. He would not stand on principle, and certainly not when its base was as narrow as it tended to be hereabouts.

He had instead taken up his role with decorum and dignity, particularly since word had reached even this outpost that certain clergymen had recently been pilloried and had their ears cropped by church authorities for marrying couples without adhering to the letter of procedure. He would not neglect any detail of ceremony, no matter how trifling.

The few participants did not tarry. They sought the relative comfort and break from the wind inside the church whose exterior walls, like many local structures built to last in this region, consisted of thick, flint work walls. This church had the rarer distinction of having a round, crenellated tower. It stood, save the occasional ancient tree above all else in the parish, including the warren lodge at Bromehill. Perhaps at one time in the past it might have been dwarfed by Weeting Castle, had the latter not already been in ruin before the tower was erected.

Inside, the unstained glass windows gave free passage to the bright sunlight this day provided. The interior was plain-spoken, where unadorned rafters and simple, secular poppy heads showed the way to the altar. The only source of color in celebration of God's glory was the large stained-glass window of simple geometric pieces on the east wall, beyond the altar.

The church did boast some fine pieces in silver; two chalices, a smaller paten, and a larger paten inscribed in Latin. Translated, it reminded those who held it of a late parishioner's generosity: *The church of Blessed Saint Mary at Weeting, given by Judith Wright, 1674.*

Nate and Thomas stood by the octagonal stone font in conversation about the weather, while Elizabeth fussed with Kitty's garments and hair. She had brought a little white powder to apply to her face and neck, rouge to give her cheeks a slight blush, and black to highlight her bright eyes. The men glanced over, smiling in appreciation of the effect.

Nate spoke, "I can see you are unsettled by this wind, Thomas."

"Indeed I am. A wind such as this, if it endures several days can be the ruin of any warren. Rabbits shun it and they may starve for holding up in their burys. 'Tis fortunate the breeding season is past, as 'twould surely have a ruinous effect on that activity. Almost certainly, dams will refuse to nurse if they are forced to lie in with their kits, which would mean their death. For now, it has simply delayed the trapping as coney cannot be forced from its burys, though we would employ ferrets and terriers."

"For how long do you think it will blow? It has been several days now, and I've heard unwelcome news is beginning to make the rounds of Lynn, Yarmouth and London."

"How so, Nate?"

"On the 17th day of September, a severe Atlantic storm caused hundreds of vessels to be lost and severely damaged. Many went straight to the bottom while others lost masts and rudders, left to founder in the wind and waves. Many, closer to the coasts, ran aground. Efforts to rescue people from these ships mostly failed because of the heavy waves crashing into them. Broken ships, bodies, and cargo litter the coast. There is talk of many thousands of lost mariners and passengers."

"'Tis indeed a tragedy. I should think the royal fleet has then suffered considerable loss."

"Hundreds of vessels have been lost, including many of the greatest men-of-war. 'Tis distressing to know this is only one of many storms that have raged this season, some worse than others. These ocean storms eventually touch the Brecks, leaving us vulnerable to strong blows."

"They must explain the fierce hailstorms that battered England some weeks past."

"Good morning, gentlemen," called a cheery Reverend Smith whose white chasuble on this occasion emphasized his point. "Come now, this is no time to be sombre."

"Morning to you, Father. Nate and I was just speaking of the weather and how it has caused much loss and disquiet."

"It has not been a serene season, has it? I have received a letter from a former colleague with whom I remain in contact. He writes with news of certain consequences suffered in his country. Since his removal to Glasgow, we have come to a more complete understanding of matters, whether politics, the colonies, or the weather."

"How should that be?" asked Nate.

"We conclude such exchanges of information, concerning events and ideas from different perspectives, affords each of us a broader perspective of the thing. Fascinating, is it not?

"He has written that snow has been falling for several days already this year. The oldest man known there cannot remember such an accumulation. The corn, which had been left upon the ground where cut, has been destroyed. As you may be aware, Scotland is a land where such losses are ill afforded. The people will certainly suffer for it this winter."

"For myself," said Thomas, "I worry the warren might suffer. Wind, rain, cold, and snow are more dangerous to the life of a warren than all the vermin to be mustered. I'll wager I must make extra provision for the hardships of this coming winter.

Just then Thomas spied Kitty and Elizabeth making their way towards them. In the hope his fellow communicants would follow his example, he deliberately cut off their discussion and lifted his expression of gloom. "Let us now turn to Kitty and Nate, who should rather be enjoying their special day."

"Then let us proceed directly, so this young couple may benefit from the remainder of this day of celebration." Father Smith moved to take his ceremonial place in the centre of the chancel, from which raised position he signalled the others to join.

Immediately following the ceremony, the four friends, and now officially two married couples, retired to Nate's cottage for dinner and celebration. It was one of ten attached cottages forming a thatched terrace. They all consisted of three rooms and a scullery, with bedrooms on the second floor accessed by a steep, narrow staircase. All entrances faced north; the south side being reserved for the residents' private garden patches.

The brick-built cottages were newly constructed as part of the Earl's plan to ensure modern accommodation for staff and labourers. This row of cottages stood between the village, the Hall, the castle, and the church. It was ideally situated for senior household staff required to run the day-to-day operation of the estate. His neighbours included the butler, valet, housekeeper, head housemaid, ladies' maid in the event any visited, cook, head gardener, head groundskeeper, and stable master.

They each enjoyed the support of hand-picked subordinates who lived in smaller cottages in the village, or for the lowliest, in secluded and cramped quarters hidden within the hall. These young maids and boys performed a multitude of tasks to make life for the lord and his guests seem perfectly ordered and simple, even effortless. The hidden truth was that dozens of hands and feet were constantly, yet invisibly at work.

Elsewhere were the purpose-built lodges for the steward, the gamekeeper, and the warrener; the three most senior positions on the estate.

The afternoon proceeded peacefully until suddenly erupted a most disturbing commotion without. Young men and women of the village appeared, making hideous noises and frantic motions. They waved coloured patches of cloth and branches and wore hats on their heads belonging to the opposite sex. A few banging pots added considerably to their merriment.

"It seems you're being welcomed into the community. You must greet them. I pray you have a shilling for their troubles. They'll want to continue their celebration and I'm certain it's over to the inn they'll be for more merriment."

"'Tis largesse they seek?" asked Kitty.

"No, the farm labourers made their rounds some weeks past. You might say this is a welcome tax, of sorts. We was not visited, perhaps as the Lodge is too distant from the community. Or perhaps," he said with a twist of his head, "there is insufficient good will towards the warrener and his duty.

"'Tis well and good they are here for you on this day."

"In such event, gladly will I contribute a shilling to their evening. No good can come of rejecting kindness so willingly and happily offered. This is a good omen for us, Kitty." At that, Nate and Kitty warmly greeted them, straining to hear the wishes offered over the clatter of the revellers, before handing over for good measure, two beakers of beer to be shared around. When Nate saw their antics beginning to fade, he slipped a coin into the hand of their spokeswoman and wished them on their way.

Having funds to start their new life was not an issue for them. Both were highly regarded and valuable contributors to the operation of Weeting Hall. According to the custom of the day, payment came after, sometimes long after services or goods had been provided.

Kitty had fortunately just received her remuneration, and according to custom she was paid for the year ending Michaelmas just past, in year 1782. Her receipt of £8 was for work in the manor kitchens. From time-to-time throughout the year Kitty received additional amounts for sewing and mending as needed. She and her mother had been living off their joint resources and as nothing was taken for granted, they did not want for anything of this world.

Now married, she followed the custom to live with her husband. Her mother remained in her Feltwell home, now anticipating the visit of grandchildren in the not too distant future.

For his part, Nate Bacon received various forms of remuneration. For the same year of work, he received £8 10s., which was not a considerable amount given his role. However, significant additional amounts, against receipts provided to the steward, were paid to him according to the activities he had supervised. From these he distributed payment to each labourer and to each provider of material, retaining a portion of the total for himself.

There was nothing dishonest in this, as it was by arrangement with Lord

Mountrath that he should receive this portion for his efforts. This was his remuneration for finding and coordinating the men and women who laboured at the various sites, and for ensuring the materials arrived as contracted for. Nate assured the right quality in the right quantity was delivered, where and when it was required.

This was a manner of remuneration experienced by his lordship in London. An essential requirement for a relationship of this nature was trust, which Nate had long secured of his lordship, for theirs was a relationship highly satisfactory to both parties. For his part, Nate was aware that his satisfaction was reliant on an abiding number of projects. Until now and for the foreseeable future, he had no complaint.

There would be other perquisites. Never guaranteed though always appreciated, he might be given the use of a horse and cart for personal use. With transportation he would visit family or help a friend in need. He might at times receive a brace of pheasant or a coney for the pot. He once received an invitation to join a group of Weeting tradesmen on a day of shooting, for which he had the loan of a fowling piece.

Nate Bacon was a satisfied and now married man, who had just been informed by the steward that in the future a single payment at Michaelmas would be made out, to Nate Bacon and his wife. An increase to £17 for the year had been promised, being 10s. more.

Later that same day, Samuel Swift perambulated the village in search of any injuries suffered from the high winds, now considerably diminished from last night. He was aware many trees, roofs, steeples, and livestock had reportedly been toppled or lost in these winds and he desired that any depredations suffered on the property be remedied without delay. This was, after all, the height of the shooting season. It would not be tolerated should any aspect of the estate appear dishevelled or in disrepair.

As he made his way past the ruins of Weeting Castle to the churchyard, he spied Father Smith hauling weeds from the neglected area behind the church, which at this time of year had simply turned to wild slashes of dark brown standing amongst the gravestones.

"Good day, Father. Do not do yourself harm. They can be quite resistant, you know."

"Thank you, Mr. Swift. I find if such is their wont, I pry them loose with my spade, against forcing their surrender to my efforts. And what fair wind, or perhaps not so fair wind on this day, brings you this way?"

After explaining his mission, Mr. Swift enquired after parish news. This opening permitted the vicar to describe in fulsome detail the ceremony over which he had earlier officiated. If ever he needed someone to speak well for him with church officials, he felt comfortable he now had the support of one credible interlocutor.

"'Tis not every day I am able to witness enjoyment in my parishioners. To my displeasure, I am more oft required for sombre occasions."

Mr. Swift surmised he referred not to baptisms, but rather to burials that seemed these days to be afflicting the very young more so than the aged.

"It strikes me you are owed a degree of sympathy, for the matter of your duties is not one reflected upon by your parishioners. To oversee as you do the very most joyful, and the most mournful events of our lives, must require uncommon discipline of humour on your part."

"I am grateful for your understanding; however, I should be better advantaged had I someone in whom to confide daily. As a single man, I find pulling weeds is best for draining my emotions."

"Speaking of emotion, I am told your sermon on the subject of that grim execution of David Tyrie has affected the women of the parish."

"In what manner do you speak?"

"I am given to understand they have taken to wagging fingers at their husbands and at children of a certain age, threatening them with perdition should they deviate from their rule."

"'Twas a violent message, no doubt. You should know, if he has not already informed you, 'twas given with the blessing, nay the encouragement of his lordship who is anxious to stem the increase in poaching and misrule in the parish. I now wonder, given the news of the loss of so many thousands on the high seas this past month, whether this is not the hand of God at work. Could there be meaning to such havoc? Do you imagine it to be a sign from God?"

"If so, Vicar, 'tis a sign God is most displeased with that odious execution of a sailor, for which he has now punished us with the destruction of our fleet."

CHAPTER XIII

MARKET DAY, NOVEMBER 1, 1782

HE HAD PLEDGED TO REMEMBER EVERY DETAIL of that day. Like a trencherman, he stuffed himself on its sights, sounds, and smells. He hoped to later conjure images of this day, but for now he bathed in the myriad details he would carry with him forever.

Thomas had kept his word and yesterday declared that today, Friday the first day of November, would be a fine day for the road. It was dry and had not been wet for several days. He also reported there were no slugs to be found and the spider webs remained long, with the threads let out. A finer opportunity may not come for some time.

If Brandon is where dealers usually take over transportation of the carcasses, on this occasion they would themselves deliver directly to John Shafton of Mildenhall, a preferred customer; the precious black pelts first being deposited with a Brandon furrier. Thomas had finally agreed Elizabeth should accompany the transport to replenish depleted reserves and to make purchases she required for new projects.

The day was to be filled with welcome new experiences for Henry. Elizabeth was not to know, but he was also given a new duty. Thomas had asked him to be especially vigilant while travelling on the turnpike, as this was to be the most vulnerable and dangerous part of the journey.

Their cargo presented an incitement to attack by highwaymen and footpads. In consideration of this risk, two reliable men were selected to accompany them. Francis and James took turns riding a shared horse and armed themselves with a stave, cudgels, and pistols. They were also to take care of the heavy lifting. Henry walked alongside the horse cart that Elizabeth rode.

Meat will exact the best price when delivered fresh and in its most advantageous state. Consequently, Thomas authorized them to take the Brandon-Barton turnpike as it alone promised the fastest, least agitated, and safest means to cover the distance. The squire so valued the higher price secured and the assurance of this important patron's satisfaction, he readily reimbursed all amounts upon presentation of the toll tickets issued.

The turnpike was not, however, free of either trouble or inconvenience for many farmers remained resentful of the obligation to pay for something they had previously accessed without charge. To make matters worse for them, toll-house keepers could be overly officious, to the point of deliberately withholding access until they were disposed to raise the gate. In spite of that, they hoped that as market day would surely bring additional traffic, the promised clement weather would bring safer travel.

Neither Elizabeth nor Henry had experience of this road. Thomas therefore took pains to explain the route as follows: "Upon departing the warren, take to the left. At the southeast road leaving Brandon you will enter the turnpike. By milestone eight, and upon arriving at a tollgate cottage, you shall abandon the turnpike. The road to the right will shortly take you into High Street where our Mr. Shafton may be found by asking any reputable shopkeeper."

They crossed the Lesser Ouse to first unload the skins at Brandon, thereby substantially reducing the weight as well as the value of their cargo before proceeding to the tollhouse. Knowing his mother was to be found in her home this time of day, Henry arranged with Elizabeth to run off to greet her and to tell her of his fortune. He promised to meet them up at the tollhouse as the church bells call people to prayer. By then, the first light of day should be arriving.

Upon reuniting, they encountered a commotion before the gate. Before them, people of various means and intentions vied for the attention of the keeper. Needless to say, each considered his own needs worthy of priority over his fellow's.

Liveried servants demanded their wealthy employers receive immediate satisfaction. Having been dispatched on errands and thus travelling without any such distinction, less fortunate servants boldly appropriated their masters' name and demeanour in attempting to gain satisfaction. It was common knowledge of two facts that simply made these late starters more anxious: all who truly were determined to sell had long since passed, and; the availability and quality of goods for sale decreased rapidly throughout the day.

Waggoneers and drovers sat unhurried atop their lumbering drays, seeming to relish their weighty contribution to the pandemonium. Carriages filled with passengers and cargo waited silently while their post horses stamped, swished their tails, and shook their heads in anticipation of running on. Peddlers of every sort spilled their wares to the ground as they jostled for advantage. The resulting confusion would be comical were the scene not tainted by growing frustration.

Elizabeth and Henry expected to progress with speed once on the turnpike and remained hopeful of a return before sunset. Although not pressed as many others seemingly were, the agitation was becoming most disagreeable.

Anxiety finally caught up to them as Francis spoke up, providing his assessment of the situation.

"Gatekeeper must calculate the toll accordin' to each, whether it be cart, carriage, chaise, or gig; large or small; narrow wheels or wide; number o' horses; whether bullocks, sheep, or swine and the number o' head. The toll paid will be marked on paper to be shown when demanded by the keepers on the road."

He nodded towards the blockage at this last reference. "Be like this each market day. I'll wager no fly-machine will pass here today for 'tis too laggardly."

As Henry watched, he identified the reason for the backup. The gatekeeper was struggling with a drover who appeared to either lack the necessary fee, or was being purposely obtuse in the hope of receiving a reduced toll fee. It did not help the toll-collector that the man's sheep were pushing him about, unsteadying him to the point of near falling to the ground.

Henry approached, sliding this way and that amongst the sheep until almost upon them, where he discovered he had mis-judged the old man. The two were simply having difficulty finding agreement as the poor beasts, worried by the drover's dog shuffled about incessantly, making the count impossible to make. At odds was the number of sheep upon which to determine his toll.

"Good day, to you. I could not but hear your quarrel, gentlemen."

"Be off with you, lad. This is not your affair." The toll-collector was evidently running low on patience.

"I may, if you grant, be of some assistance. Sir, your patrons are eager to exchange their coin for the use of your road. Should I assist you with the tally, you will speedily arrive at a satisfactory account of this gentleman's flock."

"What would you have me do? You can see for yourself this gentleman is obstructing my duties. He refuses to agree the number in his flock."

"I propose using these two wagons as a trap." As he said these words, Henry walked over to them and with hand gestures, made clear his proposal. "The drover must cut out the leaders and manoeuvre them between the wagons to the other side for the others to follow. As they move through the narrow gap, we shall count them together. I believe our numbers should sufficiently agree for you to assess your toll."

Thankfully, the toll-collector was not so frustrated and over-bearing he was blind to this solution as a speedy and face-saving way to resolve his dilemma. It might also be acknowledged by witnesses to this exchange, his attentiveness sharpened when reminded of the revenue awaiting at his lowered gate.

"I was about to suggest the very same to this gentleman when you interrupted. I would indeed be thankful for such assistance. Sir, kindly proceed as proposed and you shall soon be departed."

More slowly than they hoped, yet sooner than what might have been, they were on their way. To the left, the Breckland stretched out as one continuous warren where numerous recent plantations were in evidence. In the few hours after leaving Bromehill they successively encountered the Brandon, Wangford, Lakenheath, and Eriswell Warrens whose presence was signalled by the lodges dotting the heath that in this season, was a sea of rust and purple heather.

To their right lay the fens, their flatness marked by flailing windmills shifting water about. If Henry had expectations of destinations more interesting, he gave nary a sign of his deception as the milestones marking the distances, at once forwards and backwards, passed without his comment on the subject. Instead, and in keeping with his promise to Thomas, his gaze was reserved for those sharing the road.

Familiar with the ways of the fox, Henry estimated that someone intent on causing harm could silently lie in wait at the tollgate to mark his prey. The wagon was, after all, headed in the direction of the market and was evidently weighed down. The calculation that this charge was valuable could not be a difficult one, especially given the efforts of the horse and the presence of armed companions. He was relieved when his examination revealed no one of visibly malicious intent, or excess curiosity.

Thus far satisfied, he decided to now focus on all who approached. Though not accustomed to the ways of highwaymen, he was certain that his survival skills were solidly founded in a healthy imagination and he was determined not to fail in his promise. To ensure rigor in his surveillance, he developed a litany by which to examine each new apparition on the road. Occasionally he enlisted the others to corroborate his judgements, though in a manner not to raise any alarm with Elizabeth.

Does this lone traveller have accomplices who may be concealed?

Do those men bear concealed weapons?

Is the pace of these men too furtive?

Do any show curiosity about the contents of our cart?

Is this distraction merely a trap to isolate us?

One must not surmise that anxiety spoiled his experience. On the contrary, he found his responsibility made him a keen observer. Each examination took no more than a few moments, giving Henry enough time to enjoy the procession of life on display. He must have been deep in thought when he was suddenly aware of Elizabeth speaking his name.

"I beg your pardon. I was contemplating the sights before us."

"Well, Henry. I was asking whether you find this to your liking. I know you have not before ventured beyond Brandon. I therefore would know your thoughts, should you wish to share them."

"I will happily share with you. But I warn you, further observation may bring new thoughts."

The first concerned colour and swiftness. It was his observation these two conditions were in perfect agreement, for both grew with the station and wealth of a person. "Bright colour is reserved for those travelling in coaches drawn by well-bred horses. These splendors either dash by after advancing towards us, or retreat in the distance after leaving us behind. Colours radiate from the clothing and painted faces of the wealthy occupants and from their liveried servants, horses, and coaches."

"Equipage, Henry. I believe one calls a grand carriage and its liveried footman and horses, an equipage."

Henry nodded, registering the lesson before continuing.

"However, the greater number of people sharing the turnpike so closely resemble the land, that from a distance it is impossible to discover their presence. Upon close inspection, their faces are equally indistinct, seemingly able to fold into the earth without trace."

Henry also determined that travellers of all social ranks were interested in only their own condition. Ignoring all others appeared the rule for everyone save the innocent and the fearful, among whom he admitted to Elizabeth, he counted himself.

"I should not heed such sentiment. 'Tis no dreadful thing to observe and so enjoy what surrounds you. In this manner you will remain open to new adventure and surprise. And I add, you will doubtlessly avoid dangers others will run to. Your awareness is a noble quality for 'tis your slash of colour, as bright as the clothing of any noble personage."

She smiled inwardly. More than twice his own slim age, she had the advantage over him of a lifetime. Having lost the two brothers closest to her in age, she wondered now if he didn't remind her in some way of young Robert.

She sensed a maternal instinct rising to the fore. Already the mother of two she was once again with child. In fact, only by the narrowest of margins had this fact failed to keep her at home for Thomas had not been favourably disposed to see her depart. He decided finally not to stand between an expectant mother and her duties and desires. She did, though, show uncommon determination, and also promise in return to do something for him.

Well against noon, the party reached its destination in Mildenhall High Street, nine miles from the Brandon tollhouse. Only when a small band of men rose from a copse did Henry have a momentary concern. Francis and James showed their alarm by openly putting their hands to their pistols. Whether or not their reaction proved a discouragement they would not know, but in the event, there was no trouble. In Henry's judgement they were simply a small band of tradesmen who had stopped to rest before continuing. He saw as they passed, they paid no more heed than had anyone before, and neither did they look back upon them.

Once within Mr. Shafton's place of commerce, Henry could barely contain his enthusiasm when being introduced, impatient to ask questions.

"Hold!" Mr. Shafton laughed. "Do not fear, for you shall have much satisfaction before this day is out. All things in their time but first, young man, we must stow your charge in my larder. Afterwards we shall bait the horses in recompense for their demanding work. The coaching inn is but a short walk and once all is in hand, we shall ourselves take refreshment. 'Tis then I shall attempt to satisfy all your thirsts. Are we agreed?"

By his standard it had thus far not been a difficult day, despite his constant vigilance. Henry so looked forward to the promised conversation that to speed things up and to also work up an appetite, he assisted in transferring the meat to Shafton's larder in the rear of his shop. This advantageously provided him the opportunity to survey the premises such that when they were finished, he had a good sense of it.

Satisfied with the count and the arrangement of the meat, Mr. Shafton handed his signed receipt to Elizabeth. "'Tis pleasant to see you again, Mrs. Turner, and 'tis always a pleasure doing business with you." As she carefully stowed the receipt in her pockets, Henry said to no one, yet to everyone, "A place for everything, and everything in its place."

Elizabeth nodded, satisfied, and John replied, "Well said, master Henry. Well said. If now you agree, we shall proceed to the Clarion where all may be refreshed. Allow me to make all arrangements with the proprietor. As this is market day, he will doubtless be busy, yet I am hopeful his purveyor will find a table at his inn."

As they turned from the stables towards the tavern, James thanked Mr. Shafton for his hospitality before proposing, if it would not be inconvenient, that he and Francis should prefer to visit the market. Too seldom, you see, did they enjoy such an opportunity. Immediately arrangements for meeting afterwards were settled, they departed like two boys on a forbidden outing.

Upon entering the Clarion, one's breath was instantly taken away by the darkness and the smoke-filled interior. The tobacco smoke emanating from the host of clay pipes, that may or may not have been the smokers' own, and the smoke from the various roasts on the spit in the end wall filled the room with a dull haze. Several minutes would pass before our warreners overcame the sting to their eyes and the suffocation of their lungs.

As John predicted, he was heartily welcomed and they were seated with ceremony. He made clear that consent to his offer to be their host would honour him. Such gracious offers are only rarely declined, and this proved not to be one of those occasions. John ordered food and drink from the sideboard, enough to more than satisfy everyone, though mindful to ensure Henry was served small beer.

The Clarion was a long, red brick two-storey coaching inn situated in High Street, by St. Mary's Church. More than once it had been questioned whether the convenience of location was for the benefit of religious travellers, or for thirsty parishioners. Friday markets were a profitable source of business to complement its principal role as a stage on the north-south route serving west Norfolk and London. The little east-west travel was primarily between Bury St. Edmunds and Ely. A reputedly well-enough run establishment, it fell short of being better from the simple fact that travellers had little choice in the matter, the proprietor judging neither the expense nor the effort to improve necessary. Of comfort to our travellers was the evident pride of their host in the quality of the meats to be on offer.

Men, for principally they were all men, sat in groups of assorted sizes and configurations at long, communal tables. Some sat in chairs and others on backless benches, while yet a few sat on the tables. Wigs of all varieties were in view, where hats had been doffed to be hung on pegs or thrown on nearby seats. Some hats however remained at parade, the head beneath being either too attached to it, or too disrespectful of others to be bared.

The plentiful newspapers were being read after many fashions, but always according to the eyesight, length of arm, and space available to the reader. No customer suffered for want of a cup, and most assuredly to the delight of the proprietor, everyone had a plate.

Consistent with the public admiration for meat, the fare served was boiled or roasted, where roast beef reigned. According to the custom, pies and puddings were in abundance and accompanied by bread, roots, pickles, vinegar, and salt. To complement every meal, more puddings smothered in butter were available, along with custard and cheeses.

John and his guests drank beer although the establishment offered more potent spirits. According to the craze for cheap gin made from the overabundance of grains, copious amounts of that spirit flowed at tables where, most certainly, the customers would end this day more sadly than most.

Conversation remained light throughout their repast until, as they were concluding, John turned to face Henry, signalling his readiness to now discuss business. This was the cue for which Elizabeth was waiting. Not desirous of injuring the feelings of their important business partner and gracious host, she explained that as she was now with child, she must not forego this opportunity to return with the items needed to complete her projects before the baby arrived.

With sincerity, John rose to offer his congratulations to Elizabeth and Thomas, together. As he began what she feared would become a flood of questions to the loss of Henry's opportunity, she delicately cut him off. In this moment, she shared with him the knowledge that she was due in early summer before successfully extricating herself without offense to her host. The men were now free to take up their discourse.

Henry explained his interest much as he presented it to Thomas. John admitted there was more to the business than Henry had earlier seen at his shop, or in the mastery of sums and handshakes. He conceived that in view of Henry's interest, it would be advisable to first speak about the nature of his trade.

John then explained the purview and nature of his butchery and how it compared to, say, the business of a poulterer. "To satisfy my customers I must know to choose the finest quality, and for this I must be familiar with the nature and origin of all beasts I should deal in.

"'Twas once the custom to slaughter livestock in the autumn for the lack of fodder to sustain it through winter. Carcasses could often putrefy, making them unsuitable if not dried, smoked, or salted in the proper manner, or made into pastries. Customers often relayed their discontent with the nature of meat, claiming 'twas not possible to take breath while placing it in their mouths, for fear of the odour.

"Modern cropping methods now permit the winter foddering of all livestock, such that we now take it at will. Game and coney likewise benefit from these new methods, permitting fresh meat for our tables. You have, mayhap, noticed the changed manner of preparing food for our tables. This evolution is also changing the manner of acquiring carcasses.

"My customers in the manors and towns may not always require the whole of a large carcass, preferring I sell to them portions according to their choice. In such instances the price is according to their choice.

"While these new methods of cropping have doubtless brought many benefits, they come when agricultural workers are being forced from the land into the towns. Many see this migration as a direct result of the spread of these very same advances that so benefit livestock. A just interpretation may be to say the impacts on man are both beneficial, and harmful. For my business they are doubtless beneficial, as I will explain.

"Just imagine if you will, Henry. Cities and towns that have enjoyed stable populations since before we can remember, having to now accommodate greatly increased numbers without notice. Where are people to be lodged? What is to be their means of subsisting? Our strategies to satisfy these questions must be in harmony with the needs of society.

"I trust I do not abuse your patience. You witness that I take my civic duty to find answers to these questions seriously for as a leading citizen of Mildenhall, I am more than a butcher."

"Please continue, Mr. Shafton. I assure you I am sensitive to the nature of these questions. Although my experiences are limited, my mother took pains to ensure my education did not suffer. Should something prove important to me I will seek understanding of its meaning, and of its working, together. You speak of changes that urge men to migrate to the towns. Though I understand they are needed to work the engines, I know too little of the nature of these changes."

"Well said, indeed. E'en as we sit, the advances made by man daily change our society and the ways in which we live. It thus behooves us to better understand their nature. Did you not wish to experience the market? Perhaps we may converse as we walk.

"Before moving on, however, I wish you to know my customers will come to appreciate your effort today. Above all others, they prize your Bromehill coneys for their flavour and tenderness. Many others are wanting in these qualities. Perhaps the warrener has failed to take it at the proper age or has inexpertly flayed and bundled it. At times, the colour may be off as it has stood too long, becoming limber and slimy. Your warrener has the reputation of providing the best quality, without exception.

"My loyal customers from worthy houses hereabouts count among themselves Sir Charles Bunbury, the artist Bartram Rushbrooke, and the recently deceased Lord Chief Justice De Grey himself, may God bless his soul. You may ask why I enjoy the patronage of such esteemed persons. 'Tis that my reputation as a provider of only the best quality remains whole. This is my first rule of trade, for if my reputation suffers, my business suffers. To guarantee my reputation and my gain I circumvent with the help of Thomas, and now yourself, those intermediaries who contribute only additional delay and expense."

"What is an intermediary?"

"A person who transfers a good from one to another without adding value commensurate with the fee commanded for this service. I find him to be wasteful and an added risk, though he may provide a useful service to some. This explains the steadfastness of my dealings with your Thomas of Bromehill."

"Mr. Shafton, you further my understanding of such business matters. Are we not then indebted to each other?"

"Let us agree 'tis so, and so now proceed to the marketplace. A word of caution, I have more to say."

Making their way to the door he acknowledged certain patrons while continuing to speak.

"I attach foremost importance to my open relations with other tradesmen and shopkeepers hereabouts. I find it useful to share in what they see and experience. You will be surprised to know that if the practical nature of our trades differs, we are agreed that when it comes to our businesses, what bears on one, bears on all. We thus look to each other to understand what may lie ahead for the whole of our community. For example, we see that as the wealthy witness their exclusive hold on something weaken, so will the price they pay weaken."

"Thomas has said his forebears knew a time when coney was exclusive to noblemen and the price was equally noble. Yet in this day it is found on the table of any wealthy person, wherever he may reside, and whatever his qualification."

"'Tis further proof of what we see. Thankfully for my business, the price wealthy people will pay remains quite interesting. Although we do not yet comprehend their outcome, changes are afoot everywhere. Our agricultural advances continue, even as there are e'er greater numbers of people. I propose that one day our rabbit will be enlisted to feed these numbers and on that day, the wealthy will no longer fancy it for their tables. This will bring a decline in its price and with it, a change in the nature of our business. Mayhap, this shall be your own experience."

Henry stepped through the door into daylight, ahead of John. He stood for a moment enjoying the fresher air, letting his eyes grow once more accustomed to the light. By way of bringing closure to this chapter he said, "For the present, I am content. I am young still, and my future will surely be advantaged by the explications you accord me today."

More time was required than the journey home would afford to absorb and reason it all, so puzzling was the effect on him. Henry was certain he would riddle this for many days to come, but the market proved every bit the experience he had prayed for.

The mass of people there stirred slowly but constantly, as individuals slipped and side-stepped to avoid the path of others. Yet chaos erupted wherever peddlers, puppet shows, a dog fight, street performers, and even prostitutes vied urgently for business. Patrons in search of the unusual were readily identified by the manner in which their eyes cast madly about, while others appeared quite purposeful, ignoring all but what they sought.

Wealthy patrons of both sexes were attired fashionably in exciting colours. Fops promenaded in their outlandish conceits. Acrobats, jugglers, dancers, musicians, and clowns wore parti-coloured attire in the hope of eliciting a sign of appreciation. Shops and stalls glinted and billowed with brightly coloured trinkets, fabrics and apparel draped to best advantage. Vibrant displays of all manner of foodstuffs attracted buyers like flowers attract bees.

Yet the whole was against a backdrop so dim it only enhanced the appearance of all that was for sale. The town itself was thus afflicted, as well as all who desired to pass unnoticed. As a ploy to avoid excessive prices, servants of the wealthy were sent to negotiate prices in their most tedious attire. Pickpockets were joined by various souls who, disadvantaged by the vagaries of birth and life, plied the streets in search of a mark from whom they sought some small relief, whether freely given or not.

The first exotic notes to strike Henry's nose were the smells of our pleasantly perfumed ladies and gentlemen. Spices and fruit competed for attention with the odours of nearby ovens preparing food and baked goods. Ah, the smell of gingerbread, and an orange. These sweet and aromatic scents mixed with the smell of fume, cooking, and body odours in a way Henry found to be especially invigorating.

Yet, beneath these was the noxious stench of streets strewn with the detritus of its inhabitants and their beasts. The waste of visitors and livestock added to that of the market stalls. The river Larke served for people to deposit their waste, its funk easily closing the few hundred feet to the marketplace. Most vile of all was the stink of gin-soaked wretches lying in their own filth, too far gone, and too hard by the gin shops to extricate themselves and their children from this tragedy.

Oh, for a parade of macaronis to provide distraction.

There was no shortage of harmonious sounds. Songs, music, and storytelling of all manner provided entertainment to marketgoers. Taken together, the sounds of this multitude could be likened to the murmur of water running over stones.

Yet all could disappear in an inharmonious instant with the cry of a fervid huckster seeking to lure patrons to a nearby peep show, or cockfight. And that wailing sound, rising like a banshee, was of blades and scissors succumbing to the grinding wheels of tinkers.

"May I ask how 'tis you come by your trade?"

John did not look at Henry immediately, the question catching him off guard. He hesitated some moments before providing his answer. When he did speak, he did so while poking distractedly at the goods in a stall.

"My grandfather first opened his butcher shop in the year 1698, in the very same location you now know. He was a young man then with a family, when a contagion befell Mildenhall. I believe the year was 1711. Of those taken were counted my grandfather and his two children, leaving his widow to carry on alone. Well, perhaps not quite alone. Some months later she had a son who would not know his father. That son was my own father. I am now the third John Shafton in the same shop. So, you might say I grew into the trade." He glanced at Henry with the expression of one who had just received a visitor from his past.

"I saw today how this work requires a strong back and arms. Was this not an impediment for her?"

"She was from Cheveley to the south, where her father and brothers was tenant farmers. 'Twas agreed the youngest brother could be spared on the farm when he asked to leave to support his sister. I recall he would have been your age. She ne'er re-married, leaving the whole of the business to my father when she passed. 'Tis now mine alone."

"And do you have family?"

"My wife and three daughters are all well. Perhaps one day you shall meet them, if you like."

Somewhere in the throng was Elizabeth. No less excited than Henry, she was delighted to take in the many familiar as well as the new and exciting delights. It was no hardship to acquaint herself with the fashion of the day. Fashionable items might be neither affordable nor useful, but she could take pleasure imagining her life with them. Everything she saw would provide fodder for discussion and gossip when she next met her friends. Besides, after so many months on the warren with few other than Thomas and the warreners to converse with, she had become quite fidgety.

This day held purpose for her as her plans and projects depended on returning with the objects of her intent. Few were the servants better paid than Thomas, especially when considering their lodging, food, and land to grow food and raise animals was provided at no cost to themselves. They wanted for little.

Thomas' plan for their future required setting aside funds, which was well and good, but by agreement they would not deny the family certain comforts on the way. Using her own revenue, she could reduce the impact on his savings and still return with something for everyone. As taciturn and apart as he was from most men, Thomas still enjoyed a pleasant surprise from time to time.

Everything on her list was committed to memory, so many times had she revised it to ensure her priorities and her finances were aligned. She first surveyed the length and breadth of the market, examining the look and feel of potential purchases, mentally planning her siege. Before committing to any purchase, she would first agree a price with the vendor, and they would come this day to find Elizabeth was not easily parted with her money.

Her priorities were necessities for the growing children. Hand-me-downs from the children of family and friends were unavailable and the cold and wet of winter was near. Boots and warm woollen cloth for the children's outer clothing, a hat for John, and a bonnet and ribbon for Mary made up her first purchases. For them she would also knit scarves, stockings, and mittens from her home-spun wool. For these projects she purchased larger needles.

With plain cotton fabrics she planned to make shirts for Thomas and new underclothing for the whole family. Printed cottons would serve her own need for a new smock and dress. She decided it best to use leftovers and fragments salvaged from old garments for the newborn when it came. For a robe between the babe's skin and these garments she chose a fine, soft muslin. The vendor lamented that no finer was available since she was no longer able to import the quality that existed prior to the troubles in India. This comment was lost on Elizabeth, who in any event did not wish to dawdle and whose mind had already progressed to her next conquest.

Elizabeth was adept at imposing on others with her questions about quantities and new methods, all to render the results of her projects more serviceable and durable. And, more stylish as well.

"Well, there you are. Are you finding what you seek, Mrs. Turner?" John Shafton had spied Elizabeth and had closed the gap between them in a matter of strides.

"I'd offer to give you a hand, were it not that you have very little in hand," declared Henry. "Where are your purchases, then?"

"Your offer is most kind. I am finding what I have come for and I trust my success will continue. I am empty handed to better navigate the throng. I've asked that merchants hold items agreed until paid and collected on our way home. I find the prices more than hoped for, yet I am satisfied the prices agreed are fair and reasonable.

"If you'll excuse me, I must be on my way. The day is advancing, and we must soon take our leave for we have one more errand before nightfall. I hope you will forgive me, but I shall keep it from you until we are arrived." Without further explanation, she turned and slipped through a fold in the crowd.

Unperturbed, Henry returned to their previous discussion. "How then, will you determine the quantity of rabbit to order?"

"I record all the habits and purchases of my customers. Well in advance of the season I will write to each, remembering their past purchases and advising of my pleasure to accommodate their needs again this year. For the approaching season I ask whether their past habits will remain, and when they intend to entertain in numbers. I will also advise orders are best placed by such-and-such a date should they wish to avail themselves, once again, of the best quality for their tables. Signed, yours truly. Coney will naturally be included in their calculations."

"This is not too much effort for you?"

"My dear Henry. The effort and the quality are commensurate with the price I will charge. So long as this equilibrium remains intact, 'twill be worth the effort."

"And should they not respond promptly?"

"I shall follow up with the House-keeper or the Butler, perhaps with something extra in my saddlebag, to determine if an order is forthcoming. It may happen that plans are delayed, thus obliging me to wait. When all is finally known and tallied, I will place my order, allowing some accommodation for other, less constant customers."

For her own needs, Elizabeth settled on two bonnets and a piece of imported lace with which she would trim the collar on her new dress. Retaining both bonnets was an extravagance, certainly, yet wholly justified by her successful negotiations. Besides, she could not choose between them. Buttons, thread, and pieces of felt completed her clothing needs.

Delighted with her selections for Thomas of a new meerschaum pipe and pouch of Turkish tobacco, the smell of which she imagined appropriate for him, moleskin for a new waistcoat, and fustian for trousers, she felt uplifted and ready to set herself to household needs.

It was simply a matter of good husbandry to renew certain items from time to time. Today she wanted new linen bedsheets, pillow coats and handkerchiefs, a carving knife for the kitchen, candles made with good dregs, and soap, as she no longer had time to make it herself. Her final purchase in this category was a clockwork spit, the purpose of which was to save time she could better use on her projects and in earning more income.

And now a new cookbook to replace the one left to her when her mother died. That book was written many years previously by Eliza Smith. Although it contained some useful recipes, many more were beyond her abilities and her means, and increasingly many ingredients demanded were simply never to be found.

The broad range of cookbooks from which to choose surprised her. Many incorporated tables for values that she did not see being useful for her; or chapters of home remedies suitable for a physician. Her access to Kitty Bacon, she thought, made such selections less helpful. Many decried the French and their excesses, yet she admired their use of herbs and sauces. Eventually, she found the appropriate balance of simplicity, ease of organization, and completeness, without excessive information to confuse one. *The Experienced English House-keeper, For the Use and Ease of Ladies, House-keepers, Cooks &c. Wrote purely from PRACTICE, And dedicated to the Hon. Lady Elizabeth Warburton, Whom the Author lately served as House-keeper*, seemed practical, yet intriguing.

A delightful foray followed into the foodstuffs and provisions where the colours and smells of vegetables, fruit and spices were a welcome respite from the smell of rabbit whose odour permeated everything and everyone on the warren. Elizabeth liked that Thomas was very content with the food she prepared, so in readiness for this day she had reviewed his favourite recipes. Quantities of sugar, cinnamon, nutmeg, cloves, ginger, aniseeds, dried figs, dates, raisins of the sun, currants, lemons, almonds both sweet and bitter, orange flower water, and tea sufficient for the winter filled out her needs.

Upon reflection she added an unfamiliar ingredient, though one she believed suitable for Kitty. As explained to her by the vendor, elecampane, or elfdock as they knew it hereabouts, was difficult to find and yet prized for certain remedies. This, she wagered, would make a suitable gift for her newly married friend.

Elizabeth had no illusions that these purchases promised her a busy winter. Fortunately, her warren mates Rebecca and Esther were skilled and would not hesitate to take on more work, thus permitting her time for her projects. Her condition, together with a little of her cherished damson cheese, or some potted beef with nutmeg would go a long way to easing her burden.

Elizabeth was just stepping from the inn when James and Francis came into view. Having availed herself of the Necessary Room, a requirement made more urgent given the liquid consumption at lunch and her condition, they were readying to depart by way of the market where she would pay for and collect her purchases.

Henry and Mr. Shafton could be overheard discussing the latter's favourite recipe for coney.

"... and despite the common denigration of French methods, I do prefer rabbit with forcemeat and a sauce of provocative French mustard found only in their city of Dijon."

Elizabeth, not immune to the pleasures of the French style herself, noted the reference and determined to see if that recipe was included in her new book.

"Francis and James, I hope you have enjoyed yourselves. What is it you have been up to?" she asked of them.

James looked at Francis who appeared the more troubled, before explaining how they had been lured from their entertainment at the pillory to a cockfight where Francis had lost all his money.

"Such is life." Said John. "The market offers something for everyone. Some will return with well-found treasure. Others will lose well-earned treasure."

Our friends eventually made their way out of Mildenhall, collecting Elizabeth's well-found treasures as they proceeded. At each stop she carefully verified the contents of her packages to ensure she was not being short-measured and the goods were authentic, before handing over the agreed sum. Only in one instance was there a temporary setback, which was quickly resolved when James stepped close to ask if there was a problem.

Saying their good-byes, John spoke softly to Elizabeth, "Please convey to your husband I did with Henry in the manner requested by his lordship. He is as promised, and I believe he will be the better for our having conversed."

An afternoon wind was coming in from their left, carrying with it the vile smell off the black fen. As the Brecks beckoned, they all proved as anxious to return home as they were to leave this offense behind.

The evacuation of the town exposed the full panoply of travellers whose animation was now considerably diminished after a long day. As they dispersed in all directions they carried with them every manner of merchandise and produce that had been on hand at the market.

The general rule of travel had always been that one keeps to the left, however by all appearances on that afternoon, the left was difficult to find and hold to for on the road at this hour were many who had taken more than a swallow of gin. Horses, exempt from such abuses, thankfully knew by habit how to proceed even when their riders did not. Some riders in their lofty perches travelled crossways to their steeds, resulting in unfortunate spills and more than one coat being rent that day. Three such knights of the road pursued a brewery dray, unsuccessfully attempting to convince its driver to share a keg.

Elizabeth was anxious to make haste, but her companions wished to leave none abandoned. "We have yet one final matter to attend," she informed them, "and the turnpike is mercifully equipped with milestones by which a rider can be elevated back onto his horse." Eventually, they agreed to limit their charity to only one deed.

Between the first and the second milestones Elizabeth pointed left, to the church of St Laurence with St Peter at Eriswell where Thomas was baptised. At the third milestone opposite the former St Peter's, now standing in ruin with only a fire beacon atop its tower, they exited to the right. Minutes later they came upon the Lower Eriswell Lodge where Thomas' parents resided. Like Bromehill, it consisted of a two-storey fortified structure, twenty feet to a side. Elizabeth called out.

After greetings and introductions, Elizabeth wasted no time explaining they could not rest but a few moments, affording only the time to exchange news. Unsatisfied, old Thomas urged her to tarry. After some teasing, she admitted with hesitation her promise to return before dark, a promise she could not now keep.

"'Twill soon be black without. Permit me to take matters into hand and you shall arrive without concern for you and your fellows."

Straight away he sent a boy to fetch his warreners. The first to arrive was dispatched on a mule to advise Thomas his wife would not arrive before dark, but not to concern himself, as only his fortunate parents were preventing her from returning forthwith. Two additional armed men would escort her home; men he would be pleased to receive and to accommodate before returning the three of them tomorrow.

The others arrived presently and were asked to be prepared to leave in an hour, should this be to Elizabeth's satisfaction.

Elizabeth was satisfied Thomas would be comforted by the news as well as by the arrival of his oldest friends, for the four had grown up on Eriswell warren and known each other as brothers.

Martha Turner could wait no longer. "Now that is settled, tell us more. Would that Martha and Giles was not now visiting with George at High Lodge. How they'd have enjoyed your visit." She took a seat beside Thomas after setting out refreshments.

Elizabeth rattled on with her news. She described how Mary and John were growing and they laughed when told of her fateful play with the chicks. John, Martha proclaimed, was just like his father had been at the same age. Thomas had taken to shooting and was now quite proficient. Their good friends Kitty Sallett and Nate Bacon were now married. He was overseer on the estate and

Kitty was the cook in the Hall kitchens. For herself, she will be pleased to expect a healthy child in early summer.

The announcement came so unexpectedly, everything stood still for a heartbeat. The reason Elizabeth had insisted on stopping was in that moment explained to all, as she had wished for them to know they would once again be blessed. From that instant the conversation revolved around the single subject of her health and well-being.

The manoeuvring upon taking their leave permitted a moment for Elizabeth to pull Thomas senior aside. Quietly, she asked whether he believed poachers were increasingly dangerous. There was much talk in Weeting, and she worried for her husband's safety, despite his precautions.

A man of experience and sensibility, Thomas considered before answering. Certainly he knew of instances of great violence elsewhere in the country, but he believed in the sterner quality of the East Anglian and did not expect more violence than before. He cautioned that townsfolk often make more of this than there truly is.

"I am much relieved to hear you say this. You know well your son answers all, with his all, attacking his obligations with whatever vigour he can muster. Just now he is taken by the considerable advantages of the gamekeeper's situation and speaks of everything more he could do for us, should he hold such a situation. Yet I fear he may only put himself in greater harm than at present."

"'Tis a natural thing for a man of Thomas' ability. He sees what others achieve and can only see that he too, could be so. Should he strive and succeed, you will benefit. Should he strive and fail, he will not regret wasting an opportunity. Much will depend on his readiness should an opportunity arise."

Relieved to hear such practical words, she had a sudden realization. "Oh my, I almost forgot to give you these." With these words she withdrew from a sack three earthen pots for Martha. "My damson cheese. I know 'tis a favourite of yours." She stepped forward to hug Martha and then Thomas, leaving him with a lingering kiss on the cheek.

The journey to Bromehill witnessed a single incident. It would have been of no consequence to our friends were it not their first encounter with a true foreigner. Travelling as they were in the dark, they inadvertently aroused a man sleeping by the road. Alarmed by his stirring, he was able to reassure them he was a lonely traveller and pastor, whose strangeness was explained by his German origin. Karl Philipp Steinmetz was enjoying a walking tour of

England and had stopped for the night.

They left him with this advice from James, "You must be heedful. Many Englishmen are bein' forced onto the roads because our farms are failin' them. As poor vagrants, they're treated by others as the beggars and thieves some have been forced to become. I'm afraid you may find your welcome along the road to be direful, indeed."

CHAPTER XIV

STEPPING AT A BRISK PACE over the dewy grass, he launched a cheery greeting: "Morning, Band."

"Milord. I don't believe we've seen finer for some time."

"Have you all in place? 'Tis early in the season and I predict a fine bag."

"Everything is in readiness, milord. Shall we meet at our usual time on the bottom o' the Belvedere Plantation? As we walk up, the little wind will be in our face and the morning sun will have nicely warmed there. Norrie and the other dogs will have the advantage o' pheasant near their coverts, and partridge sunning on patches o' stubble."

"You have the sense of it, Band. We'll be conveyed in the gig for the convenience of all. The dogs will be in the bottom newly contrived for their carriage to spare them the labour of running the journey. They should thus be fresh at the start.

"Have you worked with your tyro on his shooting? I should speak to him on this matter without delay, as the reports of increased depredations are worrisome."

"Our Thomas is calm when game is sprung, showing no alarm or trepidation to overcome, and he keeps his gaze and his head steady. As for steadfastness before poachers, I'll warrant he will acquit himself well with little more effort and time."

"You was shooting game? I neglected to provide my written appointment. I take it you wasn't detained by anyone seeking your authority."

"There should be no fear on that account, sir. Thomas is authorized to take and kill game on this manor between Michaelmas and the day before

Christmas, provided such taking or killing is done in daytime."

"How do you reckon that, Band?"

"Your qualification under the Game Act milord, and your right o' free warren o'er your lands give him the right as your servant to take game for your use. As well, your tenancy agreements are consistent with your authority over game on all lands in Weeting."

"Hmnn, nonetheless, some tenants are known to entertain suits for trespass."

"As for myself, my appointment is in good standing and provides the necessary authority within the bounds o' your manor. I venture not beyond your boundaries, save with utmost care to refrain from shooting. On the day we was out I surrendered all to your kitchens, where our Kitty was grateful for two brace o' greys and one and-a-half o' pheasant for your table."

"I confess these Game Laws are bewildering. I feared poor Turner, being unqualified, could expose himself to charges of using a gun and a dog on the same day. Double the nuisance, one might say.

"By the way, I recommend you and Turner be extremely diligent in your watch for trespassers. It has come to my attention that a notice of warning against trespassing has been most wantonly attacked. It has been utterly shot through. It's remains are found by the road at Shadwell's and it must be replaced, I am afraid."

"Over by Shadwell's, you say?" Stepping aside to continue his preparations, praying his face did not betray his thoughts, "I'll advise Turner to be on the lookout and see to its replacement forthwith, milord.

"May I ask the men be reminded not to bring their pipes to the shoot? Amusing as 'tis, 'tisn't familiar to the game and the smell o' fume will get them up early."

"May I ask something of you in return, Band? As 'tis a matter of some delicacy, I wish to conceal my preference for the order of walking. I would thus ask you to assign positions in the order in which I introduce the shooters, with first being closest to the covers and the most advantageous position. I will stay at the farthest."

They eyed each other closely until the words formed an image in Jonathan's mind, when he stretched his mouth into a slim smile of understanding. They nodded in assent to their innocent conspiracy.

Jonathan Band was not one to leave anything to chance when assuring the shooters' full satisfaction with his accomplishments on the day. The weather and the skill of the shooters were beyond his control, although both seemed assured on this day. He added his own knack to purposely set a good tone. Everything else he had to make certain of, for success to be his.

By now, staging a shoot was second nature to him. Yet he insisted on his habit of working from a list, striking through each item only when he was fully satisfied each task was completed to his satisfaction. Jonathan's craft, planning skill, tact, judgment, powers of observation, and ability to lead his shooters and assistants were revealed in the performance of his duties. He was a professional.

Ultimately, his success was measured by the quantity and vigor of the game to provide a sufficient challenge to the shooters. A chief duty was thus to retain only the healthiest stock by culling the older and weaker specimens and providing quantities of untainted food and water.

Other duties were less evident. Could he ever let vermin take over even a corner of his preserve? Trapping, shooting, and poisoning them became routine.

Some duties were seasonal, such as laying in sufficient eggs to see them through a full season. His rule was always to press a shilling into the hand for every legitimately found partridge or pheasant nest, once the eggs were safely hatched.

His ability to persuade and collaborate ensured tenant farmers sowed the crops needed to retain game and provide for it through winter. He even directed the placement of crops to assure game did not venture far from the reach of the guns.

Dogs must be always in good fettle and properly trained. Mange could devastate a kennel and legs and feet were a constant worry as a lame dog was only a distraction when walking up game. Timely feeding assured eager pursuit of game, yet soft mouths for retrieval.

Several days in advance of a shoot he would scout the coverts from dawn to dusk with his underkeepers. On the last day they would scout from dusk to dawn to know the state, number, and the current habits of each type of game. He was also known to set out bait, to encourage them in the direction where the shooters would have satisfaction.

Boots were cleaned and well-oiled for the day in the event of wet. His favourite mixture for this required boiling together linseed oil, mutton suet, rosin, and bees' wax to form a paste for rubbing into the leather. Although he was not responsible for their needs, he maintained hats and capes folded at hand for guests. He also kept on hand an extra quantity of his water resist paste, in that event as well.

The only thing worse than a lack of opportunity on a shooting day was having to endure cold and wet. As in his experience the one was often blamed for the other, he attempted to ease the latter in hope of avoiding the former. Besides, being of service in adverse conditions was guaranteed to remove much unpleasantness from the situation.

On the eve, he personally inspected all fowling pieces for the day ahead regardless of how recently he had examined a piece, for in this he was meticulous. Barrels, flints, and springs could not fail. Having extra pieces on hand for repair in the field was another service he could handily provide.

He laid in quantities of tow, linens, and oils. He found the oil he extracted from sheep's feet, when freed of all impurity was nicely calculated for oiling the springs of gun locks. He preferred olive oil for cleaning the guns and for the tidy sheen it left on the barrel, both within and without.

Of course, powder and shot were also at hand. He knew the benefit of using only first quality manufactured gunpowder known by its quick fire, clean burn, and golden tinge left in the pan. The explosion of an indifferent powder, whose slow and weak kindling always failed to bring down its intended target, undid many a shooter. As for his recommended shot, he preferred an ounce of no. 6 and preached against the vulgar habit of heavy loading.

As they are to shoot in the open field before taking to the coverts, he suggested a shorter barrel would be found more convenient, although not so short as to expose a danger while loading. His selected barrel was thus thirty-three inches, sufficient to take down any bird at these distances that a lesser gun might suffer to escape. His long high-mounted stock provided the further advantages of keeping the flash of the pan farther from his eyes, when facing the oft-occurring and unpredictable Breckland winds, and presenting smartly for shooting.

Some shooters remained blithely unconcerned with these requirements and of his preparations to satisfy them. To his good fortune, Jonathan has learned to identify which distinguished gentlemen will not fail to demonstrate their gratitude for such thoughtfulness.

Long against nine o'clock of the forenoon, being the hour for meeting the shooters, he stood waiting in his brown shooting jacket, box cloth gaiters worn against the thorns and the wet, and freshly oiled boots. This, after all, was what he lived for and on these days, he was the master of all before him.

"This is what the land means to me," he thought to himself. "I've lived my whole life out o' doors amongst the trees and in the fields and spinneys. I see many things most men cannot, and for this I count myself blessed." In contradiction of himself, he closed his eyes. Through flared nostrils he sucked in a lungful of the early warming air to examine it for what it told him. He believed he could be taken anywhere in a blindfold and still know his location. This morning he ascertained the invigorating perfume of pines standing in their bed of browning needles. He picked out the decay of wheat stubble in the fields and the promised vitality of manure newly spread on the earth. From the South came the green of new cover crops and from far upwind, the headiness of stubble and peat fires. He wanted it to always be like this, free of the daily worries concerning weather, crops, the weal of his charges, and money.

As he stood in the gateway with the rising sun at his back, he relaxed his gaze. The effect was as anticipated. He instantly saw before him a spattering of precious jewels where lingering dew drops reflected brilliant violet, blue, green, red, and white. With each step he discovered a new precious horde.

He recalled another favoured sight that he named a moonbow. At rare times he had witnessed these, always on a brightly moonlit night while watching over his poults, or staking out a poacher. At such times he preferred the notion that this blessed spectacle was reserved for himself alone. Unlike say, the fall of meteors that were regularly witnessed but little noted.

Despite the many bangs he had endured, his still sharp ears caught the buzz of the last insects before they fell to the lasting frosts, the whispering of the pines in the gentle breeze, and the flapping of birds as they took to wing. Here he discovered the faraway bleating of sheep, and there, the lowing of cattle that always reminded him of his father.

When he was a boy there were few cattle left in England. His father once explained how a French plague had failed, only just, to take them all away. His father enjoyed imitating the call of all animals, yet not until he was much older did he realize how well his father had imitated cattle. Now protected by farmers and Parliament alike, they were on the rebound and to be found in great quantity.

His thoughts returning to the day's business, he acknowledged that filling his game book was unimportant to him. Stalking and walking about was the essence of the British sportsman. Raising game for it to be killed on a day like this was tolerable only in the knowledge that it was all part of God's plan, and the killing would be done in a gentlemanly and respectful manner by true sportsmen. How to present game to a shoot was one of the thorniest of a gamekeeper's divers challenges, and his final test. To succeed, he must sparingly bring his game before the line while providing an occasional spill to excite and challenge the shooters.

"And here they come along the road now," he said to himself, "riding the squire's new dogcarts, fowling pieces eagerly pointed skyward."

Introductions were made, leaving Jonathan now acquainted with Lord Charles' three guests: George Walpole, 3rd Earl of Orford, peer, career politician and man of the public, Lord of the Bedchamber to Kings George II and III and squire of Houghton Hall; Sir Frederick Haldimand, distinguished senior military officer and current Governor of the Province of Quebec; and Sir Edward Astley, Bart., former High Sheriff of Norfolk and currently Knight of the Shire in the County of Norfolk sitting in the House of Commons, resident at his family's Melton Constable Hall.

Stepping down, Charles Coote exclaimed, "Gentlemen, I hope we are all adequately recovered from our travels and yesterday's conviviality. I look forward to our days here together, although I confess to a slight fogginess of spirit which I intend to remedy throughout this day."

This brought forth mirthful exclamations and recollections of the ladies' reactions to a story of note last evening. This led to some back-slapping laughter that in his estimation showed an altogether pleasant mood was setting in for the day.

It happened that Sir Frederick was at the centre of a discourse about the Quebec situation. In his view as Governor, a role which he declares is aided by his fluency in languages, he believes many questions remain to be answered about the Quebecers, not least of which their loyalty to the British Crown.

Certainly, France did not appear to have had permanent designs or a hold on a land that is perhaps the most naturally endowed, if also the harshest to endure in his experience. The former feudal system of administration had failed to establish any significant population with a vested social order or economy in the territory. Yet where the King had failed to secure a hold in Quebec, no one doubted the hold of the Catholic Church and the suppressed Society of Jesus on the populace.

Impecunious Kings of France and their advisors had proved inconstant supporters, providing financial and military support only begrudgingly, and too late. These surely are signs of abandonment, he announced. The effects of this tenure became evident when all who could find the means returned to France with utmost haste, leaving fewer than ten thousand souls adrift, and in the hands of the British.

Although it was circulated that everyone of both means and talent had departed, Sir Frederick found those left behind to be quite sociable and resourceful, if high-spirited and unsuited to our ways.

This serious discussion took an unexpected and decidedly new direction when he introduced what had been a chief tactic of Louis XIV to induce men to settle; men who had ventured there as indentured workers only intending to return afterwards to "la mère patrie." Beginning in the year 1663, he sent some eight hundred women in the hopes they would marry and reproduce. "Les Filles du Roi" were widely reputed to be prostitutes recruited from the streets of Paris, and by sending them off to New France the King had apparently served two purposes in a single deed.

Sir Frederick professed, however, to be not of this opinion as the resident roman clergy assured him the women had been chosen for their moral and physical quality from among the lesser privileged ranks of society, to be freely transported and graced with a dowry by the King.

Whereupon the room erupted into several simultaneous asides, some resulting in laughter and others in shocked disbelief. The men shared in the former while the women were more inclined to the latter disposition.

"Dear Sir Frederick, I pray you forgive our violent reaction to your discovery last evening of the poor women of Quebec. In these times of war and violent storms that bring constant news of heavy losses both in the field and on the seas, it has been quite some time since we have enjoyed such diversion. You both educated the mind and stimulated the humours. We are all thankful to you."

"Thank you, Lord Charles. I believe the response has had a salutary effect on me, providing the opportunity to re-assess my own understanding of that situation. Methinks the truth may lie somewhere between the two extremes of possibility that have been presented to me."

Lord Charles turned to address the men as they milled around, getting their bearings and their own fogginess lifted.

"Before I ask Band to set us off, I ask one final indulgence. I believe walked up shooting brings us as close to our natural state as we may e'er be. We must keep our relationship with nature and with each other on a simple and equal footing. I propose we address each other absent style, simply as christened, and that we govern ourselves gentlemanly and humanely. Lastly, Band is to collect any fines levied by the estate in accordance with the posting in the lodge."

With nods of ascension all around, Jonathan stepped forward to name his underkeepers and assistants charged with controlling the dogs, loading fowling pieces, and collecting the kill. After explaining the morning's assault, he set up the order of walking. A final cursory inspection ensured each gun was properly equipped and in need of no further help. He then asked George, Frederick, Edward, and Charles to advance in that order, suitably spaced.

By the time their experience in the art of shooting flying had made its way along the eastern flank of the plantation, they had let off more bangs than any might have expected. They brushed the coverts along the boundary of the plantation, the grassy knolls, hedgerows, and the stubble in the field. Together they bagged eighteen brace and a half of pheasant, thirteen couple of woodcock that proved particularly quick and elusive on this day, and five hares. The dogs including our little Norrie, had performed admirably.

Most pleasantly, no fines were levied. The gentlemen were already in fine spirits when, exiting a covert they came to a small glade where a pavilion stood, beneath which awaited the other guests. Refreshments were laid out on tables and the sound of champagne bottles popped on the air.

Jonathan retired with his men and the dogs to see to their needs. It had been a busy morning, requiring they be fed and rested to continue throughout the afternoon. He and his men had roasted meats and bacon with bread, apples, and poor beer. The dogs fed on light fare and water, careful to avoid raising their scent, before the drowsy lot laid on the verge for a nap in the shade. All save Jonathan.

As the host and his guests ate and drank, they stood, sat, or mingled according to their pleasure. The chatter was lively, and none faulted the men if, braced by their recent exercise and their growing bonhomie, they engaged in a little tempered bragging of their prowess. The proof, after all, was in the bag.

Lady Ann addressed her husband, Edward Astley. "I so look forward to the end of the London Season and the run up to the Glorious Twelfth. Finally leaving the city behind in favour of an endless round of delightful house parties is exhilarating. While you was shooting, we played badminton on the lawn by the Hall. This afternoon we shall go riding where I'm told we should visit an ancient site of no small note, by the name of Grim's Graves."

"I share your pleasure of this season, and I enjoyed my own exercise this morning. I know of Grim's Graves. I'll wager you will enjoy it and the story told of its origin. I am eager for the fishing tomorrow for it is said the Lesser Ouse has excellent pike at this time of year." He frowned, "'Tis not an edible species to my mind." And then added excitedly, "Yet 'tis a good sporting fish nonetheless."

"I was very touched by Sir Frederick's comments last evening," said Lady Ann. "I can't imagine what a place Quebec must be. And those people. I don't know how he will manage to bring them around to our ways. Perhaps he never shall. I did not hear the reason for his presence in England. Do you have the answer?"

"Frederick is here principally to meet with men in London who can influence his area of responsibility. I also know, when last here he sat for a likeness by Sir Joshua Reynolds. Though long since completed, he had not returned to claim it, with the demands on him and the risks of sea voyage. I am given to understand he is most satisfied with the likeness, and now wishes to return with it to Quebec."

A small group was agreeing its aversion to the practice of running, baiting, throwing, and fighting all manner of beast, be it bull, bear, cock, or dog. These ancient and bloody pastimes of coarse folk were to be found whenever crowds gathered, often taking advantage of a public flogging, or hanging. Most alarming was the resulting drunkenness and gambling that led to brawling. "Are we not now sufficiently civilized that the men of Parliament cannot legislate against these practices?" concluded one gentle lady.

Lieutenant-General Haldimand elsewhere listened patiently as two young gentleman and their ladies expressed relief the war in the American colonies was now thankfully over, and what a splendid job our military leaders had done to preserve us from a worse fate. Britain had performed commendably in their shared estimation.

He thought better of informing them of the miscalculation that permitted the French to enter the war in a position of strength; neither did he wish to share the knowledge of the blunders, lost opportunities, misfortunes, and treacheries from within our allies. He did convey his belief in our Indian allies who had acted bravely and honourably in alliance with the King, which knowledge brought comfort to his new acquaintances.

In high spirits, Lord Charles called forth Jonathan to share with his listeners a story of which he was fond.

"Very well, Charles, I shall give the account as it concerns two o' your acquaintances. It happened one day that we was shooting in the same company. One was an excellent marksman and the other a rather indifferent shot, arising from his habit o' pinching his eyes when he pulled the trigger in anticipation o' the bang. When the birds rose up, by a stroke o' rare fortune our squinter killed two with his shot. Only just after, did our shooter hit his mark. Upon opening his eyes to witness the fall o' our shooter's bird, he unhesitatingly claimed it as his own. Without greater hesitation, yet with good nature just the same, the shooter replied, 'Very well Sir, if you have killed that bird, it must be me who knocked down the other two.' And with that he picked them up and bagged them."

A round of applause showed everyone's appreciation for this show of humour. Jonathan then excused himself as they were about to start afresh.

The afternoon was as satisfying as had been the morning, with the emphasis now being on greys and hares. Their route took them South between the Devil's Ditch, being the parish boundary with Hockwold cum Wilton, and the Western verge of The Belvedere, crossing the road to Feltwell.

Spying had informed the keepers that greys had lately taken to basking amidst the barley stubble where the later sun drenched that side of the plantation. At this time of day the wind shifted to come from the Southwest, permitting the dogs to beat up the wind where they had the better scent for them. In these conditions the birds were expected to lie well but rise quickly in their attempt to reach the coverts. Hares making for the ditch would provide added challenge and fair marks for these experienced sportsmen.

Norrie and her cohorts worked the field, the ditch banks, and the grassy edge of the plantation. They worked hard and would enjoy a well-earned rest as tomorrow was for fishing, and Monday was for hunting when a different pack would be required on the day.

The hunt was only recently added to the manor's agenda to provide sport for those guests and their wives so inclined. For Lord Charles, it also provided the opportunity to spend time with guests in different surroundings. There was after all, a serious purpose behind the sporting, games, dinners, and discussions that constituted these parties.

As the shooters walked-up over the springers, the sounds were of the whispers and whistles of the keepers, the beating and chattering of rising coveys, the shots of the guns, and the cheerfully soft exclamations of 'Bang 'er amang th' een!' Or, 'Well shot, Edward/Frederick/George/Charles!' as the case warranted.

In the event, twenty-three brace of grey partridge were knocked down and six hares taken. Jonathan noted the details of the day's bag in his Weeting Hall Game Book for the year 1782 and would provide a signed card of each shooter's success upon his departure on Tuesday, afore noon. The card would be accompanied by a hamper containing a brace each of pheasant, partridge, and hare to return home.

It had been a shooting day during which the skill and congeniality of the shooters had been a match for the vigour of the game and the beauty of the weather. His lordship was pleased. That Jonathan would be handsomely rewarded by men of this quality was not in doubt, and he had every reason to expect they would be equally satisfied with their fishing and hunting experiences in the coming days.

After a customary toast in recognition of the host and his keepers, and one in return to the gentlemanly and skillful shooters, the company proceeded to disburse just as a horseman was seen rapidly approaching in the distance. Anxious to find their rooms to ready themselves for the evening, our guests took their leave showing little curiosity at this arrival.

Singly or in pairs, according to their domestic state, they appeared in the salon at the appointed time. The men were handsome enough in their attire although no match for the women who far outdid them. They were quite simply, ravishing. Sir Frederick said as much as he bathed in the sight of their silk dresses and their matching embroidered and bejewelled stomachers. He noted jewelry was tastefully understated and appropriate to the venue. Unlike the many unkempt heads of his usual acquaintances, their freshly powdered wigs were well-groomed and sensibly elaborate according to the latest fashion. Painted faces embraced natural tones rather than the artifice to which he was accustomed.

In all, he was pleased to enjoy such sites after so long in the colonies and on the Continent. The English, he thought, are so dispassionate and practical whereas the French, while exhibiting panache, can be frivolous, even somewhat dirty.

"I have not seen Lord Charles since we separated hours ago. Has he not yet come down to dinner?"

"I am certain he is only temporarily detained, George. Surely he will be along presently." Although appearing nonchalant, Edward wondered if something alarming was afoot. The rider had approached apace, and these were, after all, days of more ill tidings than good.

Cecil Swift entered the room dressed for dinner. He mingled for a few minutes before stepping through to have words with the butler. When he returned, he begged everyone's attention.

"Ladies and gentlemen. Lord Charles requests your patience and prays you not take alarm at this delay. An important matter of state detains him. He would have us continue in his absence and advises he will join us soonest. Meanwhile, let us continue our diversions until then."

Naturally, the ensuing discussions consisted largely of speculating on the cause of Lord Charles' delay. Failed attempts to address other subjects included the weather, the upcoming fishing and hunting parties, and the ride to Grim's Graves. The most successful revived fresh memories of shooting at The Belvedere as the enthusiasm of the men, reliving the hits and the misses of their shooting, carried the conversation by shear force and energy.

They spoke highly of Band and his crew, noting especially the tireless and excellent work of the dogs. All agreed better broken dogs had never been encountered. In the end, the bag was beyond all expectations and though it was acknowledged with certain grace the bag should not be regarded as more important than the opportunity to show good sportsmanship, they collectively agreed success was largely down to the skill of the shooters.

Making their way to table, they were joined at last by their host whose sight brought immediate relief to the room. His apologies were offered and he declared all would be revealed once seated; which event happened without delay.

"Ladies and gentlemen, distinguished guests, friends, you doubtless are aware a rider has brought news to Weeting Hall this evening. You may rest assured he has brought glad tidings, which itself is uncommon in these days. He has news of a great naval and military victory at Gibraltar. Let us first raise our glasses as I wish to toast our victory before proceeding."

Lifting their glasses, Charles Henry Coote, 7th Earl of Mountrath PC, said in an uplifting voice, "I give you the King." Whereupon all raised their glasses and cheered, "God Save The King!"

"As you know, that unhappy, yet strategic outpost has been under siege by the Spanish for some years now. Thankfully, our supply flotillas have successfully run the Spanish blockades, permitting our meagre force to hold off all attempts to starve, burn, and bombard them into submission. Of late, the situation appeared decidedly bleaker as the French allied themselves with the Spanish to mount a more determined and ferocious series of attacks, using the most demonic stratagems and devices e'er conceived. This Bourbon alliance launched what they believed to be a conclusive attack on this 13th day of September. News of the outcome only reached the King some days ago. Realizing the import of the information, he immediately dispatched riders to advise his ministers and the King's Friends.

"Friends, I now tell you a total French and Spanish force exceeding one hundred thousand, supported by scores of ships of the line, Spanish gunboats, and bomb vessels, one hundred land guns and twelve floating batteries specifically conceived by the French devils that alone supported a further two hundred heavy guns, has been defeated by our force of five thousand: inferior in number although evidently not in strategy, bravery and persistence.

A resounding cry of "Huzzah!" erupted all around the table.

"The allies enjoyed the physical and moral support of eighty thousand spectators who thronged the adjacent hillsides on the Spanish border. Among them was the most noble and wealthy families of Spain as well as the Comte d'Artois and his followers. All had come to cheer on their armies and to witness what was expected to be their humiliation of our King.

At this last declaration, a disjointed number of derogatory and profane ejaculations were set off, like angry flares, round the table.

"The British Governor of Gibraltar, General Eliott, is the master of this clever and stunning victory. To his credit, our forces suffered few dead and wounded and the loss of a small number of guns. The allies suffered the loss of six thousand men, hundreds of heavy guns and their fleets was destroyed, captured, or routed. General Eliott shall be well remembered."

"The King will undoubtedly wish to commemorate Eliott's great victory. I should commend Joshua Reynolds to him, for I am quite satisfied with the representation he has completed of myself."

"I shall pass along your worthy suggestion and commendation, Frederick. The great siege is now broken with only a half-hearted and ineffectual siege now being maintained. Our forces apparently come and go at will and Gibraltar is supplied and garrisoned anew. This will surely strengthen our hand in the peace talks, and we will most surely never relinquish this prize.

"There is more to convey regarding the actions of the British naval commander Curtis, whose decisiveness and heroic action countered the chief threat, being the French floating batteries. After fighting off the Spanish gunboats protecting them, sinking two that was lost in tremendous eruptions, he boarded all twelve, setting them afire. In the ensuing panic the Spaniards reached for our boats in search of salvation. Curtis rescued hundreds of officers and men and claimed the Spanish Royal Standard from the stern of one of their lost gunboats."

Sir Frederick illuminated the subject in the following manner. "That single operation witnessed more military strength than e'er has been committed at once to North America. In such a small place it must have been a terribly wondrous sight to behold, and a spectacle like none other witnessed by an army of disappointed spectators."

"You have a rogue's humour about you, yet I wonder, Frederick," probed George Walpole, "if there are instances of heroic British action such as those of Curtis to be found among the campaigns of North America."

"Out of necessity of raising a new army after the dissolution of that which fought in the Seven Years' War, the troops under our command were obliged to recruit, impress, or hire soldiers from England, Scotland, Ireland, Wales and Germany. They also turned to native Indians and freed black colonial slaves. I am myself, as you no doubt have discerned, of Swiss origin. Certainly, many valorous men left their mark on the outcome of fighting. Yet, while I cannot think of an equal to Mr. Curtis in fame, I can certainly think of one who by his infamy, may be his equal."

More than one voice encouraged Frederick to continue.

"By way of introducing my subject I should explain the nature of the players in this rather expansive theatre of war, as this is a story of the thirteen revolutionary colonies currently negotiating their future. Therein are found a great many souls whose reasons for leaving Britain was manifold. Some left due to persecution, or resulting from their convictions for crimes committed. Others left for new ideals, or in search of adventure. Many departed for opportunity, where none existed here. Yet others, it now seems, left their homeland because they was knaves and scoundrels seeking the advantages of an open society, free from laws. To these one must add the native Indian population that comprises several distinct nations and whose land is in the process of being pillaged and appropriated by these patriots. I foresee a great challenge for these colonies will be to reconcile the different aspirations of so many peoples.

"I should distinguish between the population of the rebel colonies and those remaining loyal to the King, including many descendants of the original Dutch settlers, for their humours and ambitions are not at all similar. They continue to resist even the armed attempts of the rebels to force their surrender.

"I now come to my story. It happened that throughout 1778 and 1779 a series of brutal raids was conducted by all sides in the frontier at the westernmost region of the colonies. Our aim was to destroy farm crops sustaining the rebels and to disrupt their supply lines. We was in alliance with the Iroquois under Brant and their War Chief, a Seneca they named Cornplanter, as well as with a volunteer force of loyalists who engaged in much of the fighting on our behalf. Led by a John Butler, this force became known for its harsh tactics. Naturally, resistance and retaliation by the rebels ensued, and there was claims of atrocities on all sides.

"The rebel Continental Congress, wishing to end these disruptive raids, finally decided to mount a punitive and decisive raid of its own to eliminate the threat. We now come to our man. Washington ordered his General Sullivan to conduct a merciless campaign to target Iroquois homelands and destroy everything and everyone in its path. As this force of five thousand men moved through the undefended villages in the valley of the Iroquois Six Nations, it destroyed women and children, villages, farms, stores, crops in the fields, and animals. Many of those who fled north to safety was to die from starvation and cold in the subsequent winter. Sullivan drove on his troops so relentlessly they destroyed their own mounts. The invasion was largely successful, though it did not stop raids by Brant and Cornplanter who was furious at the brutality shown by the 'thirteen fires.'"

There was silence save for the fluttering and spitting of the candles.

George Walpole was the first to find his speech. "What utter madness. These are Englishmen in all respects we consider important. Yet they profess to seek, nay, to create a better society than that which they have thrown off, by force and the spilling of blood."

Charles Coote spoke slowly and deliberately. Being host provided one a certain privilege. "We in power, are not without some blame. Though we make some progress, and momentum is in our favour, we are still learning to organize ourselves such that our Parliamentary system more effectively governs the people. I mean to say that matters of state must be conducted for the good of all the people, not simply for the good of those in power.

"Your own grandfather, George, might agree, think you not? Robert was of unwavering loyalty to his King, his kind, and his country. Tirelessly, and sparing no expense, he extended his hand to men of all quality and persuasion to join him. His handling of the Crown and the Commons, deftly balancing the powers of one with the needs of the other, won over many more than he may have distanced with his style. His Norfolk Congress was an example of his leadership at work, bringing about policies that was favoured by the people and supported by the Crown and Parliament. He sought peace and tolerance, and supported fair taxation and opportunity."

"He may very well agree with you on this, Charles. My recollection is of a man very much larger than others, though he was of small stature. His extravagant parties at Houghton continue to be the subject of parlour gossip while his enthusiasm for shooting, hunting, and feasting are undisputed. However, 'tis no secret I inherited substantial financial obligations, which left me no choice but to sell off his grand collection of paintings. As a result, I have oft failed to reconcile his persuasiveness and moderation of policy, with his grand bearing and his excess of conviviality and misrule."

Charles continued in the following vein. "Most men are of indifferent mind on many matters, such that when presented with a strong blow, they may find themselves being transported on it. I have long believed Robert's gift for convincing others to play along was in his mastery of the detail. There was nary a question of state or policy he did not know more intimately than any other. We must be thankful to him for showing us the way forward.

"We may call ourselves Whigs or Tories, yet we know not what these terms truly signify. Presently beyond the work of your grandfather, little body of thought, policy, or philosophy binds any group of men to stir them to action while the King continues to draw his advisors from amongst his friends. I ask, will this suffice in that moment when deeply held convictions begin to stir public humours? Our failure to preserve the colonies may yet prove to be such a moment.

Charles stopped and gazed around the table to find not one pair of eyes had wandered from his own. "I beg your forgiveness. I see I preach to the converted. I beg you to find more congenial subjects and please, let us eat while supper is warm."

CHAPTER XV

HENRY'S EDUCATION WITH THE GAMEKEEPER, EARLY SHOOTING SEASON, 1784

ENRY LEAPT IN FRIGHT. He should have been prepared for it. He had been told what would happen even as he watched the movement that set it off. But he was not prepared for the violent thunderclap, the leap into the air, or the cracking of the oak stave Jonathan had moments before held in his hand.

"Thigh-crackers they call 'em. You can see why. They're placed about the coverts to catch poachers unawares."

Ardley Manning spoke. "I've heard them called man-traps and many decry their vicious nature. Once caught, a man can be hobbled for life, if not outright killed."

"I expect word o' such to spread to make poachers think twice about coming to our manor. However dangerous they may be, they're not a match for the spring guns."

Henry's query on this subject met with a brief description of these weapons, leaving him in no doubt that preservation of the lord's game was a serious business. He had not encountered such determination on Thomas Turner's warren, perhaps because access was restricted by its gorse and hawthorn armoured barrier.

"I note, Jon, his lordship has posted notices of warning about the manor and on the roads leading to it. Do you find these truly effective in keeping men out?"

"I don't leave things to foolish chance, Mr. Manning. Some manors will post warning without putting down the traps or setting the guns. I believe that's o' greater danger to poachers, as they'll only come to believe 'tis humbug."

Jonathan changed the subject.

"Henry joined me in the spring. He's since learned to raise game and to keep it at home to flourish, and not run off elsewhere. From Thomas he knows to destroy vermin and to keep this fowling piece clean and tidy. Now the autumn is upon us, he must move on to other duties. For one, to become a fine walked-up shooter himself. His lordship makes clear his desire for Henry to become a preserver o' game and sportsman o' the first degree."

"In truth, I know not why his lordship requested I accompany you on this day. I am pleased for the sport, but I have little to contribute to Henry's education on these matters. I fear I may only be a hindrance."

Jonathan turned to Henry and challenged him to reset the trap, explaining how to avoid the greatest danger of being caught in it himself. Having set him to this task he returned to Mr. Manning, leading him aside.

In a small voice he explained, "Henry has an inquisitive nature that requires more learned experience than I alone can provide. I'm certain you know o' what I speak. Lord Mountrath has many responsibilities and one is the preservation o' game in our parish. 'Tis a thing to know how to raise and take game, 'tis another to contend with the interests o' tenants, labourers, purveyors, other landlords, and poachers. Henry must now be exposed to gentlemen with such experience. I propose we shall contrive to begin this discussion together, sir, to better address Henry's predictable inquisitiveness."

"I see, Mr. Band. I willingly submit myself to your stratagem and shall follow your lead, intervening as I think helpful in that regard." They exchanged nods of satisfaction with their grand design.

Band was relieved that Henry's grandfather would facilitate his acceptance of what were to be some dumfounding truths.

For his part, Manning rejoiced in the confidence shown by his lordship in Henry's abilities and in his future.

They returned their attention to Henry as he struggled to reset the trap. "I'll give ye a hand, Henry. Truth be, 'tis something for two men." In a matter of seconds his practiced movements had returned the steel jaws to their lethal positions and with Henry's aid, disguised them with long grasses.

"There. Now you're to be in the fields and the coverts with the shooters, you'll want to know their whereabouts before walking about. You'll help set them anew every few days. Likewise, we set anew the coverts from where we spring to engage unsuspecting poachers. We can't have them comfortable moving about.

"A few hints afore we have you shooting. When game is on the wing 'tis most exposed to danger from the shooter, for should but one shot strikes its wings, its fall will be occasioned. If first it towers, you're confirmed it has been well struck and despatched mercifully."

"Thomas believes it important to kill game mercifully." stated Henry.

"Is 't not best all killing be so? Would you not wish 't for yourself, young master Henry?"

"I believe I would. I will hope to then do my best to kill well and to see other shooters do so in their turn."

Ardley Manning's chest puffed ever so slightly.

Jonathan then spoke of the manner of shooting flying game. "You've mastered your fowling piece and Thomas tells me you're adept at shooting ground game and vermin. I believe you'll find this much different. Used to be we'd shoot them where they stood or sat, but with these," he hefted his own fowling piece and swivelled it across the sky before him to make the point, "we now practice shooting flying.

"Remember the breadth o' pattern o' your shot. It provides a margin o' some inches. Distance between the gun and the game is important to judge. For fowl that traverses at a sure distance, you'll aim at the head. If farther, you should allow more for the shot to meet the bird as it passes in flight. If the game flyeth to pass o'er your head, 'tis best to shoot at the head. If from you, aim under its belly. In these manners you'll lead the bird.

"Our Norrie, here 'll spring them for you to take your shot. However, there's no guarantee how it'll fly. Traverse, lineal or oblique, be prepared and remain steady. Start o'er to that covert, along the edge o' this field where there'll be pheasant among the grain. We shall grant you the honour o' shooting first."

As they tramped through the grain still standing in the field, Henry wondered that the tenant farmer tolerated their passage. "We are certainly causing destruction everywhere we tread and surely the game must eat freely of his labours. When shooting parties trample, as they must, does he not protest?"

"He does, yet to little avail." Said Jonathan. "'Tis doubtless the extensive game and rabbit preservation at the heart o' Weeting estate has put pressure on the farmers and their crops."

"I do not understand." said Henry, "Should Lord Mountrath not compensate the farmer for any depredations suffered on his account? I have seen myself how coneys will eat turnips, or simply take out bites such that the rest spoils. Wheat and barley are regularly devastated as pheasants will eat it from the time 'tis sown to e'en when the grain is in the barn. They will go so far as to peck out the heart of newly established clover, to its ruin."

Ardley remembered his agreement with Jonathan. "The lives of many are entwined with the welfare of the manor and its landlord. Struggles will arise as the needs of one encroach on the needs of others. Flockmasters must graze their sheep in the very fields where tenant farmers sow crops and raise their livestock alongside those of labourers. The warrener and gamekeeper raise their charges in lands next those of these same farmers. Therefore, a certain willingness to accommodate is to everyone's best advantage.

"Local tradesmen, merchants, and innkeepers living on the estate are supported by the economy of these activities. The rector too, has the parish flock to tend. All rely on one another in the lord's service. Though he may fail to provide complete satisfaction, 'tis my experience Lord Mountrath strives to accommodate as best he can the needs of all, without throwing off his own interests. Is it not so, Band, we are many who profit from his lordship's stewardship?"

"True 'nough spoken. Mr. Miller, the tenant o' this farm, complains to his lordship that as the quantity o' rabbits and game increases, so do his claims for losses. He enjoys the sympathy o' those who, like himself, are also not recompensed for these damages.

"Yet e'en as it freely eats o' his labours on his own land, as Henry says, Miller is not permitted to enjoy field sports, for he has not the property qualification to hunt o' his own merit."

Ardley asked, "Does he not agree in his lease to reserve the game for the landlord and to abide by the needs of the warrener and the gamekeeper in preserving the game of the manor?"

"Aye, he does. He tolerates our passage and will abide by our wishes when sowing crops. Yet as he complains, Mr. Miller accepts his lordship's invitations to partake o' shooting on three occasions during the season. Tenants also enjoy a private shooting party at season's close."

"And does this not assuage him?" asked Henry.

"Somewhat. However, a time is near when the farmer must become our ally to repulse poachers. As they become bolder and more numerous, who better to spy on their activities and to raise the alarm at their movements? The alternative would be for them to make alliance with the poachers who'd then be most difficult to stop. What say you to this, Mr. Manning?"

Suddenly, and with no warning Jonathan stuck out his hand and spoke in a low, quick hush. "Hold! Look to Norrie to spring a pheasant. Ready yourself, Henry."

As Norrie circled an area some thirty paces ahead, Henry quickly ensured all was in readiness to shoot.

BANG!

As the bird rose straight in the air Henry's shot raced ahead, causing no damage whatsoever. "At that distance you'll have a moment to determine how you wish to shoot. Take the moment, Henry."

Resuming, Ardley responded, "My community of Brandon merchants acknowledges the increase in poaching, and we are most suspicious of the farmers. We see where greater numbers of fields are now constantly under the plough, yet fewer men are retained to labour there. What else are men to do but rely on parish charity or poach? As for the farmers, his lordship is conversant with their frustrations and is quite distressed to think his tenants may have struck allegiance with poachers for the purpose of thwarting his authority.

"To add to their woes, farmers have a new complaint, being increasingly vexed by hunters scrambling and traversing their fields with no regard for the destruction caused their crops, their livestock or their hedges. All in pursuit of the fox."

"I have heard said," interjected Henry, "the Petty Sessions are dominated by cases brought against poachers and that many of those accused are agricultural workers in distress. Their claim is that poverty made them poach and there seems to be some truth to this, as you say grandpa."

"Where have you been to hear such things?" Ardley was not certain whether to be distressed or impressed. "Some assert 'tis simply the nature of all men to be excited by the thrill of sport, or to enjoy a bracing experience in the countryside rewarded with something to take home for the pot. This applies e'en to those who are not gentlemen. Though as you say, I believe most poaching prosecutions are now for a first offense of trespass in pursuit of game during the day. As these cases are dealt with summarily, they suggest crimes resorted to casually or out of necessity. Fortunately for them, the local Justice is an educated man and not insensitive to another's plight."

"Henry will see 'tis the keeper who must bring charges and evidence against anyone he suspects o' flouting the law. I did myself bring many o' these same cases before the Justice, but not afore I ....

"Hold, Henry. Look to Norrie."

Henry waited, his fowling piece newly charged and at the ready. When the pheasant rose, he waited until its direction was known before aiming swiftly and firing as it crossed, rising obliquely. The distance was fifty paces. The pheasant towered and fell dead. Jonathan whistled softly, and in a few moments Norrie returned with the bird held softly, gratefully accepting Jonathan's scratch behind her ear with a waggle of her hind end. Everyone was pleased with this quick, smooth, and effective execution.

Ardley clapped Henry on the shoulder and congratulated him on a fine display. "You are indeed your father's son. I mean to say, naturally, your grandfather's son, and your keeper's student."

This last complement he added in haste, as one might when trying to conceal his tracks. Ardley was recovering from his faux pas, praying no damage had been committed, when he noticed that one person had fully taken note. Trained to detect the slightest of inconsistencies or changes about him, Jonathan shot him a quick glance as if to ask what he was thinking, before taking up the role of the dutiful servant.

"Your reputation as a shooter precedes you, Ardley Manning. I believe you shall now have the opportunity to prove your own skills. What do you say to that, Henry?"

Henry had shown little sign of registering the exchange, so engaged was he in examining his kill. "See here, grandpa," thumbing through the breast feathers, "three hits to the breast. A clean kill, for which I am pleased."

"You was saying, Jon?" continued Ardley.

"Pardon me? Oh yes, poaching. In advance o' bringing a case before the Justice, I confer with his lordship so's to convey his thoughts to the JP in the hope the sentence will be satisfactory to the Earl. He's proven to be a most judicious lord, treating severely only those he believes are unrepentant and repeat offenders, and those who poach for their own profit. In such cases he's predictably merciless in applying the full force o' the law."

"Are there many such cases, Mr. Band? I am unaware of them."

"There are many more than once there was, Henry. As you've seen in the marketplaces, there's no absence o' game for sale. How do you believe it arrives there, when the law forbids its sale? 'Tis our misfortune our efforts to raise increasing numbers o' game for gentlemen have only given poachers greater ambition for profit. Poached game is less costly than mutton or beef and when they've a rabbit, the skin will bring them further profit. 'Tis unintended, yet 'tis the landlords who supply the poachers."

"Are others involved in this illegal trade?"

"Many are those who conspire to take game for the marketplace. Higglers, coachmen, and poulterers are in on the game for their own profit. A man may seem more innocent than his fellow, but in my experience he's the more brazen o' them, for his intentions will be the most dishonest.

"Rabbit and hare are in great abundance. As ground game they're easily caught. This explains their prodigious consumption. To take feathered game requires a greater skill and organisation, and o' course better engines or fowling pieces. Night poaching itself requires guns or a very extensive system o' nets, making that a most dangerous activity for all."

Henry was not uninformed of the goings on in his adoptive community. "Mr. Miller does not permit labourers to keep fowl, as he fears they would steal his grain for their feed. Surely, this is further incentive for them to poach.

"You say his lordship can be merciless under the right conditions. Have you the name of one so treated, Mr. Band?"

"Aye, lad. William Cawston o' Thetford was apprehended by me while night poaching. Landlord o' the Black Thorn Inn, he was an evil-minded poacher o' bad complexion, oft convicted o' the unlawful destruction o' game. He and his fellows wore blackened faces and discharged their fowling pieces when we challenged them to halt and surrender. One o' my keepers was wounded in the arm during the scuffle. They dropped their kill and decamped o'er the heath, but we caught up with old William hiding in a thicket. He was apprehended without further resistance but refused to give up the names o' his mates. They'd taken a deer from the manor park and several pheasants that'd been sitting in the trees."

"And your keeper, did he recover?"

"He did, though he lost his arm after gangrene set in. The squire was vexed they had come at night and in disguise to steal from him. However, he was most upset that one o' his men should be wounded in their bold attempt to save themselves, once caught in the act.

"What sentence was passed on him, then?"

"Death. He was convicted o' committing a felony without benefit o' clergy. I don't know a harsher sentence, though another I recall may be a worthy rival. For now, look to your grandfather."

Jonathan had seen Ardley move deliberately to place himself before the others when Norrie changed her gait to focus on a clump of bracken. Before long she encouraged the quarry to leave this hiding and into the open. When not a pheasant, but a coney bounded from within, a surprised Ardley took an additional second to adjust his strategy. Running from them at thirty paces distant, he aimed at its ears to despatch it cleanly. As he hocked it to run his belt through the legs, he spoke with a satisfied smile, "Enjoyable as that was, I believe I should rightly take the next shot for that was not the promised pheasant, Mr. Band."

"I trust you observed your grandfather's position and hesitation before he shot that coney. 'Tis the secret o' shooters. We may both learn by watching your next kill."

"Whose sentence rivals that of William Cawston?" prompted Henry before they resumed their direction.

"He was a very bold man indeed. More recently than Cawston, just more than a year now as I recall, Matthew Page o' Swaffham was formerly a member o' the Norfolk Militia. Apprehended, yet unrepentant, violent, and threatening to return to his crimes if released, Lord Mountrath had advanced his belief the case would be better held over for the summer Assizes at Norwich where the Justices would show him no clemency. He was convicted o' poaching and sentenced to transportation for the constancy and boldness o' his transgressions. In the event, Mr. Page, then a strapping man o' twenty-four years, escaped from City Gaol with another felon in the early hours just prior to being shipped out. Posted notices o' their escape included their physical particulars as well as where they was last sighted, still in irons."

"Did they complete their escape?"

"Whoever would apprehend and secure him for the Keeper o' the Gaol was to be rewarded two guineas, and be entitled to twenty pounds under an Act o' Parliament. The two men was soon returned to gaol, then immediately sent off for a minimum o' seven years each. Mr. Page received an extra portion o' flogging for good measure."

"And what would be your sentence if e'er convicted of poaching? I ask as 'tis common knowledge gamekeepers have been known to abuse their authority."

Jonathan was struck by the unusual nature of Ardley's query. "Whatever has he on his mind?" When he responded, however, it was in his normally unconcerned manner.

"This year is the first wherein I'm required to be certified. For this I've registered with the clerk o' the peace and paid the stamp duty. If apprehended hunting game outside o' this manor, I'm liable for conviction and to pay a fine as much as £50. The more serious crime o' hunting deer on ground under my charge, without his lordship's written permission, could bring a fine o' £60, or imprisonment for one year without bail. For a second such conviction I'd be transported for seven years. In either event I'd no longer find employment as a keeper."

"Those are serious penalties. What say you to that, Henry? To where would you be deported?"

"America, I'm afraid to say."

"Aye, grandpa. Enough to discourage Mr. Band and hopefully any colleagues who may be inclined to take more than their due. I wonder poachers do not first determine the complexion of a lord and his Justice before embarking on a misadventure. I would want to avoid manors known to be harsh in penalizing those convicted."

"I am reminded of ... here, I believe I have a copy." Ardley pulled a sheet from the depths of his left pocket. "I wish to alert our Brandon leaders to a model I have discovered. It would convey our intention to fully enforce the law in protecting ourselves and our property. It seems to me that the many changes overtaking our society have disrupted the natural balance we have long enjoyed in society.

"Here, examine if you will what the Magistrates of Norwich have devised to protect the city's inhabitants. Not unlike the manner by which our game laws permit keepers to preserve and protect our game and control all destructive vermin, Norwich is to devise a Plan of Police to preserve its inhabitants through the control of human vermin."

Ardley unfolded an article that appeared in an August edition of the Norwich Mercury. Suddenly, he thrust it into Jonathan's hands before turning swiftly to shoot a pheasant rising to take wing. Once more he demonstrated his shooting prowess to the amazement of his companions.

Jonathan and Henry read together as Norrie went to work without the benefit of directions:

At a full Court of Mayoralty, held the 12th Day of August 1783. Whereas divers Burglaries, Felonies and other Trespasses have lately been committed within this City and its Liberties. The Magistrates desirous of exerting every Means for the Protection of the Persons and Properties of the Citizens, and being resolved to use and direct the utmost Vigilance for the Discovery, and bringing Offenders to Justice; do hereby request the Inhabitants to give Notice of all Persons in their respective Neighbourhoods, who have no visible means of Subsistence, or who are otherwise of bad Character and profligate Manners; also of all Houses of bad Fame, and evil Resort, such Notice is to be given either personally, or by writing to the Right Worshipful the Mayor, at the Sword-bearer's Office, or the Aldermen of the respective Wards.

And whereas divers Frauds have been practised upon several Shopkeepers and others, by a set of itinerant Cheats, known by the Term of Swindlers. It is hereby requested, that Persons taking Lodgers or Inmates, will deliver an Account of all Strangers and Persons of suspected Character who shall apply to, or be received by them, in Order that the Magistrates may be furnished with Means of detecting those who shall be found to have committed Offences in this City, or in any other Part of the Kingdom; and that the Citizens may thereby have an Opportunity of obtaining such Intelligence, as may prevent them from being subject to future Impositions.

All Innkeepers and Publicans are also, hereby, enjoined to be circumspect as to all Strangers whom they entertain and harbour, and that they may be ready to answer any Enquiries that shall from Time to Time be made under the Directions of the Magistrates. And all Constables and other Peace Officers, are strictly commanded to be diligent in executing the several Duties of their Office, especially in apprehending and carrying before a Magistrate, lewd and dissolute Women, and other disorderly Persons, who haunt and infest the Public Streets of this City, to the great Offence of Decency and good Manners, as any neglect of Duty in them, shall be certainly and severely punished. The Magistrates being determined to exert their utmost Endeavours to establish, and enforce such a Plan of Police, as shall be effectual for the Preservation of the Peace, and for the Safety of the Inhabitants of this City.

By the Court, [signed] DE HAGUE.

Having secured his kill, Ardley turned to face the others, addressing them directly to make his point.

"I believe in the ancient rights of each Englishmen to enjoy security, personal liberty, and private property; and that with respect to these rights he should have the means to defend them. The King's Bench has agreed on various occasions that keeping a gun is consistent with the laws if 'tis kept by one of suitable condition and degree, for unmalicious purpose. These same laws argue in favour of the ancient right of resistance and self-preservation. It appears to me the case for keeping arms, specifically guns, is based in a tradition that is well reasoned and consistent with our laws.

"This notice implies the sanctions of society and its laws no longer restrain the violence and oppression that threaten our rights. Here in our day, Justice De Hague is obliged to call upon inhabitants to partake in the apprehension of abusers and offenders of all venomous manner. He proposes they do this through vigilance, the supply of intelligence, and the denunciation of those of suspect character.

"The question I intend to put before our governors is whether, in addition to these measures, men of fitting condition and degree should be purposely armed and available to resist violence and oppression in the name of self-preservation."

Henry looked to Jonathan to respond, perhaps feeling inadequately experienced to summon an intelligent reply. Jonathan spoke with less than complete assurance when he ventured that, "'Tis common knowledge His Majesty tolerates a Protestant subject, though he is accused o' keeping engines and guns for the purpose o' poaching, to keep and use arms for lawful purpose. Some say 'tis a natural right to have and to use arms in such manner. Others add, 'tis the duty o' all good and able subjects to stand ready to use their arms in assistance o' those who execute the laws and defend the public peace."

"Do laws give men license to organize and employ deliberate force on condition they act within the law and according to common sense and reason?" Henry estimated this to be within his competence to ask.

Jonathan and Ardley pondered this before Ardley suggested that in his experience, the judicial decisions of magistrates had been clear on this subject.

"The answer is that Protestants, if not now also Catholics since passage of the Papists Act of 1778, enjoy the right and the duty to bear arms in defence of the law, under certain conditions as we have said. I recall to you the Gordon Riots of 1780. When we deployed a military force untrained in the fitting use of arms in defense of the law, we saw the grave danger that awaits our failure to ensure these conditions.

"Nevertheless, I say humbug to those fearing French methods on our soil. I would propose we go beyond mere requests for information our Justice de Hague calls for, so to call upon the duty of certain men to provide armed assistance in support of the Plan of Police."

"Who would govern these men?" Jonathan imagined such an armed body of men was better to be led, than let lose upon the winds of anxiety.

"I should propose they report to a senior officer who would answer to the sheriff.”

“What of those men who would take matters into their own hands, acting thus in the absence of the sheriff, if e’en in their belief they acted wisely and with common sense?”

“They, grandson, would be deemed malicious offenders, as the use of arms can only reasonably and by common sense be employed in unambiguous assistance of authorities in defence of the public peace. To do otherwise would lead to confusion, disorder and ultimately misrule.”

“Anarchy,” offered Henry. “Inevitably leading, I venture, to the loss of our fundamental rights to security, liberty and private property, as you say.”

“Exactly! Well put, lad. You see Jon, ’tisn't so opaque a proposal one cannot readily grasp the nature of it.”

“Speaking o’ Henry, I wonder if he saw what scurried under yon covert?”

“I saw the fox, Mr. Band. Shall we pursue it?”

“I’ve marked it. I’ll return to remove it anon. Any neighbouring lord ’ll pay for a healthy animal such as that.”

“Would you not remove it to plant for your own hunting?”

“I might have done, Ardley, save for my satisfaction with the concentration o’ foxes in the reserve. Not many years since, I’d kill them all as vermin. Today, my master wishes to shoot game and hunt fox, together. Despite my protestations at the difficulty, I must find a manner to keep both. I can only be thankful he’s joined those who maintain the one reserve a good distance from the other. Otherwise, ’twould be nigh impossible to preserve the game with so many foxes on the loose nearby. Whatever they didn’t kill would decamp for neighbouring coverts where they would find safer haven.”

“While the game park hard by the mansion is well known to me, I have no experience of hunting at Weeting, Mr. Band. Perhaps I have ne’er demonstrated sufficient interest to elicit an invitation from his lordship.”

“If e’er you wish to hunt, I propose you simply make your desire known. The Earl’s quite liberal with invitations as he wishes to satisfy everyone who aspires to hunt. He’s therefore devised a system to accommodate each class and hunts equally with his genteel peers as with tenant farmers, tradesmen, merchants, and lesser landowners. His greatest wish is for a high-spirited chase in pursuit o’ healthy and cunning adversaries. I’ll wager an invitation would be forthcoming without delay.”

“Then, sir, I shan’t hesitate to inform him of my appetite for hunting. However, just now, might I propose we sit here, for I am tired and in need of sustenance."

"I see Henry hasn't wasted time. He's handily dispatched two pheasants while we've been distracted. Youth's a fine thing is it not?"

As they rested and replenished themselves, Henry listened as Jonathan spoke about the duties of a gamekeeper to which he had not yet been exposed. Ardley, a man not detached from the world of shooting as we have seen, helped further the discussion while probing to see whether Henry sufficiently understood the nature and the import of Jonathan's remarks.

He explained the structure of the estate and how the warren, the game park, the hunting reserve, the deer park, the farms, sheepwalks, and the plantations were laid out by design to benefit each other. Animals of all manner thrived because of careful management of cropping fields, pasturage, heathland, quarries, sandpits, flint mines, fens, riverbank, and woodland. Even intervening spaces such as commons and waste, brakes, field margins, and hedges were managed.

His lordship holds the reins; yet he relies on servants for advice, cooperation, and to give effect to his directions. A gamekeeper at Weeting is required to be versatile for he does more than manage the parks and ensure advantageous relations with those who hold other trusted positions.

It escapes the notice of many, that the river Lesser Ouse along the southern limit of Weeting Hall falls within his purview. With the help of a river keeper he ensures it is stocked and the banks are cleared to provide suitable access for those guests who prefer angling.

The stalker similarly assists those pursuing deer, at times arranging for bagged deer to be presented for the kill. The head gamekeeper is responsible for the stalker and river keeper, together.

Planning for shooting, stalking, and angling relies foremost on ensuring sufficient quantities of game, deer and fish to satisfy expectations. This is becoming more difficult, as expectations of a large bag are increasing yearly.

Dogs for different shooting conditions must be trained and proven before introducing them to live game, and the commotion that reigns once the banging begins.

Beaters to flush game, and dog whisperers alike, must be selected to work as a team and trained to know the ground in order to flush the game according to plan.

On the day, the keeper will oversee the shooters and direct all activities, including the luncheons to be served to guests and servants.

When all is done, he will note the details of each kill in the game book, and when all have returned home with their prizes he will arrange for the sale of game not required by the kitchen.

"Mr. Band, are we not equals in the field, sharing in the destruction of game? Why then, does the luncheon for guests differ from that for servants?"

"Would that not be a sight, Mr. Manning? The servants who beat, retrieve the game, and carry equipment to and fro may receive a slab o' cold bacon, a slice o' dark bread, and poor beer to wash it all down as they sit on stumps or directly on the ground. In fine weather 'tis fairly tolerable. In the wet, 'tis much less so.

"Guests are favoured with fancy meats, with vegetable and fruit sides, pastries, cheeses, fine breads, and cakes. To wash this down they'll drink champagne, clarets, and whiskies while well seated under a pavilion to protect them from sun, wind, or rain. They're most often joined by their wives and others o' the party who do not partake in the shooting."

"I must then master humility, for I am destined to be a servant."

"That is the way for all servants." Jonathan was reminded of his day's goal.

"I now speak o' responsibilities beyond those you've known these many months. You've shown today the promise of becoming a fine shooter and sportsman. I believe your grandfather has much to be proud of." With this Jonathan placed a friendly hand on his shoulder and leaned towards Ardley in the manner of suggesting he might wish to add something.

Ardley understood. "His mother and I are proud of him. Turner has commended him for the promise he has shown throughout this past year. 'Twould appear he now applies himself to the responsibilities of gamekeeper with equal alacrity. His lordship has openly acknowledged his contentment and it is a matter of considerable satisfaction and relief to our small family that Henry is awarded such opportunities to establish himself."

With these last words he looked into Jonathan's eyes, wondering to himself, "Does he know of what I speak?"

Jonathan's gaze met his and he received his answer. Thankfully, he thought, discretion reigns over this man.

Jonathan gathered the remnants of their meal before standing to stretch his long limbs. "'Tis auspicious our Henry favors the countryside and tolerates being out o' doors in all weather. He'd otherwise be a wretched keeper. He possesses a tolerable power o' observation as well. Henry, what had that fox in his mouth?"

"Appeared to be a rabbit. As we are too far removed from the warren for him to have taken it there, I venture 'tis from one of the many burrows established by those who have escaped the warren."

"My planted foxes are restricted to the far corner o' the parish where the gorses, old pastures and brakes are reserved for hunting. There, I've established several small and secluded fox covers, spaced to give each his territory. This ensures a hunt without them running off to find refuge elsewhere. 'Twill also make it most certain they remain distant enough to restrict their predations on the game preserve and warren."

"Mr. Turner has informed me there are certain lords hereabout who've taken to killing foxes to protect their shooting. How do you prevent them from shooting your foxes if they trespass into their manors?"

"Thomas Coke, for one, is known to keep distance between his agriculture, his shooting, and his hunting. He'll abet the killing o' foxes about the park for their destruction o' his pheasants, but he's given orders to tenants not to disturb those foxes who maintain their distance. 'Tis for all neighbouring keepers and tenants to arrange together to keep them distant.

"In return for protecting the litters o' cubs and their covers, tenants will receive invitations to hunt with his friends o' similar degree. For tenants who aspire to hunt and who know their place, invitations come often enough. They may mutter at being segregated at social events, or excluded from the hunt balls, but they're satisfied sufficiently to assure their acquiescence in preserving the foxes.

"His keeper Palmer, now he's a different matter. He'd taking to shooting my foxes as he claimed they stole his pheasants and rabbits. He's fearful o' their predations on the game and losing his income from the sale o' rabbit skins. You recall, Henry, the keeper's prerogative to keep any outside the warren for his own. For men such as us, this represents a substantial sum; for which reason he had my sympathy. We therefore agreed an understanding, to which we invited our fellow keepers and tenants in the neighbouring manors to share."

"Must not farmers suffer the loss of poultry and lambs to the fox?" Ardley was no idle listener.

"Do tenants not walk the puppies and dogs of their lord's pack?" Henry had visited with farmers who had complained to him of this obligation.

Jonathan could see the questions beginning to come fast. "Though they've no love o' the fox, so wealthy have some tenant farmers become they now enjoy life in their home in a style similar to many lords. I suspect we may not know all there is to know, but there are few complaints in return for the added privilege o' riding to the hounds.

"To answer you Henry, 'tis indeed a requirement o' lease agreements. And though they may complain, they're likewise known to freely offer for sale the hunters bred from those they walk."

Having cogitated the previous train of the conversation, Ardley added, "I suspect the gentry of attempting to balance opposing forces. On one hand they risk the loss of prestige suffered by too readily accepting the newly wealthy into their society. On the other, they risk the loss of additional incomes and stirring hostility among the classes by rejecting them outright."

Henry spoke up, "Foxhunting would be less popular was the affluent gentlemen farmers not permitted to join the field. I see this as a means to lessen the gap between classes. By sharing affable diversions and by sharing the same table, so to speak, men come to better understand and appreciate one another. This has long been the lesson of armies, or so teaches my tutor. What harm in permitting men to taste luxury? They will only be the more ambitious for it."

In that moment Ardley Manning stopped seeing his grandson as a boy. His experiences and his education, due entirely to the interventions of his mother, had given him the ability to make important connections many fail to make. Henry was crossing a threshold and Ardley recognized his pride was now due a young gentleman.

"Jon, you speak of an understanding between yourself and your fellow keepers and the tenants. May we ask the nature of this understanding?"

"Ah, yes, Ardley, our keepers' grand bargain. We agreed the methods to employ and the cooperation required to preserve the fox. We are to protect cubs, plant new covers at suitable distances, dig new earths, maintain woodlands, sell each other cubs and foxes as needed, and use rabbit known to be their favourite food, to guarantee they remain where desired. Most especially, we shall only accept bag foxes from another estate as required.

"Further, we are to abstain from taking in foxes and cubs from purveyors o' uncertain character who would take advantage by selling what they have previously stolen from us. In spring, we are to prevent the hounds from destroying foxes that have gone to ground to protect the hunt later in the year."

"I would be surprised, Mr. Band, if this enterprise in support of hunting did not come at some considerable cost to their lordships. As a man of business, I can imagine the many people involved and the payments to be made. And what of your own costs? Surely you must seek restitution for the loss of a great many rabbit skins."

"In truth, I've suffered the loss o' many skins. In recompense, I receive cap money collected at each hunt for bag foxes provided. The amount will depend upon the number o' foxes brought to ground. I also receive payment from other landlords for litters brought in. In all, 'tis a satisfactory situation for the keepers.

"How's our bag, Henry? I've not been attentive, for once I saw you and your grandpa was worthy shooters, I'm afraid I lost the count."

"Two rabbits, six pheasant and three partridge. On the day, my first miss was my last. Neither you nor grandpa missed once. I pray I have demonstrated some small skill to your satisfaction."

"What say you Mr. Band, does my grandson meet with your esteem?"

Jonathan used his most approachable tone of voice while sizing him up. "Have you learned something today, Henry?"

"I have improved my shooting skills. There is a form to expert shooting, and it seems connected to a natural manner of using the eye, the hands and holding the gun. They must act as one and without undue haste. I have also learned to take my lead from Norrie. She is a wonder."

"I anticipate you shall yet become the gentleman shooter his lordship desires. Sustained practice under different conditions will prepare you for shooting where game flies in all directions, dogs brush to and fro, the guns bang away as though you was in battle, and wasted shot falls onto your head and shoulders. 'Tis near pandemonium.

"As for our little Norrie, there's none better. God bless her.

"What say you, grandpa, do you foresee us making a gentleman sportsman o' Henry?"

Ardley hesitated a few long moments. The effect of this on Henry was not lost on his elders. "Tell us, Henry, what you have taken from our discussions?"

"I better grasp the manner in which the many parts of the estate and the parish must function together. What one does may affect many others in unanticipated respects. Thus accommodations must often be found. The game preserve enjoys its place within this complex order. 'Tis a strong economic force and source of pride for the Earl. Its presence permits him to enjoy field sports, but perhaps more importantly to demonstrate 'noblesse oblige', according to my tutor, by sharing his privilege with those he deems worthy.

His generosity in this regard appears to stand above several of his peers, yet 'tis nevertheless a means to demonstrate his privilege and power over the other classes.

"I beg your pardon if this offends. I see landowners as victims of their own success in breeding. Game, rabbit and deer are raised in e'er more profuse numbers, to the great interest of poachers. As our lords aim to improve their field sports and compete for bragging rights as the best shooter, citizens are increasingly denied access at a time when they are in great need. I do not yet understand how this is consistent with a society founded on natural rights and the principles of justice.

"I also recognize, grandpa that you share with Mr. Band a manner of responding by not directly answering a question put to you." He smiled but held his grandfather's eyes until Ardley looked to Jonathan.

Their looks conveyed amazement and apprehension both, at the wonder of this growing force in their lives. Henry would not be easily distracted and if his father ever decided to reveal himself, he would find merit in claiming Henry.

BOOK THE SECOND: TRIAL & TRIBULATION

Charles Henry Coote, 7th Earl of Mountrath (1725–1802)

CHAPTER XVI

THEIR LIVES HAD DECIDEDLY IMPROVED, and Sally had become accustomed to the little luxuries his pastime provided. The fresh meat and a table at which to eat and work, a few chairs, candles, clothes, bedlinens, and some pots and irons for cooking made their lives infinitely more comfortable. They were far from where they began, and wanted for little.

Sally now enjoyed the time to pursue her favourite pastime collecting various plants, herbs, and mushrooms from the countryside. Frequent collaboration with Kitty Bacon had cemented their relationship. Their sharing of knowledge made them, together, a potent combination.

John was growing up strong, although at four years of age he showed an unnatural attachment to his first rabbit skin he still called his "benghie." Severely worn, it could not be replaced despite their efforts to give him newer and fuller blankets. John preferred to keep his old one with him day and night, refusing to break the covenant established when he was so perilously ill. He was tall for his age. Seemingly cut from the same cloth as his father, he possessed Edward's complexion, his blue eyes, and wavy blonde hair.

In 1782, Sally and Edward had another son, Nathaniel. This past summer the boys were joined by Sarah, and to avoid confusion in the household as she grew older, she would be known by her christened name. Though it was still too early to tell who she resembled, Sally hoped that Sarah might grow to be like herself.

Little John was somewhat jealous at the arrival of each bedmate, but he soon adapted to playing second fiddle to their needs. It helped that he was curious and able to spend lengthy periods exploring his environs, content in his own company.

Thanks to the many improvements suggested by Dr. Pulsford, Sally found their health much improved. Few were their inconveniences due to internal problems, with the result they were all now bigger in girth. Perhaps unsurprisingly, Sally took comfort in her greatest luxury, which proved to be the relative freedom from worry their new wealth provided.

All this contentment evaporated in a single moment when her remaining fear, one that persisted in defiance of her efforts when all others had withered and died, became a reality.

A neighbour appeared in an agitated state to inform her the Mundbridge poachers, so named for the general suspicion of their locus of hunting, were routed by keepers during the night. The ensuing battle had left dead and wounded.

In defiance of both the law and gamekeepers, Edward's failure to shun the gang had effectively confirmed his membership in it. Too fond of the rewards and the notoriety, and too little fearful of the risks, they had become bolder with time; venturing into distant parishes to often return at dawn of the following day.

As powder flashes in the pan, the absurdity of last evening came suddenly back to Sally in a vision. She shivered and gagged at the hideous memory that now seemed prophetic.

As always on the feast of Saint Stephen, the hummy dancers made their rounds collecting alms to distribute to the poor. Wearing appalling disguises, these young men challenged everyone they came upon to identify them. Their grotesque antics were accompanied by the sounds of banging on pots and a droning fiddle. Young men, some representing women as they had since the beginning of time, danced in pairs to the sounds of the hideous music.

By mid-morning and desperate to secure further details, Sally bundled the children off to a helpful neighbour under pretense of having to attend her mother, before setting off from Bromwell on foot. If anyone could help her without compromising her identity, surely it would be the Osbornes.

At The Black Feather in Mundford it took some time to locate the elusive keeper and his wife, as they were avoiding public exposure for fear of being implicated in the events of that night. She found they were no better informed than herself, having overheard only the wagging of tongues in their establishment.

As she was herself unknown to the Mundford authorities, Sally agreed to venture forth to glean what she could. When she returned, she offered this account of the disaster.

The men had invaded the preserve over to Gooderstone when they were surprised by keepers lying in wait. After being beaten off by the poachers wielding their cudgels, the keepers turned to stand their ground with raised guns, crying out they would fire upon them if they failed to surrender. Not fearful of the few confronting them, the gang refused. At once several more armed men erupted from the darkness. They were surrounded on all sides. At a signal there were many flashes and bangs unleashed with deadly intent, after which the gang appeared to surrender to the keepers' superior numbers.

However, just as they were about to be taken, our men resisted and produced once more their cudgels. Distracted by their fallen comrades, the keepers were again beaten off. In the darkness, each of the gang members escaped as best he could. Nary a one has since been seen. One is a Reverend known to them. The keepers warranty they can describe and identify the others upon sight.

"Who, then, are the wounded and dead?" asked Mrs. Osborne.

"'Tis said they'd be keepers. Our Reverend's savagely beat about the arm, yet they was all well enough to run off. A Sam Starlin' was killed directly and Will Feetom's hit in the leg. He'd be the head keeper. The coroner and magistrate are fetched. Everyone's over to the manor."

"Mrs. Leveritt, it would be inadvisable for me to venture forth in search of more details, or to help our men. It would not be long before my interest and theirs was connected by the curious. However, you might once more go forth yourself, without arousing suspicion.

"As for Mr. Osborne, it would be unthinkable for him to set out, for he might himself be apprehended if suspicion was to be aroused. Angry men are about. Before you set out anew, I should first see you eat, as you've not rested all day."

Once more set out, Sally remained determined to know of Edward's fate before she would rest. Arriving late in the day at the manor, she found the proceedings had concluded and the assembled already dispersing. Overhearing those mingling in the courtyard, she learned the accused would be hunted and held pending their trial by the justice of the peace.

Neither Mr. Starling nor Mr. Feetom being able to speak, the magistrate had taken the statements of the surviving keepers. It was their testimony that compelled him to contemplate multiple charges against each gang member, including felonies he vowed would receive the death penalty.

"Will's not gorna make it, they fear. Them poachers 'll surely hang fer th' death o' two good men. They should 'a known 'is lordship holds hard to 'is privilege."

Sally was disheartened to hear such words, for the magistrate should not fail to be encouraged were he to overhear such sentiments. There being nothing more for her to do, she turned for home.

Stopping to retrieve the children from her neighbour, she was told, "They's come in search o' Edward, but I told 'em ya wasn't about. Some be sayin' he's in great trouble. Likely goin' ter hang fer the killin' o' two keepers."

"Gwan wit' ya, Nellie. Only one's been killed, an' who's to say 'twas my Edward. Thanks, fer sittin' wit' the mites. I'll take 'em now." Sally's frustration had broken through in her speech.

"Watch yer step on th' way." With these words to her children she discharged the helpful, if insensitive Nellie.

Exhausted physically as well as being emotionally drained, she sat for some time without saying a word. At least, she believed, Edward was alive.

From time to time one of the children stirred in their sleep and the sound of it calmed her shredded nerves. Ultimately fatigue won out and she drifted off to bed, hoping dawn would bring more hope.

As she lay in their bed, Sally thought of how she would have turned to her own mother, Alice, for advice and comfort. When Sally's grandmother was widowed, she not only lost her husband and best friend, she also lost her protection. The good neighbours of Tottington, long distressed by her natural ways, ultimately ejected her and her daughter from their community of white clay lump cottages. Despite this lack of charity, Sarah, for that was her grandmother's name also, still enjoyed her good reputation abroad, and thus continued to receive the many who travelled to seek her help.

Yet her daughter Alice grew into adolescence ever more resentful of their lack of status. Introverted by nature she became distrustful and agitated, and when her own daughter Sally left home, she sought the comfort found by so many others. Like them, Alice was besotted with cheap gin and unable to help even herself.

That same night while lying in bed, Gabriel and Mary Osborne were having sober words. Fearful of getting drawn in by a misstep or a misplaced word, Mary actively shunned all about her. She believed their investment had gone bad and they would get no more from this crew. Though she remained fond of her boys, as she liked to call them, she expected they would henceforth be too shy to take to the night as before.

For his part, Gabriel reminded her of their commitment to support them in just such an event. They had profited greatly from these men and he preferred they not now be abandoned to suffer the whim of a powerful and vengeful lord. He did not admit this to her, but he equally wished to avoid having the accused turn, naming the Osborne's as accomplices, if offered an incentive by the justice.

Despite the expectation they would suffer pecuniary loss for some time, they eventually agreed the best policy was to respect their commitments, using Sally as the go-between to maintain their distance. Because of her more amenable demeanour, Mary agreed she would speak for them. The plan would rely entirely on Sally keeping their role secret.

In the morning light it came to Sally that the one person she might turn to for help was Kitty Bacon. Their collaboration in preparing tonics, ointments and other concoctions was a happy aspect of her recent life for the fulfillment she derived from relieving illness and suffering in others. They also created new edibles to ameliorate the taste of food. Without hesitation, she took the children in tow and struck out on foot in hope of finding Kitty at home.

"Friend, I have no remedy for what troubles you, and I know little of the law on this matter. I pray Nate may know of something to be done, though you must know Edward is in grave trouble. I need not remind you of what is said reserved for the guilty of such crimes." Kitty did not elaborate for fear of distracting Sally needlessly.

"For your fairness, Kitty, I hope you know we are thankful." It was Sally's turn to be artful as she avoided deliberately misrepresenting to Kitty the frequency of Edward's attendance on the warrens.

"I will speak with Nate without delay. Mr. Band, or perchance Mr. Turner may also prove helpful. I will come to you straight away I have news."

The anxiety of waiting was unbearable until, at last, Sally heard Edward's footsteps enter their cottage. He had just come out of hiding and even before finishing his account, the sheriff and his men came through the door. Events moved so swiftly she could not understand what was happening. Within moments Edward was subdued and taken away with few words spoken, save vicious threats to willingly inflict injury to him should he resist in the least.

She later discovered all four men had been identified, but only three were apprehended and secured in the manor house. Evidently some old country ways persisted, as each of them had been given up by a close neighbour.

Not waiting to be taken, Phillip Windward quietly slipped away without a trace. Mr. Osborne later ventured he feared his past catching up with him. Phillip had made a fool of the law once by escaping the gallows, he explained. To be taken in to surely face the gallows once again, would make him the fool.

Based on the depositions of the victims, Edward, Henry, and Edmund were to be prosecuted for several offenses, including murder. The victims were all servants of Gooderstone Manor, meaning the prosecution and its costs fell to his lordship.

The charges were sufficient to commit them to be bound over for jury trial at the Epiphany Quarter Sessions for Swaffham: the magistrate declaring this too serious to try summarily at his Petty Sessions. The statements and the evidence against the accused, as well as the flight of their accomplice, spoke for themselves. He fully expected them to hang within a matter of weeks.

There remained such passion over the shootings of the keeper and his man, Sally was forced to plead with the constable to be granted a visit. There she found the men in various states of shame, where his fellows greeted her well enough though Edward had great difficulty facing her.

No sooner had they explained their situation, she found herself scouring their accounts for any detail that might absolve Edward or deflect any guilt he may own. Nothing said over the next few hours brought her any comfort.

They understood one man lay dead and another, the head keeper, lay severely wounded but able to prosecute his case before the magistrate. The keepers had all given their stories to the magistrate's clerk who had drawn up the charges accusing them of several crimes, including the murder of the keeper. Indictments would next be prepared for review.

The magistrate had questioned them sufficiently for him to document their names, abodes, and occupations. He demanded to know for how long each had been poaching and whether any had ever before been charged with a crime against the game laws. He particularly sought every detail of the weapons each had carried.

He was conspicuously uninterested in their accounts or in anything the accused could say in their own defence. He had statements from the prosecutor Will Feetom, the other servants, and the coroner who had pronounced the death of Sam Starling. These, he claimed, would be all he required.

Fortunately for them, the accused had oft rehearsed their stories in the event they were ever apprehended. Salted with enough of the truth to ensure their credibility, their answers were intended to avoid worsening their lot while never admitting guilt. The result is that they gave the impression of not being organized or knowledgeable of each other, and they blamed their failure on inexperience. Of paramount importance was keeping secret the role of the Osborne's, if for no other reason than to protect their outside benefactor.

Importantly, to a man they did not recall discharging their guns when challenged. If true, they should hope this fact would be recognized at Court.

When Sally later confirmed their resolve to keep the Osborne's role secret, she was struck by Mary's demonstration of affection toward the men she called, her boys. As she waxed about their loyalty, Sally's opinion of her softened. She resolved then to never let her humours inadvertently give up their secret; as long as they continued their financial support.

Mr. Osborne would still not show himself in public though he proved true to his agreement with Mary to stand by his men. They would not be suffered to pay any fines that may be imposed by the justice. This, Sally was able to convey to the prisoners. In the event of more serious penalties, Mr. Osborne must wait to see what might be done, but they must know certain things were beyond his ability to influence.

It being widely suspected the long-running Mundford gang had finally done its worst, all agreed the future of its members did not look brilliant. To make things worse, the lord of the manor, Hollis Capell, had publicly declared he would seek the greatest penalty afforded under law.

The Rev. Mr. Edmund Spinks was relieved of his duties as curate of St. Ethelbert's following the charges against him. It is needless to remark upon the annoyance exhibited by his Archdeacon who reportedly declared, "There is a special place in hell reserved for those who would so scandalize the Church." Immaterial, was the nature of his defence, the accusation alone was enough to convict in his eyes. Absent was any concern for the pain and suffering of those Christians involved.

Henry Cranefield left behind his community of West Tofts. Not a man of conspicuous demeanour, but a highly respected master carpenter and cabinetmaker, Henry worried his patrons' incoming orders would not be fulfilled. Word reached him his loyal customers' needs were deemed to outweigh any concern they might have for an alleged breach of the game laws. They nevertheless decided it prudent to suspend all plans pending a decision by the Court.

Edward expected that as word of his involvement spread, he would no longer find work as a thatcher. He was known for the quality, if not the speed of his work due the wound he had suffered. His arm had set almost as it should, but he was left with an unnatural sensation in his arm that he struggled to conquer. Thatching provided their principle source of revenue and he very much desired to preserve his situation. He had found poaching wholly profitable, but mostly amusing, and intriguing for the agreeable stimulation and companionship he had not found elsewhere.

While the public debated the charges against the Mundford gang, the promise that their lives would come to a sudden brutal halt in a matter of weeks had not yet been absorbed by its members.

A few days following her visit to Kitty, Sally received word to meet her in their favourite wood.

"'Tis widely known at the manor the Earl will have his vengeance on the accused murderers. He expects to preside over the bench at Sessions to control the proceedings and to pass sentence himself. Some have proposed the severity of the charges demand a higher Court, though he resists this counsel. His head keeper was sorely wounded and although he will survive and give his statement in Court, he may be permanently broken. His assistant, Mr. Starling, has already been buried by his wife. The Earl payed all her expenses."

"That don't have the ring of good news, Kitty."

"One way or the other, 'tis not. I'm afraid there is more. Was you aware one of the accused has run off? Yes? The Earl declares it a sure sign of guilt, to be used to taint all those apprehended."

"There's no hope, then. My Edward 'll be lost to me and the mites."

"Nate has agreed to speak with Mr. Band when more details are known. For now, it seems the ire of Hollis Capell and his head keeper are running ahead of the trial. To hear them, one must believe there can be only one outcome.

CHAPTER XVII

T HERE WAS SOMETHING ON THE BOIL at this special gathering, and it was being stirred by the humours present. They had grown to become close friends whose collaboration had demonstrated considerable flair, but were presently discomposed for their sense of justice, nay humanity, was frustrated by forces they did not understand.

Kitty had recommended they bring Elizabeth into their confidence, for which purpose they came to visit her at the lodge. She had hoped to kindle Elizabeth's imagination in the expectation of finding a strategy to help Edward, though she also had another goal in mind, which was simply to create for Sally a distraction in the hope of easing her suffering. The return walk would help in this.

Despite the strength of the prosecution, Sally continued to assert that the accused's account of the skirmish suggested there could be confusion about the most serious of the crimes charged. Unwilling to leave Sally to resolve this impasse alone, Kitty again raised with her husband the possibility of the Earl intervening more directly. Nate proposed Thomas as the man to approach his lordship, as he had long suspected their lord of some indebtedness towards the Turners. Nothing had ever been said, but the sum of many small signals perhaps added to something that might now prove helpful.

Elizabeth listened carefully before asking, "Although what you say is imaginable, I'm uncertain of the merit of your understanding, friend. Do you truly believe all three to be in agreement, without one who influences the others? I've heard when people share an experience, particularly one involving strong humours or bad behaviour, the strongest will influence the recollection of the others. We have only to look to our children to see this at work."

"I've asked them each directly. None recalls the details as reported to be in the informations, Elizabeth. The constable has returned to see them many times as he cannot make the sum of it and there's gossip about the manor. Many say they're guilty, for 'tis proved by the disappearance of Philip Windward. Can it be that a man is found guilty by the action of another?"

"I know not the law in these matters, though it doesn't sound just to my ears. What say you, Kitty?"

"Nor to mine. I too, know not of these matters, therefore we must know more than at present. In Weeting, they say the constable is also asking questions of the prosecutors and their witnesses, tirelessly committing their every answer to his ledger. Might Thomas offer to be of help, Elizabeth?"

"I cannot say. He'll listen to me and give my request every consideration. He is of two minds at this moment. He deplores the alleged wilful theft of the lord's property and the murder of good men who were merely going about their lawful duty. It could very well have been an attack on Weeting or Bromehill in which instance, Kitty, we might now be mourning the death of our own men.

"More so though, Thomas fears and resists any wrongful doing by men in authority, for that would destroy society at large. He may attend to our plea, should he be convinced the facts are being withheld from the jury."

Sally reflected for an instant, before responding. "Such is my hope, Elizabeth, for should he not intervene I fear my Edward'll hang for certain. You've been of much comfort. We must take our leave now Elizabeth, as I wish to call also on Dr. Pulsford. As an educated man, I pray he may hold answers to our questions about the law."

Thomas arrived in his slops after a long day on the warren. The weather was colder than it should be at this time, which only made the trapping harder for man and beast. To force the coneys from their warmer burrows, ferrets were put to work. His men had to take pains to ensure no rabbit escaped the purse nets, for each was hard won on that day.

Taking him, she unbuttoned his front and slipped it off his shoulders. "Sit down a moment and rest. I have beer to refresh your throat." Elizabeth used all her wits to then lay before Thomas the nature of the situation according to her understanding. Not once did she ask for anything or propose any solution, for she durst not interrupt weaving her tapestry. When finished, she simply left it to hang for him to gaze upon.

It happened that when she had come to the end of her discovery, it was time for them to take supper, the children being already abed. As she placed the food on the table, he reached out to pull her in and laid his head on her belly. "I feel it's complaint. Do you not feel it moving about? You'll not have much longer to suffer. How find you Sally's Dr. Pulsford?"

She wrapped her arms about his oversized head and rubbed her knuckles into his hair the way he liked it. "He's kind and competent.

"Hold! You say my suffering will soon be over then? Is this what you think? And who'll take care of them little rapscallions, you will?"

He chuckled and pushed her off gently, to take her place beside him. "How was they today then? Anything to tell me?

"Mary took a chalk to the wall, just there. When I asked her what she made she said it was a list. A list, says I. Now what sort o' list would that be? And she says, ''Tis a list o' my chores with papa.' Why do you need a list o' your chores with papa? ''Cause,' says she, 'I don't want papa to forget me.' Course I couldn't make anything of her scrawls."

No father could resist the warmth that flooded his senses at that moment. "And what of the boys?"

"John tried on his new boots and after many falls, finally could run as he does in bare feet. He's quick enough. Robbie, well he still awaits his first tooth and his first steps, but both 'll be along soon enough. I thank the Lord they're healthy and they have a good papa to see to their needs."

Well, he wondered to himself what he could ever need more than this.

They finished in silence. Afterward, they cleared up together and when they closed the larder he asked in a soft voice with a certain caution, "Tell me, love, what you brew."

"Why Thomas, aren't you the wise owl. You know me well."

"Well 'nough to know when I'm being primed like that old pump outside the door."

"Truth, I don't know what I want, other than your advice and, mayhap your help. Kitty is a sister to me. That you well know, and Sally is a dear friend. More than a friend, for they are very much alike as they share the same, I don't know, I'll say gift. They won't speak about this gift, but I can feel it when they are together, and it comforts me.

"Sally believes, and Kitty too, the constable holds information he does not yet understand, but questions whether the prisoners merit the most serious charges. The magistrate holds this information to be of unusual origin as it comes not from the informations of the prosecutors. He thus ignores it. Nay, he has purposely buried it so as not to interfere with his plan."

"Surely, this is in gest. I cannot credit his lordship with such malice. He is a man of undisputed character and service to his community. What would you have me do before such a man? And for what purpose? I am a warrener; a keeper as was the men attacked. Would you not want to see justice done was I attacked in this manner?"

"I know not what you should do. What I do know is that in some few days the accused, possibly innocent of the worst of these crimes, will be sentenced to hang if the magistrate will not be stopped. Would you not approach Lord Mountrath to petition his intervention to ensure a fair trial, though the outcome not change?

"We believe his lordship may choose to step forward, in a manner befitting his condition, should he only know of the constable's discovery. Could it not be arranged for him to hear directly from the constable that although he believes the prosecutors to tell the truth as they know it, he queries the depositions as now drawn?

"I know only that Kitty and Sally firmly believe this the only manner by which to help Edward."

By the time Thomas rose from his seat he was decided to proceed without delay to speak to his lordship. He would doubtless baulk at Thomas making the case, but it was a thing to be done. Jonathan would be of like mind and would wish to accompany him, though he knew their number alone would not compel the Earl to action.

CHAPTER XVIII

TWO GENTLEMEN SAT IN STUFFED chairs with their backs to the table and their feet towards the fire. "In London, they say the French have now attributed all to a monstrous volcanic eruption in Iceland. Not a single explosion as one would expect, rather an enormous frequent expulsion of gases, lava, rock, and ash that makes it so pestilential to all life. The worst of it spewed forth between the summer of 1783 and late winter of the following year and was carried abroad on the winds. It took some time before reaching us and continues to inflict damage to this day."

The Earl of Mountrath was explaining the effects of the falling ash and sulfurous gases that had periodically killed off people, game, livestock, forest, and crops. For well more than a year they had suffered, with no hint of its end.

His neighbour added, "I recall the spring two years ago when flooding overtook the whole of the fens. Water rose the height of two men, and boats was tethered to second-floor windows. Some have said a monstrous meteor the size of which has ne'er before been witnessed fell from the heavens causing many quakes that are said to have exacerbated the volcanoes. A resulting fog was so radiant one could read by it in the night, yet in the day the same person could look directly at the sun without fear of being dazzled." William Colhoun had a fine memory for things physical. For the names of people, less so.

He continued. "In that same summer, a great ball of fire was seen flying across Britain from the northernmost parts to the southern, in less than one minute. This was followed by a shower of similar fire balls that lit up the night sky like fireworks at Versailles. From wherever do such things appear?

"I often think," Mr. Colhoun went on, "the worst is its effect on the humours of our people. They are as likely to attribute such events to the Lord, or to unnatural beings, as they are to the natural order of things. Who can blame them when violent storms leave them damaged, when the inexplicable appears before their eyes, and when alarming objects and substances fall unforeseen from the heavens?"

Charles shook his head slowly and sighed. "As when that blood-red haze returned periodically to blot out the mid-day sun, and all light with it. The accompanying heat was unbearable and brought with it a plague of flies that rendered horses frantic. Yet ice formed in late spring such that ice jammed the rivers, buildings crackled and crumbled, and the weak froze to death. Thermometers recorded temperatures ne'er before experienced and when we should have witnessed all in bloom, we had rather the withering of living things every place the gases and ash had fallen."

Charles Coote sighed once more when he finished, exhibiting his natural disposition and concern for the welfare of people. "And now we suffer drought that for the want of rain the crops are dying, and with them our livestock. Do you recall in our youth the famine that destroyed many thousands of cattle every month? In Norfolk they complained of a plague of locusts that stripped it as bare as if 'twas Christmas. I fear, Charles, such recurring calamities reinvigorate old superstitions.

"Yet despite these misfortunes we witness increasing numbers of children among the families of my tenants. As do you, William?" He shook his head in disbelief. "I cannot explain how families, or indeed the whole of the population can seemingly flourish during such times."

"Our committee of Parliament," said William, "is now taking upon itself to examine the effects of increased agricultural output, which increase is somewhat inexplicable, given such natural calamities. Many are they who see a direct relationship between improved access to victuals and the improved welfare of our people. Others claim it a matter of increased confidence spurred on by the improved productivity and economic status of the working classes. Still others credit the relative peace and relief we experience since the end of hostilities with France and the former American colonies. I dare say Charles, there is much we do not yet understand about such things and their bearing on each other."

After a sip from his glass and a moment's reflection while he swished the golden liquid in his mouth, Charles Coote returned to the discussion.

"To my mind there is great merit in understanding such things if we are to plan and to legislate for the future well-being of the nation. Mr. Adam Smith contributed to the course of our events when he proclaimed that government must not become burdensome or overly restrict the market from being open and free. Rather, its function is to keep the order, build roads and other common structures, ensure the education of all, and then defend what it has built up. I am sympathetic to his arguments.

"Britain now enjoys independence with respect to most essential goods, and we are becoming a trading nation at the centre of a world-wide empire whose colonies provide more than is required for prosperity. To keep pace with the rise in productivity we are laying in more roads, canals, bridges, and ports to facilitate the transport of goods to market. Employment is available for everyone who wishes to earn a day's wages. Where 'twill take us, we know not.

"Forgive me, William. I am easily consumed by my enthusiasm. Let us rather savour this moment."

"Ah! To savour, as one savours luxury. Take for one, your French brandy, or perhaps my new shirts. I am pleased such first quality shirts and linens are now had less dear than e'er before. I now may have my shirts fresh-laundered daily; for which I feel more wholesome of body and mind."

The two neighbours met periodically to review a wide range of issues pertaining to their mutual interests. These meetings could find them catching up on the latest ventings of London society from which they were absent during the shooting season; or debating the politics of governance about which their diverse opinions contributed to the liveliness of conversation; examining the current market conditions and the price of corn; exchanging views on relations with nearby landowners; or discussing any other subject of current interest to them. An informal meeting, it met their shared need to remain abreast of important matters and to avoid needless misunderstandings between neighbours.

Charles had chosen to sit in his library for its comfort and the warmth of the hearth where a fire had long found its stride. He took pleasure tending the fire himself. The day was sunny and brisk, making the fire a welcome companion. Shelves were lined with several books and curios. His most prized trophy was a mounted set of antlers displayed prominently over the fireplace. The Royal stag he grassed while stalking in Donegal had proved a challenge, but its proud twelve-point rack never failed to elicit praise from his guests.

The room, as did the whole of the manor, evoked a style befitting the country residence of a peer of the realm. The two shared an Irish heritage and a long familiarity with each other that, despite being at near opposite ends of the political spectrum, formed a bond deeper than their differences on current issues could break. Supper was ended, and they were just now discussing William's young daughter Grace, when new arrivals were announced.

Greetings and introductions were followed by a round of Mr. Hennessy's brandy. Taking his seat by the fire, Charles Coote commented on his pleasure at receiving this unexpected visit. Henry Babington and Samuel Stokes took this hint to introduce the reason for their visit.

"Your lordship is familiar with the mood of the country following our defeat in America. To worsen matters, 'tis now stirred by a rancor that threatens to split our nation. Many of our countrymen believe Britain to be in steady decline, that it has lost much power and prestige, never to recover. Mr. Babington and I have for some time wondered whether this pessimism is a temporary malaise or is well-founded, and thus likely to be a long-term condition.

"To find an answer we applied a scale against several attributes we believe are bound to the performance of our economy. By determining the prevailing direction and movement of each attribute against the measure of our scale, we can determine whether the sum of the results promises a worsening, or a rebounding economy as we have taken to calling it."

Mr. Babington stepped in to take up the thread. "We noted for one, the recent peace arrangement that retains Gibraltar as the vital gateway to the Mediterranean. There is then the recent arrangement with Holland. It permits our fleet to navigate freely among the Spice Islands and establishes a trading base in India where our interests are now better governed thanks to the India Act. Elsewhere, an independent America endeavours to rekindle strong trading ties with Britain, despite the manner of its departure from the empire. Britain apparently represents, after all, the safest and strongest trading partner for the former colonists."

"Further to what Henry has said, few doubt we are witnessing increased yield on all fronts, though there is yet little consensus on the relation between agricultural and industrial product.

"Lastly, our Parliament is finally on a stable footing with the competent William Pitt the Younger as Prime Minister. He enjoys both a healthy majority in the House, and staunch support from the King.

Mr. Stokes continued, "Young Pitt shows aptitude as an outstanding administrator, determined to improve the efficiency of government. He has the character to raise taxes judiciously and to keep the radicals at bay. He is also a man of integrity and great industry. He is just the man capable of orchestrating our national energies and interests to create a new order."

Mr. Babington concluded by remarking, "The populace is behind him and he is ready and capable of leading. In short, sir, we believe a resurgent Britain is on the horizon, and we wish to encourage you to position your interests for that time. To demonstrate our meaning, we have taken the liberty of preparing three proposals for your consideration."

"Mr. Colhoun, I apologize if this discourse gives offense to your political persuasion. My dear friends are not politicians, though for this they are more valuable to me as their interest in my financial well-being is undisputed."

"I assure you sir; I take no offense. Their wisdom is apparent, their enthusiasm palpable, and their concern for your interests manifest in their presence. Would that I enjoyed such advocacy myself. No, sir, if you permit, I would gladly hear what they have come to say."

"Please tell us then, how I might position my interests to take advantage of the coming return of national confidence, as you believe."

Henry Babington began by suggesting Mary Grief bring the flint knappers back to the pits to create a stockpile of gunflints. The cessation of major conflicts had brought about a considerable decrease in demand for their famous glossy black Brandon flint. But now that America was desirous of increasing trade with Britain and equipping its new army, one could expect flints from the estate would again be in great demand. Would it not prove advantageous to have a ready supply when contracts are forthcoming? Further, if his lordship strikes before his competitors, he would benefit first from lower wages than would be available in a heated marketplace, and second, from higher prices when selling in the absence of resolute competition.

They presented him with their prospectus when asked for the calculations. "I will require some time to examine this, but I promise you have intrigued me."

Henry then introduced their next proposal by pointing to the Scots black runts now fattening in the meadows to the southwest. "For the first time last year we purchased several of the spring-driven Highland cattle to fatten in our meadows and fold yards. As soon we judged the beeves of sufficient killing quality, they were taken to market. Their sale through the winter to this last autumn realized a satisfactory profit, while your tenants were very content with the foldcourse. Nonetheless, the result of our inquiries demonstrates improved profits can be achieved from the droves this coming spring."

"Please continue." The Earl was not bored.

"The greatest portion of graziers purchase their northern cattle at St. Faith's in the last weeks of October before fattening them on available marshlands nearer the coast. Their cost is lower than ours, yet 'tis said by butchers in the large urban centres the taste of their beeves, though exceptionally fine and better than that of English breeds, is inferior to meadow-fed. Nor does any farmer benefit from the effect of mucking his arable, for the absence of arable in these marshlands."

"'Tis a sight," exclaimed Mr. Colhoun, "to witness prodigious numbers of these beasts, so unpleasing in appearance, grow from skin and bones to become monstrously fat and so favoured for their agreeable taste and tenderness. I am partial to it myself, my lord, and anxiously wait to hear more."

William Colhoun was a known gourmand, and no one was surprised by this declaration, least of all Henry and Samuel. The affairs of Mr. Colhoun were well known to them and their community of peers, and despite their discretion, neither could help but wonder what his fortune would be if he were as careful with his investments as with his table. He might then avoid many of his very public financial woes.

"I listen, although I ponder the enjoyment of a plate of runt beef cooked in this brandy. I expect it could be excellent, do you not agree?"

As if by one reflex they all sipped their brandy together, imagining such a thing. After some moments of consideration, they concurred with Charles Coote.

"Shall I proceed, then?" which Henry Babington then did without waiting. "To add fat, we should add beets to their feed and for added flavour, add brewer's grains and oilcake in the weeks prior to sale. We believe our meadow-fed beeves, thus enriched, will attain a higher price at sale when their provenance is acutely proclaimed."

Anticipating his lordship's question, Samuel Stokes handed him the prospectus on this, their second proposal. "I anticipate you will wish to examine these numbers at your leisure. We believe the butchers who deal at Smithfield can be enticed to pay a superior price for beeves thus acclaimed."

"Thank you, Samuel. What is the final proposal you have for me this day?"

"The final proposal we wish to present ...."

His voice trailed off as the discussion was interrupted to welcome yet more visitors. Lord Mountrath introduced Head Gamekeeper, Jonathan Band and

Head Warrener, Thomas Turner. They declined his offer of refreshment for fear of creating a needless commotion, permitting the host to prompt Samuel and Henry to proceed with their proposal.

"It seems fortuitous, your lordship, to be joined by Thomas at the very moment we introduce a proposal involving his interest." Samuel Stokes proceeded to explain a strategy for responding to the sudden growth in demand for rabbit and its fur. The urban populations were proving ever more discerning in demanding rabbit meat when it was at its sweetest. And whereas poulterers, butchers and customers had no use for the skins, often discarding or selling them off, tanners and hatters valued them more highly than the meat itself. Because the warren habitually sold in-skin rabbits to all save a few of its best customers, they proposed henceforth making it their habit to separate the two, retaining the skins for sale.

Thomas would cull only when the meat of each rabbit was at its sweetest and the fur its richest, but by searching out those buyers who prized Weeting skins above all others, they would command unprecedented prices.

"What say you, Thomas, is this plan worthy in your estimation?"

"I confess me lord, my mind is for the most elsewhere at this moment. The plan will rely upon being ever more selective than at present. Should a warrener not submit to freeing a coney once captured, in the hope 'twould soon return as a superior coney, the warren will suffer the loss of the superior profit. The best season will be from Michaelmas to Candlemas-day and 'twill require more labour to flay the carcasses. The plan appears to have merit should it reckon these questions."

Charles looked at his banker who smiled. He then held out his hand into which Samuel Stokes placed the final document, saying, "I wish to advise you, Mr. Band, this plan does not presume to affect your right to the rabbit skins taken beyond the warren."

"Thank you, gentlemen. Your attention to the administration of my affairs constantly brings improvement to our methods. I shall return to you on these matters with little delay."

Turning to face Thomas and Jonathan he said, "Forgive me. When you arrived, we was not come to the end of our previous discussion, which proved full of promise as it turns out. I would first hear news of young Henry Manning before you proceed."

"He does well, your lordship. He grows to be a fine young gentleman. He learns quick, and if he's a mind, he can take on anything you set him to. Do you agree with me Thomas?"

"In my experience I seldom encounter young men of his mettle and canniness. He is clear spoken, which I attribute to his mother's influence and his education. I believe it also helpful he spends little time with those his own age. He's wise beyond his years, as they say. I'll wager his mother to be proud of him."

Charles digested this before inviting them to proceed with their mission.

Thomas took the lead. "We beg your pardon, your lordship. We have an urgent matter we couldn't delay bringing to your attention, as a delay would not be in your interest should you decide to act. A young and able thatcher from our parish, a good husband and father of three little ones, was apprehended during a night attack at Gooderstone. His wife is well known to our Kitty Bacon, who believes her to be a good, but ill-fated soul. She has asked for our intervention on his behalf as she fears he's been unfairly charged and is unable to defend himself. Worse, he's none to speak for him. It appears her husband's recently been caught up with the Mundford gang that's been plundering preserves and warrens across these parts."

"I am distressed for Kitty's friend. She seems to have found yet greater misfortune, though I confess I see not what you wish of me. If he is found trespassing and stealing, 'tis fitting he suffer according to the law."

This position attracted the unrestrained support of the others.

"Thomas and me, we hold the same view. Milord well knows our efforts to defend against the predations o' these villains, and how we fear the like o' what happened to those who defended Gooderstone. The keeper, Will Feetom, is a good man and known to me for some time. He was wounded in the leg. 'Tis uncertain he'll be able to hold on to his station, for the lameness that may be permanent. His man, Sam Starling, another good 'un, was shot dead in the attack. Three men are now bound over for trial, including our man Edward Leveritt."

Charles Coote was becoming annoyed and it showed on his face. He addressed his neighbour, asking his thoughts. In a rare moment of prudence, William confessed he did not see what they could want of his lordship, although he felt there was more yet to come of the story.

"There is more?" asked the Earl.

Thomas nodded and continued, to the great relief of Jonathan. "The Earl, Hollis Capell, is both victim and magistrate in this case. He's terribly agitated by the events and has publicly declared he will do his worst at trial. He leaves no doubt he's already condemned them as charged, and their fate is assured now they are in his hands."

Earl Mountrath spoke. "I am afraid I remain ignorant of what you would have of me. More so now than several moments ago, I find my sympathy, as should yours, rests with the abused Earl. Pray tell us what was found in their possession when taken?"

"They'd lurchers with them, and they carried cudgels, fowling pieces fully charged, nets, sacks and lines." Thomas looked at Jonathan for concurrence. When no challenge came, he was about to proceed, when he was interrupted.

"And what had they taken?"

"Many coney and some pheasant were killed, your lordship," answered Jonathan.

"Then prepare his wife for the worst, gentlemen. 'Twill all hang on the charges laid against each individual by Hollis Capell. You will both be aware under the current version of the law your Edward Leveritt is liable, at minimum to a severe fine or imprisonment; either one would surely be embellished with a stiff flogging for good measure. My scant understanding of the facts is this case involves the death of a man, and of course Mr. Capell's determination, which together may earn someone transportation for seven years, or imprisonment for two years with regular floggings. Most likely, however, will be the ultimate penalty of death as a felony for one or more of these men, and without benefit of the clergy."

"As you say, my lord, the facts of the case are far from certain. The constable himself has questions as to the exact events in those few deadly moments."

"Of what do you speak, Thomas?"

"When the Gooderstone parish constable returned with the weapons and equipment he had retrieved from the scene, he presented Hollis Capell with a depiction showing where each item had been recovered. This depiction also shows where each man stood at the moment Mr. Starling fell, and which weapons belonged to each individual present."

"For what purpose would he do such a thing?" asked William Colhoun.

"'Tis an attempt to determine independently the succession of events so as to test the truthfulness of each man's version of them, to aid in determining where responsibility lies."

"I share Mr. Colhoun's surprise, for I too fail to see what end he might achieve in this. Have you an explanation, Thomas?"

"I am given to believe he has learned from others in his circle. He judges it normal for a person to fail to recall with accuracy each moment of a brief and feverish activity, when so many humours and confusion abound. He declares it to be in his observances that a person cannot always recollect with certainty even his own intent and actions. He thus believes one to be even less certain when it concerns the intent and the actions of another.

"It may also be relied upon, declare the members of his circle, for each person to relate his own version of a shared experience such that a listener might well conclude they had shared little at all.

"Further, says he, one must consider the black that obscured actions on that night. The consequence is uncertainty concerning the facts. Though the magistrate resists, the constable proposes to make clear that which remains obscure, in order to permit justice to arrive at the truth of the matter. Besides, the clerk has now joined the constable in this view since taking the informations from the prosecutor and his witnesses."

"How, Thomas, does the constable propose to go about this?"

"He claims everyone's recall of that event must be examined in respect of the precise questions he has conceived. Only in this manner might he shed light on the facts, that the Court may enjoy indisputable proof to support the charges."

Charles Coote admired those who strive to apply logic and science to the world about them. It seemed somehow admirable it was now being applied to the justice system that leaves prosecution to the victims, and where the accused have little if any opportunity to prove their innocence. He began to feel a slight affinity for this man whose name he did not yet know. "What, pray, has the constable determined, if anything, to this day? What are his questions?"

"He is heedful not to inflame the ire of his lord and thus resists saying conclusively, though 'tis rumoured he is not satisfied with regard to two questions.

"And they are?" Mr. Colhoun, for one, was on the edge of his seat, staring directly at Thomas.

"The first is to answer where each man stood at the moment the fatal discharges flew at the unfortunate Mr. Feetom, and the more unfortunate Mr. Starling.

"The second is to answer to the ownership of each gun, as there is incomplete agreement on the matter."

With a quizzical expression that reflected the state of his mind at that moment, William Colhoun asked, "Whatever for? Goodness sake, can it make any difference to the outcome?"

"'Tis rumoured certain of the guns recovered remain fully charged. The constable believes the Court may wish to know who did not fire his weapon."

"This all seems too much for me, gentlemen. The men was caught in the act. In the mêlée shots was fired with the consequences we have discussed. If one is guilty, are they not all guilty by association, my lord?"

Jonathan spoke to Mr. Babington's outburst. "That is indeed the argument Justice Capell wishes to impose on the Court. Yet in defiance o' his lord's wishes, the constable remains unsatisfied as to the sum o' the evidence when matched to the informations o' the keeper and his witnesses."

"Thomas and Jonathan, you have indeed intrigued us. What would you have of me?"

"We are fearful Mr. Capell may be beyond hearing reason; most certainly from his servants. Jonathan and I would ask you to intervene with the Justice, and should you find your mind is open to him, ensure Edward has the means to defend himself. We don't support what happened, but we don't wish to see an injustice committed out of intemperance. At trial, should you eventually feel compelled by the evidence and his character to do so, we would also impose upon you to stand for Edward."

An exceptionally long silence followed.

When he spoke, the Earl used the same slow and measured tone as when addressing his peers in the House, his words coming only after careful deliberation and from conviction.

"The ill wind blowing across our nation brings changes that sweep along the victors and discard the defeated. We live on a knife-edge where a single trial can be the moment to tip everything one way or the other. Should I do as you request, I should ask my colleague and neighbour, Mr. Colhoun, to attend and support me. As men who are looked to for the welfare of those living in our parishes, and who carry some responsibility for the good governance of the nation, we share a duty to ensure emotions do not get the upper hand at the expense of fairness."

He raised his hand to display some documents.

"As for your request, I shall respond as when earlier presented these proposals. I ...," a look to William Colhoun provided an answer to the question he had wordlessly posed, "... we, shall give your request our utmost consideration."

"Your lordship, that is the most we could expect of you. Jon, we have too long interrupted our lord and his guests."

Nodding as they backed towards the door, Thomas added, "Thank you for your time and your hospitality, my lord. Good day gentlemen, we leave you to your affairs."

Elsewhere, a meeting was in progress on the very subject that Thomas and Jonathan had raised with the Earl of Mountrath. Dr. Pulsford, dissatisfied with the weakness of his responses to Sally's queries, turned to the only legally trained mind in his sphere. He invited George Hambling, clerk for the local JP, to meet with him at the Black Feather in Mundford.

"The doctrine of Joint Enterprise holds that a man may be found guilty of a violent crime by his close association with the perpetrator, unless there are circumstances which clearly absolve him of his share of responsibility. Initially conceived to deter those who might support duellists, it is now regarded as a tool in the fight against poaching gangs."

"That is unfortunate news for two of the accused, for only one gun loosed the fatal charge upon the late Mr. Starling."

"For them, 'tis indeed unfortunate, Morris. Your Mrs. Leveritt is justified in worrying for the fate of her husband. She should better have prevented his presence altogether. In his favour, there are no prior convictions as I understand, though given the gravity of the charges, this may be of no consideration."

"I believe you to be correct in this. More so now the fourth poacher has escaped what may certainly be an appointment with the hangman's rope."

"I meet in the morning with the Justice to determine the formulation of the final charges. I will then receive his instruction for preparing the formal bills of indictment. Alas, I should advise he is in a foul mood. He will undoubtedly seek to frame the bills to elicit the death penalty for all in the event the accused are convicted."

"I confess to you George, I am ignorant of the ways of the Court, particularly where homicide is in question. What means do the accused enjoy for their defence?"

"They are few, I am afraid. Justice is for the victims, where the trial is their venue to present their case. Each accused is simply expected to face the formal charges in the bill of his indictment, to make appropriate interventions if he finds a means to undo the case against him, and to give a good account of himself. The best defence is an innocent reaction and with some fortune, to have a person of quality speak well of his character. It is quite simple; the case is presented in but a few slender minutes, and the jury will render its verdict in e'en less time."

"One would believe there is hardly time to present the details of such a case in so little time. However do they move it along so quickly?"

"The indictment, as summarized by the clerk in his opening statements, is aforehand approved by the grand jury before which the justice, the prosecutors and their witnesses, the gaoler, the constable, and in this instance the coroner, will have testified to affirm their depositions and evidence. Witnesses will reassert these details to the petit jury in their short responses to any questions jury members should ask, if any. This ensures only a cursory examination is conducted at trial."

"You do not speak of the accused, or indeed of any witness who may stand for the accused being called before either jury to testify."

"They are not. As I have explained, there is no role for the accused in the pre-trial actions, and very little e'en at trial."

"Is one permitted to call witnesses in his defence during the trial?"

"Not a one."

"But he is not instructed in the law and this is not a case for petty sessions. How should he argue his defence when his life is in the balance?"

"'Tis more severe yet. Neither he, nor any barrister he may hire, is permitted to see the bills of indictment and the evidence he faces."

"What purpose could a barrister then serve, if not permitted to do other than respond as the case against his client unfolds before him? This has the markings of an unsure investment."

"The accused may first engage a solicitor to advise on forming responses and to present himself as best he can. If the accused has the funds, the solicitor may in turn instruct a defence barrister to intervene during trial, but only within strict limits as permitted by the judge. There are few instances where the judge will permit any latitude to cross-examine witnesses and to challenge the evidence.

"A judge interested in arriving at the truth above all else may tolerate interventions by the bench, his clerk, or the jury, should a point of clarification be required or should something ring untrue. Needless to say, respect for the Court, must reign.

"Such tolerance is not to be expected should the trial go to sessions where our lord intends to preside over the bench. As I have said, friend, he is of a single mind in this instance, and will likely not tolerate interventions that threaten his script."

"Where then George, should one hope to find justice, if that is what we call this?"

"You should wish for a trial at the assizes. The determination of that will be by the grand jury which sits at the next sessions."

"Is that a possibility?"

"The bills of indictment to be drawn up will seek capital punishment for each of the accused. I believe that alone sufficient to excite the grand jury to send the case at the assizes where the most serious crimes are referred. By their commission to hear and determine whether a crime has been committed, the judges of assize are commanded to make diligent inquiry into any felony.

"There, too, we find juries are more knowledgeable and thus considerate of the facts and of the character of the accused. I should recommend it."

"When is this to go forward?"

"The quarter sessions will be held in the week following the Epiphany. On the assumption the bills of indictment are not found to be ignoramus, and thus discarded for want of evidence to place before a jury, they would proceed as true bills to the Lent Assizes of the Norfolk Circuit to be held at Thetford. Of course, the grand jury could find differently for each bill and for each defendant. They may find a true bill as to the charge in one count, and ignore that in another; or find a true bill as to one defendant, and ignore that of another."

"I know not how Mrs. Leveritt will wish to proceed as she is convinced of her husband's innocence of the charge of homicide. Rather, 'tis an accidental death, not brought about by her husband."

"What is her basis for so saying?"

"She has herself examined the defendants as they sit in gaol and believes the constable has valuable information that may excuse the accused men, which the justice will not consider.

"She is not educated, George, though I can attest to her many qualities including her resolve and her intelligence. Her husband cannot do better than have her advocate on his behalf." The two stood to pull on their overcoats and hats before heading for the door.

"I doubt you not, Morris. Alas, I can think of little else to be helpful. He should hope for objectivity and a full airing of the evidence. That is surely the best approach at any trial, and one I have long sought to ensure. A good defence barrister may determine the fate of her husband."

"Psst! Psst! Husband, follow me quickly."

Mary Osborne urgently beckoned him to follow her behind the counter, signalling a need for privacy. Silently, he followed.

"Whate'er is the matter with you, wife?" These words were whispered in irritation.

"The doctor and his acquaintance just departed. I was over to yon table when I heard them conferring about the trial of our lads. I have tidings to impart without delay. Their lives may be in the balance."

"Pray, then. Tell, woman."

Mary Osborne then relayed as best she could the meaning of what she overheard. She had taken a risk, for she pretended to mop up and arrange things in the manner of preparing the room in anticipation of future patrons. To avoid hovering she would move to and fro, praying she had missed nothing of import in her absences.

"So, it is to be prayed the trial will go to assizes where the lads may put up a defence, should they enjoy the services of a good solicitor and barrister. There's a cost to this, wife."

"And they'll require persons of quality to speak for each of their characters. That too is important, husband."

"You must act soon, but do so wife, without giving up our interest in the affair as agreed."

Mary Osborne was the quicker of the two. "As estimated, the interest of Sally Leveritt is now well known. I should let the good doctor report to her before I visit. If the thing is as I believe, I will first offer the funds for a solicitor. If then matters suggest the benefit of a barrister, I will offer her that money should she ask of it, and on condition all will appear to be her idea and her money."

Softly, she added, "'Tis as much as we can do for our boys. They was good for us, husband."

CHAPTER XIX

AN AGED SERVANT PRESENTED HIM a silver plate: "This has come for you, my lord."

The Earl of Essex, lord of Gooderstone Manor, held out his hand without looking up from the papers before him. Spread across his desk was everything about this trial that had been committed to paper: his examinations, some of which were purposely rather more detailed than others; the informations of his servants Will Feetom, Sam Starling's wife, and the other witnesses; the warrants authorizing the accused be arrested and held over for trial; and the report of the coroner's investigation into a violent death.

There also, folded and out of sight, was the constable's depiction of the skirmish. Unbid by himself, it was a novel device that he proved at great pains to comprehend.

He was just now considering how best to formulate his instructions to the clerk for the bills of indictment. In his untrained but interested view, this case clearly involved a felony that merited the death penalty for all defendants.

Missing was any information helpful to the defence of the accused, for deliberately set aside from the magistrate's calculation was the discovery of the constable. In his lordship's view, the man had offended with his belief in the reliability of physical evidence as a vehicle for arriving at the truth, it being impervious to the vagaries of mortal humours and memory.

A student of Mr. Henry Fielding, the constable understood the merits of applying analytical methods to detailed record keeping and the assembly of evidence. As he explained to the Clerk, rather than rely solely on witnesses, this method permitted investigation that included consideration of the substantial.

The magistrate had no desire to grasp the import of his work to the case, his chief impediment not being its novelty, but rather the questions it purported to raise about his foregone conclusion. This was a case of trespass, theft, and murder. The culprits had been readily identified and most of them brought before justice. His role was to see that justice was now served to them.

The Earl, Hollis Capell, finally raised his head to examine what had been handed him. He was unfamiliar with the hand but not the name of its sender. Breaking the seal, he read the brief note quickly, and then stood straight as a ramrod, staring into the distance.

After several moments he lowered himself into his chair, releasing his arms to fall over the sides. Breathing a deep sigh, he fixed his eyes on the same distant object he sought whenever he needed to collect his thoughts and find his bearings. The standard hanging above the door was a reminder of his Commission of Lieutenancy for Hertfordshire. The Union Flag's red cross of St. George joined the white saltire of St. Andrew, against which were displayed the sword and the crown that were emblematic of his responsibilities. It never failed to revive his fondest memories of the years serving as the King's personal representative in that county.

One of his responsibilities was to represent the King at a wide variety of ceremonial duties. A more substantial role was to organize the militia for the county. England's long and unhappy history with respect to domestic forces was resolved when the Bill of Rights of 1689 prohibited the creation of any standing army on British soil in time of peace without the specific consent of Parliament. His Majesty's Lieutenant was the man to oversee the professionalism and effectiveness of the Hertfordshire militia, formed to repel a feared French invasion in keeping with the Militia Acts of 1757-1762. This was the period of the Seven Years' War.

The Act also allowed that Protestant subjects of suitable condition and as allowed by law, could have arms for their defence. This effectively created a shadow armed presence capable of bolstering the militia in time of need, or countervailing any misuse of the militia by a tyrannical force.

Hollis Capell, peer of England, derived satisfaction from the execution of his responsibilities and the service he provided his country. As a member of the House of Lords, he served in the creation of legislation. However the role he had most cherished, and one with which he retained a vestigial relationship, was as Custos Rotulorum, or head of the Commission of the Peace, with control of the magistracy.

Now simply as Justice of the Peace, or magistrate, he served the people of Gooderstone by dispensing justice within the scope of his jurisdiction. The case before him was to be a test of his service in upholding a law rooted in William the Conqueror's inalienable royal prerogative. In this instance the law had been flouted with deadly consequence. The clear implication was that as a peer of the realm, he too had been violated, suffering the loss of property, the maiming of one servant, and the death of another. Anyone found guilty of a wilful offense against the law should in his view, lawfully suffer the full penalty proscribed by that law.

He looked once more at the note and read:

SIR   *Weeting Hall, January 3, 1785*

Our Friend and Neighbour Mr. William Colhoun, Esq. joins me in commiserating Your recent Losses and Travails, for which we expect You have been much indisposed; indeed we are much obliged to You and Your servants for bringing to an end the Scourge of our Preserves; it coming to our attention You are preparing Indictments to formally charge the Accused at Sessions in the coming Days; we desire to lend our Support to your Cause, in a manner beyond our moral Support which is Yours without Question, for we have every Confidence in Your Judgement in these complicated and delicate Matters. It coming to our Attention Your Constable possesses extraordinary Skills and Competencies which promise to enlighten the Court, we would be most obliged if You permitted us to share in His Analysis; we ask this as it may prove instructive in our own Resistance against further wilful and malicious Felonies. Indeed, we wish You to know aforehand our Intention to attend Sessions in the Expectation of witnessing firsthand the Application of his Work. We await your decision.

You find me SIR,

Your humble Servant,

Charles Henry Coote, 7th Earl of Mountrath

His Lordship William Hollis Capell, 4th Earl of Essex

"Is this sincerity, or is this mockery? Whatever can he be up to, this kind Sir?"

Stung by the affairs of the past few days, Hollis Capell felt himself the true victim in this matter. He was slowly withdrawing, increasingly relying on the worth of his own counsel in this case. His constable, whose loyalty and reliability had never to this time been in dispute, was now found to be on a cross-grain'd course threatening his otherwise assured revenge. A small dark shadow floated across the back of his eyes, misdoubt had been aroused and of a sudden, his mind was decided.

"Fetch me the clerk!" he called out. "Advise him I will give my instructions for drawing up the bills of indictment."

When hours later the magistrate and his Court clerk arrived at certain conclusions regarding their approach, they stood to stretch their cramped legs. When they retook their seats the clerk, the only person present with legal training, summed up.

"There you have it, my lord. The first matter at hand is to satisfy the requirements of the pre-trial examinations into the alleged offences. Your warrants are in order, the accused are accordingly seized and committed as authorized, and witnesses are bound over for trial. The accused currently reside in the parish gaol, held by the constable himself. Your examinations of the victims are thorough and documented. The examinations of the accused, while cursory, provide the Court with all necessary information pertaining to their name, occupation, place of residence, age, and physical description. Dutifully, you have noted that none possesses a credible story for an alternate whereabouts at the time of the attack.

"I have here the report of the coroner's investigation. He concludes the death of Sam Starling, having occurred at the site his body was found in your park, was due a single gunshot wound, resulting in instant death so violently was he struck to the upper chest. He also concluded the weapon used was one of those retrieved by the constable at the scene. I believe we have all required to now draw up the bills of indictment for formal charges before the Court.

"The question I must now ask your lordship is, which penalty you seek for the accused?"

"I desire them to suffer the ultimate penalty, for I believe on the face of it they are guilty of the most reprehensible of crimes. I should seek death without benefit of the clergy. I won't have them transported, though that sentence has become the choice of my fellow justices. No, that is not for me, and they should all share equally in the punishment. One of them has tainted his fellows, and I say, do the lot of them in. Have we not a case for it, sir?"

"As you say, my lord, on the face of it there appears to be a case for the death penalty. Our own William Blackstone explained in his Commentaries on the Laws of England that the most principal of crimes injurious to private subjects is the taking of a life. He defined it as murder when a person of sound mind and of his own free will, unlawfully kills another with malice aforethought, either express or implied. The invasion of your park by the Mundford gang appears to satisfy the conditions for the commission of this crime.

"It then falls to me to draft the bills of indictment to justify your conclusion. I shall do my utmost to frame the charges as a matter of felonious acts involving grand larceny, a most detested property crime, accompanied by a treacherous, malicious, and wilful homicide. When completed, along with your examinations and the coroner's report, you might expect it adequate to secure your intended outcome."

"That would satisfy me, for I am victim. As I expect to chair the bench, I would thus pronounce my first death sentence as a magistrate. There is latitude in this regard which I intend to use to dissuade others who would contemplate such heinous behaviour. I have thus given much thought to formulating the sentence. I have it here to read. Pray, lend me your ear. I would have your advice."

He read from a page where he had evidently made several attempts to find the right elements and tone. "You shall be led from hence to the prison from whence you came, and from thence on the such-and-such day of such-and-such to a place of execution, and then and there you shall be hanged by the neck until you shall be dead, and afterwards your body shall be dissected and anatomized; and the Lord have mercy upon your soul."

"You go far, sir. You would take advantage of a recent extension to the ultimate penalty provided under law. Where further aggravation to the body after the sanction of death may be too fearsome a thought for many, surgeons will no doubt rejoice. The jury, being men of the community may judge it too harsh and find sympathy with the accused. You risk turning them if word of this should spread."

"And why should word of this spread?"

"Indeed, my lord." Being a man of discretion, the clerk did not divulge his feelings at his lord's indelicacy, even indecency in pursuing his vengeance.

"I foresee a hindrance which may prevent the outcome you desire. Our offenders can read, though with varying success, and there is no record of previous conviction among them. These conditions would, if found guilty, entitle them to claim benefit of clergy. If such is granted, they would escape the death penalty altogether, to be instead transported to Australia; America being no longer available."

"I can do nothing for that. It is sufficient that the case for their guilt be as strong as can be made."

"This, my lord, brings us to yet another question to be answered. We are preparing to present this case to quarter sessions. I should advise, now we have the sum of the evidence before us and your persuasion regarding the sentence, this body can be expected to commit the case to assizes. Such has been their wont for some time, and it falls from the nature of the crime, the complexity of the case involving numerous offenders, and the penalty sought.

"You recall those who made our laws contrived that a man accused of a capital crime should face his accusers only when the accusations are approved by at least twelve of his fellow subjects after all examinations and investigations have been prepared. Further, guilt can only be adjudged when another twelve of his peers unanimously confirm the truth of those accusations. Although a trial by jury at assizes may be inconvenient, I put to you the delay may be the price to pay for your justice to be served in this case."

"I regret the delay and inconvenience; however, you may be correct. I defer to your expertise in this matter, George. How do you propose to proceed?"

"There is one further matter we must settle before I am able to respond, your lordship. It is a matter of some delicacy I understand, yet undoubtedly of considerable import to the defence, the more so that should you choose not to introduce certain information, the defence will not have the benefit of it."

He had waited for his clerk to broach this subject. When finally he did, the Earl was prepared to deny him entry. "To whatever do you refer, sir?"

"I speak of the parish constable's undertaking as an official of the Court. He did go to some pains to investigate at the site, recover all materials there found, take measurements, statements from both the victims and the accused, and plot his findings in order to depict what transpired in your wood on that fateful night."

"I did not order him to do such. 'Twas impertinent of him to take such initiative and I find it incomprehensible. Who would e'er believe such a thing could prove useful to a jury?"

"Nevertheless, 'tis done, my lord. He is a devotee of new methods and has engaged with others who have employed these methods at the Old Bailey with considerable success, at times falling to the prosecution, and at others to the defence."

"Have we not fulfilled the pre-trial requirements for investigation and examination of the accused and accusers alike? Has the coroner not declared a homicide to have been committed at the scene? Has the constable not secured the weapons and the accused for trial? No one could doubt our thoroughness. The grand jury must surely assert these bills to be true. Does not justice rely on the determination of innocence based on the defendants' ability to give a good account of themselves? Their innocence will prevail should they do so."

"There are two points I must make on this matter. The one is that the accusers and their witnesses, the coroner, the constable, and you my lord, will be brought before the grand jury to respond to their questions. I cannot predict the course that will take although they should be somewhat guided in their questions by the bills of indictment.

"The other is the expected objectivity of the process. 'Twould be a failing of justice was they to hang for want of an argument to find fault in the details of the accusations, or to give good accounts of themselves rather than by a hearing of the truth. 'Twill be the role of the judge at assizes to be impartial. The constable's work contributes to that."

"Still, I am determined the Court shall not discover this work. The accused will have their say. The constable shall restrict himself to his normal responsibilities in responding. Should his own work be brought forward it must only be at the insistence of the defence.

"As you choose, my lord. I now have all the particulars before me. I shall draft the bills for your review before submitting them to the clerk at sessions for scheduling in the coming days. We should expect to be called before the grand jury. I am confident that if all goes as planned, we shall soon have our trial date at the assizes.

"I have one last suggestion, my lord. Many who sit on the grand jury will be known to you, being gentlemen who cut the finest figure in the realm. I feel certain an invitation to join you for shooting would be appreciated. They will all naturally decline given how charged their important sessions calendar will be, but the gesture will surely be noticed."

CHAPTER XX

PLANS ARE HATCHED, JANUARY 9-12, 1785

WITH OBVIOUS RELIEF, Thomas cried out: "Kitty! Sally! Children, let me see how you grow! Thank you for heeding my call. The midwife prays me not to worry, that all is as it should be. And now the cramps come sooner, 'twill not be long. Elizabeth will be comforted to know you're arrived."

Sensing his worry despite the soothing efforts of the midwife, Kitty said, "Elizabeth is strong and in good health, Thomas. Do not worry, for she's had no troubles to now. How may we help?" Yet before he could answer, Sally ushered Kitty inside.

"Come with me." Sally pushed ahead. "Let us but greet her before we see to the preparations. If somethin's yet to be done, we shall begin there."

Thomas held back Robert and John as they watched the visitors make their way up the stairway, like two geese shooing their goslings before them.

Later, Sally arranged for her John to watch over Nathaniel and the Turner brothers. Being the eldest, John was to raise the alarm should anyone wander. They all cried out to play hide-and-go-seek and as they ran past Sally she handed each a crust of bread. It was not long before their excited cries of "oyez, oyez, come for free!" were ringing through the air.

Mary Turner, the eldest of all the children had her chores to finish. Still fascinated with poultry, it fell to her to take them on their daily walk and to gather their eggs. Afterward, she would lock them in their enclosure for safekeeping from predators and give them fresh feed and water.

Young Martha Bacon and tiny Sarah Leveritt were kept close by under the careful watch of their mothers.

Like all proud women, Elizabeth kept a clean and efficient home. So energetic were Kitty and Sally, and desirous of helping their friend they did not stop to survey what needed to be done. Having taken one small step, they were soon swept along on a tide of their own making, their steady rhythm causing most things to be re-ordered in their own styles.

They found the pantry mercifully already organized and well-stocked. An experienced Elizabeth had prepared so she would not be forced to do any stoking of fires or heavy lifting for some time. Today, bed linens were washed and hung out to dry in the cold where only a few clouds rode high on the wind. Clothing and other linens were counted, folded, sorted, and stored away. The infant linens and towels were laid aside for immediate use. Tubs and pots were filled with cool fresh water drawn from the well. All surfaces were wiped down for good measure. All the while they listened for signs of progress from the room above.

As the day advanced without the awaited results, Kitty and Sally prepared supper for everyone. Sitting in the dying light of day at the table, the children safely abed, conversation turned to questions about Sally and Edward.

"He's well enough, but we do miss him. Him bein' away leaves me with no help at home and the humours of the little ones is changeful. I bring him victuals though he won't eat much. 'Tis as well he shares with his mates, as they've none to visit. The constable's fair enough, though he's taken to spying on them."

"And what of the charges? Has the grand jury accepted the bills of indictment?" Thomas knew the answer to his question but wanted to keep her busy speaking.

"They're to meet on the morrow in Swaffham. I await news. 'Tis hardest not knowing the nature of the charges."

"Why is that?" asked Kitty.

"The grand jury called the prosecutors and their witnesses, and then they called the justice, the coroner and the constable. All who'll speak to the crimes they're accused of committin' has come for'ard; but none can speak for the accused or be present to hear the charges and the evidence. Should the grand jury believe but the accusations, they're to be tried, though none has spoken for them all this time and none'll speak with me." Sally's voice began to quiver.

"At trial, will there be none to speak for them?" Thomas was uncomfortable for this did not appear to be just.

"Dr. Pulsford recommended I hire a solicitor for counsel when Edward goes to trial. I'll hire one competent in these matters on the doctor's advice. He will advise on the need for a barrister but nothing is certain, and I've none to speak for Edward. The doctor advises this is not helpful."

"Have you the money to take on such a burden?"

"I'll know more when the time comes. Edward tells me he's put some away safe." She kept her promise to keep mention of the Osborne's out of any discussion.

The evening passed without event upstairs. Gradually, everyone found a corner and a cover to purchase comfort sufficient to permit them to drift off in sleep. With the early light of morning Elizabeth began to suffer in earnest until, with the assistance of Kitty and Sally the midwife finally ushered into the world a new little girl.

As she heard its first cries, Kitty felt the early stirring of her gut that promised the arrival of her own blessed event before mid-summer.

* * *

Later that day, the grand jury at the Swaffham Epiphany Sessions met to consider the bills of indictment before them. When it came time to hear the case against the accused in the Mundford case, the seriousness of the alleged crimes created not the least ripple in the room. Without a stutter, a startle, a shudder or a squeak, the charges were read, and the evidence was tabled. Within minutes, all questions had been asked and consideration of the answers had ceased. The bills were ruled to be true bills of indictment to be sent over to the Lent assizes in Thetford, for trial by jury.

When news of this reached Hollis Capell late that afternoon, he took consolation in knowing he had achieved a major victory in the resistance against those villainous forces that threatened to tear apart the fabric of his society. He was one step closer to achieving his revenge on men who had flouted the law of the land that protected the privilege of his birthright, and who had deliberately destroyed his private property and murdered one of his constituents. These were two of the most reviled crimes that a Briton could commit against a fellow, and he had brought them forth to receive justice.

His only regret was that he would no longer preside over the trial. It would now be up to the assizes judge, the petit jury, and his prosecutorial prowess to assure justice prevailed.

* * *

When news of this reached Dr. Pulsford two days later, he immediately arranged to meet George Hambling on the following day.

After explaining the process to his friend, George stopped. "I confess to certain misgivings about this trial. I do not condone the death of the innocent Mr. Starling or the wounding of Mr. Feetom. Neither do I accept lightly the trespass on the Earl's park or the theft of his private property. Yet I remain unconvinced of the impartiality of the Earl's justice, and I fear undeserved injury awaits the accused, including your Mr. Leveritt.

"I see no other path than the employ of a sharp barrister; one well versed in the law and in the manner of discovering a flaw in the evidence tendered. Beyond this, the only hope I see is the assertion by men of superior quality to the good character and future aspirations of the accused. To do any less will assure their downfall."

"Pray tell me, to what do you allude? Do you know something you can share with me? Mrs. Leveritt stands ready to engage the service of a solicitor for counsel. I believe the expense will be burdensome, yet she proclaims to have funds sufficient for this purpose. If the matter grows, I know not her capacity to take on the additional expense of a barrister to reason before the Court."

"I suffer a dilemma, for I am of two equal minds. Perfidy not being in my nature, it pains me to divulge the confidence of a man of superior breeding and rank. At the same time, I am constrained by moral and professional allegiance to belief in the right to justice for all individuals."

"I am all ears, friend. Perhaps I may be of some assistance to you, for once."

Mary Osborne recognized them immediately they returned to the Black Feather. A practiced spy who gleans information from customers useful to their interests, Mary determined not to miss a word this time.

When they left, she considered what she had heard. That the one was alarmed by a decision taken by his lordship and JP, the Earl of Essex, was not a question. That it involved suppressing something of import to the constable was equally clear. However, the matter itself was not directly spoken of. Knowing only the one to be Doctor Pulsford who was acting in the interest of Mrs. Leveritt, she told her husband she believed the constable must be examined carefully by the defence at trial.

She would call on Mrs. Leveritt without delay.

208

CHAPTER XXI

SOMETHING ON THE AIR, JANUARY 16 - MARCH 18, 1785

IT WAS UNUSUALLY COLD for a cloudless Sunday in mid-January. On this 16th day of the month Maria Turner was privately baptized at home. The fourth child to Thomas and Elizabeth, Maria was now one week old and according to recent custom, she was baptized on her first or second Sunday for fear that if taken early, which infants often were, she would not be in the state of grace needed to enter heaven.

The private ceremony took place after that morning's church service when their few close friends were received at home. It had been so exceptionally cold that all travel abroad with an infant was discouraged. Standing for Maria were Henry Manning and his mother Mary. To all present, this honour recognized the confidence of her parents in Henry, and their newfound friendship with his mother.

Elizabeth would later explain it was Fortune herself who assured she was overtaken on that day as she was returning from the miller. She had set out on her errand in the expectation of a short pleasant walk, late on a cool autumn morning. After all, the mill was a mere twenty minutes away, and she enjoyed the use of a small barrow to take the weight of the corn from her arms, back and swollen belly.

By the time she departed the mill, the afternoon weather was suddenly turned violent; the heavy warm air threatening much rain. To protect the sack of flour from any downpour Elizabeth had removed her muffler, immediately leaving the gusts to freely whip her hair across her face: "slish-slash, and my skirts wilt-welt," she would later say, as she fought to keep her barrow upright.

"Hallo!" A voice cried out, blown almost free of her hearing by the force of the wind.

"Hallo! Halt and permit me to help you." She had not imagined the voice, for just then an unknown woman drew up beside her, coming from the direction of Weeting Hall.

Over mild protestations Elizabeth was fain to accept her offer of help, and together they loaded the sack onto the gig. Leaving the barrow to be later retrieved, they rode on to the lodge.

Once inside, and after discovering their relationships to Henry and shared respect for Lord Mountrath, they sat in comfortable discussion until a short burst of rain passed over and the sky brightened once more.

That afternoon, a dawning friendship between Elizabeth Turner and Mary Manning was undoubtedly aided by the former's respect for Henry, and the latter's respect for Elizabeth's baking as well as her excellent brewed tea.

For a newborn, Maria was strong and alert, though too young still to be responsive to the attention of the children about her. The younger ones played together inside while most of the older ones ventured out of doors to brave the cold. Elizabeth and her eldest daughter Mary sat at the trestle table with Kitty, Sally, and Mary Manning. The table was large, sturdy, and well worn. Beyond its imposing stature, it was most remarkable in that it originally sat in the Augustinian order's Broomhill Priory, whose ruins sat nearby.

Conversation was of Elizabeth, the baby's health, appetites, and whether Maria slept at night or kept them awake. As one might expect, comparisons to older children and to parents were thick.

The scene was a comfortable one, and consistent with the life-affirming conversation that is the steady heartbeat of all civilization. The sharing of such information comforts those living the experience, while it teaches and gives courage to those who are yet to live it. It confirms the joy and the pleasure that come after the pain of birth. It bonds people together, so they are willing to reach out whenever their help is called for.

The sizzling fire warmed the whole of the lodge and the smell of cooking seasoned the air. The smell of fruit pies and the bowl of oranges in particular, gave it a festive air. Tea was presently being served, and the women were settled into an interrogation of Elizabeth regarding her favourite recipes. She avoided divulging the special touches she added to her meat pies, roast fowl, and pork roast, but did give up some of her favourite touches to the rabbit ragout. "You have not yet eaten supper. You mayhap give me credit where none is warranted. You will find many of Thomas' favourite savours of mace, lemon, capers, anchovies, and his favourite, the apple smoked ham you smell."

Thomas, Nate, Jonathan, and Henry were outside where the wind whisked away the fume from their pipes. Most pipes of the day were made from clay, the stems variously shorter or longer. Not without a little pride, Thomas smoked his new meerschaum, passing it around for the others to try. The experience was appreciated. Unlike the women, their discussion was of the weather and its effect on the rabbit cull, shooting at the manor, the price of corn, and the coming planting season. If the subjects were different, they fulfilled the same purposes and produced the same soothing effect.

They examined a pony in the enclosure that Thomas thought might be lame since stumbling in a hole. He suspected a mole. The conclusion was that it had affected the beast, but all would soon pass should it not suffer further aggravation.

They did eventually turn to address the subject they had all been avoiding. The trial at the Lent Assizes would see four men, one in absentia, face an array of charges. It was widely rumoured they were to be tried for violations of the game act, the felony attempted murder of Will Feetom, and the felony murder of Sam Starling. The last was serious enough to elicit the death penalty by hanging before being delivered for public anatomization, the most dreadful outcome imaginable.

When the sum of their knowledge was known, it added to surprisingly little. They all knew that Kitty was certainly very fond of Edward's wife Sally, and their children. She believed they shared much in common and that Sally was an able woman, endowed with rare faculties.

But of the four men, only Edward was known to them, and he not very well, in truth. He was said to be an industrious and competent thatcher. Some suspected him of being a regular of the Mundford gang, though no proof of this had yet been produced. The widely respected Dr. Pulsford was said to be supportive of Sally and her husband, even providing his services and advice to them on several occasions.

They agreed that all should out at trial, when presumably all the facts would be brought forth.

A gig appeared in the distance and before long the visage of the Earl of Mountrath became clear. Before alighting, he called out, "Please forgive my tardiness. I had urgent business to attend. I trust I am not so late I have missed your celebration, Thomas."

Handing the reins to Henry he added, "I am anxious to see your little Maria.

I pray you not think me presumptuous. I bring this token in celebration, and trust you will agree brandy is quite effective against brisk weather."

"Welcome, my lord. You have arrived too late for the christening. 'Tis a wonder you did not cross paths with the vicar who departed not a half hour since. He was called away by the daughter of old John Twist who fears he will not last the night.

"I will bring you to them. Elizabeth is within and prays you will join us for supper." The Earl's answer suggested he would not miss one of Elizabeth's suppers for anything in this world. "Excellent, everyone will be pleased," concluded Thomas.

Afterwards, the men once more took to the outside. This time it was to digest their supper over a pipe. Pleasantly for them, the brandy proved an effective barrier against the chill and a loosener of tongues. Discussion of the strange weather held sway until Nate returned to where they earlier left off.

"Sally does have the three little ones in her skirts and this cannot be easy as she is alone. Yet she appears to endure her hardship as well as might be expected. She takes great comfort in my Kitty, and in Elizabeth. They have become fast friends through this ordeal."

"I often encounter Kitty and Sally searching for what only the Lord knows in the countryside. They're so often together, 'tis as though they're sisters."

Being constantly out of doors, Jonathan would know better than any their favourite places for collecting natural treasures. He continued.

"I think without such friends Sally might well succumb to a great sadness. 'Tis a nasty business Edward has found for himself. Surely poaching at night in a gang 'll earn him serious penalties alone. This business o' killing ol' Sam doesn't sit right, and I pray he'd nothing to do with it."

"Sally tells our Kitty 'tis a worse business than she could've imagined. Edward didn't shoot his gun that night. Of that he's certain. Yet Dr. Pulsford has explained that by law he's as guilty as he who did, as 'tis guilt by association. Have you an understanding of this my lord?"

"As the good doctor has explained, 'tis a legal doctrine little used until 'tis found to be helpful in resisting the threat of violent crimes where multiple violators are involved. I believe Nate, the JP in this instance may see this as a strategy to rid himself of several vermin at once, while making a public example of them."

Thomas then reminded the Earl of his promise. "Have you decided on our request, my lord?"

"I did write to his lordship, to inform him of our shared interests, and of our disposition to attend at trial in the hope of seeing justice prevail after a full airing of all information. William Colhoun joins me in this.

"Now the grand jury has sent it over to the court of assize, I am more confident the accused may be fairly treated. For one, the affair is now removed from the purview of our good neighbour. Then there is the recurrent use of jurors, meaning these men require little instruction in the essentials of criminal law and procedure. They will also receive guidance, e'en instruction from an impartial judge who can be expected to exercise his powers to comment on the merits of the case."

"How, sir, will that be attained?" Henry had been quiet, but attentive to every word.

"I also indicated my awareness of the constable's exemplary effort to portray the events of that night. I asked to review it together with Mr. Colhoun, fully expecting to be rebuffed should he be, as you presume, seized by a bias towards the truth of that night. As expected, I have yet to hear from him on this. Perhaps he sees no need for haste as the trial is now set for Easter eve, some two months hence."

"And should he fail to respond favourably to your request, sir?"

"Well Henry, that is a calculation I have yet to make. I do foresee Sally requiring a barrister to advocate for Edward and if need be, to put distance between him and his accomplices such that in the event of his innocence on the count of murder, he not be tainted by association with the guilty party."

A sudden gust whipped them, making them shiver as they huddled in the lee of the building. Wiping their running noses, they each took an appreciative gulp of the Earl's brandy straight from the bottle, having dispensed with the finer practice of using individual glassware.

"Henry, would you kindly bring my horse around? Thomas, I shall bid everyone a good night, but I must first enter to thank Elizabeth for her sumptuous hospitality. She has been most gracious, and you have together, a delightful and beautiful daughter."

Thomas accepted the cheerful cry that was sent up by Nate, Henry, and Jonathan with humour and pride.

"This has been a wonderful day, and a rare moment of joy for which I happily take some small measure of responsibility." Charles touched Thomas on the arm and gave him a wink that was barely noticeable in the dim light.

"Jon, might I save you the return walk?"

* * *

The parish gaol was a simple locked room in the constable's quarters. One of the reasons for his nomination to the role was that he came to the position with this facility. Not often put into service, it was now proving its value to the JP and to the parish.

Lying empty for extended periods had given it a fustiness that was now overpowered by the noisome presence of the three men living there for nigh on two months. Sally never ceased to be struck by it on her visits, yet she held back her revulsion to avoid making the prisoners more uncomfortable in her presence.

She did bring them fresh food and clothing from time to time. It was a duty she willingly performed for Edward, but she resented becoming the keeper of the men who had abused of her husband, despite her protestations. She sometimes believed she could take a cudgel to them herself, so full of anger their presence made her.

Once in their presence however, she would soon pity them as she did her own Edward. She often gave thanks for the financial support of the Osbornes for these, their men. This fact had remained unknown to all but the four presently in this room.

It was now four days since Maria was baptized and Sally recounted every detail of the christening and the supper that followed. The subject matter was pleasurable, but it was more the sound of her voice, like that of an angel whose sweet music played on the cords within their bodies, that created this rare moment of solace for her audience. When she came to the end, during which time she had not once been interrupted, she asked if they had learned anything since her last visit.

Not unusual in a system where the accused is discouraged, even forbidden from being heard until his moment in Court, they had nothing for her. The constable and Sally were their only contacts with the world.

"Well then, I have news." She did not bring to their attention the legal issue that might make them all equally guilty for the act of one. She was uncertain whether this would be helpful or harmful, and it would in any event be best explained by the solicitor.

"There's much said of the Earl's anger for your violation of his rights, and some unhesitatingly add, his dignity. 'Tis the death of Mr. Starlin' that permits him to seek the harshest of penalties, for he wishes each one of you to hang.

Because of his anger and his plain talk, some are takin' an interest in you. They've no sympathy for you, but they declare you must be treated fair."

She stopped to let that be digested before continuing. "Our Earl of Mountrath has written a letter to the Justice lettin' him know he and their neighbour Mr. Colhoun will attend at Court. They also ask to know what the constable is up to, as he is known to have been askin' many questions."

Edmund Spinks snorted in confirmation. "He's being a bloody nuisance if you ask me. He asks the same questions repeatedly, only in a different fashion each time, like he's trying to catch us in a lie."

"You may be right in this. We must all be careful, for we know not who to trust 'til our Earl knows the response to his request. I'm to engage a solicitor. Through others, the Earl has advised I should engage a defence barrister when the time is right. Unfortunately, he also admits there are too few able to help."

After a moment to collect her thoughts she continued.

"Dr. Pulsford's been sniffin' about on behalf of his lordship. He's found a solicitor experienced in this type of trial. Says he, "We aren't wantin' one practiced in the defence of linen thieves and pastry swipes, though that too can get you hanged in our day."

As continued references to hanging were beginning to have an ill effect on the accused, Sally now got to the point. "Mrs. Osborne and her husband will hand me the money, for they remain true to their bond. They pray me tell you that if it wouldn't make them seem involved, they'd be here alongside me."

As usual, it was Edmund Spinks who was first to find his tongue. Sally imagined that was the way of vicars. They never seemed at a loss for words, spouting on as they do in church every week. "Dear Mrs. Leveritt, you are an angel sent from heaven. We await anxiously your every visit and we are grateful for all you do for us. We see the hand of the Osborne's in this as well. Please advise them our gratitude, and our discretion, remain intact."

"I will so do, Mr. Spinks. 'Tis most unfortunate and unhelpful poor Mr. Starlin' died as he did."

"Most certainly. I could ne'er imagine one might find such an end, or that we should come to this. As Will says, you're an angel whose been caused much grief. If we're not hanged for this, we shall give eternal thanks to you, Mrs. Leveritt." Henry Cranefield at last had found his voice, despairing though it was.

"He speaks the truth, Sally. So consumed are we by our fates I e'en fail to ask after our children. Fare they well? Do they miss me, as I them? I have done the unspeakable by leaving you to struggle alone, with all in your own hands. For now, I can only pray the Lord continue to give you strength. You have my thanks and my love, and every moment brings regret for the trouble I cause you and the babies."

Rising to leave, Sally looked into the eyes of each of them. It was the look of a woman from whom many layers of innocence and youth had been recently peeled.

"I'll give your message to the Osborne's.

"I have the children and the friendship of Kitty and Elizabeth. 'Tis from them my strength comes, Edward, and I'd be lost should I lose them. For the present, 'tis they who hold me together.

CHAPTER XXII

WITNESS 1: "BECAUSE THE DECEASED went to seize him. But in my opinion, he did not die of his wound, for his skull was cut by falling with his head upon the stones."

Court: "How came he to fall?"

Witness 1: "By being shot."

Court: "Sir, do you banter the Court?"

Witness 2: "The Prisoner was taken in Bucklebury, but escaping, he turned up the alley to the Abbey and thro' Joiner's lane to the Guildhall. The mob followed and cried, 'Footpad!' The prisoner turned about, and said, 'I am no Footpad.' He was knocked down with stones and a smith threw a hammer after him. The deceased then came off a dunghill at the corner of Bridge Gate, while at the same time the Prisoner turned about, and instantly off went the pistol, but whether it was fired willingly or not, I cannot say."

Court: "Did the prisoner say nothing afore the pistol went off?"

Witness 2: "He turned about and said, 'I am no Footpad. Stand clear or I will shoot.'"

Court: "And do you believe then that the pistol went off by chance?"

Prisoner: "I fired the pistol but did it in my own defence."

Court: "We have heard the evidence against the prisoner, and you have heard his defence. Having none to stand for his character, I charge members of the Jury to return their verdict."

There was a momentary pause as the jury folded in upon itself for a brief consultation, then the foreman juror turned to face the Court.

Clerk: "You have reached a verdict?"

Foreman of the jury: "We have, unanimously"

Court: "How do you find the prisoner with this indictment, guilty or not guilty?"

Foreman of the Jury: "We find the prisoner guilty."

Sally Leveritt entered the Court feeling uncommon strange. Her legs felt heavy and a numbness was beginning to take her over. So overwhelmed was she her vision became muddled by dark clouds and tiny sparks. She neither saw nor heard clearly what was happening, but would later recall the black cloth being placed atop the presiding judge's voluminous powdered wig. By the time she cleared her senses, she heard only his final words before the bound prisoner was ushered away to his fate.

Court: "... there to be hanged by the neck, suspended between Heaven and Earth as unfit for neither, until you are dead. The Lord have mercy on your soul."

Unheard by all but two colleagues of the bench to his immediate left, the judge gave this commentary on the business now concluded: "Good news, do you not agree? The Crown may now employ its prerogative of mercy to stage a public reprieve to the satisfaction of the crowd. In these uncertain times, that is as beneficial in subduing the masses as the theatre of a public hanging followed by the gibbet."

Some weeks ago, two judges rode from London to preside over the Lent Assizes of the Norfolk Circuit. They were armed with royal commissions necessary for making all diligent inquiry into any treasons, felonies and misdemeanours assigned to them by the benches at sessions. If their inquiries resulted in the indictment of any prisoners then held in gaol, they were to hear the cases and determine their fates in accordance with law.

Judges Aaron Taylor and Solomon Forrester arrived in Thetford on Saturday afternoon the 19th day of March, to hold the last Court on this circuit. Entering at the head of a ceremonial procession, they halted before their destination. The medieval Guildhall next the marketplace stood waiting, sternly clad in the familiar black flint and stone dressings of the region.

That evening they convened the Court in a short ritual ceremony before adjourning for a feast with the sheriffs and their men. On Sunday morning they attended Mass before reconvening their respective Courts at one o'clock. Judge Taylor presided over the criminal Court, where he opened by delivering his charge to members of the grand jury so that by four o'clock of that afternoon, it had returned its first indictments. With these in hand, he was able to commence trials after swearing in the jury.

That evening, the judges entertained forty persons of the magistracy who were not kept away by their assignments to the grand jury. Justice Hollis Capell was among those being entertained.

The following morning, the 21st day of March 1785 was the most important day yet in the lives of Sally and Edward Leveritt. Sally sat in the stand overlooking the proceedings. She had made considerable effort to look as pretty as she could, for she knew that she was considered to be so. She wished this to be a sign of encouragement for Edward for if they were to never see each other again, she wanted him to have that image of her to the end. Jason Bigley, the solicitor she had hired for the defence was at her side. He came on Dr. Pulsford's recommendation after he had carefully inquired into his precedents.

For two shillings per day, Mr. Bigley was permitted to speak with his clients in gaol and any others he might gain access to, save by law any involved in the prosecution. He was not permitted to see the bills of indictment containing the formal charges and supporting evidence against his clients. He was then obliged to surmise which laws and statutes were relevant to the charges to advise his clients on their implications in his brief. This brief was the only source with which he could instruct his chosen barrister for the defence of his clients.

It was Mr. Bigley who recommended a barrister of considerable experience and some reputation. In fact, few were the barristers to choose from and fewer were those experienced in defending against seemingly impossible odds. Impossible were indeed the odds he faced, now the grand jury had completed its examination of the full body of evidence and testimony against the accused and sent over its indictments of them.

That body of evidence appeared daunting in view of the determination of the prosecutors and the seriousness of the charges. The examination of it by the grand jury resulted in unanimous conclusion there was sufficient credible evidence to proceed before a petit jury to determine the veracity of that evidence at trial. A prisoner seeking a defence would fight an uphill battle once any charge was transmitted as a true bill of indictment.

This was to be a day for a young lawyer to show his parts.

Finding the case flagged for trial on this first full morning of the Assizes, Jason Bigley was finally able to instruct his barrister and provide him with his brief for the defence. Augustus Farrow was a man of great stature, towering physically as well as intellectually above most others. He carried his black robes, wig, and responsibilities with the easy confidence of a large man accustomed to the deference paid by shorter people. He knew the law, and he knew how to address audiences despite the restrictions placed by the Courts on the defence.

The trial process was predicated on the doctrine that witnessing the spontaneous reaction to his accusers was the most reliable manner of ascertaining the truth from an accused. Because of this doctrine, the defence was constrained by realities beyond those the solicitor had been made to suffer on his way to trial. During the trial, the defence barrister could make no opening or closing statements, call witnesses to testify to facts, address the jury directly, or speak on behalf of his client. He was, consistent with the above doctrine of spontaneity, confined to seeking faults in the evidence provided by prosecuting witnesses.

A gentlemanly demeanour, a sharp mind, knowledge of the law, and an eye for the faults and inconsistencies in testimonies; these were his weapons to wield, along with the information provided him in the solicitor's brief.

Incongruously, he was permitted to call as many witnesses as were willing to spend the time at Court to speak to the characters of the accused. All of this for six guineas per day. Sally's finances were now beyond drained, making her fully reliant on the Osborne's whose support thankfully remained constant.

Searching the room for anything to bring her comfort, Sally could see the purpose to all she beheld. She had not their names, but instinctively she knew that the contest between accusers and accused is reflected in the manner this room is structured. She knew Edward and the other prisoners were meant to stand on that elevated platform she would later hear referred to as 'the bar,' and 'the dock.' They would be at a distance and facing their accusers in the witness box, which she could see enjoyed physical proximity to the table where the Court officials sat. These, as she had just witnessed, were the clerks, gentlemen of the bar showing off their lawyering skills, and scribes capturing all for the record.

On the raised dais, directly behind the Court officials, sat the judges. On this day she counted eight of them, including the presiding judge at the centre wearing a distinctly different cloak.

Stalls for the Jury that had just given up its latest verdict were hard by, and to the right of where Edward and the others would stand. This presumably permitted a clear view of their every reaction to the testimony given. Mr. Bigley had advised Courts believe the truly innocent radiate their lack of guilt. That then must explain the mirror affixed overhead. It was to reflect all available light onto those in the dock for jurors to better see them.

Voices too, were scrutinized for signs of guilt or innocence. Bigley warned his clients of the importance of their manners and their speech. Courts desired to hear defence statements directly from the accused and they were advised to avail themselves of this opportunity as it was their best, and often only means of defence. The Court desired every nuance of countenance and every inflection of voice be highlighted to better assess the validity of statements, especially as they were not sworn statements.

Applying to judges and jurors alike, Sally would learn that huddling together facilitated their consultation with each other, allowing them to arrive at decisions and verdicts quickly and without leaving the room.

The decorum she anticipated to find in Court was eroded by an informal and constant chuntering. Only when key testimonies or decisions were pronounced did all stand still, to capture every nuance. Still, she desperately sought some image to distract her, to bring a moment's comfort.

The room was redolent of lavender scented kerchiefs and Frankincense billowing from a thurible periodically swung about the room. Such fumes, she knew from her own life's work, were believed to prevent the spread of disease and went a considerable way to masking the smells of unwashed prisoners and the fulsomeness of the adjacent market. Sally fought against her stomach rising. She was extremely uncomfortable.

She wondered why so few women were present when suddenly she discerned the parts of society here represented were distinguishable by a single feature, and this found sitting atop heads. Almost smiling to herself, she watched as the big wigs of the powerful and authoritative mingled with the small wigs of professional distinction. Stylish wigs proved people of quality outnumbered their poorer compatriots, whose head pieces had long lost their lustre. Some wore theirs very prim and prettily beribboned. Here, a tousled and unkempt piece sitting askance as if proceeding at odds with its noggin: there, a head was found to be bare.

Trappings, she saw, were equally appropriate to each rank and sex. Tricorn hats, ruffles, and walking sticks or silver-tipped canes were for the men. For the women were fans, scarves of silk, feathered hats, cosmetics, and corseted bodies showing at times more breast than modesty should permit.

Sally was ultimately drawn to the wigs that were of greatest consequence to her on this day. They were both the most and the least extravagant in their length and breadth. The eight judges on the bench wore theirs descending from a great height in volumes to fall over their shoulders. The least were very slight and tied at the back with black satin ribbon. These were worn by the barristers for the prosecution and the defence.

Sally wore no wig at all, for none she possessed. Her simple bonnet spoke more to her beauty and her virtues than anything conceived by fashion.

George Hambling Acting as The Court Clerk: "Court shall rise."

Judge Aaron Taylor: "Next prisoners."

Sally Leveritt was suddenly riveted as Edward, Henry and Edmund were brought in by the constable and his men. Only now did she see they had all lost weight and the colour after months of confinement was drained from them. Only the Lord knows how they might look were it not for the food and clothing she had brought them. They appeared nervous and their eyes were downcast. Only after they were settled did Edward seek out his wife. His face was sullen, and upon meeting his eyes she felt Death place one foot upon her heart.

George Hambling Acting as The Court Clerk: "Phillip Windward, labourer, of Mundford, Edward Leveritt, thatcher, of Bromwell, Edmund Spinks, vicar at St. Ethelbert, of Mundford, and Henry Cranefield, master carpenter, of West Tofts are indicted for that they, about the hour of twelve in the night of the 27th of December past, in the year 1784, being armed with guns and other offensive weapons, did feloniously enter a certain enclosed land, called Gooderstone Park belonging to Lord Essex, setting nets thereon, and afterwards driving many rabbits and game therein: for Second Count, for unlawfully assaulting and beating William Feetom and his assistant gamekeepers, who were authorised to apprehend them and occasioning them actual bodily harm: for Third Count, they feloniously did discharge their weapons at the Person of Samuel Starling, and thereby giving him one Mortal Wound with a Gun charged with Gunpowder and small Shot, of which he perished immediately: for Fourth Count, for similarly firing upon and inflicting certain grievous and permanent bodily harm upon William Feetom, Head Gamekeeper; for Fifth Count, for Phillip Windward for failing to surrender himself to the Gooderstone parish constable. They are also charged with the like murther of Samuel Starling on the coroner's indictment."

Judge Aaron Taylor: "How do the prisoners plead?"

Edward Leveritt, Prisoner at the Bar: "Not Guilty."

Henry Cranefield, Prisoner at the Bar: "Not Guilty."

Edmund Spinks, Prisoner at the Bar: "Not Guilty."

A Voice in the Gallery called out, "They've starvin' children to feed, surely."

Another replied, "Nay, they enjoy sporting i' the night air."

There was much laughter. Many had come solely for the entertainment of sordid stories and the spectacle of raw emotion. Doubtless, there is entertainment value in Court proceedings and any who came with that interest, would find satisfaction today.

George Hambling Acting as The Court Clerk: "Call William Feetom for the prosecution."

After being sworn in by the clerk he responded to those questions required to establish his identity, profession, and experience before stating his memory of that evening.

William Feetom: "I am Keeper of Gooderstone Park belonging to Lord Essex, where game has been kept for many years past. On the 27th of December in the forenoon, as I was walking in the Park, I found a brace of coney killed, and spied the stakes for long nets placed along the west side of Lime Kiln Field. I went to the Park pales and found three of them was broken down.

"During the day I sent for my keepers to assemble against dark by the Park pales with arms. We was seven in all, me, and Sam Starling and five others was with me, Archer, Baker, Willett, Sikes, and Browne to set a watch over the field. Against midnight four men came to hang the nets and they then set the lurchers lose on the field, leavin' the tallest one to stand watch from the coverts. They did not see us as we was well hid and didn't move until I signalled.

"When they'd taken and destroyed coneys enough to fill their sacs they readied to leave. We followed them from our hiding places and came upon them to challenge them. I came first with, my men following, and when I was in their midst, I saw to a man they was armed with cudgels and guns, as far as I could see.

"I laid hold o' one and seized the gun on his shoulder. I said, 'Holloa, what have you to do here? Stand and lay down and we will take you.' He struck me in the mouth with his fist, knocking my hat to the ground. Then he struck my arm with his cudgel. I was knocked to the ground and from there I pulled the same man down to the ground where we tussled. Then stones was hurled at me, hitting me several times; all of them was throwing stones as fast as they could.

"I then heard the words, 'Damn it, it must be done.' But not in a murderous manner. In that instant a blow caught me on the side of my head that I thought must have killed me, had it not simply grazed me. We grappled more and soon we was back on our feet where one of my men seized him and threw him to the ground on his back. I was severely beat about the arms and legs and my head, and the bruises didn't go off for many weeks.

"As I believed him to be secure, I turned to offer assistance elsewhere in the scuffle. I said, 'Keep him and make sure o' him.' But the other poachers who ran away returned and rescued him.

"I then gave a whistle that my men would know what to do, as we arranged it aforehand. We retreated to form a circle about them and levelled our arms at them. They did the same and there was arms levelled in all ways, when I said, 'Don't be rash, lower your arms and we will not shoot, as we have you surrounded. We will take you to the magistrate.' A reply came, and it was the same steady voice as earlier, 'We will not be taken, you lower your guns and we'll let you depart home intact.' There was a stirring, a gun was discharged and then at once all guns flashed and exploded. Sam fell like a stone and without sound. I was struck in the leg and may ne'er be whole as afore. As I cried out, my men came to our aid. Seeing their chance in this confusion, the poachers dropped all they carried in their haste to escape."

Judge Aaron Taylor: "How was the poachers going along?"

William Feetom: "There was four o' them we could plainly see walkin' in line at the edge o' the field. The nets was stuffed in their coats' under-pockets and they carried full sacks o'er their shoulders and weapons in the crook o' their arms or slung on a shoulder."

Judge Aaron Taylor: "How could you know how many men was trespassing on this enclosed land?"

William Feetom: "We was crouched in the coverts so as we looked to them, they stood against the open sky above the field. There was the four o' them we could plainly see, as I said, walkin' in line, by the light o' the moon. By their length and breadth, by their clothes and by their hair we could see clear 'nough to describe them. Only one, Edmund Spinks, the prisoner there at the bar, was known directly by Willett, as he knows him to be vicar at St. Ethelbert in Mundford. Once we set out in the morning to search for them, our descriptions soon led us to all four. These three came along without struggle I am told, and are the prisoners in the dock, there. The fourth has flown."

Augustus Farrow, Defence Barrister: "Augustus Farrow for the defence, your honour. Mr. Feetom, can you tell the Court who paid your expenses to testify today?"

William Feetom: "It was my Lord Essex who paid."

Augustus Farrow, Defence Barrister: "And did he also pay all other expenses for your prosecution?"

William Feetom: "He did. He is both my lord and the justice of the peace for Gooderstone. He took all in hand personally."

Augustus Farrow, Defence Barrister: "So to the best of your knowledge it is his lordship who is prosecuting the prisoners and you are speaking on his behalf."

Judge Aaron Taylor: "Sir, you take too many liberties with this witness. He cannot know what his lordship's motives and full expenses are. The witness shall answer only for that which he has personal knowledge."

William Feetom: "I do not know what my lord intends nor where he spends his money."

Augustus Farrow, Defence Barrister: "Mr. Feetom, you testify the land is private enclosed land. By what manner is it enclosed?"

William Feetom: "Why sir, by the Park pales along its boundaries. The accused have removed three o' them to gain better access to the Park."

Augustus Farrow, Defence Barrister: "Did the witness see them being removed?"

William Feetom: "No sir, I did not. Yet that is where they came and went freely o' that night."

Augustus Farrow, Defence Barrister: "The witness does not in fact know that the accused simply happened upon that part of the boundary and, believing the land unenclosed, proceeded unhindered."

William Feetom: "I do not, yet 'tis well known thereabouts it belongs to Lord Essex."

Augustus Farrow, Defence Barrister: "Therefore, Mr. Feetom, if one was not from the parish, they would be unaware it was an enclosed Park belonging to his lordship."

William Feetom: "They mayhap would not."

Augustus Farrow, Defence Barrister: "Witness, I have one final question. Was the accused in disguise, by which I mean did they do anything to conceal their identities such as cover or blacken their faces?"

William Feetom: "They did not."

Augustus Farrow, Defence Barrister: "We agree then. As you have said, you found them readily by their descriptions, e'en in the black of night."

Over the next five minutes the Court heard from the four other keepers.

More details about the battle emerged providing a clearer depiction for the Court. The most colourful concerned Browne's description of his scuffle with a man he now knows was the vicar, when he described his calling out for help, "Shoot 'em Ed, they've almost broke my arm, bring your gun and shoot 'em." Notice was taken when Baker testified that, in their concern for their fallen comrades, they left most of what they had carried in the field, expecting to return later to reclaim it and their weapons.

The Clerk then called other witnesses.

Judge Aaron Taylor: "What are you?"

Josiah Wembley: "I am Josiah Wembley, Coroner for the County, residing in Swaffham."

Judge Aaron Taylor: "What is your testimony?"

Coroner Josiah Wembley: "At six o'clock in the forenoon of the 28th day of December 1784 I was awakened by a keeper to Lord Essex claiming an armed skirmish with the Mundford gang had left one of their number dead and another grievously wounded and in need of immediate medical aid. His lordship therefore required my assistance without delay and the hunt was on for the perpetrators who had fled. I was assured Dr. Pulsford had been fetched and should arrive at the manor forthwith.

"I made all possible haste, and upon arriving consulted first Dr. Pulsford who believed Feetom would survive. I examined him to find a wound in the flesh of his right leg, on the side just above the knee. On his head, he was fortunate the blow grazed his flesh, tearing a gap some three inches across. His body was marked by numerous welts that would soon show bruising. The shot had penetrated his thigh to a depth less than two inches and some was also removed from the knee itself where a piece of bone was broken off, which the doctor removed. We wait to see if he will suffer permanent hindrance of movement. He did not give his deposition to me or the magistrate until all was finished, and he had taken a tonic for his pain and his nerves.

"I then examined the deceased, Samuel Starling, concluding he died forthwith, from a single mortal wound caused by the discharge of a fowling piece charged with gunpowder and small shot. He was struck in the left side of his upper chest and neck; the wound was of the length of four inches, and depth of two inches. My inquisition is recorded in the bills of indictment."

George Hambling Acting as The Court Clerk: "At what distance do you judge the shooters to have been?"

Coroner Josiah Wembley: "I should judge the distance to Mr. Starling to have been about twenty paces. No fewer, perhaps more by three paces, from the length of the wound and the count of shot extracted, which was six. To Mr. Feetom, I similarly judge the distance to be more, by five paces."

Edmund Spinks, Prisoner at the Bar: "These keepers are gifted with excellent sight to identify any man at that distance in the black of night."

This small point, seemingly in favour of the defence, was noted by all present.

Judge Aaron Taylor: "The prisoner shall note, the identity of four accused offenders has ne'er been contested, three of whom being taken prisoner now stand before me at the bar."

The Court then heard briefly from a tearful Mrs. Starling who confirmed the hardship in the absence of her husband was somewhat offset by the goodness of his lordship who had paid his funeral costs and provided her with a pension.

George Hambling Acting as The Court Clerk: "The Parish Constable to be sworn."

Judge Aaron Taylor: "What are you?"

Parish Constable: "I am the elected constable for Gooderstone parish."

Judge Aaron Taylor: "What is your name and testimony?"

Parish Constable: "My name is James Garwood. At four o'clock in the morning of the 28th day of December 1784, I was taken from my bed by a keeper sent by Lord Essex of Gooderstone Manor. The keeper described the events of the night as he could, and I left without delay to join his lordship who required I should gather all evidence immediately, and retrieve from his park, where the conflict took place, all such weapons, clothing, and equipment that would be helpful in prosecuting the culprits.

"He also required me to organize the hunt, for the men had all fled. One suspect was believed to be Reverend Edmund Spinks of Mundford. His warrant was satisfied in the few hours that followed. With the use of the descriptions given by the keepers, my assistants took two days more to identify and bring into my custody Edward Leveritt, thatcher at Bromwell and Henry Cranefield, master carpenter at West Tofts. The fourth assailant escaped and is yet to be found. He is known to be Phillip Windward, labourer at Mundford. The lurchers have not been recovered and it is believed Mr. Windward has taken them away."

Judge Aaron Taylor: "What did you recover from the park?"

James Garwood: "I recovered equipment for trapping and carrying away game and rabbits being two long nets and their stakes and sixteen sackcloth bags containing forty-six coneys and twelve pheasants, deceased. I also recovered five hats, one greatcoat dark brown of rough cloth, two willow sticks of three feet and one oak stave of five feet. Offensive weapons was collected being four oak cudgels without stubs or spikes, several rocks that are not from the field, and eleven guns, three of which was given up by the keepers returned to the manor and eight being recovered from Lime Kiln Field belonging to Starling, Feetom, two keepers, and the four prisoners, all of whom dropped them at the scene. All is brought here for inspection by the Court."

Augustus Farrow, Defence Barrister: "If it please the Court, I should ask this witness a few questions. Do you know why these men did leave their weapons on the field?"

James Garwood: "There was three conditions which I surmise led to each weapon being left on the field; first, its owner was struck by flying shot, and dropped it from shock; second, it was left behind to facilitate the removal of a dead or wounded comrade; or third, it was found to be an unwanted burden in the owner's hasty escape. The fate of the guns recovered by me on the field are consistent with this hypothesis."

Augustus Farrow, Defence Barrister: "The coroner testified as to the distance between the shooters and the deceased Mr. Starling and the wounded Mr. Feetom. What is your judgement on this matter?"

James Garwood: "I concur with the coroner's judgement. Mr. Starling was shot from between twenty and twenty-three paces. Mr. Feetom from between twenty-five and twenty-eight paces."

Augustus Farrow, Defence Barrister: "Mr. Feetom testified they had surrounded the prisoners. How do you find for this?"

James Garwood: "I examined the markings left in the field and along the edge and they are as Feetom and others have described. I followed tracks from the place where much of the poaching took place. I found the site of the scuffle where sticks and many stones was left on the ground. There was too, the sacs with deceased coneys and pheasant. Next to this site I found where the keepers surrounded the poachers. The weapons of the accused, by that I mean to say their guns and cudgels, was all found in a line at eight to ten paces of each other in the field, at ten to fifteen paces in line with the edge. The information of the witnesses puts the poachers in this place. That accounts for four guns. Three others was found within the covering along the edge of the field. Of these, the gun of Samuel Starling was found some ten to twelve paces from the poachers and two was close together at some distance, yet still within the same line of covering. The last I found alone in the field, some twelve paces beyond where the poachers had dropped their weapons."

Augustus Farrow, Defence Barrister: "And what does this say to you, constable?"

James Garwood: "It would corroborate the testimony of Will Feetom and others they had surrounded the accused; my depiction shows it all."

Augustus Farrow, Defence Barrister: "Pray, witness constable. Of what depiction do you speak?"

James Garwood: "I examined all informations taken by the magistrate, and myself questioned each prosecutor and witness wherever I lacked understanding. I examined all evidence gathered by me personally. This constituted the body of evidence I employed to corroborate each person's recollections. I then committed each corroborated evidence to paper, in the form of a map. On it you will see how all events unfolded, but importantly you will see where each man stood at the moment of shooting, and where he reports relinquishing his gun."

Augustus Farrow, Defence Barrister: "Are the witnesses in agreement with your map?"

James Garwood: "Each has examined it and declared it precise."

Augustus Farrow, Defence Barrister: "May we presume this also indicates the declarations of the prisoners?"

James Garwood: "You may not, for the accused do not provide declarations."

Augustus Farrow, Defence Barrister: "I presume your map is to be found within the body of evidence supporting these bills of indictment. May we examine it now?"

James Garwood: "It is not in evidence."

Augustus Farrow, Defence Barrister: "I see. It is said the wisdom of the Court observes that it requires no manner of skill to make a plain and honest defence. Do you suggest this may be the reason for its absence, Mr. Garwood?"

James Garwood: "I believe it be so."

Augustus Farrow, Defence Barrister: "Nevertheless, the prisoners have been in your company for three months. Do you have information from them that is captured by your map?"

James Garwood: "None directly, as I am heedful of a man's privilege to defend himself unhindered by statements made while in my custody. He will, as you have just now said, have his day in Court."

Augustus Farrow, Defence Barrister: "Indirectly, have you encountered any information of use?"

James Garwood: "Indirectly, I have. When Mrs. Leveritt first visited the prisoners, I overheard their surprise at the shooting of Starling and Feetom, for they denied to a man having fired their guns. I was struck by these assertions, for they went against the early statements of the witnesses who also to a man believed the grievous shots was fired by the accused."

Augustus Farrow, Defence Barrister: "This must indeed have presented you with a puzzle. Did you do anything with this information?"

James Garwood: "At the time, no."

Augustus Farrow, Defence Barrister: "It is perhaps not too late then. Let us examine what more you have discovered and placed in this map."

Judge Aaron Taylor: "Mr. Farrow, you may not raise questions where there is nothing in evidence."

Augustus Farrow, Defence Barrister: "Your honour, the witness himself first brought his map to the attention of the Court. I merely pursue questions falling from that admission."

The bench consulted on this question for a full two minutes while the Court stood at ease.

Judge Aaron Taylor: "Very well counsel, you may question the witness regarding his map in so far as it depicts the evidence advanced before the grand jury."

James Garwood: "I shall respond as best I can to your questions."

Augustus Farrow, Defence Barrister: "Tell the Court then, at the time of the shooting, how distant was the accused from those who was shot?"

James Garwood: "No greater than twelve paces."

Augustus Farrow, Defence Barrister: "How far distant was the opposing lines of keepers?"

James Garwood: "I estimate twenty-five paces, perhaps a few more or less."

Augustus Farrow, Defence Barrister: "What does this suggest to you, constable?"

Judge Aaron Taylor: "I should advise the constable not to conjecture. He is to state only facts."

George Hambling Acting as The Court Clerk: "Your honour, Mr. Garwood has testified he is able to corroborate all he has committed to his map. I wonder, if he has it present whether the Court might be better informed by its examination?"

James Garwood: "I do have it with me, if it please the Court."

Judge Aaron Taylor: "Hand it to the Clerk for our examination."

As the Clerk held it aloft, James Garwood explained the scene and the evidence he had recorded on his map. It was, in fact, highly informative as the judge himself concluded. Not all justices on the bench were of this opinion, however, some being too feeble of sight perhaps to properly examine its contents.

Augustus Farrow, Defence Barrister: "What do you conclude from your examination of this corroborated evidence, constable?"

James Garwood: "To put it quite simply, it is not possible the fatal shot that felled Mr. Starling was fired by one of the accused. It also informs me similarly, the shot that wounded Mr. Feetom was equally not fired by one of the accused."

Augustus Farrow, Defence Barrister: "Are you able to corroborate this fact, constable?"

James Garwood: "Upon examining the recovered guns I found not one belonging to the accused was fired during the event."

Augustus Farrow, Defence Barrister: "Explain this for the Court, if you please."

James Garwood: "As I recovered the guns I noted from where each was collected and later corroborated its ownership with the witnesses. I am unable to attribute ownership of the prisoners' guns, as I have explained to the Court, but I can determine by their location in the field and by elimination, which four belong to the accused. Not one of those was fired. That is, when I recovered them, they was still charged with powder and shot."

Augustus Farrow, Defence Barrister: "Please explain in clear terms for the Court, the meaning of this fact."

"Clearly, they hit their own i' the dark!" For several minutes, the Court had been held in the grip of the Constable's testimony. This outburst from a spectator so released the tension in the Courtroom the judge was forced to bang his gavel while calling for order over the laughter that overtook all else. When the laughter subsided, the Constable responded.

James Garwood: "I am afraid that gentleman has the sense of it, for that is my conclusion."

Augustus Farrow, Defence Barrister: "Mr. Garwood, you have, have you not, heard the testimony of those who preceded you this morning?"

James Garwood: "I have."

Augustus Farrow, Defence Barrister: "Would you agree with me, as he who corroborates evidence, there is none to prove the prisoners entered onto enclosed land knowingly, and that having entered, there was none to say it was not simply an opportunity presented in the absence of the Park pales. Neither is there any to say they did shoot and murder Mr. Starling and wound Mr. Feetom. In fact, you have proven they did not shoot the victims. Further, there is now doubt as to how clearly the keepers could identify the poachers on that night, given they fired upon each other."

Judge Aaron Taylor: "Mr. Farrow. I warn, you are not to make speeches or to make summary statements before the jury."

Augustus Farrow, Defence Barrister: "Understood, your honour. I beg only to hear the testimony of this witness on these critical points."

Judge Aaron Taylor: "You may answer."

James Garwood: "I would agree on each of your points."

Judge Aaron Taylor: "Was this evidence presented to the grand jury?"

James Garwood: "I believe not, your honour."

There being no other prosecuting witnesses to call, Judge Taylor asked defence counsel whether anyone would come forward to speak to the character of any of the prisoners.

Augustus Farrow, Defence Barrister: "I know of none your honour; however, I now ask anyone wishing to stand for an accused to step forward and speak."

A stir from the back of the gallery resolved itself when Lord Mountrath emerged to step toward the box. At that same moment Judge Taylor handed a note he had quickly written to George Hambling, who on this day was Clerk to the Court of Assize, and who he knew to be the magistrate's clerk. It read simply, "Sir, we have Unfinished Business."

Judge Aaron Taylor: "What are you and what say you to the prisoners' character?"

Lord Mountrath: "I am Charles Henry Coote, Earl of Mountrath, owner of Weeting Hall. Edward Leveritt is a tenant on my estate. I knew his parents for the assistance they gave me when I first came to Weeting. I knew Edward well as a boy and have known of him since he married. His wife Sally sits in the Court, there, gentlemen."

As he said this, all eyes followed his arm to find Sally sitting in the front row of the gallery; she looked like a Madonna.

"He now has three small children who depend on him. A thatcher by trade, Edward is also an agricultural labourer in times of need at the manor. He is respected in the whole of our community for his work and the contributions of his family. I have ne'er known him to run afoul of the law or to disrespect his superiors in age, or in status. I have ne'er heard a thing contrary to his being a good father to his children, and friend to his neighbours. He has ne'er asked me for help although I am aware, he has suffered pains, as have most in his station. He and his wife are loyal, together. I say this because I believe him to be as equally worthy of participating in my future plans, as he is unworthy of all charges against him. If the honourable members of the jury choose clemency in the event they return a verdict against him, it will be well placed leniency.

Judge Aaron Taylor: "There being none else to step forward I now address the prisoners at the bar. Edmund Spinks, Edward Leveritt, Henry Cranefield, being charged with the crime of murder, amongst others, the prisoners shall speak for themselves in their own defence."

Edmund Spinks: "I beg mercy of the Court. Phillip Windward came seeking partners for a night as he found an unenclosed field where coneys could easily be rounded. We was each at the Black Feather when he came through the room and enlisted us. I know not these men but for our time together in the constable's gaol. Our actions of the night are proof of our inexperience. As the constable has agreed, on the principle charges, his proof shows we did not shoot at the keepers and cause murder and grievous bodily harm. For the rest, we did not know the land was enclosed, as where we passed through, we saw no pales to indicate it so. We sought merely companionship and a little sport on a fine night. As a respected vicar of the Church who has long served his community and those of all stations therein, I beg mercy of the Court, for we are innocent of these charges."

There was little doubt he was using his best Sunday voice to favorable effect on the Court. Edward was obliged to follow but was mindful not to break the spell now cast.

Edward Leveritt: "Your honour and members of the jury. We regret Mr. Starling's death and the suffering of his poor widow. Likewise, Mr. Feetom, we regret you was wounded and pray you will become again as you was before. I am a simple man, unable to add to what has been said. I remind the Court the proof is contrary to the charges, and I second the innocent plea of my partner of a night, the good vicar. I thank Lord Mountrath for his gracious words spoken on my behalf. I love my wife and children and wish nothing more than to be reunited with them. I beg you to be merciful."

Henry Cranefield: "Your honour, I am a master carpenter. That is what I know. A folly has got us here, standing before you at this bar, which I truly regret. As my partners have said, the evidence is for us. We did not go into hiding and when found at our homes we did not give any trouble but came peacefully as was our duty. We plead our innocence of the worst of these charges and beg for mercy for the rest of it."

Judge Aaron Taylor: "Gentlemen of the jury, at issue are the facts of this case and the laws the prisoners are accused of violating. The prosecution has established the identity of the perpetrators who stand before you. They are each accused of feloniously entering into the enclosed land of Lord Essex at Gooderstone Park for the purpose of taking and destroying game; that when challenged they willfully and maliciously threatened and then used deadly weapons to resist their lawful arrest; and that by such deadly intent and force they feloniously inflicted grievous bodily harm on one victim, and death to another.

"I draw the jury's attention to the challenge of these indicted facts by defence counsel. You heard the constable testify there is no evidence to prove the prisoners entered onto enclosed land knowingly. You heard the accused say, and I remind you they are not bound by oath, it was simply an opportunity found, and then wrongly presented to them by their flown partner when he discovered the absence of the Park pales. The constable has sworn the poachers was not those who shot and killed Starling and wounded Feetom. Also, there is some doubt cast on the keepers' ability to identify the poachers on that night. Finally, one of the accused, Phillip Windward, has fled justice. What does this say to the jury?

"This is a complicated case. The indicted facts have come under serious challenge. You have examined the words and reactions of the prisoners throughout the testimonies given. It is for you to now determine the truth of the evidence. I urge the jury to find these men guilty on all counts as charged, or not guilty in the whole.

"Gentlemen, you'll consider your verdict."

The jury stalls came to life, as commotion transformed the still life that had sat, unusually, in thrall to the proceedings for some time now. The jury foreman, an experienced conductor, orchestrated the consultation of members before turning toward the Court. Not two minutes had elapsed.

George Hambling Acting as The Court Clerk: "You have reached a verdict?"

Foreman of the Jury: "We have, unanimously."

Judge Aaron Taylor: "How do you find the prisoners with these indictments, guilty or not guilty?"

Foreman of the Jury: "We find them not guilty on all charges for insufficient indictment."

Judge Aaron Taylor: "I thank you. The prisoners are free to go."

As he banged his gavel a cry went up over the Court. It was a cheer of approval from everyone in that room who was not a landowner, for the acquittal was a victory for everyman, and a blow against the oppression of the squirarchy.

Unseen but by one was that a slight woman whose long-held anguish was in that instant extinguished, slipped to the floor, incapable of moving. She was drained of all emotion and energy. Edward rushed to her to carry her out of this place. He swore to Sally then, they would never again see its insides on his account.

Watching Edward make his way toward the door, Judge Taylor declared, "Remarkably, this has taken the better part of an hour from our busy schedule. Ladies and Gentlemen, we are adjourned for lunch. I fear the capon grows cold."

Outside, Edward and Sally stood to one side under the door frame where he held her tightly. They had many people to thank for their salvation, but for now they required solitude. There had been little precipitation for some months now and a hard frost had set in, yet just now, as they held on to each other, Sally shut her eyes as tiny flakes of snow began to fall on her face.

BOOK THE THIRD:
WHITE RABBIT

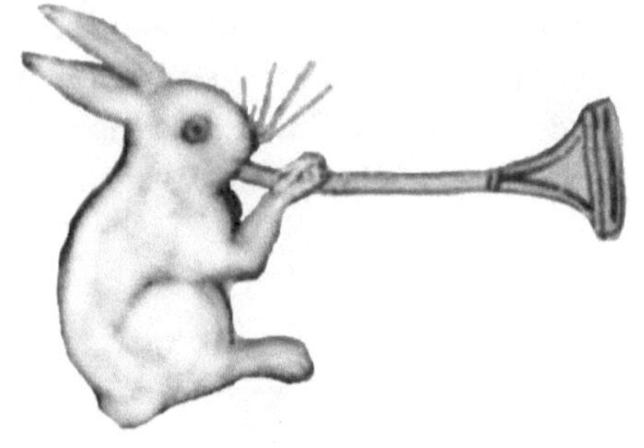

CHAPTER XXIII

THE WINDS OF CHANGE, MAY - DECEMBER 1785

SALLY WAS WRINGING HER HANDS RAW. "My husband believes he's made it quite plain he wishes no more to do with their business. Yet they persist. They chide him for the aid they provided us when he was bein' held, unable to provide for his wife and children. Yet through the troubles they was constant and good to us, as you was, dear friends. Without your help I warrant we'd be on the parish. I sometimes can't sleep, for thinkin' of those I've not thanked."

Sally was becoming flustered. Kitty and Elizabeth had witnessed this side to her in the weeks since Edward was acquitted.

Hollis Capell was dismayed at not achieving his goal, so much so he took his revenge on those closest to him: the Constable, his Clerk, and his Keeper was all turned off. Poor old Feetom was turned off as he was no longer able to get around, being too lame from his wound to fulfill his responsibilities. Despite the doctor's best efforts, the lost piece of bone proved excruciating for him, making him unsteady and unable to move about as before.

Rather than continue to insist she had sufficiently thanked them for their kindnesses, a task at which they were failing miserably, Elizabeth and Kitty rather encouraged Sally to look to the future. This too seemed to little avail.

"Sally, you must not weep so. Edward will remain true to his promise, therefore you have not to worry."

"Should they persist, he threatens to complain to the constable for should they be found guilty, he will collect a reward. I tell him this is unwise, for then his partnership with them will out and all will be drawn deeper into a trap we have only just escaped. Out of revenge, they and the others will testify against him. What is the gain in that? Oh, but he can be single-minded."

The children were outside in the spring air. Cooler than would normally be expected at this time of year it was nevertheless dry, perhaps too much so for farmers. Crops withered in the fields and the wells remained low. The coming months would prove the worst of this drought was yet to be felt.

Elizabeth made another attempt to settle her. "He is true to his promise to stay with you at night. For the rest, we must be vigilant and patient, friend."

Kitty was quieter than usual. She stepped outside to look to the children. She could see the ruins of Weeting Castle and off to the left, their church. If she turned further, she could see the roof of the Hall where Lord Mountrath would be in residence, were he not off to another of his properties somewhere in England, or perhaps Ireland. At present his absence bothered her, for she would have his wisdom on this matter.

While sympathetic to Sally's concerns, she knew not how to counsel her further. She considered for a moment it was the imminent arrival of her new baby that made her feel more sharply Sally's pain. She resolved to approach Nate on the question at the first opportunity. He would surely prove helpful.

Kitty returned to Elizabeth and Sally who were seated at her table. Elizabeth was suckling Maria, so that when she sat it was Sally's hand she took hold of. Their affinity for each other was palpable. Elizabeth watched as Kitty spoke to Sally. Although she avoided direct contact with Sally's eyes, she spoke in a tone that she immediately responded to.

"I say to you once more; you must not weep so. You must remain steady as the surface of the Lesser Ouse. Let him not see that your gut trembles and your head swims. Think of our mothers and their mothers, of how they showed us to misdirect to keep secret where we found our precious ingredients.

"You must remind him of his strength, and of your respect for him. Also remind him of the respect shown publicly by his lord. He must ne'er betray that for fear of being cast off, with you and your children too. Should he lose the silence of these people you still shelter from us, or his partners, all will be lost. Time must catch up with him, when all will be well."

She then kissed her hand before giving it back to her.

Sally thought for a considerable time and then said, "I have a plan to relieve their hold over him. We shall repay the money they gave. Do you believe this plan has merit?"

Elizabeth responded thus: "I believe Kitty's counsel is equally for Edward and you, friend. Your plan has merit but there may be more here than we imagine. Trust that Providence will come to your assistance. I urge patience on you, as you would urge it on Edward. Hold you hard until we see what shall transpire. If you wish it, we shall seek the counsel of our husbands. They have yet to fail us in this."

* * *

A pitcher was placed on the table before them. Pouring ale into both beakers, George Hambling began, "I say to you, Garwood, we may no longer be welcome in Gooderstone. His lordship has not accepted the outcome as nobly as we might have prayed."

Mr. Garwood replied, "Rather than accept your advice as the legal authority, he pursued his own course. But for the cross-examination of Augustus Farrow, he would have won the day at the great expense of the prisoners. Doubtless they was not innocent of poaching his game, but that is less grave than the charge he wished to hang upon them. I should rather say, have them hang for. The whole ordeal was immoral and certainly not consistent with the spirit of the law."

Mr. Hambling pursued that thought. "Neither would he advance the results of your investigation as they would undo his argument. His desire for revenge in this case was curiously incongruous with his education and stature. I had till then more generally found him to be lenient than harsh, and fearful of punishment meted in error.

"That is now a matter for another day. For who can say what is moral, and what is just? The immoral and the unjust have long gained free passage in the guise of judges' robes and clergy's vestments. I venture this fact holds much promise for the work we have yet to do, but for the moment, we must concern ourselves with the state of Gooderstone and our role here."

"For myself, George, I foresee my tenure as Constable at an end. It is a role I did not seek, and yet in the strangest manner I have benefitted from it. The truth may often elude us, but once seized, the great mystery is our wonder at the effort in catching it. I find the effort itself to be compelling. 'Tis for this reason I wish to dedicate my life to pursuit of the truth."

"What is it about the truth that is so mysterious?"

"Why George, it is simply that it is so apparent, it hides in plain sight."

"And thus, you intend to leave?"

"I believe London holds the greatest promise for me. There is much discord and crime in that city. It grows daily and the Court at the Old Bailey beckons, I fear. And you, friend? What do you intend?"

"I shall be patient, James. There is daily business to conduct and Lord Essex requires a clerk with legal training. There is little choice hereabouts and he cannot soon afford to find himself in trouble again. Judge Taylor has made it eminently clear to me I failed Lord Essex. Says he, I was to have been clear with him this case should have been sent over to sessions, where punishment for that which was truly unlawful was his to deliver with impunity. He over-reached, to put it simply, and failed. They will continue to oversee our sessions until satisfied they befit the Crown's expectations."

"You did not explain our Lord Essex was most resolute; that he refused to be swayed by all advice on the matter? The only recourse to salvage the truth was to have it sent over to assizes where the truth might be discovered by an impartial authority."

"In the end we was able to salvage the truth and justice both. I thank the Lord the defence counsel was astute. Had you words with him aforehand?"

"I did not. I understood you to be the canary in the coal mine. If neither of us, who then?"

"For now, it matters less who, than that it was done."

* * *

Jonathan sought Thomas in the yard where he found him attending to the repair of a harness. "I encourage you to inform his lordship without delay, Jonathan. 'Tis a good thing, and I am pleased for you. This is the time of year for it, if change you must."

"Thomas, I don't desire to make the change. This is my preserve. 'Tis where I've laboured. However, as old Will now requires a pony to get about, Lord Essex is in want of a new keeper. He's offered me higher wages and greater perquisites. At my age I should think these important. Still, it can be in the habit o' certain lords to change out their keeper after some years. Fresh blood, and fresh beginnings with the locals, if you get what I mean."

"You've been with his lordship from the beginning. I confess, Jon, I covet your position for your superior emoluments. In truth, also for the absence of the smell of rabbit." He smiled at his own humour. "Perhaps you'd put in a word with his lordship on my behalf?"

240

"Aye, Thomas, I will that. He's pleased with us for the manner we approached him. He did free Edward from his entanglement, without himself abusing Lord Essex publicly. For their class, form matters greatly. I'm certain he'll wish to show his gratitude."

* * *

In the weeks and months following the trial in Thetford life returned to normal more quickly for some, than for others. As life would have it, a new normal would become the future for some.

Kitty raised Sally's dilemma with her husband one night after putting Martha down for the night. "She is quite determined to keep her family together, yet barring help I'm afraid she may not succeed, for those who helped her now have their hooks in them. We can guess their interest in Edward."

"How do you wife? Martha has taken an interest in your belly, watching it grow with wonder. I suppose it's her age and you have encouraged her to contemplate its meaning. You are a witch, aren't you?"

"You're a strange one, husband, to think such things: more so to say them, for 'twas not long ago you would create all manner of trouble for me simply asking such a thing.

She gave him a gentle shove. "For myself, I am well, more anxious to shed this belly than anything. Will you and Thomas put your heads together once more? You was both so helpful with his lordship."

"Should I assume Elizabeth is having the same chat with Thomas, likely this very moment?"

"Don't play with witches, Nate. That will not go well for you."

He laughed and pulled her close. The smell of her, of the herbs and spices she worked with all day long; he could never get enough of it. "I shall not."

* * *

Edward was worried by the urging of Mrs. Osborne. The gang had brought considerable wealth to the victualler and his wife and he believed it was she, more than her husband, who wanted the poaching to return them the profits as afore. Its absence was surely felt and thus she sought him to replace the departed Phillip.

"They heed me not. I remind them I did not choose to involve myself in their scheme. It simply grew on me until I became fully ensnared. They reply that I shall overcome my fear."

"Truthfully, husband, I did come to value the absence of restraint and the occasional luxury the money provided. Let us look at this one more time. In their favour, they was true to you and they did procure your victuals and counsel. All went to your salvation. For that I'll forever give thanks.

"In your favour, you was on separate occasions wounded and almost captured afore your last star-crossed adventure. Yet you saved their equipment and the catch on the day. On this occasion you remained silent about their involvement, despite the easy pardon and reward money you would surely have earned for givin' them up. Too, they employed me as their go-between and to keep you fellows fed and clothed for nigh on three months. I also brought our friends into my confidence, and through them his lordship came to your support. All of this they took advantage of to protect themselves and their interest. You owe them nothin,' husband. They owe you. I therefore urge you to rid yourself of the feelin' you have disappointed them. Resist."

* * *

"Pardon me, your lordship. Might I have a word with you?"

"Come in Kitty. How does all keep? I see you have not long now."

"Your lordship is kind. I do well, as do Nate and Martha, who tries, but is not yet walking. She has a wondrous appetite; there is no denying her pleasure at table."

"I wonder from whom she receives that distinction?" He smiled and stood to meet her as she advanced. "What is it you wish to discuss? Have you found something new for me? Perhaps a dish to sample?"

"If 'twas so simple, my lord. Once more it concerns my friend Sally Leveritt and her husband, Edward. We shall not forget your intervention and the successful manner of it, for which we shall be fore'er grateful."

"I saw them together, afterwards, and they came to give me thanks. At the time they was in a delicate state. I did not wish to keep them, only long enough to say that without the intervention of the Bacons and the Turners I might ne'er have known to do anything. I explained my pleasure at the outcome and meant what I said of Edward. I trust Thomas, Elizabeth, and the children do well also."

"They do well, and little Maria is in good humour. Little thing that she is, she's the image of Thomas." They smiled knowingly, with a tinge of shared guilt for enjoying a laugh at Thomas, for he was not of the finest features. Strength of body and character were his qualities. "Do you mean to say you have a plan for Edward?"

"I have no precise plan, yet if something was to show itself, I would be favourably disposed should it promise to be of assistance."

"Thank you, my lord. May I transmit that hope to my friend?"

"You may, with my blessing. Now, what might I do for you?"

Having already secured what she came for, Kitty took another path: "Oh, 'tis a trifling. I wonder, might I go to market in search of modern ideas for the kitchen?"

"On that subject, you need ne'er ask. You are the governess of my table."

"I shan't fail to remind you of that from time to time." She smiled and curtsied before turning to leave.

As she left, he wondered at her visit. Well, no matter, it must have been innocent enough. He paused to reflect on the many who surrounded him, without whom he could not manage.

* * *

'Twas early 'fore noon on the second day of June 1785, when Jonathan entered the rooms of Cecil Swift. "Come in, Jon. This must be a strange day for you, not tending the poults as you would've."

"All's late for the cold we've had. Partridge are just now beginning to hatch. Pheasant are just now laying. I'm unsettled for the anticipation o' it. Been at Weeting so long now the change may be hard."

"I am advised by his lordship he believes you will do well. Despite his recent behaviour, Lord Essex is a man of fair reputation and his estate is a fine one. You will doubtless soon fit it to your measure when you will again enjoy the fruit of your labours. If you will sign here, yes just here, I have one hundred pounds owed you for five years' wages ending today.

"Well then, we are now settled Mr. Band. Let me take your hand and say it has been a pleasure knowing you. I wish you well in your new position. I also commend you for your recommendation to his lordship on your replacement."

"It came down to two good people. Had his lordship wished to hand off to one capable o' stepping in so no change was felt, he has Thomas, though that choice would leave him a breach to fill. He was less comfortable with his choices for warrener, and as 'tis the warren wherewith he funds his shooting, he was resistant to changing out Thomas for another.

"In the end he chose to submit to more immediate uncertainty, but all will be in the hands o' someone proven to be quick, a hard worker, and a leader o' men. He is well respected, and I am pleased. I warrant he will soon grow to be equal to this task."

"I note his lordship has a certain interest where Henry is concerned. What do you know of this?"

"I know nothing other than he has found favour with Thomas and me in the time we have been together."

"Is Thomas aware he was considered to take over from you?"

"I did tell him o' my departure, whereupon he admitted his desire to be considered should I be asked for a recommendation. I was pleased to do so as there is none better than Thomas Turner for any such position. He has not learned o' his lordship's decision from me."

"I will ask Lord Mountrath to address the subject with him without delay. He would wish to directly explain the reason for his choice."

* * *

Before the sun had reached its zenith on that same day, Lord Mountrath pulled up before the warrener's lodge on a black mare. Bess was his favourite. His route had taken him by the Mill Farm where the miller made a good living grinding corn for the manor's tenants.

Little John and Robert were playing outside at whatever is invented in the minds of small boys. Not able to guess what they were up to, Charles did note it involved sticks and stones and a bucket of water. "What have you there, lads. Might I be of help?"

Before they could coordinate their pell-mell responses, their mother had stepped outside to see to the commotion. "Greetings, my lord. Please come in. I'll pour you a beaker to wet your whistle. This uncommon dry is staying with us longer than hoped for."

"That would be a welcome pleasure, Elizabeth. Thank you."

Some minutes later, his beer now quaffed, they chatted about this and that. He played with Maria who was propped on the table. She wore a towel and in view of the weather, a little shift. Her hair was dark, thick, and standing straight above her forehead but had worn off at the back of her crown. He smiled, privately recalling the moment shared with Kitty.

"You have not come this way for beer and the sight of my little ones. You must wish to speak with my husband. He will return shortly. He's gone to the clapper to see to the does and their kits. In this dry they need more water than usual."

"I would like to see for myself. I'll just walk over. If he is returning, I'll find him on the way. You have my gratitude for the beer."

Thomas was found drawing water for his rabbits. On this sweltering day Charles Coote wore only a waistcoat over his shirt. As he commenced to say what was on his mind, he removed it to help out. "I have decided Henry Manning shall replace Jonathan. I've come to tell you personally my decision."

He let that sink in for a moment. "I regret if you had your mind set on taking over. Jonathan was for you, and I agree you are the best for that role. Unfortunately, you are too good for me here, Thomas. I have not your equal to take over from you and any loss of revenue I might suffer would be harmful to the estate. The uncertainty is too great."

"I believe you will be satisfied with young Henry, my lord. He understands raising game better for his time on the warren and I have not seen a quicker mind. He is more than fit for the work, being young and of strong constitution. He is also good with the men and is well liked. They will back him, and you may advise him should he e'er require it, he is to count on me."

"Well said and thank you, Thomas. I was certain I could count on you."

* * *

Immediately he left the Earl's company, Henry rode to see his mother in Brandon. He found her alone and her reaction was to heartily embrace him, saying it was well deserved. Mary Manning reminded her son it was his own competence that led to such a position of trust in the employ of the Earl of Mountrath. He could now be independent and think of a life of his own.

He did not tarry, though he wondered why she looked at him in a manner he did not recognize. It was a tender, motherly gaze and it warmed him. When he departed, she promised to pen her acknowledgement of the Earl's generosity that very evening.

* * *

The season was not a successful one for farmers as their crops shrivelled in the fields for want of moisture. Consequently, Samuel Stokes turned his mind once more to seeking an initiative to generate fresh revenue to support the Earl's operations. His schemes were often not intended to deliver immediate returns. Rather, their goal was to derive the most from available resources, and through diversity to lessen the impact of any single failure such as the crop failure of this year. The Earl had successfully pursued the three proposals he and Henry Babington had put to him some months ago. Would he be capable of another so soon?

He struck on the idea of transforming rabbit pelts directly, rather than selling them to furriers and felt makers in Brandon. This had now become one of their chief sources of revenue, which made this idea not without risk. In fact, his inquiries led him to identify there were several risks associated with this business, not the least of which was the sickness to workers caused using mercury substances.

A manufacturing facility would need to be found, if not expressly built for this purpose. It required specialized but not new machinery, and access to constant clean water. Bromehill would be but one source for the rabbit fur. The work force would be modest yet of necessity, properly trained in the process and the handling of the substances to prevent sickness or poisoning.

The rewards for success could be staggering.

On the evening of the Glorious Twelfth, Samuel raised the subject privately with his lordship. As he had so many times previously, his figures and notes were prepared in advance that they might be left for his lordship's later study.

In the event, he was sufficiently interested to ask who he thought might oversee the business for him. Samuel was ready with the name of a highly trusted and proven overseer, albeit not of a manufacturing process. The man he had in mind possessed all other qualities one could desire, and he said so in proposing that Nate Bacon be put in charge. If his lordship was uncertain, he could simply put him in charge of first establishing the facility, and if satisfied, he could then propose a further role. He finished by noting he thought Nate deserving of the opportunity. Lord Mountrath concurred, and promised to study the figures.

He invited William Colhoun to the next shooting party where they began with a moment of reflection on their recent success, though William deferred to

Charles' superior role in the affair.

Charles laid out his new plan. William was immediately for it. He reasoned it was to those who dared transform raw material into product that substantial profits fell. As their own warrens were to be the principal source for the raw material, they would control the entire process leaving more profit for themselves. They did not doubt the long-term demand for felt and Colhoun ventured he was prepared to buy into the operation, ready to share the cost as well as the reward.

* * *

He sat in the same quiet place he had occupied in other times. He now wore a full whisker and his clothes were changed. His hair was fashioned differently but little of that could be noticed, for he wore his hat low on his brow. When his fare was placed before him he appeared to be reading a newspaper, held before him in large strong fingers. For a man who professed to be a simple labourer, his hands were unusually clean and undamaged. Anyone who could have seen his eyes would have detected a mixture of wariness and menace.

"I thank you, ma'am."

In his voice she heard something familiar. She returned behind the bar where her husband was at work before turning back with furrowed brow.

"Hmm. Gabriel, do you know who sits yonder? I feel I should."

Glancing quickly, more to appease his wife than to be of any use, he replied he did not. Undeterred, she manoeuvred to spy as was her wont, unaware this customer was familiar with her ways. He watched, expecting her to be discreet, even praying for it, for he was fearful of being discovered by others. When she was close enough he spoke in a voice only she could hear. "G' day, Mary. Will ye not sit quietly for a bit?" He emphasized the important word, that she would understand his intent.

Startled to be both caught and known, she stiffened and searched for her husband. He was not in view. She assessed her personal risk to be low, so she sat opposite, effectively shielding him from any who might glance their way.

"Do I know you, stranger?"

"I pray you've not already forgotten me." With these words he looked straight into her eyes.

She looked back and was shaken by what she saw. She took his hand and looked about to make sure they were not the attention of anyone in the Black

Feather.

"Phillip. What do you mean returning here? You know the Constable and his men would take you in."

"I'm not so timid I could not fend off anyone if challenged. Though surely, they've no interest in me now. 'Tis six months since the trial, and more since the affray in the park. E'en so, I don't desire to attract attention."

"It galls the Earl that his warrant to bring you in remains unsatisfied. Shall I fetch Gabriel? He would wish to see you."

"Not this time, perhaps. I bring tidings I trust will please you. Let us first speak. Afterward you and Gabriel may consider my offer and decide as you wish. You may give me your answer when I return in a few days.

"Afore business, I confess I've missed your table, Mrs. Osborne. 'Tis a pleasure to see you once more."

"And you, Phillip. Speak."

He smiled at her refusal to be swayed by flattery, remembering Mary had the sharpest business mind of the two. "I hear you suffer for want of game. Cranefield and Spinks are fitful in their delivery and Leveritt is not interested. Do I understand correctly?"

"You do. Edward resists still. I remind him of our kindnesses to him, but to no avail. He tells me we have simply paid our debt to him, that he owes us nothing. Now we suffer for it, e'en to our relations with the Highlanders who'd take quantities of coneys from us."

"I'm gatherin' men and it would serve me to have an arrangement with you just as before. Our contact would be through another you'll meet when next I come. 'Twould be too much risk for me to venture repeatedly in these parts."

"Where are you now? How shall you transport the game to us?"

"I shan't tell you where to find me. 'Tis prudent for you to not know. In this manner you'll not be false should anyone suspect. The game'll come by coach. Everywhere 'tis now done. I'll arrange with the drivers to bring it here directly, should you wish."

"We will be ready when you return."

"Mary I urge you, leave Edward be. I did play him as a fisher plays a trout with his fly. He was never without remorse. His heart was ne'er in it, and his wife was miserable for it. His honesty preserved us and our equipment more than once and he would not give us up, when many these days will testify in return for their freedom and a reward. He was true to us, and I believe Gabriel could be of a mind to let him go. I tell you to forget Edward. I'm your man."

It is likely Phillip was not wholly insincere. Though he believed what he said of Edward, he also knew his words would have the desired effect.

* * *

Some days later the Earl of Mountrath took to his horse again, this time to find Nate Bacon. Cecil believed he would be found supervising the repairs and improvements to the Weeting Mill, giving it a new lease on life. A chief concern was whether the equipment would survive the proposed loads from the larger sails and grinding stone. Nate was huddled with the masons and engineers when Charles rode up.

"Good day to all," he cried out when he had come up to them.

Variations of "My lord" were given in response. All conversation stopped.

"How may I help you, my lord?"

"Nate, I was hoping to have a word, but I do not wish to interrupt your work."

"I will come right down." He turned to finish his question and bid the others think on it until he returned.

"How do Kitty and Matthew? I have not seen them since his christening in St. Nicholas. I recall 'twas midweek, the last day of July."

"They do well, sir. Martha is now two years old. Kitty is strong and she knows to care for herself as she cares for others, you and me included. We are fortunate she lives by the manor, for 'tis less trouble for her to care for the little one and keep up her other responsibilities."

"How is the work proceeding? It appears well in hand, though I am not knowledgeable in these matters. It has always amused me to see that when a site arrives at its most disorderly 'tis the sooner pulled together to arrive at its intended form. There must be a principle, or law regarding such that I missed in my education."

Nate laughed. "You are not mistaken, for that is a well-known principle of construction, the more so if the owner is watching over. What may I help you with?"

Charles explained his new scheme and how he hoped to proceed, without mention of the role he planned for Nate. When finished he asked, "How say you?"

"As I understand, 'tis ambitious, yet fitting. It accords with your interests together with the resources and the talent to accomplish the thing without recourse to outside financing. It has promise, I'd wager."

"I trust you will find it more so when I tell you William Colhoun, our neighbour at Wretham Hall to the east, wishes to partner in this enterprise. What say you to that, Nate?"

"I say Mr. Colhoun may find himself well advantaged by your plan."

"There is more. What do you say to taking the first steps with me? I require a confidant to study the ways of this business. Brandon is at hand and it should be no difficulty to visit for the purpose of spying on their operations. You would do this for me?"

"When do you require this, and what do you expect of me?"

"I am in no hurry, though there is much to plan for as no such enterprise exists in Swaffham. As for what I need, I think you may know best. Mr. Swift advises that a plan to establish premises, with equipment for the task is paramount. I will then require workers. The immediate supply of fur will be assured from the Bromehill and Wretham warrens, however I will also require a plan to secure more fur, and for selling and distributing the felt produced."

"Then we shall begin where Mr. Swift proposes. I will visit Brandon to see what such equipment and premises might be. I should visit the furriers to examine their business and to make inquiries of workers, seeking information regarding the operations as well as the availability of labour at large. I should not indicate they are informing a rival. I will report to you when I have something of use."

"Splendid, Nate. I knew I could rely on you for a plan of action. Perhaps, when that is completed the next step would be to visit Swaffham to find a suitable location."

* * *

The four had not met for some months, due merely the onerous demands of their professions. They finally agreed to put all else aside in a concerted effort to meet. Thrown together by the poaching trial that made his name, Augustus Farrow desired to remain in touch with those who unwittingly became his co-conspirators of that day. His career since then was on a steeper path to fame, if not also fortune.

His cross-examination techniques now becoming increasingly accepted in the Courts, other barristers began to apply the lessons learned, effectively setting the system on its head by overturning the underlying tenet that the accused remain "guilty until proven innocent." The change would thereafter characterise the whole of the justice system. The old guard was predictably unamused.

His Solicitor on the day, Jason Bigley, had now become a fixture in his life, the two pairing up to develop a formidable approach to defending their clients. In case after case they benefitted from a superior ability to collect and sift through the minutiae, looking for holes and counterarguments to outfox prosecutors. If their client was not in truth innocent, they could often find a technicality with which to secure if not an outright acquittal, a much-reduced punishment.

The magistrate's clerk had survived the initial glacial reaction of Lord Essex to his calamitous and very public loss. Crime continued unabated in Gooderstone and its environs, creating opportunity for George Hambling to prove his worth in support of his lay Justice of the Peace.

This evening they were received by Dr. Morris Pulsford, the man who had brought them together in common cause to resist what they had agreed was a gross injustice in the making. In their eyes, the fault lay not with one man so much as with a justice system that permitted a single person to be victim, prosecutor, investigator, and judge with the authority to direct a jury to deliver the verdict he wanted.

Dinner was a pleasant affair; the table being well furnished with everything one could desire in the way of victuals and drink. Featured in this last category was a spirit Morris had procured by way of Lord Mountrath. His source was a London banker named Hennessy whose family had secured some interests in the Cognac region of France.

The noteworthy subject of discussion on this night was the gale force blow that had so disrupted the seas and the coastline from Brittany to Wales. News was now trickling in of the damage caused throughout the first week of December. Countless ships foundered or were dashed on the rocks with the loss of cargo and the lives of many hundreds of passengers and hands. Few could recall a time when more damage was sustained, where in addition to the loss of shipping, many ports, storehouses, and dwellings were ripped apart or washed away by the tides and crashing waves that swelled to uncommon heights.

It was a sombre discussion, and one perhaps forced by the nature of the times. Being vulnerable to the vagaries and the power of Mother Nature still held much fascination for men, especially those of worldly purpose.

* * *

It was several days later and on the shortest day of the year when Lord Mountrath and William Colhoun sat to formalize their partnership. "I gather we shall be seeing much more of each other now we are partners, Charles. Your man Bacon has done a fine thing putting this enterprise together. My banker has suggested this may be one of the more astute investments I have made, although I readily admit I have made some unfortunate choices."

"Bacon does seem to have limitless talent when it comes to organizing and accomplishing even the most elaborate tasks. I wonder someone so logical and astute is not from a superior class and education. We must credit nature as the cause of his genius."

Nathaniel was indeed gifted. He had spied as planned, incidentally encountering foremen and owners whose responses helped him gather the intelligence required to formulate his plan. He afterwards accompanied Lord Mountrath to select a site for their Swaffham factory.

As it happened, a former warehouse no longer being used to store raw wool for export to Flemish mills now stood empty. The business foundered when the mechanization of the woolen cloth industry gave England a domestic capability to rival all others. The introduction of the flying shuttle and the spinning jenny were turning England into a textile giant, but it would soon eliminate the contributions of women and families everywhere.

Samuel Stokes made the arrangements on very favourable terms and it was now left for Charles Coote to enlist Nate, for he needed a leader to assemble and direct the workforce and manage the factory.

* * *

Edward was cleaning up outdoors as his wife had shown him must be done, watching over Sarah, Nathaniel, and John. Sally was busy inside preparing food and preserving her treasures from the forest and the fields. A rider approached he did not first recognize, but as the distance closed he saw it to be Gabriel Osborne.

"Mr. Osborne. Your visit is a surprise."

"How do you Edward, and your wife?"

"We do well enough. How might I help you?"

"I've come to have a word with you, together. I believe it overdue."

Not without a little suspicion given this unexpected visit, Edward put his head inside to call out. Sally greeted Gabriel with reserved civility as her latest understanding was the Osbornes remained unsatisfied with Edward's refusal to return to their former ways.

"May we sit by your fire? 'Tis cold without, and I've come some distance. I am unaccustomed to travelling about, and 'tis no easy thing for a man my age on this cold winter's day."

Seated by the fire with their mugs of warmed cider, they sipped and watched each other in silence for the longest moment. Though they were currently at odds, Sally could not find it in her to be uncivil. Her gratitude for their help when it counted had not diminished.

Gabriel's eye caught something peculiar hanging in the window. It was a sphere of colour so unlike anything he had ever seen, it held his gaze for long moments. As it turned slowly, agitated by the draft of the fire, it reflected the light of day.

"I commend you Sally, for the odors filling your house would make my customers salivate. Perhaps you may one day join us at the Black Feather."

She smiled politely and waited.

Finally, Mr. Osborne, a man generally found to be less direct than his wife, said rather directly: "I've come to say the wife and I have misjudged you both. Edward has been pressed by my wife to return to our former relationship. She has, she concedes after much debate, been quite insistent and with some good argument, for we have suffered great loss. Still, I am here to relieve you of any further worry in that regard. We ask you to keep your silence. For our part, we would release our hold on Edward and give you thanks together, for what is done. We would not speak of this again, though we pray to be counted among your good acquaintances."

Sally, herself not known to be without character, placed her mug on the floor, walked to Gabriel and wrapped her arms around him as far as his girth permitted her small arms. Edward said, "I believe you have our word on that, Gabriel."

Later, she and Edward spent time together as they hadn't for a year. Lying together with their minds still bursting with thoughts of future possibilities, Sally turned to Edward. "Do you think there is something he was not telling us?"

His reply was the last they would speak on the subject. "It matters not to me, now we are free."

* * *

On the 21st day of December 1785 Thomas Turner left the rooms of Cecil Swift after signing for the receipt of 4£ 19s. 0. It was payment for vermin killing during the quarter ending that day. On foot, heading eastward from the Hall he was overtaken by William Colhoun astride a grey. "How do you Mr. Turner? You have not far to walk?"

"I'll soon be home, thank you Mr. Colhoun. What brings you this way?"

"I've just come from your lord. We have concluded a new partnership, and one I value greatly for the promise it holds."

"Indeed. There seems no shortage of such in these times, provided one has the notion and the capital. Would I know of this venture?"

"I should think so, for it relies in part on the prodigious number of rabbits from your warren. We are opening a factory in Swaffham for the manufacture of felt, where our warrens shall be the principal sources of fur."

"I know little of it. Nate Bacon has pestered me with his ceaseless questions and reckonings. I now understand why." Thomas betrayed his annoyance with this tone.

"'Twill be some time, perhaps years, before 'tis in operation. There is much to be done and many people will become involved."

"'Twill be but one more change. There is much of that hereabouts, though I stand still."

"You do not complain surely, for you are highly esteemed and I am certain, well compensated by Lord Mountrath." Colhoun estimated the man resented not being more implicated in the planning afoot.

"I am and I have no complaint as for that." Thomas understood, and quickly changed his tone. "Elizabeth and I are content, for the moment. Yet many about me are advancing, and I wonder is anything ahead for me. I have been warrener here for many years and perhaps it is time to change, to take on more responsibility for greater reward. Is that unreasonable to contemplate, my lord?"

"I should say 'tis the thinking of every ambitious man, Thomas, yet only the few take action. Today, the ladder to riches can more easily be descended, than it can be ascended. I have been one to take action. At times it has brought me close to ruin, for though we may strive, we do not always succeed. I pray this

254

venture with his lordship may cause me to ascend the ladder one more time. For that, my warren must submit to much improvement to meet my pledge to the partnership. It is several times that of Bromehill in size and on those grounds alone, I believe we shall make good."

"I'd wager on it, sir. Tell me more of your warren, for I have no knowledge of it other than by name. Pray, who is your warrener?"

For the remainder of their short journey Thomas interrogated William on his warren and on Wretham Hall. Some may have found his inquiries intrusive, but William was a man of uncommon plainness and not averse to making comparisons with his plantations in the Leeward Islands. St. Croix, Nevis, and St. Kitts were exotic places and Thomas was momentarily carried away to balmier, more fragrant climes. It served to increase his appetite for more out of life.

They came after some time to the lodge, as it happened to be on the road to Wretham Hall some six miles further. "Would you wish to come and sit by the fire? I promise you the best beer in Weeting, or perhaps a cup of warm cider."

"I thank you. If I am no trouble to your wife, I should gladly accept."

Elizabeth eventually joined them. Though she had much work to do, she became enchanted by images of island life, of strange plants and animals, of the colours of sand and sea, of tropical smells, and of people as black as night who, when left to themselves were gentle and swayed like the palm trees in a gentle breeze. Intrigued, she kept William a full hour before releasing him to resume his return home.

They later relived his words, incredulous at the thought of what life might hold for them if they decided to make a change. They were confident that options would become available to them, but they wondered when and where they might find an opportunity and what it might resemble. Certainly, it would not resemble an island in a faraway ocean. Perhaps most importantly, they wondered how they might grasp it when it appeared.

Elizabeth had the final word before they turned in the children. "I sense some relief in you this evening. You do not show it to others, yet I see you have grown dark with fretting about your situation, and that in frustration you strike out. I fear you may risk all.

"You must heed my words, husband. 'Tis not like you to take partridge unlawfully. And I do not enjoy keeping watch that others do not discover it in my kitchen. You must know how uncommon the smell of it is on the warren.

"You have your vermin killing bounty from these many years, and I have my savings. We shall soon have the money you require to improve your position. Be patient, for I sense today is the beginning of a good tomorrow."

CHAPTER XXIV

THE SHOOTING PARTY: TIME OF THEIR LIVES, SEPTEMBER 1, 1787

THE GLORIOUS TWELFTH NEVER LOST its appeal as one of the most highly anticipated days of the year, for this was the opening of shooting for red grouse. The guns were unusually silent this year as the date happened to fall on a Sunday, a day on which all shooting and hunting was prohibited by law. Thus, in 1787 the twelfth was held on the following day everywhere but in Weeting, where the silence continued. As it turned out, the lack of water and heather moorland thereabouts did not provide a natural habitat for red grouse.

Though Jonathan had tried for many years to introduce this game fowl without success, Henry had persuaded the Earl to forego the practice of using bagged birds for the expense and for the disruption to the partridge and pheasant that did thrive on the estate. He desired to determine whether the additional weeks of peace would be to their benefit.

It was only on the first day of September the silence was broken when the estate erupted with the banging that would continue until the close of the season on the first day of February. On this first day it was usual for only the superior classes to be invited: rare were those who failed to show. The arrangements and the weather had been flawless. Lord Mountrath had proven to be steady and showed little anxiety, openly crediting Henry Manning with success on this, his first real test.

He managed well enough throughout last season, but in some ways Lord Mountrath was reluctant to credit him entirely for that success. There were a few rough spots, such as when foxes became so numerous they had the run of the place taking many young pheasant and rabbits. Thomas and his men were temporarily assigned to assist in their extermination, which loss did not sit well with neighbours who were, to a man, avid hunters.

It might also be argued that the vitality of the game was due Jonathan's planning and previous efforts, of which the Earl had long been proud. A preserve brimming with healthy game was no accidental thing.

In fact, Henry may have been due more credit than he was given that year. His ability to lead men came less from his knowledge, than from his lack of it. He understood what he did not know and refused to let pride prevent him from seeking the advice of others before taking decisions.

With willing contribution from the men and women in his charge, all aspects of the shoot came off smoothly. From arrangements to transport the shooters to and fro, to the working of the dogs, all fell together. Two dogs stood out for their enthusiasm, precision, and work ethic. Norrie had been taken by her master to Gooderstone, but of the pups she had left behind, Comet and Billy attracted the favour of the shooters.

Guests stayed on for three full days and four nights. The second day was silent and somewhat more relaxed for it fell on a Sunday. Kitty was now in charge of all kitchens where she planned and oversaw the preparation of the meals. To meet the demand they operated full time, including with a small staff during the night to satisfy any caprices of the guests.

Even the red-legged partridge obliged by presenting just the right amount of challenge for the serious sportsmen, while leaving no one on the out.

This success permitted Charles to grow more confident in his new keeper, so that it was not long before he decided a special occasion with a distinctly different guest list was in order. After all, he thought to himself, for the many reasons I have to celebrate, it does no good to do so alone.

An informal shooting party for a mixed society was therefore organized to fulfill some of his obligations and to give thanks to so many. Invitations went to everyone essential to the functioning of Weeting Hall, as well as to those with whom he had significant dealings during the past year. Some, he was determined, would receive singular treatment for their contributions.

Of invitations there were many, but few were those who would actually reside at the Hall. Most guests would come and go from their own residence in nearby villages or halls. Neighbouring lords, merchants, tenant farmers and tradesmen might shoot, but not all would attend the formal evening. Ladies would not shoot, preferring to play lawn games, attend an outing, or share lunch under a canopy and especially, attend with their husbands in the evening.

Some preferred angling to field sports. Whatever a guest's personal pleasure and level of comfort, he or she was certain to find satisfaction in Lord Mountrath's invitation.

Given the mild conditions on the day his lordship requested lunch for the shooting party be taken at Grim's Graves. The shooters were joined by the others who made their way to the tents from different directions. The keepers sat where they were most comfortable, which predictably would be as nature provided on the ground itself. Exceptionally, they were not joined by Henry Manning, as Charles had expressly asked the Head Keeper to sit at the table with his mother.

"How do you find the shooting?" Elizabeth Turner asked of Cecil Swift.

"I have been fortunate, though I suspect your husband to be a superior shooter and perhaps the best on the morning. It remains to be seen whether we can catch him up this afternoon."

"I warrant 'tis you the leader on the day, Cecil. I did not see you miss a one." Thomas chuckled and pulled on his glass of beer.

Nate was not without comment on the matter. "Let us agree, Henry has not let his lordship down. The game is as plentiful and vigorous as under Jon and the dogs are well trained."

They nodded and raised their glasses in unison, knowing full well whose success they were toasting.

When dinner had been taken and men were beginning to undo their buttons for relief, Charles spoke in a low voice to Cecil, "'Tis the moment, I believe, Cecil."

Over the next few minutes Cecil moved through the guests, drawing together under the large tent Nate and Kitty Bacon, Edward and Sally Leveritt, and Henry with his mother Mary. When these were gathered by his side, Cecil rang his glass to signal quiet, using a small silver spoon as a clapper. Servants discreetly filled every glass.

Lord Mountrath stood to speak.

"My lords and ladies, I thank you for sharing this wonderful day with me. I pray all is to your satisfaction."

This gave rise to cries of 'Here! Here!' and 'Bravo!' accompanied by cheerful clapping.

Bowing gracefully, he added: "Your happiness pleases me. For my part, I must admit to enjoying your company." This second round of cheers was gleefully meant for themselves.

"I wish to make some announcements. I can find no better time to deliver them and there are none better I wish to stand before." He turned to face Henry and Mary.

"I wish to acknowledge our satisfaction with a young man whose mother has joined us today. We thank you Mary Manning, and toast you for giving us Henry, who proved capable when thrust into higher responsibility at an age when others still apprentice. Formed by you and educated at your feet, he has fully satisfied his commitments and his obligations to me."

He turned to address his wider audience. "Your shooting successes today are proof of this. To Henry, thank you. I pray you shall long enjoy your status as Head Gamekeeper at Weeting."

He crossed the distance between them and took him by the arms, embracing as men do before battle.

When they separated, Henry replied, "'Tis I who thank you my lord, for your confidence in me. Your decision was not an easy one as you had the most excellent person at hand to replace Mr. Band." He nodded towards Thomas to avoid any misunderstanding about who this could be.

In the instant all eyes were on Thomas, Charles Coote shifted his weight and put his arm around Mary's waist to bring her in, ever so slightly, towards him. As quickly as it happened, the moment was gone. Though he doubted his act had been detected, he had not counted on the lingering blush of pink that rose on Mary's cheeks. Among his guests were those for whom her blushes might not be explained by her pride in Henry's success.

"I would say I had fine masters in Thomas Turner and Jon Band. I pray Thomas will continue to teach me, for I have yet much to learn. I also thank my assistants. They stayed on with me, and by their knowledge of the manor and their skills have made my task possible. To each of them I owe much. Bless you boys over there."

The keepers acknowledged his compliment with restrained waves and shy smiles.

Facing his mother, he added, "It pleases me you are here, for you have always provided for me and encouraged me in my endeavours. Thank you and thank you all as if named."

On saying this, he outstretched his arm to encompass the gathering, giving license for everyone to break into a jolly "Huzzah!"

Charles Coote raised his hand for silence. "The furriers of Brandon will soon face competition from Newport Furriers of Swaffham, named in recognition of my mother, Lady Diana. As you will be aware, Nate Bacon has there established a factory to transform rabbit furs into felt for the use of hat makers to the finest heads in the realm.

"What you will now know is, my satisfaction with his endeavour and success is such that Nate has agreed to take on the management of this new enterprise. In the coming months he will remove himself and his family to Swaffham in order to take full charge of the factory. I trust he remains satisfied with the terms agreed. Am I mistaken, Nate? Excellent."

"I therefore ask you to join me in recognizing Nate Bacon and his wife Kitty, who have been staunch supporters and members of our community for many years."

To more celebration Nate stepped forward to reply.

"'Twas not long ago I knew naught of rabbits and felt and hatters. From Thomas and my spying on the Brandon furriers I learned much these past months. His lordship convinced me I had the makings of something more; that he believed I could overcome new challenges to get a thing done properly. I thank you for that confidence in me. And I thank you for being good friends and neighbours. We shan't forget the many kindnesses received from you.

"Your lordship spoke of the terms we agreed. One is that I bring with me a man to take some of my burden and whose wife is as a sister to Kitty. Before you all, I now ask Edward Leveritt and his wife Sally to join us in Swaffham. You will have responsibility in the factory. What say you, Edward, and Sally? His lordship prays for your acceptance and desires this to be the final announcement."

To say they were struck as if by lightening, would perhaps not be an exaggeration. After collecting their emotions and consulting each other, Edward stepped forward to embrace, rather more enthusiastically than fine manners would normally permit, first Nate and then Charles Coote, his lord. Sally was just a step behind with her own embraces. The unrestrained joy on their faces brought tears and laughter in equal measure, for few failed to recognize the significance of this offer.

Edward then did something wholly spontaneous. So unexpectedly did he step forward he took himself off guard. Though he first checked his movement, he was ultimately compelled by a sense of gratitude to not squander this opportunity as he had others.

"May I beg permission to speak?"

With open arms, his lordship invited him to proceed. "As my fellow lawmakers might say Edward, you have the floor to reply.”

“We thank you Nate and Kitty, and your lordship together for this. We are grateful for your confidence and your friendship and we gladly accept your offer. We will do our best to be worthy of your confidence in us.”

“You have each shown us a great kindness for which we daily give thanks to the Lord. Today however, I grant we are forever indebted to your lordship for your actions on my account, and to Mr. Colhoun who joined with you in fighting for justice. Mr. Hambling, you have made the Courts fairer for all. Mr. Garwood, ’twas your determination of the truth of that night that made the difference. We pray you continued success in your work in London. Mr. Bigley and Mr. Farrow, you knew to extract that truth to the advantage of justice. Dr. Pulsford, who stands here before us, you have been our saviour in ways too numerous to count. To each of you, please accept our sincere gratitude.

“I also thank Nate and Kitty Bacon and Thomas and Elizabeth Turner for their support and friendship. Your loyalty means everything.”

He now looked out on the many faces whose gazes had not shifted for several minutes, saying, “You have permitted us to share your home with you. We have tried to honour you with our small contribution and with this further generosity we commit to do more. We accept. Together with Sally, to whom I owe the largest indebtedness of all, and our children John, Nathaniel, and Sarah, I say your generosity and your kindnesses will not be forgotten. Thank you, all.”

With these words Edward left the labouring class behind and sealed his future.

CHAPTER XXV

NATE HAD LEARNED THE ART FROM THOMAS. Rabbit pelts were not always a certain thing: everything was in their rearing, capture, skinning, and the season they were taken. Any one of these, mistimed or mishandled, would reduce the value of the fur. He had correctly assumed before describing the essentials to Edward that he already knew something of the subject.

"Pelts taken in the season between the first days of October and February provide the richest and fullest fur. This explains their cost being several times those taken in the balance of the year. 'Tis these first quality pelts we seek for our felt and though Thomas believes a competent warrener will never kill rabbits between the beginning of March and the last of September when they breed and milk, we must remain vigilant for those who would deceive us. Silver-grey is prized, but our enterprise will want the black, above all else. For this reason, we intend to procure from Bromehill and Wretham before others."

Edward spoke of a recollection that was pertinent to the subject at hand. "While sitting in the dark of gaol, Reverend Spinks often told the stories of a high learned man. On one such night he spoke of certain Catholic monks before the dissolution. Those with the right of free warren employed breeding practices that explain for example, the silver-grey and the black furs. These same monks would eat delicacies for Lent they declared was not meat. Edmund believed them wrong. Laurices, as these delicacies were named in Latin were the abandoned, stillborn, or unborn kits taken from does. They was prepared and eaten whole by the monks."

"Nothing I hear of monks surprises me. I doubt the truth of it now, still as children we was told of monks deep within their monasteries boiling children alive to be served at their tables."

"I believe those were told to make children obedient to their parents. Was you an unruly youth, Nate?

Edward finished his story. "Edmund tried to believe this practice more went hand in hand with their breeding practices. To destroy unwanted or lost little ones was to squander God's riches. Thus, they were consumed."

"Thomas advises we are to look to the feeding practice when buying from other warrens. Now better understood than in his father's time, warreners are to plant sow thistle, clover, vetch, and parsley, and provide hay and turnips in winter for the coneys.

"Also, any pelt should be shunned from a rabbit not peed off as it is killed, as should any it has touched, for the piss being strong and malodorous will ruin the fur for felt making. It will be your task Edward, to select and bring to us only the best pelts for our factory. His lordship is resolved to employ only such furs to achieve the prices he requires."

Edward: "The factory will not be in operation for some months, yet we have a goodly stock of such pelts. What quantity is required to begin work?"

"Cecil Swift will soon give me his calculation of the quantity. I have given him some details gleaned from the workers in Brandon. Black is the most valuable as it is used exclusively in clothing for the superior classes of Europe and China."

"Naturally, these are the patrons his lordship seeks for his felt."

"Naturally," replied Nate.

It was late February in the year 1788. There being no river or body from which to draw water, Nate and Edmund were in Swaffham to oversee drilling a well to supply fresh water to the factory. The building in Mangate Street sat opposite the churchyard which featured a majestic avenue lined with a score of maturing lime trees. The well had reached sixty-one yards before piercing the chalk to tap a spring sufficiently strong to supply their needs. Tomorrow, a two-handed pump to draw water would begin filling the storage reservoir. This was one of the final acts before bringing in machinery and workers.

Soon, the factory would be sufficiently advanced they could move their families into two of the many handsome houses found in Swaffham. A market town of fewer than two thousand souls renowned for their longevity, it boasted a spacious marketplace where were found many good shops and inns, at the centre of which stood by the grace of the Earl of Orford, the remarkable Butter

Cross, erected in 1783. Its lead-domed roof was mounted by a statue of Ceres, a Roman deity whose aptness was not lost on the citizenry.

This Earl's fondness for coursing hare lay behind his founding of the Swaffham Coursing Society in 1776. Headquartered in The Greyhound Inn by the marketplace, this was where Nate and Edward had taken a table just as the bells of St. Peter and St. Paul called the faithful to evening prayer.

"Kitty and Sally will surely be pleased, for 'tis a splendid church they enjoy in Swaffham. I believe they'll be most taken by the glass. The bells are pleasing as well, although I cannot imagine long enjoying them so close. Perhaps we shall learn to disregard them after some time."

Nate smiled and asked for a pitcher of beer, two mugs, and a plate for each of them. "I admire the carved angels at the head of each hammerbeam. Our Reverend Smith would doubtless enjoy the benefice afforded here. There is a fanciful story attached to this church. I wonder if you know of the tinker of Swaffham.

"You do not? Do you sit down, grab your mug, and I'll tell you about John Chapman."

And so, Nate related perhaps the most astounding story Edward had ever heard told. It was apparently a true story, the north aisle, and the tower both being paid for as a result.

"A tinker of Swaffham, you now know his name to be John Chapman, once had a dream that was so real, he heeded it. One night he dreamt that if he went to London and waited there on the London bridge, directly he would hear news that would be to his great advantage. Having travelled thither and after lolloping about for several hours, he was accosted by a nearby shop keeper who had been watching. He asked him what he was about, as he neither accosted passersby nor begged for alms. To this John replied he had foolishly come in vain on an errand communicated to him in a dream. The man replied, 'Alas, good friend! If I had heeded dreams, I might have proved myself as very a fool as thou hast; for 'tis not long since I dreamt that at a place called Swaffham in Norfolk, dwells John Chapman, a pedlar who hath a tree at the back of his house under which is buried a pot of money.' On hearing this, the tinker hastened home.

"Upon digging under the tree, he found a large brass pot full of money, and inscribed 'Under me doth lie another, much richer than I.' But hold you hard, Edward Leveritt, the inscription being in Latin, it was some time afore the tinker discovered the meaning. When he finally returned to the hole to dig deeper, he found a much larger pot filled with gold coin.”

"Never!” cried Edward. “’Tis a good story, true or not.”

They ate for some time in silence, Edward trying to figure out whether such a story could be true.

"How do you find this, then?”

They looked up to see a very engaging young woman asking them, they assumed, how they found the fare.

"Tastes wholly good to me.” Edmund didn’t wait to swallow before answering.

"Excellent! I’ll tell mater. We do like to please. You’re stayin’ at the inn, tergether, then?”

"We are. For some time until we bring our families along. We will soon be your neighbours.” Nate had found his voice.

She smiled playfully, and twirled on the balls of her feet, flaring her skirts as she turned to leave them.

* * *

Work advanced apace and finally Lord Mountrath visited to inspect progress and to tour the factory whose structure had proved sound. Edward’s first task had been to personally inspect the roof which he found in excellent condition but for one corner where a heavy blow had lifted some tiles. The damage was limited, but left unchecked could cause harm. He made the repairs without delay, despite the lack of wet that persisted throughout the year.

The machinery, ovens, racks, and other equipment were now almost completely installed, and the water continued to flow with suitable force. Covenants with warrens were in place and those for the sale, distribution, and secure drayage of the finished felt needed only the Earl’s signatures to complete; the hatters of Norwich and London having already agreed the details. His lordship would finalize all when he next visited London where Samuel Stokes was drawing up the contracts.

The Earl was pleased yet concerned to see the quantity of stored pelts awaiting the first production. The overhead stores were substantially filled and would ensure some months of continued work until the new season brought in the first of its pelts. In the meantime, its presence was a risk he resolved by hiring watchmen. These were keepers recommended by Jonathan Band who was nearby, and who proved content to have his most trusted men enjoy the light work for good pay at a time of year they would otherwise be under foot.

Despite these measures, Charles Coote remained concerned about the significant investment he had committed to these pelts. They represented his single greatest expenditure for some time, and he was anxious for production to begin returning some of his capital.

Once assured of the soundness of all preparations and with little to add, he asked to meet with the labourers and their foremen. Nate had so frequently gone to spy at other establishments, he came to know the best workers who also possessed a pleasant demeanour. He used this intelligence when the time came to create his own workforce, selecting those he found most suitable and willing to displace themselves and if needed, their families.

Nate had arranged for a table laden with refreshments. Much as for a shoot, food and drink were carried over by a victualler to be taken cold and informally. The Earl showed genuine curiosity about each person's origins, experiences, and families. Afterwards he commented that every man and woman had readily declared they were lured from their previous establishment for more than improved wages. What most pleased the Earl was their favourable impression of Nate's demeanour toward them. Seemingly, they preferred to labour for him than for another.

The Earl took advantage of his presence in Swaffham to visit a friend and peer, the Earl of Orford who was just then entertaining a Captain Gore, of the Royal Navy and nearby Palgrave Hall. 'Twas a tiring ride, for he was forced to proceed against a blow from the north. He was quite satisfied to find the hospitality awaiting him within magnificent Houghton Hall.

The conversation was congenial and Captain John Gore, despite the severity of his experiences abroad and his uninhibited descriptions of natives in faraway places, proved exceeding entertaining to his male audience. Charles spent the entire next day at Houghton before returning to Swaffham on his route home to Weeting. In the end, his excursion proved useful as well as entertaining. He learned of the Captain's plans to rejuvenate Palgrave Hall, a venerable Elizabethan structure of some renown. He also had news of William Colhoun that he prayed was a misunderstanding. His earliest attention to the matter was crucial as there was an implied risk to all he had ventured. Until he was certain, he would withhold this information from Nate. No purpose could be served by the burden of this knowledge.

* * *

By the end of spring the factory was in operation. The quality and quantity of felt produced was consistent with Cecil's estimates and revenue began flowing to the immense pleasure of Charles and William. Should this early success be maintained and nothing disrupt their plans, it seemed safe to assume their investment would return a healthy profit.

There was little to note beyond the arrival of two families to take up their new residence. They enjoyed at once the pleasure of new-found discovery, as they struggled with the anxiety of displacement. The lengthy process of establishing themselves in their new community had begun.

The Bacons and the Leveritts enjoyed the social status consistent with their new positions. Finding themselves invited to events and sought by the bourgeoisie of Swaffham, they wisely reciprocated. This had the effect of hastening their integration into that society. As happens with people, it was not long before thoughts of Weeting and those they left behind began to fade. Well, perhaps not all of those they left behind.

Meanwhile, Charles Coote pondered his options, eventually bringing his concerns about Colhoun to Cecil Swift and Samuel Stokes. "I was given private information concerning my partner in Newport Furriers. It is widely rumoured William has become financially unstable as a result of some miscalculations. First, he is become deeply indebted to purchase a seat in the House in order to advance his political ambitions. Second, his investments in the islands are floundering. People are saying a combination of mismanagement, shady dealings, and misfortune have begun to overwhelm him. He is fighting for purchase on this slippery slope by taking out mortgages at exorbitant rates."

"What do you estimate is your exposure to these events, my lord?" This came from Samuel Stokes.

"The funds for Colhoun's share of the initial investment have been transmitted to the company. His commitment to provide pelts of first quality has been met to date. These are in hand and not what concerns me.

"In my estimation the risks lie before us. Should he fail to respond to my call for ready money for instance, the greater risk falls to me. Should his creditors seek satisfaction in our joint venture, the risk again falls to me. As for the warren, many are the reasons it may founder: 'tis after all, a living thing. However, should he fail to maintain the investment required to satisfy his commitments because of pressure elsewhere, he may take a mortgage against the warren to relieve this pressure. Was I to lose control of that important supply of pelts for the factory, I could lose a great deal."

Stokes: "Those are significant risks, indeed. I can think of another. What is the risk, should he become obliged to sell his share in Newport Furriers? I believe that to be an equally ruinous upshot, as they say."

"I agree, Mr. Stokes. We require a plan to avoid such an event. Cecil, you are quiet, but not for want of something to say. Surely, you contemplate a solution."

Cecil scratched his beard while cogitating. "Hmnn. Would it be helpful to address the obvious issue at hand? By that I mean the health of Wretham Warren. Are investments lagging? Are the practices sustainable? Is the warrener competent? Has Colhoun used it as leverage?"

Charles was attentive: "Proceed, sir. We stir not."

Swift: "Thomas should visit the warren on the pretext of establishing a relation with his associate. The purpose explained would be to commence dialogue, to come to rely upon each other should the need arise, and perhaps to exchange intelligence such that their most successful practices are shared equally. Surely it could do no harm and much good is sure to come of it, if not all on this first occasion."

"What say you to this plan, Samuel?"

"I see merit in it. Perhaps the warrener is aware of a financial constraint of Colhoun's that puts the warren at risk." Samuel Stokes threw the question back to his client. "And you my lord, what is your thought on this plan?"

"It has merit, I concur. It is subtle and does not set in motion anything we cannot control. Thomas will surely be up to this.

"Cecil, I begin to believe you have missed your calling. Would you not rather have been a military commander, or a diplomat smoothing the water for Britannia abroad?"

This was once more an occasion to sample that French brandy their colleague James Hennessy was now bringing over quite regularly. His recent complaint was that he could not keep pace with the favour it found among the gentry and the wealthy urban dwellers.

* * *

Time proved Nate and Edward to be loyal customers of The Greyhound Inn. Having taken up residence in the months preceding the arrival of their families, they continued to frequent its table for the beer, the food, and for the presence of the pretty, tiny-waisted young woman who served them without fail.

Becoming increasingly friendly and close to them, she would at times sit and converse, prodding them in her sweet and bright voice for details of their experiences and their strange plans.

Rebecca Cowper, for that was her name, was not high learned but she possessed the ability to see what many others did not. She was aware of her natural endowments for even as a small child she could not ignore the ceaseless favourable comments to that effect. Her elder sister now married and departed, paid her the best compliment of all by disabusing her of the advantages of her fairness.

The lesson held, and forever after Rebecca's beauty never became her means to her ends. The strangest of creatures imaginable on this earth, Rebecca's mortal presence did not belie her moral reality; for it is one of life's greatest lessons that beauty imparts awesome power, the wielding of which is reliant on the moral strength of its holder. Happily, Rebecca's invisible touch served ends that were not selfish, or dishonourable.

She flirted with men certainly, for she was a full-blooded young woman with an easy manner. She especially took to Edward for his long limbs and blonde hair whose waves so resisted the restraint imposed by the black ribbon he tied at the back.

As for Edward, what man could resist the innocent attentions of such enchanting inquisitiveness. He enjoyed every moment, looking forward to the next encounter all the while expecting nothing beyond the enjoyment of those few moments. Nate felt it too, yet did not interfere. To his credit, he did not take his eye off the two for a minute.

By the time Sally and the children arrived, a three-way bond of friendship had developed. And so, their relationship continued, strictly within the pale of The Greyhound Inn.

* * *

Without admitting it directly, Thomas was thankful for the challenge. It was both unusual and exciting, especially as it would remove him from the routine of the summer season when rabbits were generally left to their own pleasures. The crops to feed them were growing, they were mating, the vermin were under control, and repairs to the equipment were in train. The most important task was to oversee the clappers, making certain nothing disturbed the does and their kits. Properly tasked, his men could do without him looking over them.

Once asked, it was in Thomas' nature to defy any challenge that presented itself.

The route was five miles and as straight as the crow flies. He stayed to the road, passing over open heath and through the park of Stephen Galney, Esq., until he reached Frog's Hall. Taking the northeast direction of several available, he entered Wretham Warren where he soon came to its lodge, the appearance of which held no surprise for him.

Mrs. Took gave Thomas directions for locating her husband, John. He was expecting Thomas but had to attend to a sudden commotion on the warren. Elizabeth had given him two jars of her plum cheese to offer as a sign of friendship. He handed them to her now, wrapped in muslin. This gesture was received with genuine surprise and grace. She hinted they would sup well this evening.

Thomas heard the banging before he had even left the yard. Whatever John was engaged in, he was hard at it with his gun. Must be vermin or brazen day-time poachers, thought Thomas. He loaded and primed his own gun in anticipation of having to contribute to the effort.

Approaching carefully, he came upon a scene that reminded him of the cunning his father had shown so long ago. Crows must have got at some kits, for John had set up three tripods along the edge of the covert using dead branches. To each he tied the partial remains of a carcass and then crouched in hiding within the covert, keeping his three deceits in view. As crows would approach and land, he killed them from his hide, one by one.

After introductions and the usual small talk to feel each other out, Thomas offered to help, explaining he was always glad of the practice. For the next few hours the two dispatched the better part of a murder of crows that proved, on that day more brazen than poachers. At first alighting just out of range, they would eventually show their determination by circling ever closer until they felt safe enough to land.

Bang! Credit another to the warreners.

Waiting for their next victim, Thomas and John passed the time reviewing the arrangement between their lords and the challenges it presented to them. Thomas' questions were anticipated as William Colhoun had instructed John on the reason for the visit. From John's answers as well as the questions he asked in return, Thomas felt he had a good estimate of the nature of John Took, of Wretham Warren, and of any possible vulnerability to William Colhoun's financial situation.

When the remaining crows accepted defeat and flew off, the warreners affixed the fallen to the tripods as a warning to others and turned for the lodge.

For the first time Thomas got a full view of the man. John Took had been on the warren for an exceptionally long time. He was no longer young and was shaped like a man who had landed at his mother's feet a younger version of what he now was. He was not tall. He had the belly of a fat baby and his short stout legs, as rounded as his trunk, gave him the air of a squat hourglass. Despite the warmth on the day, his head cover was a tall black hat of the sort worn by keepers, though he wore no coat. He had already earned Thomas' respect for his experience and for the answers to his prying, which he prayed was not unduly evident.

As they later sat to supper, Lydia showed her husband what Thomas had brought for them. The gesture was evidently appreciated as she had prepared a small feast of roasted leg of lamb stuck with cloves of garlic and branches of rosemary. The claret on offer was a pleasant surprise, and a welcome change from the beer he expected. He would remember to bring this to Elizabeth's attention.

The evening was congenial, and undoubtedly aided by the commonality of their experiences and their situation. Answers were only as guarded as appropriate for a first encounter. By the time they took to bed they had warmed considerably to each other, a sentiment undoubtedly furthered by the claret. Thomas was satisfied he had inquired into every aspect of John's business, and therefore Colhoun's, without raising alarm.

On the morrow Thomas took his leave. As he was about to take to his saddle John clasped his arm to say he was glad of the visit and of their discussions. His last words came as he looked him the eye, one head warrener to another. "I trust you have everything you came for."

Taken aback, Thomas answered in the manner the man deserved. "I have John. My thanks to you, together. I would be pleased to return the gesture. Should you desire, you will be welcomed at Bromehill."

Turning to push his pony forward, John softly spoke the traditional Brecks farewell, "Mind how you go," and Thomas thought to himself, "Was I less delicate than I imagined?"

What was he now to report to Lord Mountrath? Riding, he reviewed the intelligence gathered, trying to assess whether and where there might be vulnerabilities for his lordship. He saw only one significant problem, but was unsure how to present it. In the end, he decided to let the questions come at him and to respond as clearly as he knew. "Surely Samuel and Cecil will know best how to assess their risks."

Three days later Thomas was seated in the Hall's library with Lord Mountrath and Cecil Swift. For hours, it seemed to Thomas, they inquired of him everything he had learned. At one point he tried to summarize his intelligence by saying, "When all is measured, I should advise that Wretham resembles Bromehill in all save its proportions, as it is thrice Bromehill. Mr. Took obtains from his efforts what I should expect, howsoever he accomplishes it."

"And of his business, were you to learn anything of his risks?"

"No, Mr. Swift. Mr. Took understands without having the particulars, Mr. Colhoun has creditors aplenty. Yet he seems to have interests aplenty and contemplates the purchase of East Wretham to expand his park of West Wretham. I do not know what this says of his vulnerability."

"It may be nothing, or it may be everything. It all rests with the revenue he can count on and the liquidity of his assets, for it does not appear he enjoys an excess of ready cash. I am pleased to hear the warren, where lies my chief concern, is in good hands with Took, and that Colhoun is not stinting with his interest there. Surely Thomas, you must have found one weakness to inform us."

"I have given this some thought, my lord. Barring a fault in his answers or in my inquiries of Took, the only risk I see is in Mr. Took himself."

Whether intended or not, that statement made both men shift in their chairs to lean forward, fearful of missing what would next come from Thomas. "I beg your pardon. Have you not this afternoon convinced us of the excellence of his practices?"

"That is the truth, my lord. Yet I wonder, should Mr. Took fail to stay on the warren, who might then take his place such that it does not falter? Mr. Took is quite capable, but aged. I cannot believe he should enjoy many more years."

It had been no frolic. Behind this seemingly innocent scouting mission lay serious intent. Lord Mountrath proclaimed he was not decided, but would impose no further on Thomas. News of this pleased him for he had been an uncomfortable spy. For now, he was content that Lord Mountrath had claimed the intelligence he returned to be of immense service to his interests.

Lives and matters continued throughout the year until late November, when a frost descended upon the whole of the land. As frost will, it reached deeper into the ground with each day. Considerable snow fell in early December and by mid-month the hard frost gave no appearance of breaking, the 15th being the coldest day ever experienced. The wind added to the cold, blowing frost into every corner of every room. Still the cold worsened. The last day of December was so cold, water froze solid, even in rooms warmed by fire.

As the days turned into weeks without any of the usual warming spells, the frost reached further than ever known before in the history of this land.

CHAPTER XXVI

'TWASN'T ALL FROST FAIR, 1789

THE HARDSHIP VISITED UPON the people of Breckland throughout much of the present year had desiccated crops and dried the flows of water, resulting in the loss of much livestock for want of sustenance. At the close of the year the little water remaining froze through by the last week of November.

By year's end the temperature had, by some observations, plummeted in excess of 25 degrees Fahrenheit below the freezing mark, and a very hard frost had set in. Throughout the ensuing weeks the air did not stir. At times tiny crystals floated in the still air as if angel dust had been sprinkled there. Branches of trees and hedges stiffened. Evergreens shrivelled. Winter crops began poorly for want of moisture, and fared worse under the snow and sustained frost. Even the available stubble and gleanings of the fields were ruined by the unrelenting conditions.

In London, the Thames so froze over the citizens of that city held fairs on the open ice. From Putney Bridge to the shipyards of Rotherhithe were found all manner of diversion from bearbaiting to coursing, jugglers, fortune tellers, festivals, booths, turnabouts, and roasting beasts. So robust was the activity that Bartholomew Fair was declared to be less merry. For those with money there was jollification aplenty.

For the many residents destitute of employment, food, and warmth for themselves and their wretched children, this merriment must have seemed heartless. Not even the staunch benevolence and generosity of the English upper classes could respond to the want of such misery. The death toll among the poor here and across Great Britain that winter was a thing to reflect upon.

On the Continent, particularly in France, the conditions were far worse. Severe drought, followed by unrelenting severe storms that launched hailstones weighing in excess of one pound, caused the ruin of every crop imaginable. Gone were its important vineyards in every region, cereals in the north and the west, vegetables in Île-de-France, oranges and olives in Midi, apples in Calvados, and pears and plums in Alsace. So too, were lost the mulberry bushes whose precious silkworms had previously provided employment for forty thousand workers. As bad as they were, these losses were merely the prelude to a winter of crippling frost and more storms.

Ponds froze so that fish were enveloped in ice. The ice on rivers measured two feet in thickness. Deep wells froze and the wine and spirits in cellars froze. Mills could not grind wheat for want of flowing water, causing deeper famine among the poor for whom nothing could be imported, for the sea and all the ports were frozen to a distance of several leagues from the coast.

Still the temperatures descended, until trees exploded and the forests sounded and appeared as if war had erupted.

The people of Europe were unhappy. Their leaders were helpless to alleviate their suffering. The price of a loaf of bread, if one could be found, often outstripped the daily wage of a labourer.

On Bromehill Warren the frost sank deeper into the soil as rabbits clawed their way downwards ahead of the frost. One happy consequence was the quality of fur surpassed any in Thomas' experience.

During the whole of December and January, Thomas and his warreners worked ceaselessly. In their attempt to stave off disaster on the warren they carted in hay, turnips, and the branches cut from hedges and trees, as well as fresh water daily to replace that which had frozen over. To keep their bodies warm and healthy, the rabbits required many times more nourishment than in the warmer months of the year.

When news of his father's death was brought to him during that cold it was said he died on the warren carting fodder to his beloved coney. Thomas senior's body would be retained for burial when the ground thawed. There was little time to grieve as every moment was consumed by the effort to survive.

On a day less frosty, Thomas travelled to see how John Took and Wretham had suffered the conditions. He found that John and his men were holding out well enough against the weather. The same could not be said for other warreners John had news of. He expected wherever those less experienced and determined lost ground against the frost, they were surely to find ruin in their burrows come spring.

Their lords were pleased when they reported the excellent quality of the fur. How many rabbits would succumb to the cold, however, would not be known until the warm returned. Culling proceeded, although as the frost continued the numbers diminished more rapidly than was the custom.

When the thaw did come, the rivers so swollen and choked with ice, flooded the fields and towns and swept away bridges. After some relief in February the cold returned in March, thus delaying the growth of spring crops and propelling prices upwards.

This was to be followed by a stubborn heat until more storms struck in June and July of 1789, causing much devastation. The whole of the past year had been an improbable experience and one likely to mark the ages. It would doubtless leave its mark on many who would thereafter consider their primary aim to be the preservation of agriculture in order to adequately feed the population.

In the end, Death did come to the warrens, though the toll was less severe where the level of effort was almost equal to the ferocity of the occasion. Wherever the effort fell well short, the devastation was as to humans who everywhere slipped away in the silence of hunger, cold, and related diseases.

The report of damage was painful to Lord Mountrath. His own smaller losses provided little comfort as he grieved for the loss everywhere. To assess the impacts of the past winter on his affairs he gathered his advisory board at West Dereham Abbey. Being one of his many properties scattered across the islands, it was only twelve miles from Weeting Hall. Attending were Samuel Stokes and James Hennessy, Ernest Salmon and Cecil Swift, and Henry Babington.

"In France I saw and heard of such things I ne'er thought possible. My own family interests are greatly affected by the ravages of the past year. Everywhere one finds the dreariness that had taken hold of the people now gives way to anger, as those who survive gather strength. I sense things will soon change, ne'er to return as before. As e'er my lord, for those who survive, the prospect for opportunity awaits." James was impeccably dispassionate, as always.

"These are grave tidings James, for they tell of an outcome we wish to avoid for Britain. There is public unrest here as well. We risk grave danger should our blindness force an angry populace to bring about change, for it will come at a high cost. Is it not better to nip it in the bud by bringing about orderly change?"

"You speak of reform, my lord. Are your peers of the same view?"

"Some. Not enough, unfortunately, Cecil. There surely is greater merit in adapting rather than tearing down our institutions, and I for one believe the effort would benefit all."

"Perhaps not all value our institutions and traditions as do you, my lord. There are many who place no value on precedent and who prefer that all be overthrown, so as to address what lies ahead unhindered by convention."

"My friend Ernest, you speak of those who would see all men stand as equals regardless of birth, education, colour or creed. That may be an honourable goal, but would require many more a valiant heart to achieve than now exist."

"To return to your own affairs sir, what is your estimation of our reports?"

"The answer to your question eludes me still, Henry. What is your view?"

"We do not forget past storms weathered together. Like oxen struggling beneath the single yoke we have learned to pull together. However, this present tragedy has left us disordered as ne'er afore, and disconsolate. I feel you are better served to wait some time afore taking decisions. With time, humours will settle and opportunities may present themselves of their own."

"Answer me this then, gentlemen. What is the greatest benefit we can bring to man that is within our realm to address? I ask without guile, as I truly seek the answer." Indeed, by the expression on his face, Charles Coote sought a candid reply.

No truly apt response came until this from Ernest Salmon. A man for the people, he estimated that within the sphere of his lordship's influence lay his role as a lawmaker, wherein lay his foremost opportunity to benefit man. However, within the sphere of his business interests lay his ability to feed man. Those of his affairs most germane to this issue were the farms and the warren, although to his thinking they differed in one chief aspect.

When asked to explain, he reminded them the law of the land assures that warrening shall chiefly benefit the private owner, which benefit he achieves through the sale of his coney. Barring exceptional circumstances, coney would multiply and thrive if left to its own in the wild, free for all men to pursue equally, according to nature.

Grain on the other hand, requires man to deploy several costly practices to obtain the most from its sowing. Left to its own, it would fail to achieve the bounty now regularly attained in our fields.

He reasoned that must one choose between the two methods of feeding man, the latter appeared more reliant on his intervention than the former.

"You have all provided me much to think on, though above all else I find the reasoning of Ernest to be most fascinating. As is the wont of such discourse, gentlemen, I have much to ponder."

"I should hasten to add a reminder," said Cecil, "of the agitation suffered upon the tenants. The farms have been a chief source of profit under the care of able tenants, yet this year has proven difficult for the double ruination of the reduced yield due to severe weather, followed by the surfeit of rabbits invading their fields as they struggle to find sustenance. Your tenants now witness reduced returns as yours from the warren increase, seemingly at their expense.

They argue this threefold injustice is reason to withhold rent in retribution until you bring about satisfactory control of the rabbits, though I suspect they should be satisfied to be given the right to take rabbits they find on their land."

"Do I not ignore their transgressions? They know they are perfectly welcome in these times to take any rabbit found destroying their crops."

James Hennessy spoke after holding his silence, "I believe them to be more shrewd than Cecil believes. The problem is exaggerated to make a point, and so I ask, 'What is that point?' 'Tis that tenants will remain unsatisfied until they are granted the right to take coneys without your permission, as freely as it may be given."

"There is another approach."

"We listen, Henry. What would you say to us?" Lord Mountrath was growing tired as it was now late.

"You might eliminate the problem altogether."

"How so, friend?" asked James.

"The warren occupies land once found unsuitable for cropping. Through the adoption of new practices, it could now be turned over to crops, plantations, and livestock. In this manner you would eliminate the complaints of tenants and permit them to freely take unenclosed coney while obtaining greater revenue from tenant leases and increasing your park land for shooting. I venture your leases to be more valuable and you would also export timber and wheat at immense profit."

"That is an unconventional notion whose merits escape me in my fatigue. I bid you all a good night for I must to bed.

"Yet now a further question comes to mind. What say you to divesting myself of this Abbey? Does it serve me sufficiently I should continue to invest in its preservation? I leave you with that. You may continue as you will, however I am off to sleep on these matters. Gentlemen."

With that he left them alone.

"I say, we have seen some interesting things in our day, have we not?" James spoke to no one in particular.

"'Tis ten years or more since we recovered from another such disaster. This is infinitely worse than then; or has time merely diminished the ability to recollect?"

"I believe you are correct, James. For myself, I remain uncertain of the status of Newport Furriers. Surely the losses suffered on the warrens will affect the success of that enterprise."

Cecil had intimate knowledge of this situation as Thomas had prepared him for this meeting. "Despite every suspicion to the contrary Samuel, the quality of fur this winter is unsurpassed by any previously achieved. Thomas credits the cold and the adequacy of nourishment the rabbits received, for the warreners went to great lengths to cart fodder and water to them. Decidedly, the numbers culled at both Bromehill and Wretham are much reduced, yet the remaining quantity of fur is sufficient for their needs. They could do nothing for kits bred during the cold as they succumbed to the frost reaching into their burrows. Should they enjoy normal weather this year, the remaining stock will see them through. Many warrens encounter another fate, where their prior indolence now suffers them to struggle for survival."

"Newport should then thrive?"

"Such is my assessment, James. However, should his lordship transform the warren I would not venture to estimate the duration of that success, as a primary source of the prized black would be lost to it. Whether the much larger Wretham can fill the void, is a question to be answered. Whether success can be achieved using pelts of lesser quality, is another. I cannot say here and now. We travel next to Swaffham to examine the factory."

"These, gentlemen are further questions to ponder." James rose and stretched. "I am off to bed. I too bid you a good night."

"We too are exhausted. Should that route be decided it will fall to someone to find the way to tell Turner." Cecil's respect for Thomas was evident in this show of concern.

"To whom would that deed fall? Another thing to ponder." Turning to leave, James said once more, "Good night"

✳ ✳ ✳

Being a mere eleven miles from Swaffham, for this was their destination, Charles Coote and Cecil Swift enjoyed a more leisurely pace than their comrades who had earlier departed on their respective routes homeward. On the road they largely avoided the subjects of last evening save for his lordship confirming with Cecil his recollection of the questions he must consider.

"One. How to resolve the dissatisfaction of tenants with rabbits that destroy their crops.

Two. Whether to transform Bromehill to farms and plantations.

Three. Whether to sell the Abbey. Have I all?"

"Would 'twas that simple. After you retired, we devised more questions for you.

Four. Should you transform Bromehill, could Wretham alone fill the void?

Five. Should it not, could Newport succeed using pelts of lesser quality obtained elsewhere?

Six. Who will inform Thomas and what shall become of him?"

"These are splendid questions, all! We have much to think on."

Reaching Swaffham by late afternoon, they left their mounts with the stabler in the marketplace and walked the short distance to the factory.

They later repaired to The Greyhound for refreshments. Seeing Nate enter in the presence of two superior gentlemen, Rebecca instinctively kept a respectful distance.

The essence of the Abbey meeting was scrutinized anew for Nate's benefit and comment before any decision was taken that would affect the future of his operations.

Nate agreed their understanding and assumptions were consistent with his own. The quality of fur this season had indeed more than compensated for the diminished numbers of pelts. For the moment there did not appear to be any further risk, as the warrens from which they procured fur were expected to quickly return to normal. Should the supply be permanently reduced, it would be felt only in the next year.

Respecting the relationship between Nate and Thomas, and also perhaps fearing putting up the rabbit too early, as the saying went, they withheld the discussion of Bromehill and its possible closure.

The Bacon residence hosted dinner that evening. Everyone formerly of Weeting was invited so they might together share in news of old friends and acquaintances. In their turn, Charles and Cecil learned of Swaffham and its notable citizens and local gentry. Before retiring, they had agreed an entertaining evening was had by all. Lord Mountrath, in respect of his reluctance to sleep in hired quarters, was offered the master bed for the night while Nate, Kitty, and Cecil were accommodated in other rooms.

Charles toured the factory in the morning, resolved to defer all decisions until he had considered his positions more thoroughly. During his inspection he greeted each worker, relishing the climate of productivity and harmony. The workers he would never meet, for they worked in their own homes, were the women who hand plucked the fur from the treated skins.

Mountrath rarely relaxed his responsibility for oversight, regardless of his comfort with past decisions. On this day he particularly sought indication of Nate's success as the manager of his business, and was gratified to confirm he had one less question to ponder.

By early afternoon they were back on the road, heading home to Weeting.

Their route would take them south across the Swaffham and then Pickenham Heaths, to the river Wissey that would lead them on to Hilburgh. From there the Mundford Road would lead them to Ickburgh, Mundford, and beyond into Weeting, only thirteen miles distant. At a walk, it was expected they would reach home in under four hours. The weather was fair and dry. Charles rode black Bess, and Cecil, his chestnut gelding.

Opposite South Pickenham they came to a wood, wherein they spied a man leading his horse some little distance ahead. His back was to them. Approaching, Cecil called out for him to move aside. There was no response. Seemingly, he had not heard the call. As they pulled up behind him, two mounted men emerged from the wood to their rear. In that very instant the dismounted man turned with a pistol, cocked and pointed directly at his lordship. They could neither advance nor retreat.

"What is the meaning of this," cried Cecil in a voice full of authority, demanding an answer.

"Stand and deliver, gentlemen, or we shall take your lives!" came the gruff answer from the one with the pistol.

"Highwaymen, I wager you'll want our money and valuables." Charles was not about to argue the point.

"Thass right, there bor. Gi' us yer money." The oldest of the three was the apparent leader of this gang. He and his fellow brandished their bludgeons as if to strike from the rear.

Under the threatening gestures the horses were becoming jittery, particularly Bess who sensed her rider was no longer relaxed in his saddle.

"Do as they command, Cecil, and pray we come to no harm."

They pulled out their purses and dropped them well short of the thief with the drawn pistol. The highwaymen had chosen their ground well and despite the cover provided by the trees, had no interest in prolonging this encounter.

Stooping to retrieve the purses, Saint Nicholas' clerk suddenly straightened, coming up into Bess' head. She took a small step forward and in that instant flicked out her hoof, catching him in the leg. His recoil from the shock and the pain was such that he discharged his pistol.

His one ball spent; the highwayman now became vulnerable. Seizing the advantage, Charles quickly spurred her forward and Bess kicked out once more. This time the crack of his leg could be distinctly heard. He buckled.

At the same instant Cecil turned with his crop to place a wicked blow between the eyes of the rear guardsman's horse directly within his reach. "Oh, for want of my hanger," he was heard to growl as he turned fully to face his opponent whose rearing mount almost unhorsed him. The oldest, and their presumed leader stood his ground until Charles pulled from its concealment a small pistol, and cocking it, aimed it straight at his wicked heart.

"I believe you no longer enjoy the advantage of us. Leave the purses where they lie, take your man and depart immediately, or I shall fire upon you, sir."

They were forced to dismount that they could lift their broken companion, no longer able to mount or walk, across his horse face down, buttocks skyward. They were last seen on foot taking a small trail into the woods away from South Pickenham.

The ambush had failed. The rout complete, Cecil dismounted to retrieve the purses. After securing them, he discerned he was now in need of regaining his saddle.

Walking alongside Charles in search of the next milestone, Cecil responded to a question. "I had my crop made special in Norwich, following a cavalry officer who once showed me his last line of defence. 'Tis lead weighted and quite lethal, you know." Turning to share the moment with his eyes, he noticed blood staining Charles' boot.

"I say, you've been wounded."

"The ball has struck my leg. I fear I may not be with you much longer for I am losing blood."

"You must remain in the saddle. We must get you to Swaffham without delay. Where are you struck, man?"

In a manner unsuspected of Cecil, he went into action without a single further word. He assessed the damage, which he found to be a single wound to the thigh about two inches deep. He tore the sleeve from his linen shirt and fashioned a tourniquet above the wound. Leading his horse into the wood in search of a fallen tree, he quickly returned to lead them back to Swaffham from whence they came. At a fast trot, made more difficult for his lordship's wound and failing strength, they soon arrived directly at Kitty Bacon's door, their horses in a lather and near blown.

Kitty dispatched little Martha to quickly fetch her father at the factory and ordered that he return immediately with the surgeon. "Tell him a musket ball has struck his lordship."

Aided by passersby, they lowered an ashen Charles, by now greatly weakened and slipping from his saddle, to lay him on the ground where Kitty had spread some covers. Those who had come to help were dismissed with appreciation and when they were alone, she knelt at his side, removed the tourniquet, and placed her hands on him, speaking in words and in a voice unknown to Cecil. The bleeding stopped.

"I suspected as much."

She quickly lifted a hand and put a finger to Cecil's lips to stop him saying more. "Then you'll know what you must ne'er do, together."

It seemed an eternity had passed before the surgeon arrived. At least his lordship was alive and breathing although he seemed oblivious to their presence. The surgeon extracted the ball and with the aid of Kitty applied potions and bandages, promising at the door to return on the morrow to see how he was mending.

While Kitty prepared a tonic in her kitchen to revive him and give him strength, four hardies from the factory carried him upstairs to the very bed he had rolled out of only hours before.

Charles and Cecil did not wait until the last to do their duty. As soon as he was strong enough to recount the ordeal, the sheriff was called to Charles' bedside to record their informations. Should the highwaymen be discovered they stood ready to prosecute. Given the descriptions of their assailants, including details of the broken leg, the sheriff believed their arrest should not be delayed.

Over the next few days the surgeon applied his remedies while Kitty ministered hers. Whether one was more effective than the other, Charles was on his feet and walking, or rather limping slowly with the aid of a crutch within a week. After a fortnight he appeared ready to return to Weeting with an armed escort. To avoid undue pressure on the wound, which was not entirely healed, Charles rode a gig with Bess tied behind.

* * *

Before she was unable to travel, Kitty returned to Nate's mother in Feltwell for the last weeks of her pregnancy. Her own mother had unexpectedly taken ill and was too weak to abide the imposition. On the 30th day of April Maria was born, and on the 2nd of May 1789 she was christened at St. Mary's Church. Elizabeth and Thomas stood for her. Sally and Edward were present as well.

Standing to one side, the men shared the latest information on the highwaymen. Identified as a father and his two adult sons, the one now deceased from the shock of his corrupted leg, warrants were drawn up to bring them to trial. However, in advance of the sheriff seizing them they took flight, and were now declared dangerous villains and highwaymen.

"How fares Charles?" asked Nate.

Thomas explained how his humour was affected by the favour he showed the one leg. He had taken to using a cane.

In the churchyard the children played a game of tag among the headstones. A light drizzle fell on them making their hair hang heavy. Their heads were covered in fine to coarse, curly to straight, and fair to black hair, displaying the diversity of their heritages.

They screamed excitedly as they twisted and turned trying to avoid the touch that would transfer the plague to the unlucky 'it.' Avoiding the more complex rules of the game, they were happy to simply chase each other until exhausted, with no respite save the touch of the one stone they had agreed upon.

John Leverett with his siblings Nathaniel and Sarah were there, as were Martha and Matthew Bacon. So were Mary, John, Robert, and Maria Turner. Missing was the baby Elizabeth never knew. For fear of rushing back too soon and risking the loss of another, she had become somewhat indifferent in their lovemaking.

The women had their own matters to discuss.

"'Twas sweet on his part, but when I told him that bringin' broom in flower into the house will bring ill-luck, he turned and placed them in a glass on a stone without."

"Poor Edward. Some men know little of such things. Thomas once complained an apple tree was blighted and died. He asked me had I been cutting any trees about that time. I'd meddled about with a barberry to make some poultices and tonics as you once instructed me, Sally, taking what I needed. He explained he'd seen his father chop down a barberry tree only to see the wheat in the next field become blighted. He said I may be to blame for the loss of the apple tree, for meddling with the barberry tree. I remember well. I was with the child I then lost."

"He should be believed, Elizabeth. My mother has said likewise, and that a woman with child is to avoid the barberry for fear of losing it."

They mulled this until Elizabeth said, "Do you believe that is the reason for losing my child?"

Kitty answered, "I cannot know for certain, yet it is possible, friend."

* * *

In view of his long convalescence, William Colhoun agreed to meet Charles Coote at Weeting Hall. To ensure the trip would not disappoint, Charles organized a small shooting party involving a few local lords. James Hennessy and Samuel Stokes were also invited, as he thought it prudent they be present in the event any financing questions arose. He might also have been unsettled by the relentless rumours regarding Colhoun's financial troubles.

The weather did not entirely cooperate. Mild enough for mid-September, it rained on and off throughout. This was to the delight of the dogs who readily picked up the scents, but the shooters found it difficult to sight with the rain falling in their eyes.

The poor weather and shooting conspired to keep everyone in close quarters, making it difficult to have the privacy Charles sought. He was finally able to get William alone, save the presence of his bankers, under pretext of seeking his advice on a common boundary issue between the parishes. He then made known his plans insofar as they relate to the welfare of Wretham Warren.

"In honesty, I feel much improved now the wound is scarred over. I suspect my leg will ne'er be as strong as it once was, but that is a minor irritation. I give full credit to Swift for his quickness of thought and determination, and to Kitty Bacon for ministering her potions, poultices, and tonics: dreadful all, but seemingly efficacious."

"Rumour has it you was obliged to fend off the highwaymen yourselves. That is uncommon courageous, Charles."

"One might imagine that to be, however we would not have done so had my Bess not first kicked out and destroyed the man's leg. That altered the balance and Cecil, seeing the change, quickly wielded his weighted riding crop to make good our advantage by unhorsing a second thief. I was able to reach my pistol despite taking a ball to the leg. With it I held their leader in check."

"I must have such a riding crop."

"I have ordered one for myself. You shall see it yourself when next we meet, and you will know then whether to order one for yourself.

"Let us get to the point, William. Bromehill, though prodigiously successful, simply no longer serves my most important aims. I wish to improve the land for farming. I do not wish to damage our partnership and therefore seek to join forces in seeking answers to avoid any unfavourable outcome for Newport."

"I appreciate you bringing this to my prompt attention. This is a courtesy too infrequently extended in business.

"The question is, how best to replace your Bromehill commitment for furs? At present my commitment is equal to yours, while Wretham is thrice the area of your Bromehill. I cannot say whether Took can extract more from Wretham, but the possibility seems to be present. To my mind, this is the first question to resolve.

"If Took is incapable of this, then other questions come to mind. Can another achieve such a deed? If so, then what is to become of Took?"

"I may answer one of your questions. Turner has been a superior head warrener for several years, to my great profit. He has a family and is proven to be reliable. I know no man more commendable for his qualification, suitability of character, and vigour. His relative youth may interest you for the longer term. It is my sole regret in this business that I should lose a fine man and contributor to our community."

"I see. You wish to find a situation for Turner in advance of advising him of your plan."

"If such is possible. Turner admires Took for many of the qualities I have just credited to him. Took may very well be able to increase the take on the warren, but he has few years in him. Perhaps you have something he can take on to the benefit of all?"

"Newport has proven its value and any reduction of the revenue it occasions would be intolerable. I assure you; it is a boon where many others of my investments fail me. I will give your situation my utmost consideration,

Charles. I will see what is possible."

"Should e'er you wish to speak with Turner you should know that I find him to be unstinting, generous, and capable when he takes the bit in his own mouth. It would be advantageous to give it the appearance of seeking his advice.

"I must now see to other guests. I leave you with these gentlemen to answer your questions of finance. I am certain you will appreciate the news they bring you, and should Wretham fill the void Bromehill leaves behind, it would prove immensely profitable to you, William."

He smiled warmly and raised his glass to toast their understanding.

* * *

At Frog's Hall he took the road due east for half a league to arrive at Wretham Hall. Not a particularly noticeable residence, it was older and sat by the remains of the ancient and now deserted hamlet of West Wretham, far from any road and not frequented unless by some compelling force to do so.

Before reaching the Hall, he came upon the ancient and much neglected St. Lawrence Church with its unusual and impressive western tower. Standing taller than others he had seen, it narrowed slightly as it rose in three equally tall sections. The bottom two were square and the uppermost eight-sided, where each side had a large pointed belfry opening. Its battlement having once served to defend citizens against raiding parties from across the North Sea, was now broken in places like an old warrior's smashed mouth.

Throughout the entire church, stone quoins provided shape and strength to the flint and rubble walls that were faced with rough courses of unknapped flint. Here and there remained patches of mortar facing. The roof was severely damaged, likely affecting the interior he thought, and one wall had partially collapsed. Thomas thought it might be one of the oldest churches he'd seen and being ill preserved, not likely to last much longer. Its fate was seemingly cast he thought, for the growth that had started to choke it off from everything else was no longer being cut back.

Wretham Hall was surrounded by a small park and stood on an otherwise barren, un-parked landscape. Thomas was not struck by anything so much as the evident need of the manor for much improvement, and for this, much capital.

He had considered what William Colhoun's plans might be. Charles Coote had agreed Thomas could be helpful to him, this much he had been told. He was therefore invited to discuss important matters with Colhoun, and to provide advice to him in advance of his taking decisions.

It was late October and with the cull well in hand, Thomas decided this to be a good day to visit. He had sent a message ahead by one of his warreners. The weather being calm and warm for the season, William offered to show him the grounds, claiming Thomas would benefit from the sight as it was to be the subject of their discussion.

At a walk, for the distances were not great, he showed him first three unusual bodies of water encompassed within the Park. Mickle Mere and Hill Mere being the two largest and several acres each in area are, he said, full of mystery for their origins are unknown: there being no flow of water into or out of any as they self-regulate from below. The water seems to come and go according to some age-old pattern that constantly varies their size.

"They are a bellwether for the price of corn. 'Tis said, as the water rises or falls so follows the price of corn. There are those who assiduously measure and report to others on this. I wish 'twas so simple." Sighing wistfully, he added, "There are many such meres hereabouts."

"My lord tells me you have plans for Wretham."

"You see yourself there is much to be done here. Yes, I think you must. Those who once resided in the tiny village have long departed, there being nothing for them here. The land is wretched for agriculture. 'Tis fit for plantations, sheepwalks, and warrens only; or perhaps a game park. I have attempted to improve some brecks without success as there is truly little earth to work with; nought but sand and fathomless bog. The most we can pray for is to grow crops for the warren.

"Come this way. I would show you something."

They rounded Mickle Mere heading north and after only a few minutes of travel in silence, William stopped before an expanse of land. "Yonder is Black Rabbit Warren with beautiful blacks from the very same Methwold stock as your own Bromehill. To our right will become Galley Hill, where I will have blacks as well."

He turned westward, travelling north of the former village toward Sturston Lodge, before turning south by Wretham Warren to Fowl Mere, and then back by way of Thorpe Farm. Along the way he pointed out many things of note and explained he had purchased the Wretham Estate from Eton College in 1755. Since that time, he has been amassing funds and making his plans for parkland, plantations, a mews, and larger culls from his warrens. He also described the new Hall to be built commencing well against next Lady Day.

"Your plans are ambitious, Mr. Colhoun. You will commit large sums to make this all come to pass."

"I will require every penny I can muster to pay for it. Steady revenue from business investments is the key, I believe. I must ensure each investment is carefully chosen to ensure sustained success; no flash in the pan so to speak, though there are no guarantees. Business is business, after all. I believe you understand my meaning."

"Though not a man of commerce like yourself, I have learned a few things as head warrener."

"I suspect you have. Let us take some refreshment." When seated he said, "Money is one key. As I have said, I will require every penny I can place my hands on. Do you know another? Good people. That is one important lesson I learned in the islands. For without good people, one might just as well toss his money on the wind."

Thomas did not yet see how he could contribute to this. "What is it you would ask of me?"

"I require a good man, a man perhaps such as yourself to augment the culls of my black conies now they are in e'er greater demand. Now I have shared with you my plans, you must surely understand the import of this requirement. I thus ask myself, where might I find such a man, and what might entice him to come to Wretham."

"How so? All such good men are presently in a situation."

"I pray 'tis you who will advise me, how so. Do you see an opportunity opening before you?"

"I am uncertain."

"Are you ready to take it?"

"As for being ready, we have saved for an opportunity. Yet the shape of this eludes me."

"In truth, Thomas I seek your advice on it and you must work with me as I do not possess all the answers. I intend there to be three warrens with only glorious blacks. Should there be a surfeit to the needs of Newport, they shall be sold elsewhere. At present I have two head warreners in whom I am confident, Took and Hawes, but I must consider the age of Took. Neither is the man I seek."

Thomas said: "You pointed to Galley Hill where you will have a warren. It does not appear to be vast."

William: "Do you think it suitable for a man to take on in his senior years? A challenge requiring all his skill and knowledge, while less daunting physically?"

Thomas: "You would see Took at Galley Hill. That would leave an opening at Wretham for someone."

William: "I understand you have some knowledge of Wretham. However, the man I seek will also be required to oversee all consignments to Newport; a man worthy of my trust." He paused slightly, and before Thomas could speak William gave him a look that made unnecessary the words on his tongue.

"I see." Said Thomas, looking at nothing in particular on the ground. Well, he didn't quite see, but over the next hour they both came to see a very new future for themselves. When they had almost concluded, Thomas said he had only a few concerns.

One. He desired to deal with the Earl directly. He did not wish to leave him abruptly for fear of damaging the prospects for Bromehill.

Two. He wanted to review the financial aspects with Cecil as he was confident to receive an assessment he could rely upon.

Three. He wanted to ensure his wife would accept the change. She was his partner and wherever they were it was important they work together.

"I would have it no other way, Thomas. I will have the contract drawn as soon as you advise me."

William was comfortable with the first two stipulations, for he knew in advance the Earl's plan and the financial advantage for Thomas was plain to see. As for his wife, he knew nought on that score but surmised the conversation would not have advanced to this point if Thomas had serious doubts about her desire to embrace a change for the better.

Returning homeward, Thomas reviewed the discussion and its outcome. This was an unexpected turn of events and he was fearful he had overlooked something important in the moment. Thankfully, William had agreed time for him to consider. He went over it once more in his mind.

"As tenant of Wretham Warren, I'm to receive an agreed portion of the sale of each carcass and each pelt. Farmers are to heed my advice to improve the land and to crop for the needs of the three warrens, as well as the game park. I shall conduct the selection of furs from the three warrens sent to Swaffham. This will require taking measures and providing direction to warranty all is of the first quality. For these undertakings I am to receive an additional fee, married to the quantity of pelts. Should this plan come to pass, I would see my family removed to Wretham against next Lady Day."

He was anxious to return to Elizabeth.

"Pa, I know you're watching over me now. What do you see? Shall I yet become a gentleman farmer?"

CHAPTER XXVII

NEW BEGINNINGS, FEBRUARY - SEPTEMBER 1790

THOMAS TURNER SENIOR WAS FINALLY LAID TO REST on the last Saturday in February, when the frost had sufficiently loosed its grip on the hard ground. His family and fellow warreners joined to say goodbye in a brief and simple ceremony conducted at the Church of St. Laurence and St. Peter, in the village of Eriswell.

The New England Company did not delay in replacing Thomas as head warrener. Martha had only time to remove her belongings before vacating the lodge that had been their home for more than thirty years. With a heavy heart she departed Eriswell, having also lost her daughter Martha on the 6th day of November past. Fortunately, she was laid to rest before the deep frost that prevented her father's burial until now had set in. Father and daughter now shared the same stone.

Martha had gone to live with George and his family, as it was his duty being the eldest to take her in. They now lived over by Little Hockam, beyond Wretham where George had been a licensed gamekeeper and servant to William Colhoun, Esq. for almost five years.

She would have been welcomed in either son's home. However as Mary's health had never been a sure thing, an extra pair of hands about the home would prove invaluable in raising three young boys. George junior would soon be fifteen, Thomas thirteen in a matter of days, and Timothy was eleven years of age. According to custom, all three boys were following in the steps of their father.

Elizabeth spent much of the morning at the side of the woman who had come to replace the mother she lost when she was twelve years old. Martha

Turner had always been a happy but pragmatic woman, but the loss of her daughter and husband in the same month, on the eve of a mercilessly cold and difficult winter, had changed her considerably. She had grown joyless and wore the tracks left by grief on her face.

Thomas and George stood aside from the funeral crowd talking in the manner of brothers who so valued their words, they used them only sparingly.

"How is ma? Does she want for anything?"

"Seems well enough. You know she keeps so much within 'tis difficult to know. She's doughty, as all may see for themselves."

"We can thank the Lord for her strength. Your boys are growing. In no time they'll outstrip you, brother. Will they make good keepers in the way o' their grandpa?"

"'Tis uncertain. George and Thomas take to it and are a help. Wing shooting is more Timothy's liking. We shall see. He's young and taken with the modern style from the continent the French call *battue*. They drive the game over a line of stationary guns to be taken in prodigious numbers. 'Tisn't the way of sportsmen to my mind. Says we shall soon refer to shooters themselves, as guns.

"And you Thomas, you'll take over at Wretham on Lady Day?"

"Hmnn. Required most every penny of our savings to make up the lease, yet such was our wish. You know Took to be a good man. The warren he left behind is healthy and amply stocked. Sufficiently so for him to seed Galley Hill."

"And Took?"

"Professes contentment. Good land to work with, less onerous for his old bones, and no change to his payment or perquisites. Wife's closer to her folks. Only half the distance now to her family."

"He'll be closer to me in Little Hockham. Strange twist, to find us with Colhoun, together. He's been good to me, though I hear rumours his finances are precarious." Thomas wisely opted for discretion on this subject.

George offered to move the conversation along. "Elizabeth is happy to make the change?"

"She can be like ma. I mightn't know. Lydia Took is a proud woman and Elizabeth assures me the lodge is as she herself would have it. I believe she's happy, though she suffers the absence of her good friends now in Swaffham."

Not wanting George to feel disrespected by his refusal to pursue the previous subject, Thomas finally offered an answer which he prayed would satisfy, while putting the subject to bed.

"I believe Colhoun to be a complicated landowner. He has failures, 'tis certain, yet he has his successes. Let us pray we may be counted among these."

* * *

The remarkably mild winter of 1789-1790 felt much milder for the memory of the suffering endured last winter. On the 2nd of April it rained to the satisfaction of all who knew to collect Good Friday rainwater as a remedy for sickness of the eyes. Elizabeth was confident that as she collected this water in Wretham, so Kitty and Sally did in Swaffham.

By then, turnips were so plentiful they could not be given away and cases were reported where money was being offered to those who would cart them away.

On the 3rd day of May, Elizabeth noted her first sightings of swallows in the year. It was also the day she received Lydia Took, come on behalf of her daughter. Ann Took had married Joseph Adcock, a shopkeeper and tailor of Great Hockham where it happened that children of the small town recently contracted an illness leaving them with the squits and feeling listless. Curiously, the very same illness recurred each spring. Their small appetite had kept them in a weakened state for weeks. Concerned for her grandchildren, Lydia sought a remedy from Elizabeth to keep the illness at bay.

Elizabeth suggested a remedy that she was glad to take home with her. "I should gather up a goodly number of ordinary snails and tie them in a muslin bag. The bag should be placed where it will hang so the slime falls and is collected in a beaker. When small doses of this are given to children, 'tis said to ward off this sickness. 'Tis Sally Leverett who swears by this."

Their first moments together were spent cautiously circling each other, feeling each other out. What could be their relationship when the one had dislodged the other from her lifelong home? After some time they each developed an appreciation for the sensibility and grace shown by the other. Respect was growing with the understanding the burden of closing the gap between them would be equally shared.

"I feared losing the things I have come to love. I have always found the smell of the wild thyme and heather to be soothing. And the breath of the wind whistling in the pines sang to me. I am happy to find they exist at Galley Hill as well."

The gap closed a little more.

"What can you tell me, Lydia, of the British Home Defence?"

"I know nought of it, though it does sound ominous." Lydia adjusted her barnacles, as she called them. "What of it?"

"Thomas has been asked by the publican of the Dog & Partridge to volunteer for a force of armed men. They are fearful the French troubles will incite them to heed their longstanding threats to invade England."

"'Tis awful business, their turmoil. My son Joseph tells me the journals constantly report on the latest, being all hunger, disorder, strife, and bloodshed. I could not imagine such a thing descending upon us."

"Nor Thomas. He's sorely tempted to join them. It is asked he teach others to shoot, in readiness to repel French forces when they land on our Norfolk shores."

"I pray they do not ask John, for he is too old to be parading around or fighting those mad Parleyvoos."

"Thomas is not convinced they will invade; he fears training for our defence to be akin to rabbiting with a dead ferret."

The gap closed even more.

* * *

Swaffham, a wealthy town with an entirely wholesome aspect sat on the crown of a gentle rise that sloped away in all directions to arable, meadow, and wooded parkland. Its large and well-built residences testified to its role as a destination for the influential families of Norfolk who came in season for the waters and the society. The Assembly Rooms were their venue for social events and balls, where lords, ladies, warriors, politicians, and businessmen came to mingle and make important connections.

George Walpole often came from his home at Houghton Hall to gamble at the racecourse where he was always welcomed, being both a luminary of society and a founding member of the Coursing Club.

Lady Caroline Townshend attracted many to the Assembly Rooms for the opportunity to bask in her influence and her renowned beauty.

On leave from his duties at sea might be seen Horatio Nelson with his wife as they strolled the streets, or attended events.

Three times a year the town was transformed as people from afar came together for the fair. This, the first of the year, was held over three days beginning the second Wednesday of May. Ostensibly held for the sale of cattle, sheep, pigs, and other livestock, it had long ago grown to encompass a variety of amusements as a means to release humours so long fettered by winter. Centred in the marketplace, the fair had grown to now spill out into adjacent streets and the Camping land where that violent medieval sport was still played.

Hucksters, hawkers, and vendors bargained with the wary and the innocent who sought household necessities and luxuries, personal care items, utensils, and exotic merchandise. The haggling alone proved to be highly entertaining for gapers.

The sights and smells of food were calculated to entice. The smells of roasting, baking, exotic fruits, and spices stimulated the stomach while everywhere the smell of nutmeg confirmed its popularity with the English. Tasty puddings, fancy cakes, and baked items vied with succulent roasted meats, the whole of which was washed down with lemonades, beer, cider, or claret.

Knives were sharpened, fortunes were told, and most appetites were satisfied. A cockfight held at some distance from the marketplace provided men of all ages a wager or two: the noisy cheering only heightening the urge to participate. There were also the desperate, offering themselves and their services for rent or for sale to prospective employers.

Crowds will forever harbour the unprincipled who navigate therein to prey upon the unwary. Pickpockets, thieves, and cozeners relied on their skill to move easily through this crowd. Gamblers and whores, in contrast, preferred to stake out a corner where they fought tooth and nail to protect their territory, to the added delight of spectators.

To project a semblance of control and authority, soldiers were casually stationed about the fair. Often more for appearance than for any real protection of citizens, they added considerable flair when marching to the beat of their drums and the sound of their pipes.

The carnival atmosphere so enjoyed by visitors was in fact calculated to seduce them through an array of sights, smells and sounds that assailed their imaginations. Listen to the vendors loudly proclaiming the virtues of their wares; hearken to the children squealing with delight and surprise at the puppet show. All came together in a perpetual and electrifying motion. Jugglers, acrobats, and dancers were so close you could feel the air move about them.

For one moment people are almost equals, rubbing shoulder to shoulder in pursuit of similar distraction. Who would bemoan his fate when standing before the most curious forms of man that exist, or can be devised? The Bearded, Tattooed, or Three-Breasted Lady; The Hottentot Venus; The Dwarf King; The Painted Indian, and; The Centaur, are some of these. As are those with genuine birth defects, amputations, and rare skills. Each is eagerly anticipated and available to see, for a price.

The fair was also an occasion for the romantically inspired. The Assembly Rooms and Halls provided the wealthy with venues for young women and men to meet outside of their normal contacts. The streets and the amusements provided the same opportunity for the less favoured.

Inns and alehouses did brisk trade as people repaired to these establishments for respite and refreshment. The merriment reflected as much the good humour, as the inventions and boasting of storytellers that so delighted their audiences.

It is at The Greyhound where the Turners, the Bacons, and the Leveritts have settled in to celebrate.

Absent each other's company for several months, they had arranged by exchange of letters to meet in Swaffham at the time of the fair. They had just spent the afternoon in service to the children. Having joyfully raced through the booths and the attractions, until now spent of all energy and ready money, they were retired to the safety of their beds at the Bacon abode in the care of servants.

The parents had stolen away for an evening of relaxation where they began by ordering plates of sliced roast from the pork on the spit, scotched collops and pease pottage, pickled salmon, sage cheese, lamb's lettuce, and pickled vegetables. In their hunger they had already despatched the bread earlier placed on the table, and for drink, they had chosen the Inn's own best beer.

"I enjoy everything here," said Edward. "'Tis the curious nature of all that excites me."

"I suspect the archery contest requires the most skill. I think that is my favourite."

Elizabeth looked at Thomas thinking that was perfectly logical, and so like her Thomas. "And you, Nate, do you have a preference?"

"Naturally, friend. I think the jugglers very talented fellows. To keep so many things flying through the air and to know where they will land is a feat.

What is yours, then, Elizabeth?"

"I would say the oddities."

Thomas laughed, "You surprise me, wife. I should not have imagined such a thing of you."

"'Tis not for their oddities I am drawn to them. I find them sad for their misfortune, yet admirable for what they accomplish despite that same misfortune. The thrill lies for the most with the barker, when he teases us to enter. 'Tis then we conjure images of things in this world we know not of."

Rebecca brought them port and plates of fruit tarts and rice pudding while her helpers removed the cleared plates.

"There's a sensible young woman. I wonder, is she married?"

"She is too sensible and fine, Kitty, for many of the men who enter here."

"How do you know of such things, husband?"

Nate looked at Edward and gave a look as though to say, "I might as well confess, for she'll have it out of me later."

"She unfailingly serves us, even sitting when she's not occupied. She is a fair and level-headed woman, we agree."

Edward nodded his ascent.

"She is not married then." Sally seemed to have something on her mind.

"Speak, Sally, for I know thee. Say what you will."

"I may surprise you, for 'tis not as you think, husband." She said with a little shove. "I am not jealous. I merely see someone perhaps suitable for Henry. What say you, ladies?"

Elizabeth nodded her concurrence. "Sally, we must bring him to Swaffham at the first opportunity. No woman can long fend off advances should the right man present himself."

"I recall the day his lordship spoke when last we was together at Weeting Hall," ventured Sally. "Did I alone notice the blushing cheeks of Mary Manning?"

In fact, Elizabeth had noticed the blushing as he squeezed her, but she curbed her tongue from long habit and respect for his lordship's privacy.

Kitty said, "I did see her blushes Sally, as well as their cause. I perhaps imagine something not there, for I find Henry is seemingly e'er more like the Earl himself."

I think wife, you imagine such a thing, for we are too far distant to take note."

"I disagree Nate, for 'tis the distance that permits me to see the thing."

In an aside to Elizabeth and Kitty, Sally said, "I believe we all saw John take to your Mary. He did not leave her side all day and took her by the hand at every opportunity." They all three smiled, accepting Sally's assessment. Despite their combined powers, they had evidently not the ability to see into the future.

Edward tried to revive the previous light-hearted mood. "I believe Nate, we have seen many young gentlemen of means turned off with a cold gaze from our Rebecca."

Tilting her head towards each of her two allies, Kitty Bacon returned to her usual wit. "Men will ne'er understand what they hold for us."

"And women know all too well what it is they hold for us. Is that not a fact, gentlemen?" Thomas lightly squeezed Elizabeth just above her knee.

An expression was shared between the wives, before it changed into another they turned on their husbands.

Rebecca brushed against Edward without subtlety, reaching to remove what remained of the fruit tarts and rice pudding. Straightening, she smiled and asked what more she could serve them.

"I believe we have all we need, thank you." Sally's expression, as she looked at Edward, left no doubt they should settle with Rebecca and return home.

After making certain the children were down for the night, Edward and Sally, Nate and Kitty, and Thomas and Elizabeth continued in the pleasure of each other's company well into the small hours.

Two days later, their short stay at an end, kisses and embraces were shared all around. Though too soon to be aware of the changes that would soon take hold of their bodies, when the ladies said their farewells to each other it was with more warmth and tears than even their special friendship might have warranted.

After the Turners had departed, Sally tugged at Kitty excitedly and stood silently, facing her for several moments. Suddenly, as though coming to a long-considered decision, she took something from her skirts, placed it carefully into Kitty's hands, and covered them while holding her gaze.

When Sally nodded and released her hold, Kitty looked at her hands before opening them to reveal the glass ball that had hung in her window.

"Why Sally, your witch's ball given you by your mother. How kind. And how generous!"

"We wish you to have this. For all you've done 'tis little enough. And for bringin' us with you to Swaffham."

Late in the day Thomas turned off the road to cut across the warren to the lodge. There before them, sitting in the dying rays of the sun, they saw something neither Thomas nor Elizabeth had seen in many years, and certainly not together.

"Look there! children, a long-eared white coney with pink eyes."

Elizabeth prayed Thomas to hold up for them to gaze upon it. "Promise you will not take it, in this or any season."

"You have my promise, wife. Woe betide he who wishes it harm." said Thomas.

* * *

Some two weeks after the culling season had begun, Thomas was found overseeing the early days of the harvest on Wretham Warren. His mind was elsewhere, as it tended to often be these days. He was preparing his plans for increasing the cull, now he had spent the last months assessing the warren. It would require additional men to take on the heavy lifting. Given the terms of his leasehold, he was aware the added expense would be to his own account. Should he be successful however, the profits would also be to his account.

Thomas enjoyed the full support of his family in taking this important step on the way to his dream. Also behind him was his squire, William Colhoun, for as Thomas prospered so would he. He thus waited anxiously for news of Thomas' strategy.

He returned home late in the day to find his brother sitting with Elizabeth and the children. Never seized by the warren and its vastness, or its smells, George had some years ago decided he preferred small preserves where he could work alone with his own boys. George, Thomas, and Timothy were now quite adept at raising and taking game. In fact, George junior was ready to take on his own responsibilities should a situation present itself. In the meantime, his father became licensed for more than one preserve at a time, permitting him to often leave the one in his eldest son's care.

"George, this is a pleasant surprise. How are Mary and the boys?"

"The boys are well. Mary does poorly. She grows weaker and more quiet."

"And ma?"

"Mam passed last night. I think we should send her home to be with pater."

ABOUT THE AUTHOR

Steven Turner's father did a tour of duty in Metz, France, at the height of the Cold War when France was in the founding years of its Fifth Republic and dealing with the aftermath of the Algerian War. While teens 'back home' perhaps thought of going to the lake or to a movie on the weekend, his family toured the battlefields of two world wars and the cemeteries that dot the landscape of northeastern France, paying homage to those who fought and the many who paid the ultimate sacrifice. Later, he enjoyed a long and distinguished career in public service where his responsibilities took him far and wide, although too frequently away from his family. His various mandates were a constant source of challenge, as well as an opportunity to contribute to the well-being of Canadians for which he was awarded various distinctions, including the 125th Anniversary of the Confederation of Canada Medal, and the Queen Elizabeth II Golden Jubilee Medal for service to his country.